PRAISE FOR *BETWEEN THE RIVERS*

"Historically intriguing, splendidly textured, and full of stimulating ideas."

—*Kirkus Reviews*

"The author's cadenced prose imparts an epic feel to this tale of humanity's attempt to forge its own destiny."

—*Library Journal*

"This book is as well executed as the author's magisterial alternate histories, as Turtledove turns his attention to a venerable SF theme—the struggle of reason against faith—and as he uses all of his historiographical and narrative skills, plus his inimitable wit, to elevate his version to the same high level occupied by (among others) L. Sprague de Camp."

—*Publishers Weekly*

"This new version of the old SF concept of the triumph of reason over fate Turtledove renders excellently, thanks to his customary historical scholarship, narrative gifts, balanced judgment, and dry wit."

—*Booklist*

# TOR BOOKS BY HARRY TURTLEDOVE

# HARRY TURTLEDOVE

# BETWEEN THE RIVERS

**TOR®**
**fantasy**

A TOM DOHERTY ASSOCIATES BOOK
NEW YORK

BETWEEN THE RIVERS

Copyright © 1998 by Harry Turtledove

Edited by Patricia Nielsen Hayden

A Tor Book
Published by Tom Doherty Associates, LLC
175 Fifth Avenue
New York, NY 10010

www.tor.com

Tor® is a registered trademark of Tom Doherty Associates, LLC.

ISBN 0-812-54520-6
EAN 978-0812-54520-3
Library of Congress Catalog Card Number: 97-29844

First edition: March 1998
First mass market edition: April 1999

Printed in the United States of America

0  9  8  7  6  5  4  3  2

# BETWEEN THE RIVERS

# 1

Sharur was walking back toward his family's shop and home on the Street of Smiths when a fever demon that had been basking on a broken mud brick soaking up heat sprang at him, its batlike wings glistening in the sun. He leaped back so it could not breathe sickness into his mouth and pulled out an amulet marked with the eyes of Engibil, patron god of the city of Gibil.

"Begone, foul thing!" he exclaimed, and made the left-hand gesture every child in the land of Kudurru learned by the age of three—every child, at any rate, that lived to the age of three. He thrust out the amulet as if it were a spear. "Greater powers than you protect me."

Screeching in dismay, the nasty little demon fled. Sharur strode on, his back straight now with pride. He returned the amulet to its proper loop on his belt. The belt, which also bore a couple of other amulets, a bronze dagger, and a stylus, held up a knee-length linen kilt that was all he wore between stout leather sandals and a straw hat shaped like a short, broad cone. Slaves—and some freemen of a class poorer than Sharur's—dispensed with shoes and sometimes with kilt as well. No one went without a hat, not in the land between the Yarmuk and the Diyala.

The streets of Gibil were narrow and winding. Sharur's sandals scuffed up dust and squelched in muck. A farmer coming at him leading a donkey with baskets of beans tied to its back made him squeeze up against the front wall of one of the two-story mud-brick homes lining both sides of the street: a prosperous home, because that front wall was whitewashed. The shiny white coating did not make the sun-baked mud any less rough on the bare skin of his back. Farmer and donkey plodded on, equally oblivious to having annoyed him.

His grandfather's ghost spoke in his ear: "You should follow that fellow and break a board on his head for the bother he caused you."

"It's all right, father to my father. He's on the way to the market square; he had to get by me," Sharur answered re-signedly. His grandfather had been quarrelsome while he was alive, and was even more bad-tempered now that no one could break a board over *his* head.

"If only that fellow had known me in the flesh, I'd have hit him myself," the ghost grumbled. "He deserved it."

"It's all right, father to my father," Sharur repeated, and kept walking.

His grandfather's ghost sniffed. "All right, he says. It's not all right, not even close. Young people these days are soft—soft, I tell you."

"Yes, father to my father," Sharur said. The ghost, he knew, would keep on haranguing him and trying to meddle in his affairs as long as he lived. He consoled himself by remembering that it would have no power over his children, whenever they might be born, for they would not have known his grandfather alive. *And when I'm a ghost myself*, he thought, *I hope I don't plague the people who recall me*.

He turned a last corner and stepped onto the Street of Smiths. It was probably the noisiest street in all Gibil, but he found the racket familiar, even restful, having lived with it all his life. Smiths banged and tapped and hammered and rasped and filed. Fires crackled. Molten metal hissed as it was poured into molds of wet sand.

Behind the racket, power hovered. Smithery was a new thing in the land of Kudurru, and thus in the whole world, however big the world might be. In the days of Sharur's grandfather's grandfather, no one had known how to free copper and tin from their ores, much less how to mix them to make a metal stronger than either. These days, smiths stood on an equal footing with carpenters and bakers and potters and those who followed the other old, established trades.

But smiths were different. The other trades all had their old, established tutelary gods, from Shruppinak, who helped carpenters pound pegs straight, to Lisin, who got spots out of laundry. Smithery, though, smithery was too new for its great power to have coalesced into deities or even demons. Maybe it would, in time. Maybe, too, the smiths would keep the power in their own merely human hands.

Whenever that thought crossed Sharur's mind, it frightened him. If Engibil saw it there, or, worse, if one of the greater deities—sun god, storm or river goddesses; the ugly, sexless demon that squatted underground and caused earthquakes with its quiverings; many more—did so, what would they do with the smiths, to the smiths, for seeking to gain power thus? Sharur neither knew nor wanted to find out.

At the same time, though, knowing himself to be a worm in the eyes of the gods, he longed to be a strong worm. His eyes traveled down the Street of Smiths to the lugal's palace at the end of it, the only building in the city that came close to Engibil's temple in size and grandeur. Kimash the lugal gave Engibil rich presents, of course, but he ruled Gibil in his own right, as had his father and grandfather before him.

One or two other cities in the land of Kudurru had lords who were but men. The rest were about evenly divided between towns where ensis—high priests—transmitted the local god's will to the people and those where the gods ruled directly. Sharur was glad he did not live in one of *those* towns. Everyone who did struck him as a step slow.

Thinking of power, he almost walked right past Ningal without seeing her. "Well," she called as he went by. "Don't say hello."

"Hello," he said, and felt very foolish.

Ningal set down the basket of eggs she was carrying back to her father's smithy: had she kept holding it, she couldn't have set both hands on her hips to look properly annoyed. "Sometimes," she said, "I think you live too much of your life inside your head instead of in the world out here."

"Not when I look at you," Sharur said. Ningal's smile said he'd gone partway toward redeeming himself. Like other well-to-do women of Gibil, she wore a linen tunic that covered her from the neck almost to the knee, but it clung to her in the heat and did little to hide her shapely figure. Her eyes sparkled; all her teeth were white; her hair fell to her shoulders in midnight curls. Sharur went on, "With the profit I make from my next trip to the mountains, I'll have enough to pay bride-price to your father."

"How do you know I'll want you to, when you don't even notice I'm here?" she asked with a toss of her head that sent those curls flying.

Sharur felt his cheeks heat, though he doubted Ningal could see him blush. Like her, like everyone in the land between the rivers, he was swarthy, with dark hair and eyes. In Laravanglal, the distant southeastern land whence tin came, the people were the color of dark bread, and men grew beards scanty rather than luxuriant. A few of the mountaineers of Alashkurru had eyes of green or even gray, and hair that might be brown or even, rarely, the color of copper instead of black. More, though, looked like Sharur and his countrymen.

He said, "Well, if you don't, you can always tell your father."

"Do you think he would listen to me? I don't. He's set on marrying me to you, to join our houses together." Ningal's smile showed a dimple in her cheek. "And so I guess I won't bother telling him that."

"Fair enough." Sharur tried hard not to show how relieved he was. He very much wanted the marriage to go forward. As in every other marriage in Gibil, the partners would join at their families' instance, not their own. But Ningal and he had known each other since they were toddlers playing in the dust of the Street of Smiths. They'd always got on well, even as children. And ever since he'd thought of marrying anyone, hers was the face he saw in his mind.

" 'Fair enough'?" she mimicked, exasperated at him again. "Is that the best you can do?"

He knew she wished he were more demonstrative. He took off his hat, then stooped, picked up a handful of dust, and let it fall down into his hair, a gesture of mourning and contrition. "O gracious lady, please forgive your slave," he wailed, his voice cracking convincingly.

Ningal made as if to throw an egg at him. Laughing, she said, "I may—eventually." She carried the basket into her father's smithery. Sharur watched her hips work under the clinging linen.

Once she was out of sight, he went on to his own house. His father, Ereshguna, was counting leather sacks of ore. "Seventy-two, seventy-three . . . Oh, hello, son." He got to his feet and bowed to Sharur. The two of them looked much alike, though his face was more strongly carved by the years and gray flecked his hair and elaborately curled beard.

Sharur's younger brother, Tupsharru, also bowed. He held a tablet of damp clay in his left hand, a stylus in his right. "Do you want to finish this lot now, Father, or shall we set it aside for a while?"

"It will keep," Ereshguna answered. "That tablet's not going to dry up if you set it on the table. You'll still be able to write on it after we all have a cup of beer." The jar of beer and several earthenware cups sat on a small table made of golden, fine-grained wood brought down from the mountains of Alashkurru. Only palms and poplars grew in Kudurru. Their lumber, while cheap, was neither lovely nor particularly strong.

Ereshguna poured three cups full. He and his sons murmured thanks to Ikribu, god of barley, and Ikribabu, goddess of brewing, before they drank. The sour beer washed some of the dust from Sharur's mouth. "That's good," he said, and praised the god and goddess again.

"Here, give me a cup, too," his grandfather's ghost said.

"Yes, my father." Ereshguna held the jar over an empty

cup and tilted it, not far enough to let more than a couple of drops of actual beer come out. Symbolically, though, it was full. Ghosts dwelt more in the symbolic world than in the material one, in any case. The efforts of Sharur's grandfather's ghost to drink the actual beer made the cup quiver on the table, but that was all.

"It is good beer," the ghost said, judging by the essence, "but I remember a jar I drank when I was a young man. It—"

Ereshguna rolled his eyes. He'd heard that story more often than Sharur and Tupsharru put together. It had been boring when his father was alive. It was deadly dull now. At last, the ghost finished and fell silent.

Trying not to show how relieved he was, Ereshguna turned to Sharur and asked, "What do the harness makers say?"

"They will have the new straps ready when we need them, at the price on which we already agreed. I can lead the donkey train to Alashkurru when the goddess Nusku carries the boat of the moon a couple of days past full, as we had planned."

"Good. That's good," Ereshguna said. "We don't want to run low on ore." He and his family brought more copper and tin into Gibil than anyone else, along with whatever other interesting things they found along the way. When Sharur laughed and pointed to the sacks he'd been inventorying with Tupsharru, he shook his head. "Those will go soon enough, my son. Almost all of them are already spoken for. We need more. We always need more."

He pointed toward the clay tablet and stylus Tupsharru had put down. His younger son picked them up again and said, "The last one you counted was number seventy-three."

"Yes, that's right. Seventy-three. It was this one right here. Then Sharur came in." Ereshguna pointed to the next sack and resumed his count: "Seventy-four, seventy-five . . ." Tupsharru made fresh tally marks in the damp clay.

Sharur listened to the reckoning with half an ear. Inventory was necessary, but not exciting. He was about to go upstairs when a customer came in and gave him something to do. Bowing, he said, "How may I serve you, honored Irmitti?"

Irmitti was a plump man who looked as if his stomach pained him. "I've come to give you another payment on those dozen fancy lamps and the perfumed oil that goes with them you sold me," he said, and tossed Sharur a gold ring. "It should be the last."

Sharur caught it out of the air, hefted it, bit it, and nodded. "It is good gold." He walked over to a small balance and set it in one pan. In the other, he set weights that he took from a cedarwood box. "It weighs one keshlu, and a quarter part, and a half of a quarter part. Let me examine your contract, honored Irmitti. If it is too much, I shall repay to you whatever the excess weight may be."

He rummaged through a basket of clay tablets till he found the one he needed. Syllable by syllable, he sounded out the words written there. The polite smile faded from his face, to be replaced by a polite frown.

"I am sorry, honored Irmitti, but the amount you still owed was three keshlut of gold. The writing is very clear. That means you have left to pay"—he worked out the answer on his fingers—"one keshlu's weight of gold, and a half part, and a half of a quarter part. When I have it, I will give you the tablet, and you may break it."

"I will give you the rest of the gold when I have it," Irmitti said. "One keshlu, and a half part, and a half of a quarter part." He repeated the amount several times so he would remember it. Having done that, he went on, "Truly I thought I owed you only this smaller amount."

"Memories can slip," said Sharur, who thought Irmitti was probably telling the truth. He added, "Mine often does," which was not true but was calculated to console the customer. He hefted the clay tablet. "The writing here, though, is the same as it always was. It does not forget. It cannot forget."

As he spoke, he wondered whether writing might not prove an even greater creator of power than smithery. Prayers, invocations, spells . . . all centered on words. And writing pinned them down. It made them stay as they had always been. And it let a man command more of them than he could hope to do with even the capacious and accurate memory Sharur enjoyed. If that wasn't the raw stuff of power, what was?

Irmitti's thoughts had run along different lines. A discontented look on his face, he said, "My great-grandmother's ghost tells me that, in her time and the time of her father, only a few priests scratched marks on clay. A man's unaided memory was enough to take him through his whole life, and a tablet did not strike like a snake and make him out to be a liar."

"Honored Irmitti, I do not take you for a liar, only for a man who forgot," Sharur said. "We have more things to remember than they did in your great-grandmother's time."

"Life was simpler then," Irmitti said. "Life was better then, I think. I mean no offense to you and your family, but are we better for having so much bronze in the city? The smiths make it into knives and swords, and we kill each other with them. A wood sickle edged with polished stone was good enough for my great-grandfather. Why would anyone need a bronze tool now, when you metal merchants have to travel to the ends of the world to find the stuff the smiths use to make it?"

"You may be right," Sharur said with a small bow. Never insulting a customer was a merchant's first rule. But he did not believe what he was saying, not for a moment. Where new things seemed to frighten Irmitti, they excited him. He could hardly hold still, he so much wanted to point out all the interesting, useful, beautiful things that were easy to accomplish with metal but slow and difficult if not impossible with stone.

After grumbling a little longer, Irmitti left. Ereshguna looked up from his counting and said, "You did well there, son. The worst sort of fool is a man who does not know he is a fool."

"Irmitti could be worse," Sharur said. "Some forget they owe us anything, not how much they owe us. Then the lugal's men have to remind them."

"Oh, yes, I know that, and you are right," Ereshguna said. "But when he talks about sickles edged with stone, from where does he think the stone came? It did not come from the land of Kudurru. Here between the rivers we have water and mud and the things that grow from them, not much else. Merchants brought the stone here, as we bring in ores today. But he does not want to think of that, and so he does not."

"If he wishes for things to be as they were in the time of his great-grandmother . . ." Tupsharru let that hang, for what he meant was unquestionably something like, *He would wish Engibil ruled the city in his own right once more.* Saying such things aloud was dangerous. The god might be listening. If he was, he might choose to punish the speaker in any number of unpleasant ways. Or he might even decide to overthrow the line of lugals and resume his direct rule. That was the last thing Sharur and his family wanted; they had gained too much from the changes over the past couple of generations.

Engibil might also be listening to Tupsharru's thoughts. If the god chose to do so, he could go through a man's mind as Sharur had gone through the basket of tablets looking for what he wanted. Engibil had no particular reason to be listening to Tupsharru's thoughts, but that did not mean he wasn't.

Sharur took from his belt the amulet with which he'd routed the fever demon. He covered Engibil's eyes with his own two thumbs for a moment, symbolically masking from the god what was passing in this house. His father and brother imitated the gesture. Each of them looked nervous. They did not know for certain whether the charm bound the god, or merely distracted him, or in fact did nothing to restrain him. They did not want to find out.

Ereshguna said, "Sometimes I feel like an ant in a line of ants crawling up a wall inside a house. We think we are doing something fine and grand. But one day the kitchen slave will notice us crawling there and smash us with her hand or sweep us away with a broom."

"We are ants who know copper and tin," Sharur said. As his brother had before, he spoke with great care. One of the things for which metal was better than stone was making weapons. But he had not spoken of fighting the gods, nor even come close. "We are ants who write down the way to the dates in the larder. Even if the kitchen slave smashes us, our brothers will know where they are."

"We are still ants," Ereshguna said. "We would do well to remember it."

For the late meal, Sharur, a hungry ant, ate locusts. The cook, a slave woman captured from the nearby city of Imhursag, had roasted them with coriander and garlic and now served them up on wooden skewers along with thin sheets of barley bread, onions, melons, and dates preserved in sesame oil.

Sharur's mother, Betsilim, was not in a good mood as the kitchen slave brought in another tray loaded with sliced onions and melons and set it on a stool. "We should have had beans, too," she grumbled. "I told her three different times to put them in the pot, but she forgot."

"I'll whip her, if you like," Ereshguna said. "Will that make her remember?"

"If I thought it would, I would tell you to do it," Betsilim answered. "But I do not think she is lazy. I think she is stupid."

"Remember, Mother, she is without the voice of her god in her ear, too," Sharur said. "Enimhursag rules his city himself. He has no lugal, he has no ensi. He watches over all his people all the time."

"He can't do that in Gibil!" said Nanadirat, Sharur's younger sister.

"No, he can't, and he never will," Sharur said. Now, instead of trying to conceal his thoughts from Engibil, he wanted the god to know he was glad Engibil still protected Gibil even if he no longer directly ruled it. Gibil and Imhursag were neighbors and rivals in Kudurru. Engibil and Enimhursag were also rivals. Each god wanted more land and more worshipers. Over the years, Engibil had succeeded at Enimhursag's expense. Sharur knew how jealous the other town's god had to be, and how angry.

Ereshguna said, "Imhursag would be more dangerous to us if the town god let his people be freer. They would soon think of ways to fill our canals with sand."

"Yes, but Enimhursag fears they would think of ways to fill his canal with sand, too," Tupsharru said.

Giving his brother a reproachful look, Sharur took out his amulet again and covered Engibil's eyes. Ereshguna did the same. A moment later, so did Tupsharru himself. He put on a shamefaced expression. If Enimhursag's people might trouble him on being given more freedom, what of Engibil's people, who had gained more? Would they now trouble their god as a result? Those were not the sort of thoughts any man who valued such freedom as he possessed wanted the city god having.

"Let us drink some wine," Betsilim said hastily, and clapped her hands. "Slave, bring us the wine and cups and a strainer."

The kitchen slave—she had no name, not in Gibil; it was left behind in Imhursag—carried in the jar and the cups and the bronze strainer. "Ha!" Tupsharru said, pointing to it. "I'd like to see Irmitti make a strainer out of stone."

"What did they used to be before they were made of metal?" Ereshguna asked the air. No family ghosts answered. They were all off doing something else. That gave supper an unusual feeling of privacy.

Timidly, the slave said, "In Imhursag, the strainers are made of clay and baked like pots and dishes."

"Ah. Well, there you are," Ereshguna said. The slave poured the thick fermented juice of dates through the strainer into the cups. Twice she had to rinse the strainer in a bowl of water to clear the sticky dregs from it.

Like anyone well enough off not to have to make do with water, Sharur drank beer with almost every meal. Date wine was for more special occasions. After pouring out a small libation to Putishu god of dates and to Ikribabu's cousin Aglibabu, who made the dates into wine, Sharur sipped. The wine was very sweet and strong and made his heart merry.

He and his family drank the jar dry. The kitchen slave cleared away the bowls and pots in which supper had been served. As she carried them out of the dining room, she hummed a little hymn to Enimhursag. Sharur did not think she even knew she was doing it; no doubt she had been doing it all her life. It would not help her, not in this city where the people worshiped Engibil. Hum, speak, scream: her god would not hear her prayer.

"When will you be leading the trade caravan to the mountains?" Nanadirat asked Sharur.

"A few more days," he answered. "I was seeing about donkeys today, before I came home and saw Irmitti. Why? Do you want me to bring you back something special?"

"A ring or a bracelet with the blue stones they have there," his sister said at once. "They're pretty. I like them."

"I'll see what I can do," Sharur told her. "They know we like those stones, and they want a lot for them."

Betsilim said, "I'm going up on the roof."

"I'll come with you," Ereshguna said. Nanadirat nodded and got to her feet, too. After supper, most families in Gibil, as in the other cities between the Yarmuk and the Diyala, went onto their roofs to escape the heat that lingered indoors. Most of them slept up there, too. Sharur's blanket was there waiting for him. He would lie on it, not under it.

He and Tupsharru rose at about the same time. Sharur was about to follow his parents and sister when Tupsharru touched him on the arm. Sharur stopped and lifted one eyebrow, a gesture he shared with his father. Tupsharru asked, "Were you going to have the kitchen slave tonight?"

"Ah." As the older brother, Sharur could take her ahead

of Tupsharru, just as Ereshguna, if he felt like putting up with Betsilim's complaints, could take her ahead of him. "No—go ahead if you want to," Sharur said. "I've taken her once or twice, but I don't think she's anything special."

"I don't think she's anything special, either," Tupsharru said, "but she's here and I feel like it, and this way I don't have to go out and find a harlot and pay her something. So if you're not going to, I will."

With purposeful stride, he headed off toward the kitchen. Sharur went up the stairs and onto the roof. Twilight was fading. As he watched, more and more stars appeared in the darkening bowl of the sky. He murmured prayers of greeting to the tiny gods who peered out through them. Most of those gods were content to stay in one place in the sky day after day, year after year, accepting the absentminded reverence people gave them.

A handful, more enterprising, moved through the heavens, some quickly, some more slowly. They were tricksters, and had to be propitiated. Sharur, who was going to move over the land, reminded himself to offer to them before he set out.

Ereshguna had carried a lamp up with him, and used it to light a couple of torches. More torches and lamps and thin, guttering tapers burned on other roofs in Gibil, making an earthly field of stars as counterpoint to that up in the heavens. Somewhere not far away, a man was playing a harp and singing a song in praise of Engibil. Sharur nodded. The god, who was vain, would like that.

Catching himself in a yawn, Sharur shook out his blanket to make sure he would not be sharing it with any spiders or scorpions. He took off his sandals, shifted his kilt so he could piss in the old pot the family kept up there for that purpose, and lay down.

He was just about asleep when Tupsharru came up onto the roof. His brother whistled a happy tune. As Sharur had done, he shook out his blanket, eased himself, and lay down, a man happy with the world and with his place in it.

Down below, in her sweltering little cubicle, the kitchen

slave, like the rest of the slaves Ereshguna owned, would also be going to sleep. What she thought, what she felt, never entered Sharur's mind as he began to snore.

A line of donkeys, each but the leader roped to the one in front of it, stood braying in the Street of Smiths. Sharur went methodically down the line, checking the packs and jars tied to the animals' backs against the list written on two clay tablets he held in his hand.

"Linen cloth dyed red, four bolts," he muttered to himself. He counted the bolts. "One, two, three, four . . . very good." He used a stylus to draw a little star by the item on the list. The clay was dry but not baked, so he could incise the mark if he bore down a little. "Wool cloth dyed blue with woad, seven bolts." He counted, then frowned. "Harharu! I see only five bolts here."

If a donkeymaster was a good one, he knew where everything in the caravan was stored. Harharu, a stocky, middle-aged man, was the best donkeymaster in Gibil; Ereshguna would have settled for no one less. He said, "You're talking about the wool dyed blue, master merchant's son? The other two bolts are on this beast three farther back."

And so they were. "I thank you, Harharu," Sharur said, bowing. He set the star beside the item. On he went, making sure he was in fact taking all the date wine, all the fine pots, all the little flasks of the rock-oil that seeped out of the ground near Gibil, all the medicines and perfumes, all the knives and swords and axes and spearheads, and all the other things on his list.

"Always strikes me funny, taking metal things up to the mountains when that's where we get our copper from," Harharu remarked.

"The Alashkurrut have plenty of copper," Sharur said, "but they have no tin. Our bronze is harder and tougher than any metal they can make for themselves, so they are happy to get it. They give five times the weight of copper or fifteen times the weight of ore for good swords."

Harharu grunted. "And sometimes, when they feel like it, they use their good swords to take whatever a caravan brings, and they give nothing for it but death or wounds."

"We are not going by ourselves, you and I." Sitting in the shade of a wall, talking or dozing while they waited for the caravan to get moving, were a dozen stalwart young men who had proved themselves with spear and sword and bow in the latest war with Imhursag. Along with trade goods for the men of the mountains of Alashkurru, the donkeys carried their weapons, their shields of wickerwork and leather, and their linen helmets with bronze plates sewn in. When the caravan left the land of Kudurru, the guards would carry their gear themselves.

Seeing Sharur's eyes on him, the leader of the guard contingent asked, "How much longer, master merchant's son?" Mushezib might have been carved from stone, so sharply chiseled were the muscles rippling under his skin. The scar on his cheek above the line of his beard and the bigger scar that furrowed the right side of his chest might have been slips of the sculptor's tools.

"It will be soon now," Sharur answered. His bow and spear were packed on a donkey, too. He had never yet had to fight up in Alashkurru, but that he never had did not mean he never would.

When he'd satisfied himself nothing was missing from the caravan, he nodded to Mushezib. The chief guard growled something to his men. They got to their feet and swaggered over to take their places on either side of the donkeys. There were caravans where the guards ended up running the show, they being both armed and used to fighting. That had never happened to any caravan Sharur led. He was determined it wouldn't happen this time, either.

"All right, let's go," he said. "May Engibil give us a profitable journey." Several of the guards took out their amulets to help ensure that the city god heard and heeded the prayer. So did Harharu and a couple of the assistant donkey handlers.

Sharur gave Harharu the lead rope for the first donkey,

committing the caravan into the donkeymaster's hands. But before Harharu could take the first step, ram's-horn trumpets rang out on the Street of Smiths. In a great voice, a herald cried, "Behold! Forth comes Kimash, lugal of Gibil! Bow before Kimash the mighty, the powerful, the valiant, beloved of Engibil his patron! Forth comes Kimash, lugal of Gibil! Behold!"

The trumpets blared again. Drums thundered. Surrounding the lugal were warriors who made the men Sharur had hired seem striplings beside them. Even Mushezib looked less formidable when set against their thick-thewed bulk.

Sharur's grandfather's ghost spoke in his ear: "All this folderol over a mere man is a pack of nonsense, if anybody wants to know. The lugal in *my* day, Kimash's grandfather Igigi, didn't put on half so much show, and the ensi before him didn't put on any at all, to speak of."

"Yes, father to my father," Sharur answered, wishing the garrulous spirit would shut up. His grandfather's ghost often started chattering at the most inconvenient times.

Besides, the ghost wasn't so smart as it thought it was. The ensis who had ruled Gibil before Igigi had had no need for fancy displays of power, not with Engibil speaking directly through them. The lugals, on the other hand, were faced with the problem of getting people to obey them even though they spoke for no one but themselves. No wonder they made themselves as awesome as they could.

Sharur bowed low as Kimash's retinue came past the caravan. He was not altogether surprised when the procession stopped. Kimash favored smiths and merchants and scribes. They brought new powers into Gibil, powers that might be manipulated against Engibil's long-entrenched strength.

Kimash's guards stood aside to let the lugal advance. He was a man in his early forties, not far from Ereshguna's age, still vigorous even though gray was beginning to frost his hair and beard. He wore gold earrings, and bound his hair in a bun at the back of his neck with gold wire rather than a simple ribbon. The hilt of his dagger was wrapped in gold wire, too, and gold buckles sparkled on his belt and sandals.

"You may look on me," he told Sharur, who obediently straightened. The merchant reached out and set his hand on Kimash's thigh for a moment in token of submission. The lugal covered it with his own hand, then released it. He said, "May Engibil and the other gods, the great gods, favor your journey to the mountains, Sharur son of Ereshguna."

"I thank the lugal, the lord of Gibil," Sharur replied.

"May you be fortunate in bringing back ingots of shining copper; may your donkeys' panniers be laden with heavy sacks of ore," Kimash said.

"May it be so indeed," Sharur said.

Abruptly, Kimash abandoned the formal diction he used when speaking as lugal—the diction handed down for rulers since the days when the lords of Gibil were ensis through whom Engibil spoke—and addressed Sharur as one man to another: "I want that copper. We cannot have too much of it. Imhursag is stirring against us once more, and some of the towns with gods on top of them may send men and weapons to help in the next war."

"If I can get it for you, lord, I will," Sharur said. "I wouldn't be heading off to the Alashkurrut if I didn't think they would trade it to me."

"I know. I understand," the lugal answered. For all his power, for all his vigor, he was a worried man. "Bring back curiosities, too, things never seen in the land of Kudurru. Let me lay them on the altar in Engibil's temple to amuse the god and give him enjoyment."

"Lord, I will do as you say," Sharur promised. "The god of the city deserves the rich presents you lavish upon him."

He and Kimash looked at each other in mutual understanding. Neither of them smiled, in case the god was keeping an eye on Kimash. But they both knew how venal Engibil was. Igigi had been the first to discover that, if he heaped enough offerings on Engibil's altar, the god would let him act as he thought best, not merely as Engibil's mouthpiece. Kimash followed the same principle as had his grandfather. The god remained vastly stronger than the lugal, but Engibil was distracted and Kimash was not.

"I shall have Engibil's priests pray that you enjoy a safe and successful journey," Kimash said. Sharur bowed. Some of the priests, no doubt, resented the lugal for ruling, but, with the god content to suffer it, what could they do? And some, the younger men, served Engibil, aye, but served Kimash, too. The lugal said, "My prayers will go with theirs."

Sharur bowed again. "I thank the lugal, the lord of Gibil."

"One thing more," Kimash said with sudden abruptness. "Whatever word of Enimhursag's doings you hear in the wider world, bring it back to me and to Engibil. That god hates this city, for we beat Imhursag and we prosper though men rule us."

"I shall do as you say, lord," Sharur promised once more.

Kimash nodded, turned, and went back to his place among the palace guards, who fell in around him. His retinue started down the Street of Smiths once again, the trumpeters blowing great blasts of sound from their ram's horns, the herald announcing Kimash's presence to everyone nearby as if the lugal were equal to Engibil when the god (or, these past couple of generations, a statue of him) paraded through the city on his great feast day.

Harharu and Mushezib, the assistant donkey handlers and the guards, all looked at Sharur with new respect. Harharu had surely known Kimash favored Ereshguna's clan. Mushezib probably had known it, too. The others also might well have known it. But knowing it and being reminded of it were not one and the same. Everyone in Gibil knew the lugal's power. When he walked with guards and trumpeters and herald, he reminded people of it.

"Do you see, father to my father?" Sharur murmured.

He'd really been talking to himself, but his grandfather's ghost heard. "Oh, I see," it answered. "That doesn't mean I like it." The ghost left. He could feel it go. He smiled to himself. His grandfather hadn't liked much as an old man, and liked even less now that he was dead.

Sharur didn't suppose he could blame his grandfather's ghost. When the last person who remembered him alive died, the ghost would no longer be able to stay on earth, but would go down to the underworld and dwell in shadows forever. No wonder he reckoned any and all change for the worse.

One day, Sharur thought, that fate would be his, too. But he was young. Strength flowed through him. He hadn't yet married Ningal, and had no children, let alone grandchildren. Life stretched ahead, looking long and good. He did not intend to become a ghost for many, many years.

"Let's go!" he said. Harharu, as he had been on the point of doing when Kimash came over to Sharur, pulled on the lead donkey's line. The donkey stared at him with large, astonished liquid eyes: the idea of actually going anywhere had long since vanished from its mind. Harharu pulled again. The donkey's long ears twitched. It brayed indignantly.

"Give it a good kick," Mushezib suggested.

"Patience." Harharu's voice was mild. He tugged on the lead line again. The donkey started forward. That took up the slack on the line connecting it to the next beast, which brayed out its own protest before reluctantly following. The hideous clamor ran down the line. Here and there, a donkey balked. The handlers encouraged the animals to go, sometimes gently, sometimes by methods akin to Mushezib's. At last, the whole caravan was moving.

Dimgalabzu the smith, Ningal's father, came out of his house as Sharur led the caravan past it: a tough-looking, wide-shouldered man whose bare belly bulged above the belt upholding his kilt. He was carrying a big wicker basket full of rubbish, which he flung into the street. "Going off to get more copper for us, are you, Ereshguna's son?" he called.

"Just so, father to my intended bride," Sharur answered. "And, when I return, we shall talk about payment of the price for your daughter."

"You think so, do you?" Dimgalabzu said, not as a true threat but because he enjoyed making his prospective son-in-law squirm. "Well, we shall see, we shall see." He waved to Sharur, winked, and went back inside.

Mushezib chuckled. "I hope for your sake, lad, the girl takes after her mother."

"In looks, you mean? She does," Sharur answered. Ningal also had a good deal of her father's bluff, sometimes disconcerting sense of humor. Sharur said nothing about that. His fiancée's intimate personal characteristics were not the concern of a caravan guard.

He had turned off the Street of Smiths and was well on his way to the western gate when he led the caravan past a family who were knocking down their house. That happened every so often in Gibil. The sun-dried mud brick of which almost everything in the city save Engibil's temple and the lugal's palace was built was hardly the strongest stuff. Sometimes a wall would collapse under the growing weight of the roof as one season's mud chinking went on top of another's. Sometimes a wall would collapse at what seemed nothing more than the whim of a god or demon. Sometimes a whole house would fall down. When that happened, people often died.

No one seemed to have been hurt here, not by the cheerful way in which the family and a couple of slaves were biting chunks out of the one wall still standing with hoes and mattocks, and spreading and pounding the crushed mud bricks to make a floor for the new house they'd soon build on the site of the old one. They'd carefully saved their poplarwood roof beams and set them in the street next to the stacks of bricks from which the new house would arise.

The street had been narrow to begin with. Wood and bricks slimmed it further. And, of course, a crowd of people had gathered to watch the work and offer suggestions. "After you're done with your house, why don't you knock down mine?" somebody called.

"Knock down your own house, Melshippak," the man of the laboring family answered, in tones suggesting that Melshippak was a close friend or a relative. "Me, I'm going to enjoy being on a level with the street for a change, instead of taking a big step up every time I want to go out my own front door. This is the first time we've had to build in more than twenty years.''

Over twenty years, a lot of people had, like Dimgalabzu, pitched their trash into the street. No wonder its level had risen in that stretch of time.

Sharur, however, did not care how high the street was, only how wide, or rather, how narrow. "Please move aside," he called to Melshippak and the other spectators. When they didn't move, he shouted, "Make way!" That shifted a few of them, but not enough. He nodded to the caravan guards. They swaggered forward. Even without any weapons but fists and knives, they were large, impressive men. With them at his back, Sharur shouted, "Clear out, curse you! Stop clogging this canal!"

People stared at him as if they hadn't had the slightest idea he or the donkeys or the guards were anywhere nearby. Slowly, grudgingly, they gave way. One after another, the donkeys squeezed past the bottleneck. As soon as they had gone by, the crowd flowed back.

Like the god's temple, like the lugal's palace, the city wall was built of baked brick, far more costly than the sun-dried variety but far harder and more nearly permanent. In the Alashkurru Mountains, they made houses and walls out of stone, but in Kudurru that would have been even more expensive than baked brick.

"Engibil's goodwill and all good fortune attend you, son of Ereshguna," one of the gate guards said. They were Kimash's followers to a man, and so well inclined toward traders and smiths.

Sharur led the caravan down the low hill atop which Gibil sat and onto the floodplain at the base of that hill. He had descended the hill countless times, never once thinking about it. Now he looked back and seemed to see it with new eyes. Had it always been there, a knob sticking up from the flatland all around? Or had Gibil-that-was started out on the floodplain and slowly risen, one basketful of trash, one knocked-down house, at a time, till now it stood some distance above the plain all around? If that went on for another thousand years, or two, or three, would Gibil end up sitting atop a mountain? Maybe it would, but not with him here to see it, nor even his ghost.

The road that ran west toward the Yarmuk River—a beaten track in the mud—passed any number of small farming villages. A few of the better houses in them would be made of sun-dried brick, like those of Gibil. Most, though, were built of the reeds that grew along riverbanks and, where untended, choked canals to death. Those huts resembled nothing so much as enormous baskets turned upside down.

"I wouldn't want to live like that," Sharur said, pointing toward one such hut in front of which a couple of naked children played. "You couldn't go up to the roof to sleep without rolling off on your head."

Mushezib's laugh bared a fine set of strong, yellow teeth. "I grew up in a village like this one, but, after I'd gone into Gibil a few times to trade, I knew that was where I wanted to live out my days."

Harharu nodded. "My story is the same. So many people, though, are happy to stay in the fields all their lives." His wave over the landscape encompassed farmers weeding the growing wheat and barley, their wives tending garden plots of beans and onions and cabbage and melons and cucumbers, a couple of men digging mud from the bank of a canal and plopping it into square frames to make bricks, a woman spanking a child that had been naughty, and a fellow spearing fish out of a stream with a sharpened reed.

Sharur would have bet all those people would stay in their village till they died. He was lucky enough to have been born in Gibil, in a city that traded to east and west, north and south, and that boasted whole streets not only of smiths but also of potters and dyers and basketmakers and other artisans. Had he not been born there, he knew he, too, would have found a way to make it his home.

Then he thought again of Gibil-that-was, the town he imagined down on the valley floor rather than standing tall on its hill. In the time of his grandfather's grandfather's grandfather, would it not have been a village much like any of these others? He wondered what had made it grow while they stayed as they always were.

*Engibil*, he thought. The god had always dwelt there. People who came to petition him would have stopped to trade and simply to gossip with one another. That alone might have been enough to push Gibil ahead of the neighboring villages. Sharur smiled nervously. He, a modern man, tried to stay out of the god's shadow and stand in his own light as much as he could. Strange to think he might have been enabled to become a modern man because Engibil caused a city to come into being.

That night, the caravan camped by a village still in the territory ruled by Gibil. One of the donkeys carried trinkets to trade for supplies along the way. A few necklaces strung with pottery beads, brightly colored stones, and small seashells from the Sea of Rabia (into which the Yarmuk and Diyala flowed) got Sharur enough bread and beer and sundried fish to feed his men. He unrolled his blanket on the ground and slept till sunup.

"Come on," he said as he splashed water on his face from a canal to help wake himself up. Several of the donkey handlers and guards knelt by the edge of the water with him, doing the same. Others, a little farther downstream, pissed away the beer they'd drunk the night before. Still yawning, Sharur went on, "This was the last night we'll be able to rest without posting sentries. By tonight, we'll be in the lands that belong to the city of Zuabu. Nobody with any sense will trust the Zuabut: they're thieves."

"That's Enzuabu's fault," Harharu said. "They used to have another god there, a long time ago, but Enzuabu stole the city from him and chased him out into the desert. Of course the people take after their god."

"I heard it the other way round: that the city god takes after the people, I mean," Sharur said. "I heard they were such thieves that they raised a power of thievery in their land, and that was how Enzuabu got to be stronger than the god they used to have."

"It may be so," the donkeymaster answered with a shrug.

"It's not the tale I'd heard, but it may be so. Whether it is or it isn't, though, you're right—they steal."

The caravan came to the border between Gibil's lands and Zuabu's not long after noon. The two towns, the two gods, were at peace. No guards patrolled the frontier, as they did between Gibil and Imhursag to the north. A bridge of date-palm logs stretched across a canal. Once over it, Sharur went on down the road to the west through Zuabu's land.

Before long, Zuabut, curious as crows, came flocking to the caravan. They were as full of questions as they were of gossip, which was very full indeed. As they chattered away, they eyed the donkeys—and the bundles on the beasts' backs—with bright, avid eyes. Mushezib and the rest of the guards all did their best to look fierce and vigilant. Sharur was mournfully certain something would turn up missing; he hoped it wouldn't be anything too valuable or important.

You never could tell how much attention you ought to pay to anything the Zuabut said. Sharur listened to the story of Nurili, the ensi of Zuabu, impregnating all fourteen of his wives on the same night with the amount of incredulity he thought it deserved. "The god spoke through him," insisted the man of Zuabu telling the tale.

"The god poked through him, you say?" Sharur returned, pretending to misunderstand the hissing Zuabi dialect. His own men laughed. After a moment, when they realized Enzuabu wasn't offended (or, at least, hadn't noticed), the Zuabut laughed, too. Sharur went on, "That's what it would have taken, I think."

But not all the tales were tall ones. Another man of Zuabu said, "Three days ago, a caravan from Imhursag came through our land, also heading west. If you meet on the road, I hope you do not fight."

Zuabu was at peace with Gibil. But Zuabu was also at peace with Imhursag. Sharur said, "We will not be the first to fight. But if the Imhursagut quarrel with us, we will not be the first to leave off fighting, either."

"That is good. That is as it should be," the Zuabi said, nodding. "It may be, too, that you and the Imhursagut will not meet."

"Yes, it may be," Sharur agreed. "Whither are they bound?"

"To the mountains of Alashkurru, even as you are," the man of Zuabu replied. "Still, it may be that you and they will not meet. Three days is much time for travelers to make up on the road."

"This is also true," Sharur said. He did not believe it, though, not down in his heart. Had he had a three days' lead on the men of Imhursag, he would have been sure they could never catch him up. Being three days behind them, he reckoned it likely he would pass them on the road. People from towns where gods ruled directly never seemed to move quite so fast as those who did all their own thinking, all their own planning, for themselves.

The Zuabi pointed. "Look there in the sky!" he said, his voice rising in excitement. "It is a mountain eagle, flying to the west. This is bound to be a good omen for your caravan."

For a moment, Sharur's eyes did go to the sky. Then they swung back to the man of Zuabu, who was stepping rapidly toward the closest donkey. In his hand he had a little knife of chipped flint, the sort of knife everyone had used in the days before bronze. Sharur reached out and grabbed his wrist. "I do not think you would be wise to cut any bundles open. I think you would be wise to go away from this caravan and never let us see your face again."

"This is how you pay me back for warning you of your enemies?" the man said indignantly.

"No. This is how I pay you back for lying to me about the omen and for trying to steal my goods." Sharur spoke without heat. The people of Zuabu were given to thievery, and that was all there was to it. "Put away your little stone knife and go in peace. That is how I pay you back for warning me."

"Oh, very well," the man of Zuabu said. "You should have been fooled."

"I have been through Zuabu and the lands it rules before," Sharur answered. "I know some of your tricks—not all of them, but some."

The donkeys plodded on. Toward evening, they approached the city of Zuabu. Only one building was tall enough for its upper portions to be seen over the top of the city wall: the temple to Enzuabu. Sharur knew the ensi's residence was only a small annex to the temple, not a palace in its own right, as Kimash the lugal enjoyed back in Gibil.

"Shall we go up into the city for the night, master merchant's son?" Harharu asked.

Sharur shook his head. "I see no need to pay for lodgings, not when the weather is fine and we can sleep on our blankets. We have not been traveling so long that we stand in need of special comforts. On the way home, maybe we shall bed down in Zuabu, to remind ourselves of what lies just ahead."

That satisfied the donkeymaster. It also satisfied Mushezib, who, from everything Sharur had seen, liked going out on the road better than living soft in a city, anyhow. If the assistant donkey handlers and ordinary guards had different opinions, no one bothered to find out what they were.

Some time in the middle of the night, one of the guards, a burly fellow named Agum, shook Sharur awake. The moon had risen not long before, spilling soft yellow light over the land between the rivers. Sharur murmured a prayer of greeting to Nusku, then said, "What's wrong?"

Agum pointed toward the walls of Zuabu. "Master merchant's son, I'm glad we're not in that city tonight. Look—Enzuabu walks."

A chill went through Sharur. As gods went in the land of Kudurru, Engibil was a placid sort. Had it been otherwise, he should never have allowed merely human lugals to rule Gibil these past three generations. He was content, even eager, to accept the offerings the lugals gave him, and to stay in his temple to receive them. He had not gone abroad in his city since Sharur was a boy.

But, as Engibil had once done, other gods played more active roles in the lives of their cities. And so, his eyes wide with awe, Sharur saw Enzuabu's moonlight-washed figure, twice as tall as the walls of Zuabu, go striding through the streets. The god's eyes would have glowed whether the moon was in the sky or not; looking at them put Sharur in mind of the yellow-hot fires the smiths used to melt bronze for casting.

Across a couple of furlongs, those eyes met Sharur's. To the merchant's horror, Enzuabu paused in his peregrinations. He stared out toward the caravan as if contemplating paying it a visit. If he did, Sharur did not judge from the way his great form tensed that the visit would be a pleasant one.

Sharur's hand closed over the amulet he wore on his belt. "Engibil is my lord," he said rapidly. "Engibil has no quarrel with the lord of Zuabu."

For a moment, he thought Enzuabu would ignore that invocation and reminder. But then the god lowered his burning gaze so that it fell within the city once more. He reached down onto, or perhaps through, the roof of one of the houses there. When he straightened, the hand with which he had reached was closed—on what or whom, Sharur could not see. He thought that just as well.

Agum's voice was a bare thread of whisper: "If we'd been in there, he might have grabbed us like that."

*He might have grabbed* me *like that*, Sharur thought. For whatever reason, Enzuabu had taken him for an enemy, although, as he'd said, Enzuabu and Engibil were at peace, no less than their cities were. Sharur scratched his head in bewilderment. He'd come through Zuabu and its hinterland several times, going to and from the Alashkurru Mountains. Never once had the god of Zuabu taken the least notice of him.

A thought much like that must have crossed Agum's mind, for the guard asked, "Did you somehow anger Enzuabu, master merchant's son?"

"Not in any way I know," Sharur answered. "Come the morning, though, I will make a forgiveness-offering even so."

"It is good," Agum said. "I do not want a god angry at us."

"No, nor I." Sharur watched Enzuabu until the god shrank down to accommodate himself to his temple once more. Only then did the merchant think it safe to lie down and go back to sleep.

He greeted the rise of Shumukin, the lord of the sun, with a prayer set to the same music as that for Nusku the night before. Shumukin was, without a doubt, the most reliable god the folk of Kudurru knew. His one failing was that he sometimes did not know his own strength.

After telling Harharu and Mushezib what Agum and he had seen in the night, Sharur said, "I will buy two birds for the forgiveness-offering," and started back toward the village closest to Zuabu.

"Why not go into the city?" Mushezib asked. "It's right here before us."

Sharur shook his head. "I do not wish to enter the stronghold of Enzuabu on earth before offering to the god, not when I do not know how badly I may have offended him." Mushezib ran a hand through his thick, elaborately curled beard before finally nodding.

Having traded jewelry for a pair of trussed doves, Sharur carried them to the caravan. He laid them in a fine bowl, one for which he had intended to gain a high price from the men of Alashkurru. No help for it: an offering of his worst would have inflamed Enzuabu against him had the god not been angry before.

He held the bowl with the two doves out toward the walls of Zuabu and humbled himself before the city god: "Lord Enzuabu, if I have enraged thee—forgive, I beg! Lord Enzuabu, if I have affronted thee—forgive, I beg! Lord Enzuabu, if I have insulted thee—forgive, I beg! Lord Enzuabu, if I have offended thee—forgive, I beg! Lord Enzuabu, if I have slighted thee—forgive, I beg!"

After running through a long litany of the ways in which he might have incurred Enzuabu's displeasure, he twisted off the doves' heads and let their blood fill the bowl. Then, using only the first two fingers of his right hand, he sprinkled the blood on his chest and his kilt. He beckoned first Harharu and then Mushezib forward, and did the same with them. Last of all, he sprinkled the lead donkey with the doves' blood. The donkey snorted and twitched its big ears. It did not like the smell of blood.

"Lord Enzuabu—forgive, I beg!" Sharur cried. "May thy wrath be shattered like this bowl I give to thee!" With all his might, he dashed the thin, lovely bowl against the hard ground. It smashed into a hundred pieces. The doves' blood made a red star on the dirt.

"It is accomplished," Harharu intoned, almost as if he had expected it would not be. "Now let us continue."

"Now let us continue," Sharur echoed. Harharu pulled on the rope to get the lead donkey moving. But, as the caravan passed Zuabu by, he got no sense that Enzuabu had in fact forgiven him. True, the god did not rise up in fury, as he might have done, but he yielded nothing, either. He simply bided his time.


West and north of the lands Zuabu ruled was a barren, unirrigated stretch of land no city or god claimed. Little dust demons swirled around the caravan, now nervously running away from the men and donkeys, now skittering up close to see if they might cause some mischief. When one of them got under his feet and tried to trip him, Sharur took from his belt the eyed amulet of Engibil. "Begone!" he cried, and, with little frightened gasps, the dust demons fled from the power of the god.

Wild donkeys fled from the caravan, too; the power of man sufficed to put them in fear. Their hooves kicked up more dust than all the dust demons in the world could have raised. Sharur sent Agum and one of the assistant donkey handlers, a wide-shouldered man named Rukagina, after them with bows. The hunters returned later in the day with a gutted carcass slung from a pole.

Sharur led the cheers for them. "Tonight we feast!" he

cried. Wild donkey might not be so flavorsome as mutton or beef, but everyone would be able to gorge himself on meat.

The caravan crew were not the only hunters on the plain. Not long after Agum and Rukagina came back with the donkey, a lion roared nearby. That fierce, thunderous cough made Sharur's hand fly to the hilt of his knife before he realized it had done so. It also made the donkeys of the caravan, which had been restive at the sight and smell of one of their kind slain, suddenly become docile as lambs.

Harharu chuckled. "They depend on us to protect them from the wild beasts, and they know it," he said to Sharur.

Off in the distance, the wild donkeys threw up a great cloud of dust. The roar sounded again, and several more after it in quick succession. Vultures spiraled down out of the sky, as they had done when Agum and Rukagina killed. Then the birds could feast on the offal the men had left behind. Now they would have to wait until the lions were done before taking their share.

Sharur set his hand on the neck of the lead donkey. "We will give them what they expect, then," he said. The donkey snapped at him. He jerked his hand away in a hurry. Harharu laughed out loud.

That evening, the guards and donkey handlers gathered brush and dry donkey dung for a couple of cookfires by a tiny stream. They and Sharur held gobbets of donkey meat over the flames on sticks, roasting them till they were charred black on the outside but still red and juicy within. Sharur burned his fingers, burned his lips, burned his tongue. He did not care. His belly would be full.

Rukagina's eyes glowed in the firelight. For a moment, Sharur, seeing that, simply accepted it. Then he knew something was amiss. The eyes of dogs and foxes, wild cats and lions, gave back the fire that way: he had watched the beasts prowling round the edges of many camps. Men's eyes did not normally reflect the light in the same way.

Demons' eyes did, though. "Rukagina!" Sharur said sharply.

Rukagina stared at him. The donkey handler's eyes

glowed brighter still, as if the fire were behind them, not in front. "Rukagina, yes," he said, as if he did not recognize his own name. Then he laughed, a hideous cry that made all his companions exclaim in alarm. "Rukagina is eaten, eaten!" he roared.

"A pestilence!" Harharu said. "A demon of this desert has seized him."

"Yes," Sharur said, and brandished Engibil's eyed amulet, as he had at the little dust demons on the road.

This one was made of sterner stuff. Its laugh came again through Rukagina's mouth. "I am the spirit of this desolation," it declared. "Your god is far from home, and lazy even in his own city. He has no power over me here. The desert is my city. Here I am a god. Maybe with this man I shall cause a true city to rise here. Then I shall be a true god, a great god, greater than your god."

Maybe the demon could do that. Maybe Engibil had been just such a wandering desert spirit once. But Sharur did not intend to let the demon aggrandize itself at the expense of one of his men. "Seize him!" he shouted, and the caravan guards piled onto Rukagina.

With the demon in him, the donkey handler fought back with more than human strength. But he was not stronger than all the guards together. They held him down, two men on each arm, three on each leg. He howled like a fox. He hissed like a serpent. He snarled like a lion, and tried to bite like one. And ever and always, he kept seeking to throw the guards off him.

Mushezib drew his bronze knife from its sheath. "Maybe I should yank up his beard and cut his throat like a sheep's," the guard captain said. "That would make the demon flee."

"Yes, but whom would it seize next?" Sharur asked. "You, perhaps?"

"Avert the omen!" Mushezib exclaimed, and spat to his left side.

Sharur walked over to the packs the men had taken from the donkeys' backs when they stopped for the night. Had he paid less attention to the way the beasts were loaded, he might have searched till sunrise without finding what he sought. As things were, he ran it to earth like a cheetah bringing down a gazelle gone lame: a small, plain pot, its stopper sealed with pitch.

"What have you got there?" Mushezib asked.

"Essence of the marigold," Sharur answered. "The Alashkurrut esteem it highly, and every caravan sells many jars to them. It's sovereign against scorpion stings—of which they have many—snakebite, jaundice, toothache, stomach trouble, difficult breathing, diseases of the privates . . . and possession by a demon."

"Strong stuff!" the guard captain said admiringly.

"Engibil grant it be strong enough." Sharur used the point of his own knife to scrape away the pitch and pry up the lid to the pot. He was used to being glad Engibil took less part in human affairs than a god like Enzuabu or, worse, Enimhursag. But when a desert demon mocked his deity, he wondered if he should have second thoughts.

A sweet, spicy odor rose from the pot when he opened it. Beckoning for Mushezib to come with him, he walked over to demon-possessed Rukagina and squatted beside him. Seeing—and perhaps smelling—what he bore, the spirit made the donkey handler clench his jaws tight, like a two-year-old who refused to eat his mashed parsnips.

Mushezib seized Rukagina's beard and pulled with all his formidable strength. Altogether against the demon's will, the donkey handler's mouth came open. Sharur poured half a potful of essence of marigold down him. Rukagina was trying to cry out at that moment, which meant the medicine all but drowned him. Instead of being able to spit it out, he coughed and choked . . . and swallowed.

He let out a cry that frightened into silence the small crawling and creeping, piping and cheeping creatures around the caravan's campfires. His entire body convulsed, so violently that the men holding him were flung from his limbs. Something dark came forth from his mouth and nose, from his eyes and ears, and was gone before Sharur could be sure he had seen it.

Rukagina sat up and looked around. A hand went to his chin. "Who's been pulling my beard?" he demanded. Had Mushezib yanked on Sharur's whiskers like that, his chin would have been sore, too.

"Look at the fire," he told the donkey handler. When Rukagina did, Sharur studied his eyes. They did not flash as they had before. "The gods be praised: we have driven the demon from you."

"Demon?" Rukagina said. "What demon? I was sitting by the fire, eating a slice of the donkey's liver, and, and . . ." His voice trailed away. "I do not remember what happened after that."

"As well that you do not," Sharur said, to which the rest of the caravan crew nodded in unison, as if a single will controlled them.

"Tell me!" Rukagina said. His companions were happy enough to oblige him.

Thoughtfully, Sharur replaced the stopper in the pot of marigold essence. Among the supplies the caravan carried was a small pot of pitch: no telling when someone might need to stick something to something else. As he used a twig to daub it on and reseal the stopper so what was left of the medicine would not spill, Mushezib came up to him and said, "That is a strong medicine."

"Yes, it is," Sharur agreed. "Now that I can tell the Alashkurrut I saw with my own eyes how it routed a strong demon, I can charge more for it."

"True enough," the guard captain said. Eyeing the pot, he went on in musing tones: "If it works as well for diseases of the privates as for driving out demons, it is a very strong medicine indeed."

"Ah." Sharur looked down at the pot he held in his hands. He hefted it. "Do you know," he said, "I very much doubt the Alashkurrut would want a pot that has already had half the medicine drunk from it. Why don't you take it, Mushezib? You can dispose of it as you like."

"The master merchant's son is kind." Mushezib made sure he did not seem too eager. "I shall do just that."

# 2

Past the haunted desert, three cities lay between Gibil and the Yarmuk River. In neither of the first two, both ruled by ensis, did the caravan encounter any difficulty with men or gods. Sharur still wondered why Enzuabu had seemed so hostile. Even the demon of the desolation had mocked Engibil. The omen struck Sharur as worrisome. "I wonder if the demon troubled the caravan out of Imhursag," he said to Harharu.

"I doubt it," the donkeymaster answered. "The Imhursagut have their heads so full of their god, there's no room in them for anything else."

"In that case, I am glad to be empty-headed," Sharur said, and Harharu laughed. So did Sharur, though a moment later he wondered what was funny. If Enimhursag protected his people and Engibil did not protect his, which was the stronger god?

But a city's strength, as Sharur well knew, depended on more than the strength of its god. It was the strengths of god and men together. Engibil might be weaker than some, but Gibil, as the metal merchant knew, was by no means to be despised. Where gods were weak, the strength of men could grow, as could their ability to act for themselves. He cherished what freedom he had: cherished it and wanted more.

Instead of going through the territory of Aggasher, the city that controlled the usual crossing point for the Yarmuk,

Sharur swung the caravan north through the debatable land just to the east of it. Eniaggasher, the city's goddess, ruled it in her own right. He found dealing with men who were hardly more than mouthpieces for their city's deity tedious at any time. Now he also feared they would try to delay him or, worse, to help the cause of the caravan from Imhursag, whose men remained similarly in the hands of their god.

"I know what you're doing," Harharu said when Sharur ordered the turn. "This wouldn't work in springtime, you know."

"We're not in springtime," Sharur said with a smile. "The sun is high, and the river is low."

A couple of herdsmen and a couple of peasants stared as the caravan came down to the Yarmuk. They were folk of Aggasher. One day, Eniaggasher would chance to look through their eyes when a caravan from Gibil used this ford to avoid crossing by the city. Then there might be trouble. But it had not happened yet. Eniaggasher paid little attention to these outliers under her control, in the same way that a man, under most circumstances, paid little attention to his toenails.

A goddess dwelt in the Yarmuk, too, of course. Before venturing into the river, Sharur walked up to the bank, a gleaming bronze bracelet inset with polished jet in his hands. "For thee, Eniyarmuk, to adorn thyself and make thyself more beautiful," he said, and dropped the bracelet into the muddy water.

The sacrifice made, he took off his sandals, pulled down his kilt, and stepped naked into the Yarmuk to test the ford. The sand and mud of the river bottom squelched up between his toes. Little fish nibbled at his legs. The cool water seemed to caress his body as he advanced. He took that for a sign the river goddess had accepted his offering.

Up to his knees he went, up to his thighs, up to his waist and beyond. If the water got much deeper, the donkeys would have trouble crossing. "Let us be able to ford in safety, Eniyarmuk, and I will give thee another bracelet, like unto the first, when we reach thy farther bank," he said, and pressed on across the river.

Before long, his navel, and then his privates, too, came out of the water. He kept on until, wet and dripping, he emerged on the western bank of the Yarmuk. From there, he waved back at the rest of the caravan. Guards and donkey handlers got out of their clothes. Rukagina thoughtfully picked up Sharur's kilt and sandals and carried them above his head along with his own gear. The men led the donkeys into the river.

As Sharur had prayed they would, they made the crossing without incident: almost without incident, at any rate, for a couple of men and a couple of donkeys came out of the water with leeches clinging to their legs. They had to start a fire there by the riverbank, and use burning twigs to make the worms' heads let go. The guards cried out in disgust. One of the donkey handlers cried out, too, when a donkey kicked him. Despite the leeches, Sharur gave Eniyarmuk the second bracelet.

He went up and down the length of the caravan to see if the trip through the ford had damaged anything. A couple of bolts of red-dyed linen were soaked, but everything else seemed all right. He sighed. "Well, we're not going to get much for those, not with the color running and stained with mud," he said.

"For a fording, we did well," Harharu said.

"I know that," Sharur answered. "And we saved ourselves trouble from Eniaggasher, unless I miss my guess. But even so——" He scowled. He did not like anything to go wrong, and was still young enough to be easily aggrieved when perfection eluded him. He also begrudged the time spent going down small paths back to the main road.

West of the river, as far as canals took its waters and those of a couple of small tributaries, the land might as well have been part of Kudurru. The people were of the same stock. They spoke the same language, although with a rather singsong intonation. They worshiped the same great gods and lived in the same sort of reed-hut farming villages.

But they had no cities, and no city gods. None of the demons dwelling in this part of the world had been strong enough to consolidate any great number of people under his control. Like the spirit that haunted the waste west of Zuabu, the demons west of the Yarmuk might have had ambitions, but as yet lacked the power to make those ambitions real.

West of the Yarmuk, too, more and more stretches of ground were bare, dry wasteland: country that might have been fertile if water reached it, but that was too far from any stream or rose too high to be irrigated. The mountains of Alashkurru rose higher above the horizon here. Back in Gibil, they were visible only on the clearest days: a deep, mysterious smudge denting the edge of the sky. Not here. West of the Yarmuk, Sharur felt them looking down on him.

Two days after the caravan forded the river, irrigated land became the exception, dry, scrubby country the rule. There was enough forage for the donkeys; Sharur bartered some of the water-damaged linen for a couple of sheep from a herder driving his flock not far from the road. That night, he and the donkey handlers and guards ate roast mutton with wild garlic.

The next morning, they caught up with the caravan from Imhursag.

Sharur had known they were gaining on the Imhursagut. Had he not taken the detour, they would have caught them sooner . . . so long as everything went well at the main river crossing by Aggasher. He doubted that would have happened.

When the donkeys of the other caravan went from being hoofprints on the road to shapes in front of him, Sharur ordered the guards to don their helmets and carry weapons and shields. "You just can't tell what the Imhursagut will do," he told Mushezib. "If Enimhursag wants them to attack us, they will, even if we should outnumber them. A god does what he thinks best for himself first, and worries about his people only afterwards."

"I've seen that myself, in the wars we've fought against Imhursag," the guard captain said. "The Imhursagut would throw themselves away for no purpose anybody with even a bare keshlu of sense could see. But they think we're crazy, because each one of us acts for himself instead of as a piece of our god's plan. Goes to show, you ask me."

*Goes to show what?* Sharur wondered. Instead of asking, he ran a finger along the edge of his bronze spearhead, then tapped the point. He nodded to himself. It was as sharp as he could make it.

Up ahead, the Imhursagut were also arming themselves. Sharur saw shields, spears, swords, bows. The other caravan looked about the same size as his own. If the two crews came to blows, they were liable to wreck each other.

"It will be as I said in the land ruled by Zuabu," Sharur declared. "We shall not begin the fight here. But if the Imhursagut begin it, let our cry be, 'Engibil and no quarter!'" The guards nodded. Some of them looked eager to fight. Some did not. All of them looked ready.

Closer and closer the caravan drew to that from Imhursag. Soon they were within easy bowshot of the rearmost donkeys from the rival city. Almost all the Imhursagut had dropped back to the rear to defend the beasts against the men of Gibil.

Sharur strode out ahead of his lead donkey. "Gibil and Imhursag are not at war now!" he shouted. That was true. It was also the most that could be said for relations between the two cities.

One of the Imhursagut walked back toward him and held up a hand, not in peace but in warning. "Come no farther, Gibli!" he cried. "Halt your donkeys. Do not approach us until you have made known your desires to Enimhursag, the mighty god."

"You also halt your donkeys, then," Sharur said. "We will parley, you and I." He suppressed a sigh. They would parley: Sharur and the man of Imhursag and Enimhursag himself. It was liable to take a while, for the god would have only a tiny part of his attention directed toward the caravan.

Sure enough, the Imhursaggi stood as if waiting for orders for several breaths before nodding jerkily and saying, "It shall be as you propose." He turned back to the rest of the Imhursagut and ordered them to halt. Sharur waved for his followers to come no closer. Then the man from Imhursag demanded, "Why are you pursuing us? The god told us some time ago that you were following in our wake."

"We are not pursuing you," Sharur answered. "We are going our own way, down the same road as you are using, and we happen to be moving rather faster. Let us go by without fighting. You will breathe our dust for a little while, but then it shall be as if we never were."

"It could be so," the man of Imhursag said. But then, while he seemed on the point of adding something more, he suddenly shook his head. "No. Enimhursag does not believe you. You seek to get ahead of us to disrupt our trade with the Alashkurrut."

Only the certain knowledge that laughing in a god's face was dangerous made Sharur hold his mouth closed. The city gods of Kudurru were a provincial lot, Enimhursag more than most. Though his power touched his followers far beyond the land he ruled, he had no true conception of the size of the world and its constituent parts. "Alashkurru is a wide land," Sharur said soberly. "We can trade in one part of it and you in another. Even if we get there first, it will not matter."

"It could be so," the Imhursaggi said again.

"If you are a merchant, you will have made the journey to the mountains of Alashkurru yourself," Sharur said, speaking to the fellow as one man to another: always an uncertain proposition when dealing with folk from a god-ruled city. "You will know for yourself how wide the mountain country is—more like Kudurru as a whole than any one city within the land between the rivers. Your caravan and mine can both trade there."

"It could be so," the man of Imhursag repeated. Sharur

started to be angry at him for his stupid obstinacy, but
checked himself. He realized the Imhursaggi did not dare—
or perhaps simply could not—come straight out and disagree with his god. That did not rouse anger in Sharur, but
pity and fear.

"Let us past you without fighting," he said gently. "In
Engibil's name, I swear my men will start no quarrel with
yours as we go by."

"How can you swear in your god's name?" the Imhursaggi—or was it Enimhursag himself?—asked. "Engibil
does not speak through the Giblut. We have seen this, to
our cost. The words of the men of your city have only their
own wind behind them, not the truth of the gods."

For the first time, Sharur realized deep in his belly that
he and the rest of the folk of Gibil were as strange and
frightening to the Imhursagut as they were to him. "I speak
only for myself," he admitted, "but Engibil is still my god.
If I lie in his name, he will punish me."

"That has not always been so," the man of Imhursag
replied. But then, abruptly, his whole tone changed. He
threw back his head and laughed. When he looked at Sharur,
he seemed to look straight through him: Enimhursag was
looking out through his eyes. Sharur shivered and reached
for Engibil's amulet. No assault came, though, neither
against his body nor against his spirit. "Go on," the Imhursaggi said, in a voice not quite his own. "Go on! Alashkurru is wide, you say. See if it is wide enough for you."
He laughed again, even less pleasantly than before.

As quickly as Enimhursag had taken full possession of
him, the god released him once more. He staggered a little,
then caught himself. Sharur wondered if he would remember
what the god had said through him. He proved he did, turning to his own caravan crew and ordering them to move
their donkeys to the side of the road to let Sharur and his
companions pass. Men of Gibil would have argued. The
Imhursagut, feeling the will of their god press on them,
obeyed without a word.

To Sharur, the Imhursaggi spoke as himself once more:

"Go ahead. You Giblut are always so eager to go ahead, so eager to sniff out a keshlu's weight of silver in the middle of a dungheap. Go ahead, and see what it profits you now."

"What did your god tell you?" Sharur asked. "Why did he change his mind like that?"

"I do not know why," the man of Imhursag answered. "I do not want to know why. I do not need to know why. It is not my place to know why." He spoke with pride, where Sharur would have been furious at being kept in the dark. "As for what he told me, he told me no more than I told you."

Was that true? Sharur wondered. But the Imhursaggi was less naive than some men from god-ruled cities with whom he'd dealt, and so he could not be sure. Muttering under his breath, Sharur went back to his own caravan. "Forward!" he told the guards and donkey handlers, adding, "I have sworn in Engibil's name that we shall not be the first to start any fight. Be ready for trouble, but begin none yourselves, lest you leave me forsworn."

"Do you hear that, you lugs?" Mushezib growled to the guards. He set down his spear for a moment so he could thump his chest with a big, hard fist. "Anybody who gets frisky when he shouldn't have answers to me afterwards."

Warily, Sharur led his caravan past the one from Imhursag. The Imhursagut did not attack his men. He had not thought they would, not when Enimhursag, speaking through their leader, had agreed to let him by. They did jeer and hoot and make horrible faces: they obeyed their god, but their manner declared what they would have done had he given them leave.

Perhaps they were trying to make the Giblut lose their tempers and begin the fight. Wanting to prevent that, Sharur pointed to the Imhursagut and said, "See the trained monkeys? Aren't they funny? Why don't you throw them a few dates, if you're carrying any in your belt pouches to munch on as we walk?"

As he'd hoped, the guards and donkey handlers laughed. A couple of them did toss dates to the Imhursagut. Their rivals plainly did not know whether to be glad of the food or angry at the way they received it: Enimhursag did not know, and had not told them. They were still waiting for their god to respond by the time the last of Sharur's donkeys and the last of his men had passed them by.

Harharu said, "That was well done, master merchant's son. When men from a god-ruled city act in ways they have acted before, they are as quick and clever as we. Give them something new to chew on, even if it be only a date"—he and Sharur smiled at each other—"and they wave their legs in the air like a beetle on its back until their god decides what they should do."

"I was hoping that would happen," Sharur agreed. He raised his voice: "Well done, men. Now the Imhursagut will be breathing our dust and stepping in our donkey droppings all the way to Alashkurru. Let's step it up for the rest of the day, so we can camp well apart from them."

His followers cheered. They complained not at all about moving faster. The donkeys complained, but then the donkeys always complained.


Sharur picked his campsite that evening with great care. He would not be satisfied until he found a small rise the caravan crew could easily defend against an attack in the night and from which he could see a long way in all directions. "The Imhursagut won't trouble us here," Mushezib said, nodding vigorous approval. "They'll be able to tell we'd give them lumps if they tried it. That's the best way to keep someone from bothering you."

"My thought exactly." Sharur looked toward the east. He spied what had to be the Imhursaggi camp, fires twinkling like medium-bright stars, a surprising distance away. "We did walk them into the ground this afternoon."

"Of course we did." Mushezib's massive chest inflated further. "Master merchant's son, if we can't outdo the Imhursagut, we aren't worth much. You tell me if that isn't so."

"Well, of course it is." Sharur had as much pride in his comrades, the men of his city, as did the guard captain. Walking back to the rest of the guards and the donkey handlers, he asked, "Does anyone have a ghost traveling with him?" He had never thought he would wish his bad-tempered grandfather had joined him on the caravan instead of staying back in Gibil, but he did now.

Agum the guard looked up from his supper of dried fish and dates. "I do, master merchant's son. Uncle Buriash guarded a couple of caravans himself, so he likes traveling this road."

"That is good. That is very good," Sharur said. He had never known Agum's uncle, who therefore might as well not have existed as far as his senses were concerned. "I want him to go back to the camp of the Imhursagut and listen to their talk for a while, to see if he can spy out why their leader—why their god—changed his mind and decided to let us pass. He should also see if he can learn why their leader mocked our chances for good trading in Alashkurru."

Agum cocked his head to one side, listening to the dead man's voice only he could hear. "He says he'll be glad to do that, master merchant's son. He doesn't like the Imhursagut any better than we do. In one of the wars we fought with them—I don't quite know which—they stole all his sheep."

"Thank you, Buriash, uncle to Agum," Sharur said. Even if he could not hear the ghost, the ghost could hear him.

"He says he is leaving now," Agum reported. "He says he will return with the word you need."

Sharur was just sitting down to his own supper when Harharu came wandering over to him. The donkeymaster spat out a date pit, then said, "Sending the ghost out is well done, master merchant's son. Not many would have thought of it, and it may bring us much profit." He grimaced and chuckled wryly. "My own ghosts, I'm just as well pleased they're back in the city far away."

"I was thinking the same thing about my grandfather," Sharur answered.

Harharu nodded. Because Sharur outranked him, he chose to come round to what he had in mind by easy stages. "Would we not be wise to wonder whether what we do, others might do as well?"

"Ah," Sharur said around a mouthful of salt fish. He saw where Harharu was heading. "You may speak frankly with me, donkeymaster. I shall not be offended, I promise."

"Many people say that. A few even mean it." Harharu studied him. "Yes, you may be one of those few. Very well, then: if the Imhursagut think to send a ghost to spy on us, can we trap it?"

"I suppose we can try," Sharur answered. "After tonight, it will not matter, for we shall be too far ahead of them for one of their ghosts to catch us up. And now it will be hard for us to tell an Imhursaggi ghost from a curious ghost of the countryside, just as Buriash may well seem such a ghost to them."

"What you say is true, master merchant's son," Harharu agreed. "And yet—"

"And yet," Sharur echoed. He tugged at his beard. "It might be done. A ghost from Imhursag will bear the scent, so to speak, of Enimhursag, where a ghost of the countryside will not."

"It is so," Harharu said. "If you can use this difference without offending the ghosts and demons and gods who make this land their home—"

"I shall take great care, donkeymaster—believe me in that regard," Sharur said, and tugged at his beard again. "I think it can be done. You are right. I do not want to offend the unseen things here. I shall make a point of letting them know we do not claim this country forever, only for a night."

"Ah, very good," Harharu said. "Any man would know you for your father's son by your resourcefulness."

"You are kind to a young man." Sharur inclined his head in polite gratitude.

Setting a small pot on the ground out where the light from the fires grew dim, he walked around the encampment, chanting, "Tonight, let the land in this circle belong to the men who follow Engibil. Until the rising of the sun, let the land in this circle belong to the men who follow Engibil. Tonight, let Engibil protect the land in this circle. Until the rising of the sun, let Engibil protect the land in this circle. Tonight, let Engibil ward off and drive away Enimhursag and the things of Enimhursag from the land in this circle. Until the rising of the sun, let Engibil ward off and drive away Enimhursag and the things of Enimhursag from the land in this circle."

On he went, slowly, ceremoniously: "Before we, the men who follow Engibil, encamped here, the land in this circle belonged to the unseen things that dwell here always. After we, the men who follow Engibil, depart hence with the rising of the sun, the land in this circle shall again belong to the unseen things that dwell here always. We, the men who follow Engibil, seek only our god's protection this one night for the land in this circle."

He repeated his prayer and his promise the prayer was for the night only over and over again, until he approached the spot from which he had begun the circle. Continuing to chant, he peered around and finally spied the pot he had used to mark his beginning point. With a sigh of relief, he stepped over it and walked on for a few more paces, making certain the circle was complete.

"That is a good magic, master merchant's son," Mushezib said when Sharur walked back to the fires. "May we have much profit from it."

"May it be so," Sharur said. His own prayer was that the magic would prove altogether unnecessary, that the Imhursagut would never think to send a ghostly spy to his camp. He would not know one way or the other, for he could hardly hope to sense the spirit of a man or woman with whom he had not been acquainted in life.

He turned to Agum. "Has the ghost of your Uncle Buriash returned from the Imhursaggi camp?"

"No, master merchant's son," the guard replied. "But he wouldn't be back yet anyhow. He has to go there from here, and then here from there, and he'll want to listen a good long while in between times. I don't expect him till after I go to sleep." He grinned at Sharur. "He'll yell in my ear then, never fear."

Sharur nodded. "He sounds like my grandfather. Good enough. When he does come back, you wake me. I shall want to know what he says as soon as he says it. Why did Enimhursag change his caravan leader's mind?"

"I shall obey you like a father," Agum promised.

But Sharur woke only with morning twilight the next day. Angrily, he hurried over to Agum. The guard was already up and about, with a worried expression on his face. "I would have wakened you, master merchant's son, of course I would," he said. "But Uncle Buriash never came back. I finally went to sleep myself, sure he'd wake me when he returned, but he never did."

"Where is he, then? Where can he be?" Sharur uneasily looked eastward, back toward the camp of the Imhursagut.

"I thought—I was hoping—the circle you made last night might have kept him away," Agum said.

Sharur frowned. "I don't see why it should have. Your uncle's ghost is no enemy to Engibil, no friend to Enimhursag."

"No, of course not," Agum said. "Still, I did not want to go beyond the circle and maybe break it to find out if he was waiting there. If he is, I'll hear about it soon enough." His chuckle sounded nervous. "First time in a while I'll be glad to have the old vulture yelling at me, let me tell you."

"I know what you mean." Sharur slapped the guard on the back. "The circle will break of itself when Shumukin brings the sun up into the sky. Then Buriash can harangue you to his heart's content."

The sun rose. The caravan headed off toward the west once more. But Uncle Buriash did not return to Agum when the circle of magic was broken. Agum never heard Uncle Buriash's voice again. All that day, and for days to come, Sharur kept looking back in the direction of the caravan from Imhursag. What he felt was something uncommonly like fear.

The land rose and, rising, grew rough. Streams dwindled. Near them, a few farmers scratched out a meager living. The land a little farther from them could have been brought under the plow, too, had anyone dug canals out to it. Not enough people lived along the streams to make the work worthwhile.

Instead, herders drove large flocks of cattle and sheep—larger than any in crowded Kudurru—through the grass and brush that grew without irrigation. Lean, rough-looking men, they watched the caravan with hungry eyes. Guards and donkey handlers and Sharur himself always went armed. Thanks to Mushezib, the guards acted as tough and swaggering as the herdsmen, and so had no trouble with them.

"You can't let them think you're afraid of 'em," Mushezib said to Sharur one evening. "If they get that idea into their heads, they'll jump on you like a lion on a lame donkey."

"Yes, I've seen that," Sharur said. "The Alashkurrut are the same way." His eyes went to the west. This country blended almost seamlessly with the foothills of the Alashkurru Mountains. He sighed. "Another few days of traveling and only a few folk, the folk who make a habit of trading with us, will speak our language. The rest will use the words of the Alashkurrut."

Mushezib used a word of the Alashkurrut, a rude word. He laughed a loud, booming laugh. "A guard doesn't need to know much more. 'Beer.' 'Woman.' 'Bread,' maybe. 'How much?' 'No, too much.' Those do the job."

"I suppose so." Almost, Sharur wished he could live a life as simple as Mushezib's. When all went well, the guard captain had little more to do than walk all day and, when evening came, have someone give him food and beer and silver besides, so he could buy a woman's company for the night or whatever else he happened to want. To a peasant living in drudgery the whole year through, that would seem a fine life indeed. It had seemed so to Mushezib, who had made it real for himself, just as at the beginning of days the great gods had made the world real from the thought in their minds.

For Sharur, though, the reality Mushezib had made from his thought was not enough. The guard captain cared about no one past himself, about nothing more than getting through one day after another. When he died, his ghost would not remain long upon the earth, for who would remember him well enough for the spirit's voice to linger in his ears?

Sharur walked down to the edge of the little nameless stream (nameless to him, anyhow; whatever god or goddess dwelt in it had never drawn his notice) and scooped up a handful of muddy clay. Mushezib followed, saying, "What are you doing, master merchant's son? Oh, I see—making a tablet. What have you found here that you need to write?"

"I'm practicing, that's all," Sharur answered. "I practice with the spear, I practice with the sword, and I practice with the stylus, too." So speaking, he took the stylus from his belt and incised on the soft clay the three complex squiggles that made up Mushezib's name. The guard captain, who could neither read nor write, watched without comprehension.

*Hear me, all gods and demons of this land*, Sharur thought. *I mean no harm to the man whose name I erase.* He crumbled the tablet in his hands, then washed them clean of mud in the running water.

"Didn't the writing come out the way you wanted it?" Mushezib asked.

"It was not everything it could have been," Sharur replied. Mushezib's life was like that: a tablet that would crumble and weather and be gone all too soon after writing covered its surface. Sharur wanted the tablet of his life to go through the fire after it was done, to deserve to be baked hard as kiln-dried brick and so to have the writing on it preserved forever in the memories of Gibil and the Giblut.

Mushezib had his own ideas about that, though. Laughing again, he said, "What *is* everything it could be?" Sharur, to his own embarrassment, found no good reply for the guard captain.

The demon sprawled in the roadway. It looked like a large wild cat with wings. Its eyes glowed with green fire. It lashed its tail, as if to suggest it had a sting there like a scorpion's.

At the sight of it, Harharu had halted the caravan. He did nothing more. Doing more was not his responsibility but Sharur's. Sharur approached until he was almost—but, he made sure, not quite—within reach of that lashing tail. Bowing, he spoke in the language of the mountains: "You are not a demon of the land of Kudurru. You are not a demon of the land between the rivers. You are a demon of Alashkurru. You are a demon of the high country. I know you, demon of the high country."

"I am a demon of the high country." The demon sprang into the air and turned a backwards somersault, for all the world like a playful kitten. "You are one of the new people, the people from afar, the people who travel, the people who bring strange things to Alashkurru."

"I am one of those people," Sharur agreed. Men from Kudurru had been trading with the Alashkurrut for generations. To the demon, though, they were *the new people*. They would likely be *the new people* five hundred years hence as well. The demon showed no sign of moving aside. It lolled in the sunlight, stretching bonelessly. "Why do you block our path?" Sharur asked. "Why do you not let us travel? Why do you not let us bring our new things"—he would not call them *strange things*—"to Alashkurru?"

"You are the new people," the demon repeated. It cocked its head to one side and studied Sharur. "You are one of the new people even among the new people. You listen to your own voice. You do not listen to your god's voice."

"That is not true," Sharur replied. "Engibil is my god.

Engibil is my city's god. All in Gibil worship Engibil and set fine offerings in his temple.''

"You play with words." The demon's tail sprang out, like a snake. Sharur was glad he had kept his distance from it. "Your own self is in the front of your spirit. Your god's voice is in the back of your spirit. You are one of the new people even among the new people." By its tone, the demon might have accused him of lying with his mother.

"I do not understand all you say." Sharur was lying. He knew he was lying. The demon laid the same charge against him and his fellow Giblut as Enimhursag had done. He took a deep breath, then went on, "It does not matter. We come to Alashkurru to trade. We come in peace. We have always come in peace. The wanakes, the chieftains, of Alashkurru profit by our coming. Let us pass."

Lash, lash, lash went the demon's tail. "You trade more than you know, man of the new people even among the new people. When you talk with the wanakes, the chieftains, of Alashkurru, you infect them with your new ways, as an unclean whore infects a man with a disease of the private parts. There are wanakes, chieftains, of Alashkurru who have spoke with great wickedness, saying, 'Let us put our own selves in the front of our spirits. Let us put our gods' voices in the back of our spirits.' The gods of Alashkurru grow angry at hearing such talk, at hearing such thoughts."

"I trade metal. I trade cloth. I trade medicine. I trade wine," Sharur said stolidly. Under the hot sun, the sweat that ran from his armpits and down his back was cold as the snow atop the highest mountains of Alashkurru. "If I speak of Engibil to the wanakes, the chieftains, of Alashkurru, it is only to praise his greatness. Let us pass."

"It shall not be," the demon said. "The gods of Alashkurru are angry. The men of Alashkurru are angry. Go back, man of the new people even among the new people. You shall do nothing here. You shall gain nothing here. Go back. Go back. Go back."

Sharur licked his lips. "I will not hear these words from a demon in the road. I will hear them from the lips of the wanakes, the chieftains, of Alashkurru.'' The demon sprang into the air again, this time with a screech of rage. Sharur spoke quickly: ''I will not hear these words from a demon in the road. I know you, demon of the high country. Illuyankas, I know your name.'' He hated to try to compel a foreign spirit, but saw no other choice.

The demon Illuyankas let out another screech, this one a bubbling cry of dismay. Off it flew, as fast as its wings could take it. Knowing its name, Sharur could have worked great harm on it.

The donkey handlers and caravan guards clapped their hands and shouted in delight at the way their leader had routed the demon. ''Well done, master merchant's son,'' Mushezib said. ''That ugly thing will trouble us no more.''

''No, I suppose not,'' Sharur said absently. He noticed that Harharu seemed less jubilant than the rest of the caravan crew, and asked him, ''Donkeymaster, do you not speak the language of the Alashkurrut?''

''I do, master merchant's son,'' Harharu said. ''I do not speak so elegantly as your distinguished self, but I understand and make myself understood.''

''Then you understood what the demon Illuyankas, the demon of ill omen, and I had to say to each other,'' Sharur persisted. At the donkeymaster's nod, he went on, ''The demon's warning comes close to what the men of Imhursag told us.'' Harharu nodded once more, even less happily than he had the first time. Sharur said, ''If the men and gods of Alashkurru will not treat with us, what shall we do?''

''Here I have no answer, master merchant's son,'' Harharu said. ''I have never heard of the Alashkurrut refusing trade. This I will tell you: they have never refused trade before, not in all the years Gibil has sent caravans to their country.''

''I have not heard of their doing so, either,'' Sharur said. ''Perhaps it is a ploy to force us to lower our prices.''

''Perhaps it is,'' Harharu said. Neither of them sounded as if he believed it.

\* \* \*

Tuwanas was the first Alashkurri mining center to which the caravan came. By that time, Sharur's spirits had revived. The peasants on the road to Tuwanas had been friendly enough. None of them had refused to trade bread or pork—it was a good swine-raising country—or beer to him and his men. Their gods, whose little outdoor wooden shrines were nothing like the great brick temples of the gods of Kudurru, had not cried out in protest. Sharur took that as a good omen.

He led the caravan up to Tuwanas in the midst of a rain-storm. The guards who were making their first journey into the Alashkurru Mountains looked up into the heavens with fearful eyes, muttering to themselves at what seemed the unnatural spectacle of rain in summer.

Sharur reassured them, saying, "I have seen this before. It is the way of the gods in this part of the world. See— even though Tuwanas lies by a stream, the folk here have dug but few canals to bring water from the stream to the fields. They know they will get rain to keep their crops alive."

"Rain in summertime." Agum shook his head, which made some of the summertime rain fly out from his beard, as if from a wet dog's coat, and more drip off the end of his nose. "No stranger than anything else around these parts, I suppose." He pointed ahead to Tuwanas. "If this isn't the funniest-looking place I've ever seen, I don't know what is."

There Sharur was inclined to agree with him. By the standards of Kudurru, it was neither a village nor a proper city. The best word for it, Sharur supposed, was "fortress." He would not have wanted to take the place, not when its wall was built of great gray blocks of stone so huge, he wondered if they had been set in place by gods, not men.

Sighing, Harharu said, "The Alashkurrut are lucky to have so much fine stone with which to build. Mud brick would be nothing but mud in this climate."

"I see," Agum said. "Even the peasants live in stone houses here. Does the straw they put on the roofs really keep out the rain?"

"Better than you'd think," Sharur told him. "The peasants and the potters and the leatherworkers and the smiths and such live outside the walls, as you see. They take shelter inside when the other Alashkurrut raid Tuwanas."

"The smiths," Harharu murmured.

"Yes," Sharur said. No matter what Enimhursag and the demon Illuyankas had told him, he had hope for the smiths. In Alashkurru no less than in Kudurru, they were men of the new, full of the power control over metal gave them, a power so raw it was not yet divine.

"Who lives inside the walls of Tuwanas, then?" Agum asked.

"The Alashkurri gods, of course," Sharur answered, and the caravan guard nodded. "A few merchants have their houses in there, too. But most of the space the gods don't use goes to Huzziyas the wanax and his soldiers."

"Wanax." Agum shaped the foreign word, then laughed. "It has a funny sound."

"It has a funny meaning, too," Sharur said. "There is no word in our speech that means just the same thing. It's half-way between 'ensi'—because the Alashkurri gods do speak through the wanakes—and 'bandit chief.' A wanax will use his soldiers to rob his neighbors—"

"—And his own peasants," Harharu put in.

"Yes, and his own peasants," Sharur agreed. "He'll use his soldiers, as I say, to make himself rich. Sometimes I think a wanax would sooner steal one keshlu's weight of gold than put the same amount of trouble into getting two by honest work."

Agum clutched his spear more tightly. "I see why you have guards along, master merchant's son."

"Huzziyas has more soldiers than you could fight," Sharur said. "So does every other wanax. Sometimes, though, when the wanakes aren't robbing one another, a band of soldiers will get bored and start robbing on their own. *That* is why I have guards in the Alashkurru Mountains."

As they talked, they squelched up the narrow track between thatch-roofed stone huts toward the one gate in Tuwanas' frowning wall. Most of the men were out in the fields—rain made weeding easy—but women and children stood in doorways and stared at the newcomers, as did artisans who labored inside their homes.

In looks, they were most of them not far removed from the folk of Kudurru. Men here, though, did not curl their beards, but let them grow long and unkempt. Men and women put on more clothes than they would have done in Kudurru, men wearing knee-length tunics of wool or leather and the women draping themselves in lengths of cloth that reminded Sharur of nothing so much as oversized blankets.

And, now and again, more than clothes and hairstyles reminded the caravan crew they were in a foreign land. Sharur heard one of the donkey handlers wonder aloud if a striking woman with coppery hair was truly a woman or a demon. "Don't say that in a language she can understand," the caravanmaster remarked, "or you're liable to find out."

The guards at the gateway leading into the fortress of Tuwanas stood under the overhang to stay out of the rain. But for their wild, shaggy beards, they would have fit in well enough among Kimash the lugal's guardsmen. Sharur recognized a couple who spoke the language of Kudurru. One of those guards recognized him at about the same time. "It is Sharur son of Ereshguna, from the city between the rivers called Gibil," he said.

"It is," Sharur agreed. "It is Nenassas son of Nerikkas, of Tuwanas. I greet you, Nenassas son of Nerikkas." Nenassas hadn't greeted him, merely acknowledged his existence. He did not take that as a good sign.

Nenassas still did not greet him, but asked, "What do you bring to Tuwanas, Sharur son of Ereshguna?"

"I bring swords and knives and spearheads of finest bronze," Sharur said, pointedly adding, "such have always delighted the heart of Huzziyas son of Wamnas, the mighty wanax of Tuwanas. I bring also wine of dates, to delight the heart of Huzziyas in a different way; strong medicines''— he gestured toward Rukagina—''and many other fine things.''

Nenassas and the other guards put their heads together and talked in low voices in their own language. Sharur caught only a couple of phrases, enough to understand they were trying to figure out what to do with him, and with the caravan. Their attitude alone would have told him that much. He kept his face an impassive mask. Behind it, he worried. They should have been delighted to greet a caravan from Kudurru.

He got the idea they would have been delighted to greet most caravans from Kudurru. A caravan from Gibil, however . . .

At last, Nenassas said, ''What you tell me is true, Sharur son of Ereshguna. Your wares have delighted the heart of mighty Huzziyas. Still, that was in the days before our gods spoke to us of the city between the rivers called Gibil.''

''I do not seek to trade my swords and knives and spearheads with the gods of Tuwanas,'' Sharur replied. ''I seek to trade them with the mighty wanax of Tuwanas, and with his clever merchants.''

''See!'' one of the other Alashkurri guards exclaimed in his own language. ''This is what the gods warned us against. He cares nothing for them.''

''That is not so,'' Sharur said in the same tongue. ''I respect the gods of Tuwanas, the gods of Alashkurru. But, Udas son of Ussas, they are not my gods. My god is Engibil, and after him the other gods of Kudurru.''

Udas seemed disconcerted at being understood. The guards put their heads together again. Sharur heard one phrase that pleased him very much: ''Those swords *do* delight the heart of the wanax.'' More argument followed. A couple of times, the guards hefted the spears they were carrying, as if about to use them on one another. Finally, Nenassas said, ''You and your caravan may pass into Tuwanas, Sharur son of Ereshguna. This matter is too great for us to decide. Let it be in the hands of the mighty wanax and the gods."

"For this I thank you, Nenassas son of Nerikkas, though it grieves me to enter this place without your greeting," Sharur replied. But he got no greeting from Nenassas, only a brusque wave ahead. Scowling, Sharur led his men and donkeys into Tuwanas.

"See what I have here." Sharur set out a row of swords on top of a wooden table. In the torchlight, the polished bronze gleamed almost as red as blood. "These are all of fine, hard metal, made strong with the tin we of Gibil bring in at great risk and great expense. They will cut notches in the blade of a copper sword until it is better used as a saw than as a weapon. Alashkurru is a land of warriors, a land of heroes. No one will want to be without such fine swords. Is it not so, Sitawandas son of Anawandas, my friend, my colleague?"

Sitawandas put Sharur in mind of an Alashkurri version of his own father—a large, solid man who knew his own mind and who was intent on wringing the most he could from any deal. He picked up one of the swords Sharur had taken from their woolen wrappings. His grip, his stance, showed he knew how to handle it.

"This is a fine blade to hold, Sharur son of Ereshguna," he said. "I would have looked for nothing less from you." Gently, he set down the sword and took from his wrist a copper bracelet. "May I test the hardness of the metal, to be certain it is as you say?"

Sharur bowed again. "I am your slave. If the buyer is not pleased and satisfied in all regards, how can there be a sale?"

Sitawandas took up the sword once more, using the edge against the bracelet as if he were slicing bread. He stared at the groove he had cut in the copper and said, "Yes, man of Gibil, this bronze is as fine as any I have ever seen."

"Many warriors will want swords like these," Sharur

said. "They will give you silver and gold for them. Do I ask silver and gold for them? No—only copper and copper ore, as you well know."

"I know the terms on which we have dealt, yes." Sitawandas put down the sword again, as carefully as he had before. "And you speak truly, Sharur son of Ereshguna: a warrior of Alashkurru would be proud to carry such a blade in his sheath." He let out a long, deep sigh. Sharur thought he saw tears in his eyes. "Truly I am sorry, man of Gibil. It is as you say. I could gain gold and silver for such swords. I have copper and copper ore in plenty in my storehouse, to pay to the man who could give such swords to me. But it shall not be. It can not be."

Sharur's heart sank. "I understand the words you say, Sitawandas son of Anawandas, but not the meaning concealed within them." He did not, he would not, let the Alashkurri merchant see his dismay.

"For myself, I would like to gain these swords," Sitawandas said. "I am forbidden from trading with you, however. I am forbidden from trading with any man of Gibil."

"Who forbids you? Is it Huzziyas, the might wanax of Tuwanas?" Sharur set a finger by the side of his nose and winked. "Let one blade, two blades, three blades come into the hands of Huzziyas for no gold, for no silver, and surely you shall be able to do as you please with the rest of them."

Sitawandas sighed again. "Huzziyas the mighty wanax would be proud to have such blades. This cannot be denied." The guards at the gates of Tuwanas had said the same thing. Sitawandas went on, "But, Sharur son of Ereshguna, Huzziyas the mighty wanax is no less forbidden than I from trading with you. I pray I shall not be punished even for speaking to you as I do, though that has never been formally prohibited for us."

"Once a sword is set in the hands of a warrior, he will not care whence it first came," Sharur said. "Once a knife is set in a sheath on the belt of a warrior, he will not care whence it first came. Once a spearhead is mounted on a shaft, he will not care whence it first came. If you have these things, Sitawandas son of Anawandas, you can trade them to your countrymen at a profit. No one will ask, 'Is this a blade of Gibil, Sitawandas, or is this a blade of Imhursag?' The only question you will hear is, 'Will this blade help me slay my enemies, Sitawandas?' ''

The Alashkurri merchant licked his lips. "You tempt me, man of Gibil, as a honeycomb lying forgotten on a table tempts a small boy who is hungry and wants something sweet. But what happens to a small boy when he snatches up that honeycomb?"

"Nothing, often enough," Sharur answered with a grin. "Did you never steal honeycomb when you were a boy?"

"As often as I thought I could get away with it," Sitawandas said, also smiling. "But sometimes my father was watching, or my grandfather, or a family ghost, though I knew it not. And when that was so, I ate no honeycomb, but got a beating instead, or ate of it and got a beating afterwards. And sometimes the honeycomb lay on the table and I spied my father or my grandfather standing close by, or a family ghost spoke to me of some other thing. And when that befell, I stole no honeycomb that day, for fear of the beating I would surely earn."

"I do not understand," Sharur said, though he did, only too well.

Sitawandas said, "You are not a fool, Sharur son of Ereshguna. You are not a blind man." Sharur said nothing. Sitawandas sighed. "Very well. Let it be as you wish. I shall explain for you. Huzziyas the mighty wanax stands here for my father. If I gain these blades from you, he will chastise me. The gods of Alashkurru stand here for my grandfather, or for a family ghost. If I gain these blades from you, they may see without my knowing, and they will chastise me."

There it was. Sharur could not fail to understand that, no matter how much he might wish to do so. "Why does the wanax, mighty Huzziyas, hate me?" he cried. "Why do the gods of Alashkurru hate me?"

Sitawandas set a hand on his thigh. "I do not think mighty Huzziyas the wanax hates you, Sharur son of Eresh-

guna. I think he would have these things of you, if only he
could. But, just as a father chastises a small boy, so also
may a grandfather chastise a father.''

"You say the gods of Alashkurru will chastise Huzziyas,
the mighty wanax, if he gains the swords and spearheads
with which to defeat his enemies?'' Sharur asked. "Do your
gods then hate Huzziyas?''

"Never let that be said,'' Sitawandas exclaimed, and
made a sign the Alashkurrut used when a man of Kudurru
would have covered the eyes of his god's amulet to keep
the deity from seeing. "But the gods fear the wanax will
walk the path you men of Gibil have taken. When the gods
declare a thing shall not be, the man who stands against
them will not stand long.''

That was true. Sharur knew it was true. Kimash the lugal
ruled in Gibil not by opposing Engibil but by appeasing him,
by bribing him to look the other way and flattering him so
he thought his power was as great as it had ever been. No
man could directly oppose a god.

Indirectly, though—''Suppose—merely suppose, mind—
I were to lose some of these swords at such-and-such a
place: suppose a donkey handler were careless, for instance,
so they fell off the beast. And suppose again, a few days
later, that you were careless enough to lose some ingots of
copper at some other place. If I chanced to find them there,
I do not think I would ever tell you about it.''

"No, eh?'' Sitawandas licked his lips. He knew what
Sharur was saying, sure enough. Sharur made himself stand
calm, stand easy, as if, since they were discussing things
that might not be, those things were unimportant. Sweat
sprang out on Sitawandas's forehead. He was tempted to do
business by not seeming to do business; Sharur could see
as much. But at last, convulsively, the Alashkurri merchant
shook his head. "I cannot do this thing, Sharur son of Ereshguna. I dare not do this thing. Should my gods take notice of the doing—No.'' He shook his head again.

"However you like.'' Sharur spoke carelessly. "If you do

not care what might be found in out-of-the-way places—''

"I do not care?" Sitawandas broke in. "Never let that be said, either.'' He let out a long, shuddering sigh. "Treating with you here, man of Gibil, I understand better and better why the gods of my people have come to fear you so."

"Is it so?" Sharur shrugged, outwardly careless still. "Men are always wise to fear gods. I cannot see how gods, with their power, are wise to fear men."

"There—do you see? You can speak well, when you care to. But, when you care to, you can also speak in ways that frighten men and gods alike." Sitawandas brushed the sweat from his face with a hairy forearm. "Most frightening of all is that you have no notion how frightening you are."

"Now you speak in riddles, Sitawandas son of Anawandas.'' Sharur made as if to start rewrapping the weapons he had displayed, then paused one last time. "Are you sure you will not trade with me?"

"It is not that I will not." Sitawandas paced back and forth across the stone-enclosed chamber. "It is that I dare not."

"Then who may?" Sharur demanded. "Has Huzziyas, mighty wanax of Tuwanas, the power to do with me as his people and mine have done with each other in peace and for common profit for generations?"

Sitawandas said, "Sharur son of Ereshguna, I do not know."


Even being allowed to go into Huzziyas's palace and see the wanax took longer and cost more than Sharur had expected. The longer he stayed in Tuwanas doing no real business, the more he begrudged every bangle, every broken bit of silver he paid out for nothing better than living from day to day. Paying to gain access to a man who should have been glad to see him—who had been glad to see him the year before—galled him even more.

In the end, with patience and bribery, he did obtain an

audience with Huzziyas. As he strode up to the massive doorway to the palace, he reflected that that was not the ideal name for the building. Just as Tuwanas was more nearly fortress than city, so the wanax's residence was more nearly citadel than palace. The stone walls were strong and thick, the only windows slits better suited to archery than vision, the roof sheathed with slates on which fire would not catch.

Many of Huzziyas's guardsmen carried bronze swords Sharur knew they had got from him. They wore copper greaves and breastplates and caps, and had their shields faced with copper, too. Copper was softer than bronze, but easily available here in Alashkurru. Huzziyas's men used armor far more lavishly than did Sharur's, or even Kimash's guards back in Gibil.

Some of the guardsmen greeted Sharur like an old friend, remembering the fine weapons he and his family had brought to Tuwanas over the years. Some would not speak to him at all, remembering the admonitions of their gods. Two of the silent ones led him through the narrow halls of the palace and up to the high seat of the wanax.

Sharur thought he would have been likelier to meet Huzziyas in a roadside ambuscade than as wanax of Tuwanas. Tuwanas' ruler below the gods was a tough fifty-five, gray thatching his hair and shaggy beard but his arms and chest still thick with muscle. Scars seamed those arms, and the bits of leg showing between tunic hem and boot top, and his rugged, big-nosed face. One of them barely missed his left eye.

After the bows and the polite phrases required of him were done, Sharur spoke as bluntly as he dared: "Mighty wanax, what have I done to offend, that you and yours will not buy what I have to sell even when buying it works more to your advantage than mine?"

"Understand, Sharur son of Ereshguna, you have not offended me personally," Huzziyas replied. They both used the tongue of Kudurru, in which the wanax was fluent. "Had you offended me personally, you would not be treating with me now. You would be lying dead in a ditch, the dogs and the kites and the ravens quarreling over your bones.'' He sounded more like a bandit chieftain than the ruler of a city, too.

"Do I understand you rightly, mighty wanax?" Sharur asked. "Do you say I have not offended? If I have not offended, what keeps you from trading for the fine wares I have brought from the land between the rivers?"

Huzziyas's eyes glinted. "I did not say you had not offended, man of Kudurru, man of Gibil." He made that last into an insult. "I said you had not offended me. Were I the only one who spoke for Tuwanas, we would trade, you and I. But you and your city have . . ." He paused, looking for the right words.

"Angered your gods?" Sharur suggested bitterly.

"No." The wanax shook his head. "You and your city have done something worse. You and your city have frightened the gods of Tuwanas, the gods of Alashkurru. Unless my ears mistake me, you and your city have frightened the gods of Kudurru, the gods of the land between the Yarmuk and the Diyala."

"The gods of my country are no concern to you, mighty wanax," Sharur said. "And I, mortal worm that I am, I should be of no concern to the gods of Tuwanas, the gods of Alashkurru. Neither I nor my city is a foe to Tuwanas, to Alashkurru. I want only to trade in peace and to return in peace to my city."

Huzziyas looked now this way, now that. Sharur could not help looking this way and that, too. He saw nothing. He wondered what Huzziyas saw, or what he looked to see. The wanax said, "For myself, I am fain to believe you. My gods still fear you lie. They fear I will become like you, a liar before the gods."

He glanced around again. Now Sharur understood what he was doing: he was trying to find out whether his gods were paying close attention to him at this particular moment. Sharur smiled. If Huzziyas had not yet become what the gods of Alashkurru feared, he was on the edge of it. He wanted the swords and spearheads and knives Sharur could trade to him. Unless Sharur misread him as if he were an unfamiliar sign pressed into clay, he would not be overfussy about how he got them, either.

"I am not a liar before the gods," Sharur declared, as he had to do. As he had so often on this journey, he declared his loyalty to Engibil. The more emphatic his declarations got, the less truth they seemed to hold.

"As I say, I am fain to believe you," Huzziyas answered. "But if my gods will not believe, what can I do? My hands are tied." His mouth twisted. His gods still held him in the palm of their hands. He wanted to slip free, but had not found a way. So Igigi's father must have felt—he had been ensi to Engibil, but had not managed to become lugal, to rule in his own right.

Casually, as if it had just occurred to him, Sharur proposed to Huzziyas what he had proposed to Sitawandas: trading as if by accident. The wanax of Tuwanas sucked in his breath. Sharur watched the torchlight sparkle in his eyes. Sitawandas had lacked the nerve to thwart the will of the gods of Alashkurru. Huzziyas, now . . .

Huzziyas twitched on the high seat. He looked surprised, then grimaced, and then, as if he had given up resisting whatever new force filled him, his face went blank and still. Only his lips moved: "Man of Gibil, what you say cannot be. Man of Gibil, what you say shall not be. The gods of Tuwanas, the gods of Alashkurru have declared the men of Tuwanas, the men of Alashkurru shall not trade with you. The men of Tuwanas, the men of Alashkurru shall heed what their gods have declared. I, Huzziyas, mighty wanax of Tuwanas, have spoken."

But it was not Huzziyas who had spoken, or not altogether Huzziyas. The hair on Sharur's arms and at the back of his neck prickled up in awe. The wanax had been wise to wonder whether his gods were watching him. They were, and had kept him from breaking free of their will. Back in Gibil, Engibil had been content to let Igigi and his son and grandson rule for themselves alone. The gods here intended to stay unchallenged lords of this land.

"I am sorry, mighty wanax," Sharur said softly.

Little by little, Huzziyas came back to himself. "It cannot be, Sharur son of Ereshguna," he said, echoing the words the god had spoken through him. "You see why it cannot be." The gesture he began might have been one of apology. If it was, he never finished it. He looked angry: the gods were still watching what he did, what he said. He sighed. He was not a lugal, free—even if only narrowly free—to chart his own course. With the gods of his country so watchful, he would never be a lugal.

Sharur did not care about that, not for its own sake. He cared about trading. "Mighty wanax, will your gods hearken to me if I speak to them face to face, to show them my wares and to show them I am not dangerous to them?"

Huzziyas cocked his head to one side, listening to the gods of Tuwanas, to the gods of the Alashkurru Mountains. Sharur felt the power in the chamber, pressing down on him as if with great weight. Then it lifted. The wanax said, "They think you brave. They think you a fool. They will hear you." After a moment, he seemed to speak for himself rather than the gods: "They will not listen to you."


Like the wanax, the gods of Tuwanas, the gods of Alashkurru dwelt in what was to Sharur's eyes a citadel: a formidable tower of gray stone. He had visited that temple on his previous journeys to Tuwanas, to offer the gods incense in thanks for successful trade. He had no success for which to thank them now, and did not know what to offer to gain one.

Huzziyas accompanied him to the temple. The wanax looked nervous. True, the gods spoke to him and through him. But they also knew he pined for the freedom Sharur and the rest of the men of Gibil enjoyed. The priests who served the temple and the temple alone looked at Huzziyas from the corners of their eyes. What had the gods said of him to them? By those glances, nothing good.

Tuwanas had no single tutelary deity who ruled its territory as his own, as did the cities of the land between the rivers. All the Alashkurri gods were present here, though one of them, Tarsiyas, spoke with the loudest voice. His stone statue was armored in copper and held a bronze sword, making him look as much like a bandit as any of the humans who reverenced him.

Sharur bowed before that clumsy but fierce-looking image. "Tarsiyas, great god of this town, great god of this land, hear the words of Sharur son of Ereshguna, a foreigner, a man who has traveled long to come to Tuwanas, a man who wishes the folk of this land and the gods of this land only good."

The stone lips of the statue moved. "Say what you will, Sharur son of Ereshguna. We have said we will hear you." The words resounded inside Sharur's head. He did not think he was hearing them with his ears, but directly with his mind, as if the god had set them there.

He said, "You are generous, great god." Had Tarsiyas truly been generous, Sharur would not have had to beseech him so. But Sharur assumed the god was, like most gods of his acquaintance, vain. Like all gods, Tarsiyas was powerful. That was what made him a god. He had to be handled more carefully than a poisonous serpent, for he was more deadly. Sharur pointed to the sword in Tarsiyas's right hand. "Is that not a fine blade, great god of this town, great god of this land?"

"It is a fine blade," Tarsiyas agreed. "It is better than the blade I bore before. Huzziyas the wanax gave it to me." The stone eyes of the statue fixed Huzziyas with a stare Sharur was glad to see aimed at someone other than himself.

"I delight in giving the gods rich presents," Huzziyas said. Sharur almost burst out laughing. The wanax sounded like Kimash the lugal, and no doubt wished his hypocrisy were as successful as Kimash's.

"Tarsiyas, great god of this town, great god of this land, do you know whence this sword first came?" Sharur asked.

"I do not, nor care," the god replied. "Huzziyas gained it; Huzziyas gave it. It is enough. I am well pleased."

Again, Sharur fought to keep his face straight. Tarsiyas and the other gods of the Alashkurru Mountains might work to keep the men of Alashkurru under their rule, but they were no less greedy about receiving presents from those men than was Engibil, back in the land between the rivers. Sharur said, "Great god of this town, great god of this land, the sword with which you are well pleased, with which I am glad you are well pleased, is a sword the smiths of the city of Gibil have made, a sword the men of Gibil traded to Huzziyas the mighty wanax. And now you say—"

He got no further than that. His head filled with a roar as of a thousand wild beasts of a hundred different kinds all bellowing at once. The din in Huzziyas's head must have been worse; he groaned and clapped his hands to his ears. At last, the god's cry of rage boiled back down to words the two mortals could understand: "Wretch! Fool! You gave me a gift from the hands of men who set their gods at naught?"

"We do not set our gods at naught," Sharur insisted stubbornly.

And Huzziyas added, "Tarsiyas, great god of this town, great god of this land, my master, when I gave you this sword, you had not said you did not want such work. No other god said he did not want such work. No other goddess said she did not want such work. The work being proper for giving, I gave with both hands. I did not stint. I gave of the finest I had."

Tarsiyas's voice swelled to an unintelligible shout of fury once more. The god clasped the sword in both stone hands and, in a motion too quick for Sharur's eyes to follow, broke it over his stone knee. He hurled both pieces of the blade away from him; they clanged off stone with bell-like notes.

"I reject this!" he cried, as those clatterings drew priests who stared in wonder and terror at his unwonted activity. "I reject all gifts from Gibil. Let them be taken from my treasury. Let those of metal be melted. Let those not of metal be broken. I have spoken. As I have spoken, it shall be. I, a god, will it."

This was worse than anything Sharur had imagined. He wished he had never come to the temple. "Tarsiyas, great god of this town, great god of this land, may I speak?" he asked.

"Speak," the god said, an earthquake rumble of doom in his voice. "Tell your lies."

"I tell no lies, great god of this town, great god of this land," Sharur said. "The gift Huzziyas the mighty wanax set in your hand pleased you. If the gift be good, how can the giver who gave it with both hands, who gave it with open heart, be wicked? How can the smiths who made it with clever eye, with skilled fingers, be wicked?"

"They made it of themselves, with no thought for the gods," Tarsiyas replied.

"Smithery has no god, not yet; it is too young," Sharur said. "This is so in Kudurru, and it is so here."

Huzziyas gave him a horrible look. After a moment, he understood why: the gods of Alashkurru were liable to try to forbid their men from working in metal at all. But that did not seem to be Tarsiyas's most urgent concern. The god said, "You take no thought for the gods your land does have."

"That is not so," Sharur insisted. "The weavers of fine cloth reverence the goddess of the loom and the god of dyeing. The winemakers worship Aglibabu, who makes dates become a brew to gladden the heart. The—"

"They are the small gods," Tarsiyas said. Scorn filled the divine voice. "Even here, they have let themselves become men's servants as much as men's masters. But you men of Gibil would reduce your great gods to small gods, your small gods to demons, your demons to ghosts that chitter and flitter and are in a generation forgotten. The riches you gain in this world tempt you to forget the other world. You shall lead no one here astray. You shall lead no one here away from the path of the gods. As I have spoken, it shall be. I, a god, will it."

"But—" Sharur began.

Huzziyas took him by the arm and pulled him away from Tarsiyas's image. "Come," the wanax said. "You have made trouble enough already." Trouble for himself, his glare said he meant. With his gods watching him so closely, how could he escape them, as the men of Gibil had begun to do? But Sharur had troubles of his own. Without the profits from this caravan, how was he to pay Ningal's bride-price?

# 3

Donkeys brayed and complained. They'd got used to the soft life of the stables of Tuwanas, with nothing to do but eat and sleep. Now they had packs on their backs once more, and handlers making them go places. The world seemed as unjust to them as it did to Sharur.

"We go on," he insisted. Bowing to his will, the caravan headed west along the narrow, winding path toward the next fortresslike town of Alashkurru.

Harharu coughed. "Master merchant's son, what you do now is brave. What you do now is bold. What you do now—is it not also foolish? You have said the god of this place told you that you would get nothing in Alashkurru. The god of this place told you that we would get nothing in Alashkurru. Would you openly fight the god?"

"Donkeymaster, I would not," Sharur said. "I am not a fool: if all the gods of this place oppose us, we have no hope of profit here." *And I have scant hope of making Ningal my wife.* But that was not Harharu's concern. Aloud, Sharur continued, "The hand of every town in Alashkurru, though, is raised against every other. If it were not so, they would not build as they do here. Where the men are in discord, will the gods agree?"

"Ah," Harharu said, and bowed. "Now I see what is in your mind. You think that, while we gain nothing in Tuwanas, while Huzziyas will not treat with us, while Tarsiyas speaks harshly against us, some other town, some other wanax, some other god may prove more hospitable?''

"That is what is in my mind, yes," Sharur agreed.

"Truly you are your father's son," Harharu said, and now Sharur bowed to him.

As they made their slow way up to the top of the hills separating the valley Tuwanas dominated from the next one deeper into the mountain country, they met a party of eight or ten Alashkurrut coming the other way. The men of Alash-kurru were armed and armored like Huzziyas's guards. They led a few donkeys themselves, all the animals far more heavily burdened than those of Sharur's caravan.

At Mushezib's sharp orders, the caravan guards rushed forward to show the Alashkurrut they were ready to fight at need. Because they were ready to fight, they did not have to fight. The . . . bandits, Sharur supposed, did nothing but nod and tramp on past them.

Seen from the hills, the fortified town of Zalpuwas looked even more formidable than Tuwanas had. As the caravan approached the fortress, peasants came running from the fields to stare and point and jabber. They found the men of Kudurru, who wore clothes different from theirs and curled their beards, as funny as a troupe of mountebanks with trained dogs and monkeys.

Looking to sow goodwill, Sharur passed out bracelets and bangles. He also opened a small jar of date wine and let that pass from hand to hand among the peasants. Everyone who got it took a small swig before passing it on to whoever stood next to him till it was empty. Sharur had been sure it would happen so. In Gibil, someone would have been greedy and gulped down half the jar. He was sure of that, too.

In Gibil, men thought more of themselves and less of the gods than they did here. Sharur chose not to dwell on that point.

The woman who did finally empty the jar returned it to him, saying with a smile, "We have never seen a caravan-master so generous before." Her stance and the sparkle in her eye suggested that, did he choose to be a little more generous, she might give him something in return.

"We trade with all," Sharur declared loudly, and many of the peasants exclaimed to hear him speak in their language. "We trade great for great; we also trade small for small." None of the gods of Alashkurru had forbidden their people from trading food and donkey fodder for his trinkets, for which he was duly grateful.

Surrounded by an excited crowd of peasants, the caravan passed through the stone huts ringing the stout walls of Zalpuwas and up to the gateway into the fortress. One of the guards said, "Is it Sharur son of Ereshguna, out of Gibil in the land between the rivers?" His voice broke in surprise, as if he were a youth rather than a solid warrior with the first threads of gray in his beard.

"Yes, it is I, Malatyas son of Lukkas," Sharur replied. "I pray that your mighty wanax, Ramsayas son of Radas, flourishes like the wheat in your fields. I pray that he flourishes like the apple trees in your orchards. I have many fine things to trade with him, or with the merchants who are his servants: swords and spearheads and knives and medicines and—"

He broke off. Malatyas was paying no attention to his polished sales pitch. The gate guard burst out, "Are you not come from Tuwanas, Sharur son of Ereshguna?"

"Yes," Sharur admitted.

"And when you were there," Malatyas persisted, "the gods did not warn you to come no farther into the mountains of Alashkurru?"

"They did not," he said truthfully. Tarsiyas had warned him of many things, but not of that. Perhaps the god and his fellows had assumed Sharur would be so downhearted, he would not continue. They were not his gods. They did not know him well. In reasonable tones, he went on, "Had the gods forbidden it, how could I be here now?"

"It is a puzzlement." To prove how great a puzzlement it was, Malatyas scratched his bushy head. "We were certain that—"

"Since I am here, since I have goods the mighty wanax

Ramsayas will surely covet, may I enter great Zalpuwas?''
Sharur broke in.

As had the guards back at Tuwanas, Malatyas and his
comrades plainly wanted to forbid the caravan from going
into their town. As had those guards, these found themselves
unable. ''The mighty wanax will attend to you according to
his wishes,'' Malatyas said, which sounded more like warning than welcome. But he stood aside and let Sharur and his
companions pass into Zalpuwas.

Being deeper in among the mountains than Tuwanas, Zalpuwas received visitors less often, and was not so well prepared to accommodate them. The couple of inns were small
and dingy and dark, with sour straw in the stables. Their
sole virtue, in Sharur's eyes, was that their proprietors made
no fuss about accepting beads and bangles and broken bits
of silver to house the caravan.

''The Alashkurri gods may be against us,'' Mushezib
said, sipping beer made bitter with the flowering head of
some plant that grew in the valley, ''but the innkeepers
aren't so fussy.''

''Are you surprised?'' Sharur answered. ''When have you
ever heard of a god who would bother taking notice of an
innkeeper?'' Mushezib's laugh sprayed beer over the top of
the table where the two men of Kudurru sat.

But Sharur's joke soon turned as bitter as the local beer
to him, for none of the copper merchants of Zalpuwas took
notice of him or of his caravan. When he went to greet men
with whom he had traded on previous journeys, their doors
were closed against him as if they had never heard his name.
He sent word to Ramsayas son of Radas, requesting an audience. No word came back from the wanax.

Finally, in growing desperation, Sharur sent Ramsayas
not word but a sword, one of the finest swords he had
brought from Gibil. Where nothing else had, that did prompt
the wanax to send a servant to seek out Sharur. Sharur
bowed to the servant as he might have to the master, saying,
''Tell the mighty wanax I am honored that he deigns to
notice me.''

"Ramsayas son of Radas, mighty wanax of Zalpuwas, notices everything and everyone that passes inside these walls," the servant answered.

"Of this I am truly glad," Sharur said. "Does he likewise notice everything that passes outside the walls of his fortress?"

"No, he does not claim that," the servant said. "He is not a god, to have so wide a purview, only a servant of the gods."

"I thought as much," Sharur replied. "He should know that I sent him the sword in token of what he does not see: other wanakes in other valleys arming themselves and their retainers with such weapons. If he would not be left behind his neighbors, he might think on the wisdom of gaining more such blades."

The servant's mouth fell open. "I cannot believe other wanakes would—" He checked himself. "But who knows into what depravity men of other valleys might sink?" After coughing a couple of times, he went on, "I shall take what you say to Ramsayas son of Radas. Let his judgment, not mine, rule here."

Ramsayas sent for Sharur the very next day.


Sharur bowed before the wanax of Zalpuwas as he might have done before Kimash the lugal of Gibil. "I am honored, Ramsayas son of Radas, that you deign to notice me," he said as he straightened.

Ramsayas grunted. Actually, he put Sharur more in mind of Mushezib than of Kimash: he was a fighter, first, last, and always. He had a narrow, forward-thrusting face with a nose hooked like a hawk's beak and almost as sharp. The way he leaned toward Sharur in the tall chair on which he sat emphasized that seeming inclination to attack.

"Oh, you are noticed, Sharur son of Ereshguna. Rest assured, you are noticed," he said. His voice had a harsh rasp to it; too much shouting, perhaps, on too many raids against too many nearby valleys. "Now, what is this you say about my neighbors' buying blades from you?"

"I said nothing about their buying such swords from me, mighty wanax," Sharur replied, though that was the impression he had wanted to leave with Ramsayas's servant. "I said they are acquiring them. Gibil is not the only city of Kudurru trading with the many valleys, the many fortresses, of Alashkurru, but our blades—and our other goods of all sorts, I make haste to add—are among the finest to be had. You have dealt with me; likewise, you have dealt with my father. You know these words I say to you are true."

"I have dealt with you. Likewise, I have dealt with your father." Ramsayas ran his tongue over his lips. "That was a splendid sword you sent me."

Sharur bowed. "A wanax deserves nothing less than a splendid sword."

"And yet, you are of Gibil." Like Huzziyas before him, Ramsayas seemed of two minds. Part of him plainly wanted what Sharur had brought up to Alashkurru from the land between the rivers. That was the part Sharur and his father and other men of Gibil had always seen when they dealt with the Alashkurrut. The rest of Ramsayas, though, the rest was afraid.

"Yes, I am of Gibil," Sharur agreed. "I was likewise of Gibil when last year I also came here to trade. You were glad to see me then, Ramsayas son of Radas. You were glad to trade with me. You were glad to buy from me." He knew he sounded bitter. He had reason to be bitter. He *was* bitter.

Ramsayas's fierce eyes went up to the timbers of the ceiling. Having so much fine timber, the men of Alashkurru often used it in what struck Sharur as profligate style. He had even seen, in some valleys deeper into the mountains than that of Zalpuwas, whole buildings made of wood. Ramsayas's eyes flashed past Sharur to the far wall of the audience chamber. Sharur realized he had succeeded in embarrassing the wanax. That might bring him profit, or might bring only trouble if embarrassment turned to anger.

To his surprise, embarrassment turned to regret. "Yes, I was glad to see you then, Sharur son of Ereshguna," Ramsayas said with a sigh. "Yes, I was glad to trade with you. Yes, I was glad to buy from you." Suddenly, the wanax looked more hunted than hunter. His hoarse voice dropped to a whisper. "As a man, I am still glad to see you. But I am more than merely a man. I am a man who obeys his gods. I may not trade with you. I may not buy from you. So my gods have ordered. My men obey me when we war against our neighbors. I obey the gods."

"But we are not at war, you and I!" Sharur cried.

"No. This is so," Ramsayas said. "But you Giblut, you are at war with the gods of Alashkurru, I fear. Do I understand rightly that you are at war with the gods of Kudurru as well?"

"No," Sharur said. "I say ten times, a hundred times, a thousand times, no. Engibil is my god. I and all of Gibil worship him."

"But he does not rule you," Ramsayas said, and Sharur had no reply. "That is at the heart of why the gods of this town, the gods of this land, fear you and will not let you trade with us. They do not want the men of Alashkurru to become as the Giblut are."

"So I have seen, though I tell you, mighty wanax, this fear is groundless," Sharur said. "I worship my god. I fear my god." That was certainly true. The merchant went on, "And I would not, I do not, try to seduce you away from—"

"No," Ramsayas broke in. "I will not hear you." To prove he would not hear Sharur, he stuck his forefingers into his ears, so that he looked rather like a three-year-old refusing to hear what its father told it.

Back in Tuwanas, Huzziyas had quivered with eagerness for a chance to get around his gods and trade with Sharur. He would have disobeyed them had they not forced obedience upon him. They had won this battle. Sharur did not think they would win the war in Tuwanas, not if Huzziyas stayed on as wanax there and was not overthrown. Huzziyas wanted, panted, to be a lugal, or whatever the Alashkurrut would call a lugal: a man who ruled in his own right. He had not been able to take this chance to do it. He would surely try again. Sharur guessed he would succeed, sooner or later.

Ramsayas—unfortunately, from Sharur's point of view—was different. Like Huzziyas, he was a rough, strong man. Like Huzziyas, he would have liked to trade with Sharur for the fine weapons the man of Gibil had brought. But unlike Huzziyas, he was not willing to risk defying or deceiving the gods to get what he wanted. He was either content with the arrangement he and his forebears had long known or simply afraid to try to change it.

Sharur held up a hand. Ramsayas asked, "Does that mean you will speak on something else?" Sharur nodded—the wanax of Zalpuwas still had his fingers in his ears. At that nod, he removed them, wiping one against the wool of his tunic. "Very well then, Sharur son of Ereshguna. Speak on something else."

"By your leave, mighty wanax, I should like to speak to your gods." Sharur had no great hope anything would come of that. The same gods dwelt in Zalpuwas as in Tuwanas. But Tarsiyas did not speak with the loudest voice here; that place belonged to the goddess Fasillar. If the gods of the Alashkurru Mountains knew discord—as the men of the mountains did, as the gods of Kudurru did—perhaps Sharur would find those strong here more friendly to his cause.

Ramsayas's eyes got a faraway look, as if he were listening to someone Sharur could not hear. That was exactly what he was doing. As Huzziyas had back in Tuwanas, he said, "They will hear you." And, as Huzziyas had, he added, "They will not listen."

When Huzziyas had said that, he had appeared to be speaking for himself. Ramsayas sounded more like a man delivering the words of the gods. That was not a good omen, not so far as Sharur could see. He had had few good omens since setting out from Gibil. He hardly even missed them anymore.

* * *

Had the gods been besieged in their temple in Zalpuwas, they could have held it even longer than was so for their citadel back in Tuwanas. Sharur felt, and was no doubt meant to feel, like nothing so much as a tiny insect as he walked into the great stone pile. The weight of the stone-work, and of the power indwelling there, made him want to shrink down into himself, making himself of even less account when measured against the gods of Alashkurru.

Fasillar, the Alashkurri goddess of birth, was depicted enormously pregnant. By Sharur's standards, the statue was earnest but clumsy work; it might have been carved by the brother of the man who had shaped Tarsiyas's image back in Tuwanas. Ninshubur, the goddess of birth in Kudurru, was also the goddess of new ideas. Sharur did not think that was so for Fasillar; as best he could tell, the Alashkurri gods actively discouraged new ideas.

Ramsayas stretched himself out at full length on the ground before the cult image of Fasillar. Sharur bowed low before it. He respected the gods of the Alashkurru Mountains (more accurately, he respected the power of the gods of the Alashkurru Mountains), but they were not his gods.

The goddess spoke: "Whom do you bring before me, Ramsayas son of Radas? Why do you bring him before me?" Did Sharur imagine it, or was that last question full of ominous overtones?

"Mistress of the mysteries of birth, provider of warriors, great goddess of this town, great goddess of this land . . ." After the honorifics, the wanax of Zalpuwas took a deep breath so he could come to the point: "I bring before you Sharur son of Ereshguna, a foreign man, a man of the distant land between the rivers, a man of the town of Gibil." He did not raise his head as he spoke, not once. Indeed, he reckoned himself far more a servant of the gods than did Huzziyas of Tuwanas.

Sharur wished the wanax had not mentioned Gibil. Fasillar surely knew whence he came, but reminding her of it would do his cause no good. He bowed again, saying, "I greet you, great goddess of this town. I greet you, great goddess of this land."

Fasillar's stone eyes swung in their sockets till they bore on Sharur. "You are the foreign man who spoke with Tarsiyas my cousin in the town of Tuwanas."

"I am that man, great goddess of this town, great goddess of this land," Sharur acknowledged.

"Tarsiyas my cousin made it plain to you we do not want what the men of Gibil have to trade," Fasillar said. "Tarsiyas my cousin made it plain to you that we do not want the men of Alashkurru to take what the men of Gibil have to trade. Tarsiyas my cousin having made that plain to you, why did you not leave this land? Why did you not return to Gibil? Why did you go deeper into these mountains, into this land, to disturb another town, to disturb Zalpuwas?"

"Great goddess of this town, great goddess of this land . . ." As he spoke the honorifics, Sharur used the time they gave him to gather his own thoughts. "I understood from Tarsiyas your cousin, great god of that town, great god of this land, that he rejected dealings for the things of Gibil, dealings with the men of Gibil." He licked his lips. "I did not understand him to mean all the towns of this land, all the gods of this land, rejected my city and the men of my city."

Fasillar's stone eyes blazed. The nipples of her swollen stone breasts sprang out and pressed against the rich wool wrappings in which the folk of Zalpuwas had decked her. "You knew what Tarsiyas my cousin told you, Sharur son of Ereshguna. You knew what Tarsiyas my cousin meant, man of Gibil. In your heart, you chose to misunderstand, to twist the words of Tarsiyas my cousin to a shape more pleasing to you. That you do this, that you *can* do this, shows why all the gods of Alashkurru hate you."

Still down on his belly, Ramsayas moaned. Again, his was a different kind of fright from Huzziyas's. The wanax of Tuwanas had been frightened because Sharur had got him in trouble with his gods. The wanax of Zalpuwas was frightened because Sharur had got himself in trouble with the Alashkurri gods. Huzziyas wanted to be out from under them, but could not escape. Ramsayas was content down to the bottom of his spirit to remain their servant.

Their anger frightened Sharur, too, for it meant he would not return to Gibil with his donkeys' packs nicely burdened with copper and copper ore. It meant he would not return to Gibil with rare and beautiful things for Kimash the lugal to set on Engibil's altar, which might in turn make Engibil angry at Kimash and at the rest of the men of Gibil.

And it meant he would not return to Gibil with Ningal's bride-price. She would have to remain in the house of Dimgalabzu the smith, her father. Perhaps Dimgalabzu would offer her to someone else, someone who had not been so rash as to pledge a bride-price from profit and then come home without it. Ereshguna would not be happy to see this marriage alliance fail, for he wanted his family joined to Dimgalabzu's. Sharur would not be happy to see this marriage alliance fail, for he wanted himself joined to Ningal.

He said, "Great goddess of this town, great goddess of this land, I will appease you and the other gods of this town, the other gods of this land, with any contrition-offering you ask of me, short of my life or the lives of my countrymen. I want no more from you than to trade my wares for the wares of this land and to return to my city, to return to my god, in peace."

"No," Fasillar said, and Ramsayas moaned again at that blunt rejection. The goddess went on, "A contrition-offering depends upon true contrition. You, man of Gibil, you would make the offering and speak the words of contrition with your mouth, while your heart laughed within you. For the gods of this town, for the gods of this land, to accept such an offering would be for us to eat of poisoned fruit. Better it were never made."

Sharur bit his lip. Fasillar had indeed seen what was in his mind: he would have made the offering as part of the price of doing business in the Alashkurru Mountains, not because he repented of being what he was. Bowing his head before the superior power he could not help but recognize, he asked, "What am I to do, then, great goddess of this town, great goddess of this land?"

"You have but one thing to do." Fasillar's voice was implacable. "Leave this land. Return to Zalpuwas no more."

"Great goddess of this town, great goddess of this land, I obey." Sharur bowed his head again. Even as he spoke, though, he saw how he might bend the Alashkurri goddess's words to his own purpose.

As the caravan pressed deeper in among the Alashkurru Mountains, Harharu asked, "Are you sure you know what course you take, master merchant's son, the goddess having told you to quit this land?"

"Donkeymaster, I obey Fasillar." Sharur's smile was crooked. "We quit the land of Zalpuwas, do we not? When we leave these mountains, we shall not leave them through the land of Zalpuwas, but by another route."

Mushezib laughed. "Thus did I obey my mother after I got too big for my father to beat me." The guard captain eyed Sharur. "Are you too big for these gods to beat you, master merchant's son?"

"Not a chance of it," Sharur answered. "If the gods— any gods—take it into their minds to beat a man, they will beat him. My hope is that they will not take it into their minds to do any such thing, that I can make myself too small to draw their notice."

That satisfied Mushezib. It did not satisfy Harharu, who said, "Master merchant's son, on what do you pin this hope? Slice words as you will, the goddess told you to quit this land, and you press deeper into it. Before long, we shall halt in another valley. Before long, you shall present yourself before another wanax's chief merchant, or more likely before another wanax himself. Before long, you shall be brought into the presence of the Alashkurri gods. How can you fail to draw their notice?"

"Before long, we shall halt in another valley," Sharur agreed. "I know the valley in which we shall halt: the valley of Parsuhandas. The trading in the valley of Parsuhandas has long been good for Gibil. But I shall not present myself before Wassukhamnis, the chief merchant of the valley of Parsuhandas. I shall not present myself before Yaddiyas, the mighty wanax of the valley of Parsuhandas. Most especially, I shall not be brought into the presence of the Alashkurri gods in the valley of Parsuhandas. I shall not draw their notice."

"Ah. Now I understand." Mushezib boomed laughter. "You will trade swords and spearheads and good date wine to the peasants of the valley of Parsuhandas, and we will go back to Gibil with our donkeys piled high with cucumbers." He laughed again.

"The peasants of the valley of Parsuhandas are Alashkurrut like any other Alashkurrut," Sharur said. "No doubt, could they pay for them, they would be glad to have fine swords of bronze, and fine spearheads of bronze as well. Could he pay for it, any man would be glad to drink good date wine. But we have in Gibil cucumbers aplenty. I would sooner bring back to our city copper and copper ore. And this, if matters go as I hope, I shall do."

Harharu's frown remained. "And you will not see Wassukhamnis, chief merchant of the valley of Parsuhandas? And you will not see Yaddiyas, mighty wanax of the valley of Parsuhandas? Master merchant's son, what will you do?"

"I shall present myself before Abzuwas son of Ahhiyawas," Sharur replied.

Harharu considered that for as long as a donkey took to walk five paces. Then the donkeymaster bowed so deeply to Sharur, his hat fell off his head.


Rain spattered down from a cloudy sky as the caravan entered the valley of Parsuhandas. By that time, guards and donkey handlers had stopped exclaiming in dismay at summer rain, and most of them had stopped making signs and charms against the evil omens to be drawn from such a phenomenon. For his part, Sharur took the evil weather as a good omen: rain made it more difficult for the gods of the Alashkurru Mountains to peer down and see what he was about.

Stronger than both Tuwanas and Zalpuwas was the fortress town of Parsuhandas, which seemed to have sprung from the stony ground rather than being built. The valley of Parsuhandas was narrow and steep, the fields of the valley small and cramped. Nevertheless, Parsuhandas prospered.

Parsuhandas prospered because many black-mouthed holes had been dug into the sides of the valley, most often where it was steepest. Men went into those holes and grubbed at the ground with copper picks and with pry bars made from branches and shod, sometimes, with copper, and with shovels more often of bone and wood than of copper and wood. Not many men went down into the mines, for the mountains of Alashkurru were like any other land in that their peasants could not raise food enough to support more than a few who were not peasants. But miners there were, who brought copper ore and, every now and again, masses of native copper up from the darkness into the light of day.

Near one of those mines, the largest in the valley of Parsuhandas, dwelt Abzuwas son of Ahhiyawas. A great pillar of smoke rose from his stone home, guiding Sharur and the caravan thither. Yet that home was not afire. Like so many in Gibil, it was also Abzuwas's place of business, and he the busiest and most clever smith in the valley of Parsuhandas and, probably, in all the Alashkurru Mountains.

As if Abzuwas had been a man of Kudurru, he wore only sandals and a linen kilt. He did it not to ape the men from the land between the rivers, but because he spent so much time tending his forges, and would have steamed in his own wrappings had he donned the usual Alashkurri tunic.

He stood outside the stone building when Sharur led the donkey train up to him: outside and, too impatient to wait for the rain to do the job, pouring a big jar of water over his head and hairy torso, both to clean himself and to cool his body after some long stretch of sweltering work. "I greet you, Abzuwas son of Ahhiyawas, master of metal," Sharur called out as he approached.

Abzuwas shook himself like a wet dog. Water sprayed out from his hair and beard. He rubbed at his eyes to get the water out of them, too. "Well, well," he said, his voice deep and rolling like the voice of a big drum. "Well, well. *I* greet *you*, Sharur son of Ereshguna, master merchant's son. For a man from the land of Kudurru, a man with the knowledge of bronze, to call me a master of metal is praise indeed. It's more praise than I deserve, but a man fool enough to turn down praise would also be fool enough to turn down a woman if she offered him her body, and, whatever kind of fool I may be, I am not such a fool as that. Welcome, Sharur son of Ereshguna, welcome!"

He walked forward to enfold Sharur in a wet, smelly embrace. No matter how wet and smelly it was, Sharur was glad to have the hug. Since he had come into the Alashkurru Mountains, Abzuwas was the first person to have fully returned his greeting. Since he had come into the Alashkurru Mountains, this place was the first place he had felt welcome.

As he freed himself from Abzuwas's massive arms, he realized that was literally true. Here by the smithy, he did not feel in the back of his mind the unfriendly presence of the gods of the Alashkurrut. Metal had power, and gave a man power—power that was not, or was not yet, the power of any god.

"So," Abzuwas boomed. "So! I had not heard you were in the fortress of Parsuhandas. I had not heard you were treating with Yaddiyas, the mighty wanax of Parsuhandas. I had not heard Yaddiyas, the mighty wanax of Parsuhandas, had sent you to me." He shrugged his broad shoulders. "But so what? When I get to working, when the metal pours bright into the mold, I do not hear anything, even things many men think they tell me."

"Abzuwas, my friend, I will not lie to you," Sharur said. "I was not in the fortress of Parsuhandas. I was not treating with Yaddiyas. Yaddiyas has not sent me to you.''

"Well, well," Abzuwas said again, in a different tone of voice. "So you came straight to me, did you? Why did you come straight to me? Why did you not go into the fortress of Parsuhandas? Why did you not treat with Yaddiyas, the mighty wanax of Parsuhandas?"

"I came straight to you because I felt sure you would trade with me," Sharur replied, sounding more confident than he felt. "I did not go into the fortress of Parsuhandas, I did not treat with the mighty wanax Yaddiyas, because I did not think he would trade with me."

Abzuwas frowned. "And why is that, Sharur son of Ereshguna? The mighty wanax Yaddiyas has always been glad to gain your swords. The mighty wanax Yaddiyas has always been glad to gain your other goods. I can give you only copper and copper ore in trade. Copper and copper ore are all I have. The mighty wanax Yaddiyas has many different things. He can give you many different things in trade."

"Copper and copper ore will do nicely," Sharur said. "They are what draws the men of Kudurru to the Alashkurru Mountains."

"You did not answer my question." Abzuwas folded his arms across his chest and looked straight at Sharur. "Why did you come to me, and not go into the fortress? Why would you treat with me, and not with the mighty wanax?"

"For no reason I can see," Sharur said, almost truthfully, "your Alashkurri gods are angry at me. They have forbidden the wanakes of this land from trading with me. They have forbidden the merchants of this land from trading with me. So far as I know, they have not forbidden the smiths of this land from trading with me."

"Ah, the gods." Abzuwas spoke in some surprise. "Yes, the gods." Sure enough, he needed to be reminded of them, just as a smith in Gibil might go for days without worrying about the will of Engibil. The gods were stronger than he, yes, but they did not much impinge on what he did in his daily labors. "They are angry at you, you say?" Reluctantly, Sharur nodded. Abzuwas asked, "Why should they not be angry at me, then, if I give you copper and copper ore in trade for your goods? Why should they not be angry at me if, of a sudden, I trade Gibli swords and wine and cloth and whatever else you may have?"

"Because you are a smith," Sharur answered. "Because you have your own power. Because here in this place I do not feel the weight of the Alashkurri gods on my shoulders." *Because you are more like a man of Gibil than any other Alashkurri I know, even Huzziyas the wanax who would be a lugal if only the gods here would let him.* But Sharur did not say that aloud, not knowing how Abzuwas would take it.

The smith understood it even if he did not say it. "I cannot take this chance, Sharur son of Ereshguna. You and I, we are not so much alike as you would think."

"But we are," Sharur insisted. "We both have more freedom from the gods than is common here in your mountains or in the land between the rivers."

"No." Abzuwas shook his head. "You are nearly right, but you are not right. I have freedom under the gods. I do not have freedom from the gods. I do not desire freedom from the gods."

"It amounts to the same thing in the end," Sharur said.

But Abzuwas shook his head again, sadly. "I have seen you Giblut. Whether the gods give or not, you snatch. Such was never my way. I am content. Are you?"

"Content?" Sharur had, so far as he was able, been holding in his temper in the presence of the Alashkurrut and their gods. Now, for the first time since he'd entered the mountains, it escaped him altogether. "Content?" His voice rose to a shout. "No, I am not content! I have fine goods to trade here, and no one will trade with me. I am going to face a loss, not a profit, because no one here will trade with me. Your gods have the foolish notion—your gods have the stupid notion—I have some sort of a disease of the spirit, and that I am liable to give it to you, and so they will let no one trade with me. I shall not have the bride-price for the woman I want, the woman who wants me, because no one will trade with me. And you ask if I am content? Would you be content, standing where I stand?''

He was dimly aware of the donkey handlers and caravan guards staring at him while he raged. What gossip they would have when they got back to Gibil! Most of his attention, though, centered on Abzuwas the smith, who, he had thought, was more like a Gibli than any other man of Alashkurru.

''If the gods made it plain to me they did not want me to trade, I would not trade,'' Abzuwas answered. ''The gods have made it plain to me they do not want me to trade, and I will not trade. Whether they are right, whether they are wrong, they are the gods. They are too strong to fight. I will not fight them.''

He *was* like a Gibli: he had come so far out from under the rule of his gods that he could see they might be wrong. And he *was not* like a Gibli: he accepted their rule nonetheless, on account of their strength, and did not seek to work around that strength with such strength as he and his fellow men possessed. Sharur did not know what to make of him, how to reckon him.

''What should I do?'' Sharur asked the question at least as much of himself as of Abzuwas.

Abzuwas answered it nonetheless: ''Go home to Gibil, Sharur son of Ereshguna. You cannot profit on every journey. In your heart, you must know this is so. If you do not earn the woman's bride-price here, perhaps you will find another way of getting it. You Giblut are clever in such things, as in so many others.''

*I cannot, not in this*, Sharur thought. But he had not fully shared his reasons for concern even with his own father, even with Ningal his intended, and he would not take them up with a foreign smith, even with a sympathetic foreign smith.

Harharu came up to him. The donkeymaster chose his words with great and obvious care: ''Master merchant's son, if Abzuwas son of Ahhiyawas will not trade with us, no

Alashkurri will trade with us. Is this the truth, or is it a lie?''

"It is the truth," Sharur said dully.

"If none of the Alashkurrut will trade with us, do we not waste your substance, do we not waste your father's substance, by persisting in this land where the gods hate us and the men obey the gods?''

"We do," Sharur admitted, dully still. He let out a long sigh. "I understand your words, donkeymaster, however much my heart rebels within me at yielding to them. But you are right. Abzuwas is right, or partly right. We have failed here. We shall go home to Gibil." He pretended not to hear the muffled cheers that rose from his followers.


The caravan had no trouble leaving the mountains. The Alashkurrut were willing enough to trade food for Sharur's trinkets, even if they would engage in no commerce that meant anything. No bands of raiders, no wanax's guardsmen (these two groups sometimes being difficult—sometimes being impossible—to distinguish one from the other) beset him or tried to rob him of the swords and wine and medicines for which the Alashkurri great men refused to bargain.

That puzzled Sharur as much as it relieved him. The Alashkurrut sometimes plundered caravans for the sport of it, even when their gods were not ill-inclined toward the foreign merchants in their land. If their gods hated him so, if their gods hated all men of Gibil so, why not seek to wipe him from the face of the earth?

He pondered that as day followed day and bandits continued to stay far away from his donkeys. Nor was he the only one pondering it. As the caravan encamped one evening, Mushezib came up to him and said, "Why are they leaving us alone, master merchant's son?" He sounded aggrieved at losing the chance to fight.

By then Sharur had devised an answer that, if not provably true like a question of arithmetic, at least helped him toward understanding this strange part of the world. "Guard captain, we know the gods here hate us."

Mushezib nodded emphatically. "All the more reason for wanting to be rid of us by hook or by crook, wouldn't you say?"

"They want to be rid of us, yes," Sharur said, "but I think they fear us too much to try to slay us or despoil us. Perhaps they are afraid of what our ghosts might do if we were murdered in this country. Perhaps they are afraid of what the living men of Gibil might do if we were murdered in this country. So long as we are willing to leave their land, they seem willing to let us leave in peace."

"Gibil is a long way off, and is only one city," Mushezib said. "How could the living men of Gibil hope to avenge us against Alashkurri bandits?"

"Against Alashkurri bandits, I do not think they could hope to avenge us," Sharur said. "Against Alashkurri gods, I think they might. The gods of Alashkurru fear the men of Alashkurru will slip out of their hands, as we Giblut have to some degree slipped out of the hands of Engibil." He spoke softly as he made to his countryman the admission he would not make to the Imhursagut or Alashkurrut.

"How does that help the living men of Gibil avenge—?" Mushezib held up a hand. "Wait. I think I see. If many Giblut came here—"

Sharur nodded. "Just so, guard captain. Trading with us, talking with us, has already made many Alashkurrut much more like us than they were even a generation ago. If enough Giblut came and traded and talked, sooner or later a wanax would do what Huzziyas could not do, and would make himself into a lugal, a ruler in his own right. My guess is, the gods of the Alashkurrut believe that, if all the men of Gibil leave this land, if none has any reason to come here, Alashkurru shall remain forever as it has always been."

Mushezib weighed that, then grunted. "Do you think they're right?"

"What an interesting question," Sharur said, and did not answer it. He thought the Alashkurri gods likely—almost certainly—wrong, but was not so rash as to say so where they could hear. "Shall we drink some beer, Mushezib?"

"That's a good idea, master merchant's son." Mushezib always thought drinking some beer a good idea.

Two days later, in the valley dominated by the fortress-town of Danauwiyas, to the north of the valley of Zalpuwas (through which Sharur dared not go, not now), the caravan met that of the men of Imhursag, which it had left in the dust long before reaching the Alashkurru Mountains.

Sharur recognized the Imhursagut before they figured out who he was. He would have been angry at himself had it been the other way round. If a man from Gibil, a man who thought for himself, was not more alert than the Imhursagut, drunk with their god as they got drunk with wine, what point to being a Gibli?

Then he bethought himself that the caravan from Imhursag would have made a fine profit here in the mountains. He knew in his heart he would have made more even on the same shoddy Imhursaggi goods—if, that is, any of the Alashkurrut would have consented to deal with him. Since the Alashkurrut, as he had seen to his sorrow, would not deal with him under any circumstances . . . what point to being a man of Gibil now?

"Pride." Finding the answer, he spoke it aloud, and then addressed his companions: "Show pride, one and all. Do not let the Imhursagut know we are downhearted; do not act like slaves before them. Follow my lead in all I do. If the Imhursagut think we have done well here, it will confuse them. If they think we have made a profit here, it will confuse their god."

Where nothing else might have served, that raised the caravan crew's spirits. Putting one over on Enimhursag was sweeter to the Giblut than dates candied in honey, more satisfying than a great bowl of stewed lamb and lentils.

And so, by the time the men of Imhursag realized the men and donkeys approaching them came from the city that was their hated rival, by the time they scurried around and readied themselves for a fight that might or might not come—by that time, Sharur and the caravan guards and the donkey handlers showed new life in their step, new cheer on their faces. Striding out ahead of them, Sharur marched confidently toward the Imhursaggi caravan.

An Imhursaggi came toward him, too: the same man with whom he had spoken on the road to Alashkurru. "Gibil and Imhursag are not at war. Engibil and Enimhursag are not at war," Sharur said. "Let us by in peace. We shall let you by in peace. We are homeward-bound."

The Imhursaggi cocked his head to one side, as if listening. Listening he was, to no voice Sharur could hear, to no voice Sharur cared to hear. Having learned the will of his god, he answered, "We shall let you go in peace. Go home to your city, Gibli; go home with your tail between your legs."

"When I get home to Gibil, I shall thrust my tail between the legs of my Imhursaggi slave woman," Sharur retorted. "Why do you mock me? Why do you insult me? May you make as much profit on your journey as I have made on mine."

He knew how he meant that. He did not think the man of Imhursag would. He did not think Enimhursag would, either, when the god heard the words through the man's ears. He proved right on both counts. Angrily, the Imhursaggi said, "Profit? How can you have made a profit?"

"Why do you ask? Don't you know how yourself?" Sharur's smile was easy, lazy, happy, as if he had just had the Imhursaggi slave. He knew how much effort holding that smile on his face required. By holding it there, he hoped to keep the man of Imhursag from seeing that effort.

And he succeeded. Swarthy though the Imhursaggi merchant was, he flushed angrily. "You cannot have made a profit in the Alashkurru Mountains!" he shouted. "You cannot! The gods of this country hate you. They know what Giblut are. They know what Giblut do."

Sharur's smile only got wider. With a shrug, he answered, "Enimhursag hates the men of Gibil, but we trade all through Kudurru, and make good profits. We do not trade with Enimhursag. We trade with men. We do not trade with the gods of this country, either. We trade with men."

From dark and ruddy, the merchant of Imhursag went pale. He understood what Sharur was saying. Enimhursag understood what Sharur was saying, too. "You have made the Alashkurrut into Giblut—men who cheat the gods," the merchant gasped.

"They will tell you otherwise," Sharur said. "They will insist it is not so. They will deny they ever traded with me. They will sound as if you should believe them. But how will you know for certain whether they speak the truth?"

"You are worse than a demon of the desert places," the Imhursaggi said, horror in his eyes—a horror that was a window into a place deeper and darker than the bottom of his own spirit, a window into all the fears Enimhursag felt. Putting the god of Imhursag in fear felt almost as good as making a profit would have done. Almost.

"We shall go by now," Sharur said. "We shall go by in peace now. I told you once and now I tell you twice, man of Imhursag: may you profit here as I have profited here."

He wondered if Enimhursag would change his mind and order the Imhursagut to attack his men rather than letting them pass in peace. The merchant with whom he spoke evidently wondered the same thing, for he stood poised, his eyes far away, awaiting any orders his god might give. No orders came. The merchant slumped, ever so slightly. "We shall let you go by in peace. Go home to your city."

As warily as they had west of the Yarmuk, the caravan from Gibil and that from Imhursag sidled past each other. The Imhursagut scowled frightful scowls at Sharur and his companions. At his command, his own guards and donkey handlers did their best to pretend the caravan crew from the other city did not exist. Not a word was said on either side.

Continuing east, back toward Kudurru, back toward Gibil, Sharur looked over his shoulder. Looking at him was the Imhursaggi merchant who led the other caravan. When their eyes met, the man of Imhursag flinched, as if from a blow. Quickly, he turned his gaze in another direction.

Sharur told his own caravan crew how he had confused

both the Imhursaggi merchant and Enimhursag. His fellow Giblut laughed and cheered and clapped him on the back. Harharu said, ''The only way the tale could be better, master merchant's son, would be for our donkeys in truth to be heavily laden with copper and ore and the other goods of Alashkurru.''

''If the Alashkurrut *were* like us—if they truly were their own men first and took care of their gods to keep them quiet—we would be heavily laden with copper and ore and the other goods of Alashkurru,'' Sharur said, from out of a strange place halfway between frustrated fury and amusement. ''But they are not, worse luck. And so Enimhursag wins this game.'' *And so I lose it.* That was even more to the point.

''But Enimhursag, stupid ugly blind fool of a god that he is, doesn't even know he's won,'' Mushezib said with a scornful laugh. ''He's back there in his temple in Imhursag, hiding under the throne with his thumb in his mouth.''

Such cheerful blasphemy, aimed at a god Sharur despised above all others, was bracing as a draught of strong wine. And the guard captain was likely to be right; Enimhursag's followers had been well and truly fooled, which meant, at such a remove from his own land, that their god was also almost sure to be well and truly fooled. That gave Sharur some consolation: some, but not enough.


As the caravan wound its way out of the mountains of Alashkurru toward the lower, flatter land to the east, eerie laughter floated down out of the sky. Sharur stared this way and that, but could not spy the demon. Nevertheless, he shook his fist and cried out, ''I curse you, Illuyankas demon of this land, by your name I curse you for mocking me. May you eat the bread of death for mocking me, Illuyankas demon of this land; may you drink the beer of dying. May your face turn pale, like a cut-down tamarisk, Illuyankas demon of this land; may your lips turn dark, like a bruised reed. May the gods smite you with the might of their land.

I curse you, Illuyankas demon of this land, by your name I curse you for mocking me."

Only silence after that, silence and the sound of the breeze sighing through saplings. "That is a strong curse, master merchant's son," Harharu said, "a strong curse, but one you shaped with care."

Sharur nodded. "Yes. Not having seen Illuyankas, I cannot be certain that demon is the one whose laughter we heard. I would not lay a curse on a demon for something of which that demon is innocent. If Illuyankas was not the demon mocking us, the curse will not bite."

As always, the herders who roamed the land beyond the reach of life-giving water from the Yarmuk and its lesser tributaries eyed the caravan as a hawk overhead eyed a shape on the ground, wondering whether it was a hare that would be easy to kill or a fox that would fight back. The guards carried their shields and their weapons and wore their helmets, suggesting that any of the wanderers who might attack would pay dearly.

The lean, fierce herders were persuaded. When they approached Sharur's donkey train, it was to trade sheep and cattle for trinkets. "You will have nothing better for us than the scraps of your goods, not coming east from out of the mountains," one of their leathery chieftains said. "It is always thus—the men of Kudurru gain more for their goods in the mountains than here, and more for the goods of the mountains in Kudurru than here. This leaves us with little but what we take for ourselves." His eyes were bright and fierce and avid.

"If you try to rob us, what you will take for yourself and your kinsmen are wounds and sorrow," Sharur said. Mushezib strutted by then, not quite by chance, looking as if even a hundred herdsmen might not be able to pull him down.

"It could be done," the chieftain said. Sharur gestured with one hand, casually, as if to answer, *Well, what if it could?* The chieftain sighed. "As you say, it would cost us dear. Strange how those who have so much fight so hard to keep those who have little from getting any more."

"As strange how those who have little think they deserve more without working for it," Sharur returned. The herder showed his teeth, as a desert fox might have done. Sharur kept his voice elaborately calm: "By the will of the gods, we have with us a few finer things than usual. Would you see them?"

"Only if it pleases you to show them," the herder replied, sounding as indifferent as Sharur. That was how the game went. "If it would be too much bother, you need not trouble yourself."

"They might amuse you," Sharur said, and the chieftain did not say no. Sharur set out before him date wine and medicine and linen cloth—the herders did more than his own people with wool. He also set out a few, a very few, swords and knives, as if to suggest that the Alashkurrut had acquired the rest.

"True, these are not things traders show us every day," the herder chieftain said. He looked down at the ground to disguise the eager glow in his eyes. But, tent-dwelling no-mad though he was, he was neither a blind man nor a fool. "All these things come from the land between the rivers. Nothing comes from the high country." He pointed first east, then west. "By the will of the gods, you say, you have these things to show us. Was it the will of the gods that you not trade in the mountains?"

The herders did not know gods well, or, to put it another way, the gods hardly found the herders worth noticing. The chieftain smiled as he asked the question. But the smile disappeared when, in a stony voice, Sharur replied, "Yes, that was the will of the gods."

"Ah." The herder plucked at his beard. He had dyed red streaks in it with henna. Turning away from Sharur, he entered into a whispered colloquy with some of his own people. When he turned back, his face was troubled. Slowly, he said, "It may be that you are not lucky men. It may be that any who trade with you will not be lucky men. They are fine goods." He sighed regretfully. "They are fine goods, but, as with robbing you of them, they might cost us dear.''

He and the herders he led vanished into the night, a few at a time, until they were all gone. Mushezib said, ''Well, we won't need to worry so much about the cursed thieves this time through, anyhow. They're as bad as the Zuabut, sometimes.''

That was the best face anyone could put on it. Sharur wrapped up the weapons and nostrums and wine and cloth the herders had not wanted. ''I shall return to Gibil in failure,'' he said. ''Better I should not return at all.''

''Your father will not say this, master merchant's son,'' Harharu answered. ''Your mother will not say this. Your kinsfolk will not say this. They would sooner greet you in the flesh than hear your ghost whine in their ears. In the flesh, you may yet redeem yourself, and so, no doubt, you shall.''

Harharu might not have had any doubts. Sharur was full of them. The donkeymaster had meant the words kindly, though, and so Sharur inclined his head to him and said nothing more than, ''Well, we shall go on.'' He nodded. That sounded right. Seeing him push the brief moment of self-pity behind himself, Harharu nodded, too.


The morning sun shone off the Yarmuk River, turning its muddy water to molten silver. As he had done on the westbound journey, Sharur brought his caravan to the Yarmuk at the little-used ford north of the city of Aggasher rather than to the usual crossing point by the city. He did not know what Eniaggasher, the goddess ruling the city, might do to him and his men, and he was not anxious to learn.

When he drew near the river, a frog leapt in from the nearby mudflat. Ripples ruffled the silver surface, then subsided. All was calm once more. Sharur brought a bracelet to the water's edge and said, ''For thee, Eniyarmuk, to adorn thyself and make thyself more beautiful.'' He tossed the sacrifice into the river.

Ripples spread from the bracelet, as they had when the frog leaped into the river. Unlike those ripples, these did not subside. They grew larger instead. More appeared, more and more and more, till the surface of the Yarmuk might have been the sea in a storm. But it was not the sea, and no storm roiled it.

Something flew out of the river to land at the feet of Sharur, who had jumped back away from the water's edge when the unnatural tumult started. Now, as it eased, he stooped and picked up the bracelet he had offered to the river goddess.

"Eniyarmuk has rejected the sacrifice!" he exclaimed, blank astonishment in his voice. "What do we do now?"

"One thing we don't do, I reckon," Agum the caravan guard said: "I don't reckon we try and cross the river right now."

Harharu said, "I don't know how we are to return to Gibil without crossing the Yarmuk River." He stared at the stream. "I have never heard of Eniyarmuk rejecting a crossing-offering, never in all my days."

"Can we cross anyway?" Mushezib asked.

"I wouldn't care to try it," Sharur said. He thought of the storm the goddess had raised in the river, and of what such a storm—or a greater storm—would do to the men and donkeys of the caravan. "If the goddess is angry, we would be no more than toys in her hands."

Mushezib, a true man of Gibil, growled, "The goddess is a stupid bitch." But even he realized he had gone too far, for a moment later he hastily added, "But we can't fight her, that's certain sure. No man can take a goddess by force."

"There you speak truth," Sharur agreed. He stood on the riverbank and pondered.

"Even a woman taken by force isn't all that much fun," Mushezib went on, more to himself than to anyone else. "They scream and they kick and they wail and they try and bite—more trouble than they're worth, if you ask me." He came out of his reverie when Sharur darted back toward one of the donkeys. "What are you doing, master merchant's son?"

"Taking a woman by force is more trouble than it's worth, as you say," Sharur replied. "Sometimes, though, if you go with her to a tavern and buy her wine, she will smile and be happy, and you have no need to take her by force." He carried a sloshing jar down to the bank of the Yarmuk.

Using the point of his knife, he chipped pitch away from the stopper until he could pry it up. The rich sweetness of fermented dates filled his nostrils. He walked upstream from the ford, perhaps half a bowshot, then bowed low and, with great ceremony, poured the wine into the water. That done, he tossed a stick into the river and followed it back until it had drifted past the place where the caravan waited to cross.

When it was past the ford, he waved men and donkeys forward, saying, "Eniyarmuk has now drunk a jar of wine. If she is not too sozzled to take notice of a few mortal men, she never will be." He slipped out of his own kilt and sandals and led the first donkey into the river.

He knew what the goddess could do if she was not too sozzled to take notice of a few mortal men. His fear grew with every step, for he believed she *would* do it if she was not too sozzled to take notice of him. Those thoughts did not fill his mind alone, either. Harharu and Mushezib called out to their men with quiet urgency, seeking ever greater speed. The donkey handlers and guards would have pressed ahead without those admonitions; with them, they pressed harder. Even the donkeys acted less balky than usual.

Sharur came up onto the dry land—well, the muddy land—of the eastern bank of the Yarmuk. A great sigh of relief gusted from his lungs. He hauled on the lead line to bring the first donkey out of the water. The others, and the rest of the caravan crew, followed in rapid succession.

"Come on," Sharur told them. "We're not done yet. Let's get away from the river, as far as we can, before we get into our clothes and set everything to rights."

"Good thinking, master merchant's son," Mushezib said. "Don't want to be close by when the river goddess sobers up, no I don't. You get a woman drunk and have your way with her, she's liable to be angry in the morning, yes she is.''

''Just so,'' Sharur agreed. Naked still, he pushed the pace, begrudging the time he would need to pause and belt on his kilt. The sun quickly dried the Yarmuk's water on his body. *The drier, the better*, he thought: less lingering contact between himself and Eniyarmuk's domain.

He chanced to be looking back over his shoulder when the river goddess realized he had muddled her wits and deceived her. The surface of the Yarmuk suddenly boiled and frothed. Water leapt into the air, then splashed down. In unmistakable fury, the river began to pursue the caravan. Men and donkeys cried out in alarm together and hurried eastward as fast as they could go.

So long as the questing tentacle of river remained in the bed the Yarmuk occupied during full flood, it came on after them more swiftly than their best pace. Beyond the riverbed, though, the fierce flow faltered: outside her domain, Eniyarmuk's power was much diminished. At last, sullenly, the waters drew back toward their proper channel.

Panting, sweating, Sharur held up a hand. ''We have escaped the anger of the river goddess,'' he said. ''Let us give thanks and rejoice, hymning Engibil's praises.''

The hymn rang out, loud and triumphant. Only when it was through, only after he had covered his nakedness, did Sharur think to wonder about the propriety of praising one god for having escaped (*no, for having beaten*, the defiant part of his mind thought, though he dared not say that aloud) another.

''Master merchant's son, your cleverness let us get by no small problem there,'' Harharu said. ''Had we not got past Eniyarmuk, we might have had to go down to the regular ford, and then we would have had to go under the eye of Eniaggasher. That likely would have been worse. Your father will be proud of you.''

''No doubt,'' Sharur said. ''He will be proud of me for going up into the mountains of Alashkurru and coming back down with the same goods I took up. He will be proud of me for coming back without copper, without copper ore. He will be proud of me for coming back down without rich things, strange things, unusual things, to lay on the altar of Engibil.'' *Ningal will be proud of me for coming back without her bride-price.*

Quietly, the donkeymaster said, ''He will be proud of you for doing as well as you could, for doing as well as you did, in harsh circumstances not of your making.''

''Were those circumstances not partly of my making?'' Sharur asked. ''Did I not go up into the mountains of Alash-kurru before? Did I not speak with the Alashkurrut? Did I not show them what we men of Gibli are, by my words, by my deeds? Did I not help make some of them want to be like us Giblut? Did I not help frighten their gods because some of them wanted to be like us Giblut?''

Harharu bowed his head. ''If you are determined to be angry at yourself, master merchant's son, I cannot stop you. If you are determined to cast scorn upon yourself, I cannot prevent it.'' He strode off to check on the donkeys, which, while stubborn, knew not bitterness nor worry ahead of time.

Sharur strode on, alone no matter how close the rest of the caravan might be. What would his father say, what would his father do, when he came home from the mountains without having been able to trade the goods the Alash-kurrut were known to crave? Caravans had come back to Gibil with less profit than they might have (though never one headed by a man of his clan). Caravans, sometimes, had failed to come back to Gibil at all, having met with robbers in the mountains or the desert. But never, so far as Sharur knew, had a caravan returned without doing business.

And what would Kimash the lugal say? Kimash had relied on him to bring rich things, strange things, unusual things back to Gibil to lay on the altar of Engibil. The lugal had said as much, when the caravan was just departing his father's house. Sharur had failed Kimash, too, and in failing Kimash had failed the men of Gibil. For if Engibil grew

discontented with Kimash's rule of the city—if Engibil grew
discontented with the way Kimash praised and rewarded
him—the god might yet rise up and, instead of resting comfortably and lazily in his temple, as he had been wont to do
for three generations of men, might walk through Gibil as
Enzuabu walked through Zuabu. He might seize men's spirits, as Enimhursag seized the spirits of the Imhursagut. And
the little freedom the men of Gibil had known would die.

Grim though that prospect was, it was not the prospect
uppermost in Sharur's mind. What would Ningal say, when
he came home from the mountains without the bride-price
to pay to Dimgalabzu her father? Sharur had sworn a great
oath to Engibil to earn that bride-price with the profit from
this caravan. Now he came home without profit, a forsworn
man. Would Dimgalabzu give her to another? Sharur kicked
at the dirt. The smith would be within his rights.

"But he can't!" Sharur exclaimed.

"Who can't, master merchant's son?" Harharu asked.
"And what can't he do?"

"Never mind." Sharur's ears went hot at having let others see into his thoughts. The trouble was, Dimgalabzu
*could.* And, if he decided to, Sharur would not be able to
do anything about it. Muttering curses that surely would not
bite on the gods of the Alashkurrut, he trudged east toward
Gibil.

When the caravan entered the territory ruled by Zuabu,
Sharur felt he might as well be home. After so long among
so many stranger peoples, the Zuabut seemed as familiar to
him as his next-door neighbors along the Street of Smiths.
His comrades must have felt the same, for almost to a man
they were grinning and laughing among themselves as they
automatically took the precautions they needed to keep the
Zuabut from stealing them blind.

"Keep your eyes open, boys," Mushezib called to the
caravan guards under him. "We all know the stories about
the caravans that came into the land of Zuabu with a profit

and went out with a loss, even though they hadn't done any trading while they were there. That isn't going to happen to us . . . What are you making horrible faces about, Agum? Donkey stepping on your—? Oh.''

Mushezib shut up, several sentences too late. Sharur, also intent on making sure the Zuabut could have no fun with their light fingers, pretended he had not heard the guard captain. This caravan could hardly see its profit disappear in Zuabu, for it had no profit. Making a loss worse somehow seemed much less important, even if the value vanishing from the caravan was the same in either case.

As had been true when he was setting out for the Alashkurru Mountains, Sharur could have taken the caravan into the city of Zuabu to spend a night. As he had then, he camped away from the city. Then, he had begrudged what he would have to pay for food and lodging. He still did, but he had more pressing reasons for avoiding the city now. He did not want to, he did not dare to, enter into Enzuabu's center on earth, not after the city god had sent such a menacing stare his way on his westbound journey, and most especially not after everything that had happened since.

As had been true then, so now someone shook him out of sound sleep. As had been true then, it was Agum now. What he said, though, was something any caravan guard might have said on any journey through Zuabu: ''Master merchant's son, we've caught a thief.''

Sharur yawned till he thought his head would split in two. ''Why tell me about it? Give the fellow a beating and send him on his way. He'll try to steal from the next caravan that comes through, but he won't try stealing from us again.''

''Master merchant's son, we were going to do as you say, the very thing, but then the wretch had the nerve to claim Enzuabu ordered him to steal from us, and that the god would punish him if he failed.'' Agum made a small, unhappy sound. ''What with all that's gone on this trip, we thought you had better see him.''

With a sigh, Sharur got to his feet. He did not bother pulling on his kilt, but followed Agum naked to the fire beside which three more guards were holding down the thief. Yet another guard fed dry reeds and small dead bushes into the fire to build it up and throw more light on the Zuabi.

He was a small, skinny man, supple as a ferret and with a face to match. "He looks as if he'd steal from us whether Enzuabu ordered him to do it or not," Sharur remarked to Agum.

"So he does," Agum agreed. The guards holding the man shook him till the teeth rattled in his head. Agum put a growl in his voice: "You cursed river leech, you tell the master merchant's son the lies you've been grizzling out to the rest of us."

"Yes, lord," the Zuabi said, as if Agum were his ensi. "I *am* a thief. I am the best of thieves. Would Enzuabu have chosen me were I less? Would Enzuabu pull a plow with a hen, or make a pot out of beer? I was suited to my god's purpose, and his voice sounded in my mind, summoning me to his temple, that he might give me orders there. I obey my god in all things. I went to the temple, and he gave me orders there."

"And what were the orders he gave you?" Sharur asked.

"Lord, he told me a caravan of Giblut was encamped outside Zuabu, in such-and-such a place at such-and-such a distance. He told me to rob this caravan of Giblut. He told me you Giblut oppose the gods, and that robbing you Giblut is only right and proper because of this. He told me your caravan had in it rich goods of your city, and that robbing it would profit him and me alike."

Sharur scowled. The thief had been caught before he could rob the caravan. How could he know what goods it had, unless Enzuabu told him? Unless Enzuabu told him, would he not think it had goods from the mountains of Alashkurru? His words were too much like those Sharur had heard from gods and demons for comfort.

"You have not robbed us," Sharur said. "What will Enzuabu do with you, now that you have failed?"

"Lord"—the thief shuddered in the grasp of his captors—"he will smite me with boils, and with carbuncles he will smite my wife and my concubine and my children."

In a judicious voice, Sharur said, "Would it not be fitting, then, to send you away from this place, to send you back to Zuabu, to let your own god punish you as you deserve? In some cities, the gods punish thieves who succeed. Only in Zuabu does the god punish thieves who fail."

Agum and the other guards laughed. The thief wailed. "Have mercy on a man who sought only to obey the command of his god!" he cried.

"You would have tried to rob us anyhow," Agum said roughly. "You deserve your boils, and may your concubine get a carbuncle on her twat."

The guards laughed again. But Sharur held up a hand, and the laughter stopped. If Enzuabu had sent out the thief, Enzuabu deserved the punishment. And, deliciously, Sharur saw how he might give it. "Let him up," he said.

Startled, the guards obeyed. Even more startled, the thief rose. Sharur rummaged in a pack until he found a necklace of painted clay beads, as near worthless as made no difference. He laid it on the ground and turned his back.

"Here," he said. "Steal this. Lay it on Enzuabu's altar. You will have obeyed your god. He cannot smite you with boils, nor your wife and your concubine and your children with carbuncles."

When he turned around again, the necklace was gone. So was the thief. From out of the night came a soft call: "My blessings upon you, lord, whatever—" *Whatever Enzuabu might say?* The thief was wise to stop speaking when he did. But he would not stop thinking. In the silence, Sharur nodded slowly, once.

# 4

"It is Sharur, the son of Ereshguna!" the Gibli gate guard exclaimed. He bowed to Sharur, who led the caravan as it returned to his home city. "Did you fare well in the Alashkurru Mountains, master merchant's son?"

One of Sharur's bushy eyebrows rose. His mouth twisted into a wry smile. "I am back from the Alashkurru Mountains. I am back in Gibil. Is that not faring well, all by itself?"

The gate guard laughed. "Right you are, master merchant's son. Not enough copper, not enough silver, not enough gold to make me want to visit those funny foreign places, not when I live in the finest city in Kudurru, which means the finest city in the world." He stood aside. "Not that you want to hear me chattering, either, no indeed." His voice rose to a shout: "Enter into Gibil, city of the great god Engibil, Sharur son of Ereshguna, you and all your comrades!"

Sharur would sooner have entered Gibil quietly, with no one knowing he was there until he came to his family's house in the Street of Smiths. He had not got any of what he wished on this disastrous journey, and knew ahead of time he would not get to enjoy a quiet entrance, either.

Where the Zuabut were known throughout the land between the rivers for their nimble fingers, the men of Gibil were known for their nimble minds. They buzzed round the caravan as flies buzzed round a butcher shop, calling out greetings to Sharur and to the donkey handlers and guards they knew, and, most of all, calling out questions: "Did you make a profit?" "How big a profit did you make?" "How much copper did you bring back?" "Any of that fine-grained red wood that smells good?" "Carved jewels, master merchant's son?" "Are the Alashkurrut really ten feet tall?" "Did frozen water fall out of the sky on you?" It went on and on and on.

As Sharur had asked of them, the caravan crew said as little as they could. Giblut were also known throughout the land between the rivers for talking to excess, but neither Sharur nor the donkey handlers nor the guards lived up to that part of their reputation. That the men were to receive the last installment of their pay at Sharur's home helped persuade them to hold their tongues.

Some of the Giblut assumed that quiet meant the caravan had not done so well as they would have expected. They were right, but Sharur gave no sign of it. Some assumed the quiet meant the caravan had done far better than expected. They were wrong, but Sharur gave no sign of that, either. Arguments broke out between pessimists and optimists, distracting both groups from the caravan.

Not everyone in Gibil used shouted questions to try to learn how much wealth the caravan had brought to the city. One of the fanciest Gibli courtesans simply pulled off her semitransparent shift and stood magnificently naked in the street, saying without words, *If you can afford me, here I am.* With his men, Sharur stared longingly and walked on.

Word of their return ran through the city ahead of them. By the time they reached the Street of Smiths, the workers in bronze had come forth from their smithies, sweat streaking through smoke stains on their torsos. Their questions were the same as those of the other Giblut, but more urgent, as the answers were more immediately important to them.

By then, Sharur had been answering questions by not answering them for so long, he had no trouble making the smiths believe he'd told them much more, and been much more encouraging, than he actually had. But then Ningal

came out of Dimgalabzu's establishment and called to him,
"Did you bring back my bride-price, Sharur?"

"I . . . will have to reckon up the accounts to make sure
I have enough," he answered. He fought for a smile, and
managed to achieve one. "I hope so."

The smile must have been better than he thought, for Ningal returned it. "I hope so, too," she said, and went back
indoors.

"You will be a lucky man, master merchant's son," Harharu said, "if that is your intended bride."

"Yes," Sharur said, hoping his voice didn't sound too
hollow. He was, in a way, glad the donkeymaster, not Mushezib, had come up to him. The guard captain would have
phrased essentially the same comment in so pungent a way,
Sharur might have felt he had to hit him. Had the caravan
succeeded, he would have taken any and all chaffing in good
part. Without Ningal's bride-price here, he was ready to lash
out at anyone and anything. Only realizing as much let him
keep his temper from being even worse than it actually was.

At last, the donkeys plodded up to his own home. Standing in front of it in the narrow, muddy street were his father
and his brother Tupsharru. Ereshguna folded him into an
embrace, saying, "Welcome home, my eldest son. It is good
to see your face once more."

"Thank you, Father." How would Ereshguna think it to
see his face when he found out Sharur had returned to Gibil
without a profit? Sharur knew he would learn that soon—
too soon. For his family's sake as well as his own, he
wanted to keep the rest of Gibil from learning that too soon.
He said, "Father, I should particularly like to commend the
donkey handlers and caravan guards, who served better than
we dared hope. Along with their last payments, which are
due now, I suggest you give them bonuses in silver, to reward them for their loyalty."

"What?" Tupsharru said. "We've never done anything
like—Ow!" Without being too obtrusive about it, Sharur
had contrived to step on his brother's toes.

Ereshguna, fortunately, was quicker on the uptake than

his younger son. If Sharur proposed an unprecedented bonus, he assumed Sharur had some good reason for proposing it. "Just as you say, so shall it be," he said. "I had the final payments prepared and waiting inside, but I can add to them. I shall add to them." He went back in to do just that.

Sharur addressed the caravan crew: "For your diligence, for your perseverance, for your courage, and for your discretion, you shall be rewarded over and above your final payments."

A few muffled cheers arose. In a low voice, Mushezib told one of the guards, "That means keeping your mouth shut, you understand?"

Tupsharru noticed the most important word, too. "Why are we paying them above the usual to be discreet?" he asked, also quietly.

"Because we have reason above the usual to want them to be discreet," Sharur replied, which was true and uninformative at the same time.

Ereshguna and a couple of the house slaves came out then. The slaves led the donkeys off the street and into the courtyard at the heart of the house. Ereshguna carried on a tray leather sacks full of scrap silver: smaller ones for the ordinary guards and donkey handlers, larger ones for Mushezib and Harharu, who had led them. On the tray also gleamed silver rings. "Every man take one over and above your final payment," he said, "save the guard captain and donkeymaster, who are to take two." He still asked no questions of his son. Later would be time enough for that.

And then, as the men of the caravan crew were taking their pay and their bonuses and offering up words of praise for the house of Ereshguna and for its generosity, the ghost of Sharur's grandfather shouted in his ear: "Boy, when you led that caravan to the mountains, did you stand out in the sun too long without your hat? You've brought back all the stuff you set out with. No, you've brought back *some* of the stuff you set out with"—his grandfather's ghost sniffed—"but nothing you set out to get."

The ghost had not bothered to speak to him alone. By the

way Tupsharru's head came up in startlement, he could tell his brother had also heard the angry words. Sighing, Sharur murmured, "I will tell this tale presently, when I can tell it in more privacy."

Some of the donkey handlers and guards were murmuring, too, as ghosts that had not left Gibil greeted those who remembered them on their return. Agum was shaking his head and talking vehemently under his breath. Sharur wondered if he was trying to explain why the ghost of his uncle had not returned with him.

He got only a moment to wonder, for his grandfather's ghost shouted again: "Kimash the lugal will be angry at you for coming back with nothing you set out to get. He's not so much of a much, Kimash, but for what he is, he'll be angry at you. And Engibil—Engibil will be angry at you, too, for coming back with nothing you set out to get."

Sharur sighed again. "Yes, I know that," he muttered. It hadn't crossed Tupsharru's mind; he stared toward Sharur. Ereshguna also looked in Sharur's direction. Whatever he thought, he kept to himself.

Only after the men of the caravan crew departed, many of them praising the generosity of the house of Ereshguna, did the head of the house turn to his elder son and say, "Come into the house. Come into the shade. Come: we will drink beer together. And you will tell the tale of your journey to the Alashkurru Mountains."

"Father, you will not rejoice to hear it," Sharur said.

"I rejoice that you are here. I rejoice that, being here, you may tell it," Ereshguna said. "Set against that, nothing else has the weight even of a single barleycorn. Whatever it may be, we have the chance to set it right."

"It will take a good deal of setting right," the ghost of Sharur's grandfather said. "For what he brought back, he might as well have stayed home. In my day, caravans that went out to trade went out to *trade*, if you know what I mean."

Ereshguna ignored the ghost's complaints. He led both his sons into the house and called for beer. A slave fetched a jar of it, and three cups. After spilling out libations, after offering thanks to the deities of barley and brewing, Eresh-guna and his sons drank. Only after the first cups were empty did Ereshguna turn to Sharur and ask, "We have less of profit, then, than we had hoped?"

"We have no profit," Sharur said. "Father, I shall not dip this news in honey, though to speak of it is to put a bitter herb in my mouth. The gods of the Alashkurrut refused to let them trade with us, save only in small things such as swapping bread and beer for trinkets. But of refined copper I have none. Of copper ore I have none. Of fine timber I have none. Of jewels I have none. Of clever carvings I have none. Of the herbs and spices and drugs of the Alashkurru Mountains I have none. I have only what I took with me from Gibil, less what I traded for food and used for bribes that failed in the course of my journey."

Ereshguna stared at his son. "You had better tell me this whole tale," he said.

And Sharur did, starting with Enzuabu's menacing stare and going on through the meeting with the Imhursagut, the encounter with the demon Illuyankas, the Alashkurri gods' preventing Huzziyas the wanax from trading with him, his failure at Zalpuwas, his inability to get even Abzuwas the smith to deal with him, Eniyarmuk's rejection of his crossing-offering, and the Zuabi thief's attempt to rob the caravan at the command of his city god.

Ereshguna said not a word while Sharur detailed his misfortune. Once his son had finished, the trader let out a long sigh. He set a hand on Sharur's thigh. "You did, I think, everything you could have done."

"I did not do enough," Sharur said. "It eats at me like a canker."

"You did more than I would ever have thought to do," Tupsharru said.

"Against the gods, a man fights openly in vain," Ereshguna said. He took out his amulet to Engibil and covered its eyes. As Sharur and Tupsharru did the same, their father went on, "Only in secret and by stealth can a man hope to gain even a part of his way in the gods' despite. Now, it seems, the gods beyond Gibil have awakened to the knowledge of how much we have gained over the years, how much we have gained over the generations. They wish to force us back into full subjection once more.''

''The caravan from Imhursag traded among the Alashkurrut,'' Sharur said gloomily. ''It came away with copper. It came away with copper ore. It came away with the other good things of the mountains. If the Imhursagut can trade and we cannot, Imhursag and Enimhursag shall be exalted among the cities and gods of Kudurru, and Gibil shall slide into slavery.''

''You speak of Gibil,'' Tupsharru said. ''You do not speak of Engibil.''

And Sharur realized he had not spoken of Engibil. His city counted for more in his heart than his city god. Everything of which the gods of other cities, the gods of other lands, had accused him was true. He did not feel shamed. He did not feel sorry. To the extent he could, he was glad to be his own man.

Ereshguna said, ''The word you bring back to Gibil, my son, does not affect the house of Ereshguna alone. It affects the other merchants and the smiths. It affects the city as a whole. And it affects Kimash the lugal.''

''I know, Father.'' Sharur hung his head. ''I did not bring back rich offerings for Kimash to lay on the altar of Engibil. I was prevented.''

''Tomorrow,'' Ereshguna said, ''tomorrow we shall go to the palace of Kimash the lugal and make known to him what passed on your journey.'' Ever so reluctantly, Sharur nodded. What choice had he?


At supper that evening, Betsilim and Nanadirat listened to Sharur tell his story all over again. His mother and sister exclaimed indignantly over the injustice he had suffered at the hands of the Alashkurri gods, and even more at the injustice he had suffered from gods dwelling closer to home.

"Eniyarmuk had no business rejecting your sacrifice for the crossing, none whatsoever," Betsilim declared.

"I didn't think so, either," Sharur answered. He turned to the kitchen slave. "Bring me more roast mutton, and garlic cloves to rub on it." She bowed and hurried away. The family had laid on a feast to celebrate his return, although, as far as he could see, only the fact that he had returned at all was worth celebrating.

His mother was not finished. "Had I been standing on the bank of the Yarmuk, I should have given the river goddess a piece of my mind," she said.

Sharur believed her. "No wonder the foreign gods fear us Giblut," he said, which made his father laugh.

Betsilim gave Ereshguna a sharp look, then resumed: "And Enzuabu! Enzuabu has no quarrel with Engibil. The Zuabut have no quarrel with the folk of Gibil. The Zuabut are thieves, surely, but how wicked for the god to set a thief on my son's caravan."

"Would it have been all right for the god to set a thief on the caravan of someone else's son?" Ereshguna asked. His wife ignored him.

Nanadirat said, "Worst of all, though, is that the Imhursagut and Enimhursag got the chance to gloat because the Alashkurri gods were so foolish." She clapped her hands together. "Slave, more date wine for me."

"I obey," the Imhursaggi war captive said softly. She held the strainer above the cup of Sharur's sister and poured the wine through it.

Sharur also held out his cup to be refilled. The kitchen slave rinsed the strainer, then gave him what he wanted. He nodded to her. She did her best to pretend she did not see him.

After the feast was over, Sharur's parents and brother and sister went up onto the roof to sleep. "I will join you in a while," Sharur said. He walked back toward the kitchen. By the light of a couple of dim, flickering torches, the slave from Imhursag was scrubbing bowls and plates and cups clean with a rag and a jar of water. Sharur set his hands on her shoulders. "Let us go back to the blanket on which you sleep."

With a small sigh, she set down the rag and dried her hands on her tunic. "I obey," she said, as she had when Nanadirat asked her for more wine. But, as she and Sharur walked down the narrow hall to her hot, tiny, cramped cubicle, she said, "You have not required this of me for a long time."

"And now I do require it," Sharur said. The kitchen slave sighed again and walked on.

Inside the cubicle, it was black as pitch, blacker than midnight. Linen rustled as the slave pulled her tunic off over her head. Sharur shed his kilt. He reached out. His hand closed on the firm round softness of the woman's breast. He squeezed.

"Do you know why I do this?" he asked as they lay down together. In the darkness, he found her hand and guided it to his erection.

"Because you own me," the slave answered. "Because you have been long away and you have no wife and you want a woman."

He shook his head. "You know I came home without profit," he said, and felt her nod. "In the mountains, far away, I met a caravan of Imhursagut. They mocked me. They said I was going home with my tail between my legs. I told them that, when I got home, I would thrust my tail between the legs of my Imhursaggi slave woman. And so"—he entered her—"I do."

"Oh," she said, and nodded again in the darkness. "You do this in fulfillment of a vow."

"Yes," he answered, drawing back and thrusting, drawing back and thrusting, forcing his way deeper each time even though she was dry.

"A vow should be fulfilled," she said seriously. "It is a duty to your god." She still thought like an Imhursaggi.

And then something strange happened. The other handful of times he had taken her, she'd simply lain there and let him do as he liked until he spent himself and left. Now, suddenly, unexpectedly, her legs rose from the blanket and clenched his flanks. Her arms wrapped around his back. Her mouth sought his. The way into her, which had been difficult, grew gloriously smooth, gloriously moist.

She made several small noises deep in her throat, and then, at the moment when pleasure almost blinded him, a mewling cry like a wild cat's. He slid out of her and sat back on his knees. "You never did anything like that before," he said, his voice almost accusing.

"Other times you have had me, it was only for your own pleasure," she said. "This time, you made good your word to your god—and to mine." Softly, under her breath, she murmured, "Oh, Enimhursag, how I long for thee."

Sharur was a young man. One round took the edge off his lust, but did not fully sate it. When he heard the slave woman shift and start to rise, he set his hand on her chest, in the valley between her breasts. "No. Not yet. I will have you again."

She lay back; a slave's duty was to obey. He mounted her once more. Save that she breathed, she might have been dead beneath him. So it had been every time until this evening. So it was again. Eventually, his seed spurted from him.

As he groped for his kilt, he said, "I was no different the second time from the first. Yet you took pleasure—I know you took pleasure—the first, and none at all the second. How is this? Why is this?"

"I told you," she answered. "I took pleasure in helping fulfill your vow: I am one who respects the gods, and I rejoice when you Giblut do likewise. The second time, it was only you. The gods were far away."

He pulled on the kilt, rose, and left the dark cubicle without another word. When he went up onto the roof, he found his parents were already sleeping. He lay down beside Tupsharru. "The Imhursaggi slave woman?" his brother asked.

"Twice," Sharur said.

"Twice?" Tupsharru coughed. "My dear brother, you *have* been without a woman a long time. Once, of course; once is always sweet. But twice? Did having her fall asleep

while you were at work make you want to go in again so
you could see if she would stay awake all the way through
the second time?''

"Surprises everywhere, my dear brother," Sharur answered through a yawn. "Yes, surprises everywhere."


When morning came, Sharur wanted to go to the house and
smith of Dimgalabzu to discuss revising the arrangements
for paying bride-price for Ningal. Ereshguna would not hear
of it. "Everything in its own place, Sharur," he said. "First
we call on Kimash the lugal. He needs to know of the misfortune that befell you in the mountains of Alashkurru so
he can decide what to do next."

"Dimgalabzu also needs to know, because—" Sharur began.

Ereshguna folded his arms across his chest. "I am your
father. I say we will go to Kimash. You shall obey me."

"You are my father." Sharur bowed his head. "We will
go to Kimash. I will obey you."

And so, instead of walking down the Street of Smiths to
Dimgalabzu's, Sharur and Ereshguna walked up the Street
of Smiths to the lugal's palace. As they passed, smiths and
other metal merchants popped out of the buildings in which
they worked to ask how Sharur's journey had gone. None
of them seemed unduly concerned; the bonuses Ereshguna
had paid to the caravan crew must so far have persuaded
the guards and donkey handlers not to say too much.

Nor did Sharur and Ereshguna say too much now to their
colleagues. "We go to speak of the caravan with Kimash
the mighty lugal," Ereshguna said several times. "Kimash
deserves to hear first the news of what Sharur traded. The
mighty lugal deserves to hear first the news of what Sharur
brought back."

That satisfied the smiths and the other metal merchants.
It did not satisfy Sharur. *What did I trade? Nothing*, he
thought bitterly. *What did I bring back? What I set out with.*
And what would the smiths and the other metal merchants

say if they heard that? What would the smiths and the other metal merchants do if they heard that? Sharur was glad he did not have to find out, not yet.

A procession of slaves and donkeys carrying costly baked bricks on their backs made Sharur and Ereshguna stand and wait outside Kimash's palace. "See, he is building it larger again," Ereshguna said. "Soon, I think, it will be larger than Engibil's temple."

"I think you are right, Father," Sharur answered. Neither man said what he thought of that. Just for a moment, Sharur covered the eyes of the amulet he wore on his belt. He did not want Engibil looking at him then. He did not want Engibil looking into his heart then. He did not want Engibil seeing how he hoped the lugal's palace would outdo the god's temple.

When the last braying donkey and the last sweating slave had passed, Sharur and Ereshguna advanced to the doorway of the palace. Guards with spears and shields stood stolidly, enduring the building heat. Ereshguna bowed before them. He said, "When the mighty lugal Kimash should deign to cast his eye upon us, we would go into his presence. When the mighty lugal Kimash should deign to hear us, we would have speech with him."

"You are Ereshguna and Sharur," one of the guards said. "I will tell Inadapa the steward you are come. Inadapa will tell Kimash the mighty lugal you are come."

He hurried away. When he returned, Inadapa accompanied him: a bald, round-faced, round-bellied man with a beard going gray. "Kimash the mighty lugal bids you welcome," the steward said. "Welcome you are, he says, and welcome, and thrice welcome. You will come with me."

"We shall come with you," Ereshguna and Sharur said together. Without another word, Inadapa turned on his heel and went back into the palace. They followed.

Sharur wondered how Inadapa found his way through the rabbits' warren of corridors that made up the palace. The building had not grown up according to any unifying plan, but haphazardly, by fits and starts, as three generations of lugals decided again and again that they needed more room—and more rooms—to house all that was theirs, or to store away the old so that they might enjoy the new.

Here was a room full of stools and tables. Should Kimash decide to give a great feast, they might come forth once more. Meanwhile, they simply sat in twilight. In the next room, pretty young women brewed beer, chanting hymns to Ikribabu as they worked. The chamber after that was piled high with bales of wool; the powerful oily smell of sheep filled that stretch of the hall.

Jars and pots held wine, beer, grain, dates . . . who could say what all? The stores in the palace might feed Gibil for a year, or so it seemed to Sharur.

Presently, Inadapa led his father and him past a chamber where more pretty young women were spinning wool into thread. As Sharur had in the brewing chamber, he noticed them because they were young and pretty. If Kimash summoned one of them, she would come, and, Sharur was sure, she would not lie beneath the lugal as if half a corpse. Kimash had opportunities for pleasure beyond those of an ordinary man.

Ereshguna noticed something else. To Inadapa, he said, "Steward to Kimash the mighty lugal, would these women not get more work done if the wool they spun were in the chamber next to theirs rather than halfway across the palace?"

Inadapa stopped in his tracks. "Master merchant," he said slowly, "in days gone by, wool *was* stored in the room next to this one. For some reason or other, it was moved. No one ever thought either to move it back or to move the women closer to the chamber where it is now held. Perhaps someone should give thought to such things." Shaking his head, he strode down the hallway once more.

"How many other such cases are there in the palace, if only someone would look?" Ereshguna murmured under his breath to Sharur as they followed the steward.

"I wonder if any one man knows everything the palace holds," Sharur whispered back.

Ereshguna shook his head. "Inadapa's grandfather—maybe even his father—might have, but the palace was smaller in those days."

Sharur started to answer, but just then the hallway opened out into Kimash's audience chamber. The lugal sat on a chair with a back; its legs and arms were sheathed in gold leaf, and it rested on a platform of earth that raised Kimash above those who came before him. Inadapa went to his knees and then to his belly before Kimash. Sharur and Ereshguna imitated the steward's action.

"Mighty lugal, I bring before you the master merchant Ereshguna and his son Sharur," the steward said, his face in the dust of the rammed-earth floor.

"In my day," Sharur's grandfather's ghost said with a scornful sniff, "in *my* day, I tell you, we only groveled in front of Engibil, not in front of some upstart man who thought he was as fancy as a god."

"Not now, Grandfather," Sharur whispered under his breath.

"Father, Kimash may be able to hear you," Ereshguna added, also muttering into the dust. "He knew you well in life, recall."

The ghost gave another loud sniff, but said no more. Kimash gave no sign of having heard. He probably heard a lot of ghosts; as lugal, and before that as lugal's heir, he had come to know a great many Giblut. All he said was, "Rise, master merchant Ereshguna. Rise, Sharur son of Ereshguna."

"We greet you, mighty lugal," Sharur and Ereshguna said together as they got to their feet.

"And I greet you in turn," Kimash said. "You are welcome here. You will drink beer with me." He clapped his hands together. "Inadapa! They will drink beer with me."

"Yes, mighty lugal." Inadapa clapped his hands together. A lesser servant came running. Inadapa pointed to Sharur and Ereshguna. "They will drink beer with the mighty lugal."

"Yes, steward." The lesser servant hurried away. Soon a

slave came in with a pot of beer and three cups.

After libations and thanks to the gods, Kimash, Sharur, and Ereshguna drank. Setting down his cup after a deep draught, Kimash said, "I am glad you have come home safe from the Alashkurru Mountains, son of Ereshguna; I am glad no harm befell you."

"I thank you, mighty lugal," Sharur said, less comfortably than he would have liked. He could see the track down which the caravan of this conversation was heading. A lion lurked at the end of the track. It would leap out and devour him unless he turned the conversation aside—and he could not turn it aside.

Kimash said, "I have not heard how your caravan fared in the distant mountains. With most caravans, I know this before they come into Gibil. But the house of Ereshguna holds its secrets close." He smiled at Sharur's father, more approvingly than otherwise.

Yes. There was the lion. Sharur could hear it roar. He could see it lash its tail. Very well. He would cast himself into its jaws. He said, "Mighty lugal, my father and I have come before you on account of what passed with the caravan in the mountains of Alashkurru."

"Good." Kimash leaned forward in his high seat. "What offerings have you that I can lay on the altar of Engibil? What strange things, what rare things, what beautiful things have you? The god has been restive of late; the god has been hungry. I must show Engibil I can sate him; I must show the god I can satisfy him. I do not wish to risk his anger."

Feeling the lion's teeth close on him, Sharur exchanged a glance of consternation with Ereshguna. His father nodded slightly. He knew what that meant: better to be eaten all at once than to have chunks bitten off him. His own thought had been the same. But oh, how bitter, oh, how empty was the truth: "Mighty lugal, I have no strange things, I have no rare things, I have no beautiful things for you to lay on the altar of Engibil. I have brought back no offerings for the god; I have brought back no profit for my father. The Alashkurrut would not treat with me, for their gods have come to hate and to fear the men of Gibil.''

Kimash scowled. ''I feared it might be so.'' His voice was heavy. ''When a caravan returns successful to the city, it blares forth the news with trumpets. When a caravan returns with profit, it blares forth the word with drums. Failure is wreathed in silence. But so, sometimes, is success extraordinarily large. So, sometimes, is profit extraordinarily great. I hoped that might be so. Tell me now why it did not come to pass.''

As Sharur had for his father, he spun out the tale for the lugal. When he finished, he asked, ''What are we to do? The gods are stronger than we men. If they will that we fail, fail we surely shall.''

''If all the gods will this together, and it stays in all their wills long enough, fail we surely shall,'' Kimash replied. ''But the gods are contentious, no less than men. How could it be otherwise, when we are created in their image? Therein lies our hope: to wait out this flood until their anger against us recedes within its banks and the sun shines on their quarrels once more.''

Ereshguna said, ''Mighty lugal, your words are as pure as a nugget of gold. Great Kimash, your words shine like polished silver. From the anger of all the gods we may yet win free, as a hare may chew through the noose of a snare if the hunter is lazy and does not return soon enough to his trap. But Engibil presses on us always. How shall we escape the wrath of the city god?''

''I had hoped to ease his spirits with gifts from the Alash-kurrut; I had hoped to soften his heart with presents from the men of the mountains,'' the lugal answered. ''Master merchant, you press on the wound where it is sore. Now I shall have to find some other way to appease Engibil. If I do not . . .'' He let out a long, harsh sigh. ''If I do not, things shall be as they were in the days of my great-grandfather, and of his great-grandfather before him.''

''May it not come to pass,'' Sharur exclaimed. ''May you

rule us, mighty lugal. May Engibil remain content with worship and presents.''

"That is also my desire, I assure you." Kimash's voice was dry.

"It is the desire of all within Gibil, mighty lugal," Ereshguna said, covering the eyes of his amulet to hinder Engibil's senses. "We see the god-ruled cities around us, where men are toys or at best children, from whom obedience is required and who are punished without mercy when they obey not. You are a man. You know men. We would sooner have your judgment and your guidance."

And Kimash the lugal inclined his head to Ereshguna. "For your generous words I thank you, master merchant. Generous they are, but not, I believe, altogether true. Merchants and artisans: yes, you would sooner a lugal or an ensi ruled you than a god. But the peasants? Who can say? A god gives certainty. A god gives not freedom of thought but freedom from thought, in the same way as does the beer pot. Have you never known men who found this desirable?"

"My heart is heavy within me, for I cannot deny what you say," Ereshguna replied. "I wish I could show you speak falsely. Then my spirit would rejoice."

"But what are we to do?" Sharur broke in. "How are we to keep Engibil content to rest lazily in his temple?"

Kimash cocked his head to one side. Then, to Sharur's surprise, he smiled. "The ghost of Igigi my grandfather says he managed it when Engibil was less used to rest and more used to rule than he is now. My grandfather's ghost says I had better manage it as well."

"Your grandfather was a wise man, mighty lugal. No doubt his ghost remains wise," Ereshguna said. "Does the ghost tell you how you are to accomplish what you desire?"

"Oh, no." Kimash smiled again, this time wryly. "He simply tells me what I must do, not how I must do it. Such is the usual way with ghosts in my family. Is it otherwise with yours?"

"No, mighty lugal," Sharur and Ereshguna said together. Both of them were resigned to the way of ghosts.

"I heard that," Sharur's grandfather's ghost said sharply. "I heard that! I don't care for your tone of voice, not even a little bit I don't."

As best they could, they both ignored him. Sharur said, "Mighty lugal, what are we to do? Do you know how to appease Engibil even without the strange things, the rare things, the beautiful things I should have brought back from the mountains of Alashkurru? Do you know how we Giblut can trade if the gods outside our city remain united against us in hatred?"

"I can appease Engibil a while longer, I think," Kimash said. "It would have been easier, son of Ereshguna, had your caravan succeeded. You know this as I know this. But I can go on. To answer your second question, we Giblut cannot trade if the gods outside our city remain united in hatred against us. Our hope must be that they do not remain united in hatred against us. Our prayer must be that they cannot remain united in hatred against us."

"Thank you, mighty lugal, for showing my son forbearance," Ereshguna said. "Bless you, mighty lugal, for showing him kindness."

"I know the worth of the house of Ereshguna," Kimash replied. "He is your son, master merchant. Had he been able to do more, he would have done more. I wish he had done more, but against the gods a man contests in vain. Now let us all think on how we may yet profit ourselves and satisfy our city god."

He nodded to Inadapa, signifying that the audience was over. The steward led Sharur and Ereshguna out of the palace through the maze of halls by which they had come to the lugal's audience chamber. When Sharur reached the entranceway, the sudden strong sunlight made him squint and blink.

"Now," he said, "to the house and to the smithy of Dimgalabzu, the father of my intended. He, too, must know what passed in the Alashkurru Mountains, though I would sooner sup with snakes and scorpions than have to tell him."

\* \* \*

As they walked back along the Street of Smiths toward the house of Dimgalabzu, Ereshguna said, "Son, do not fret over what the smith will do. Do not worry over what Dimgalabzu will say. His family wants this match between you and Ningal to go forward. Our family wants this wedding to take place. Where the will on both sides is good, a way will open."

"But I cannot pay the bride-price to which we agreed," Sharur said.

"You are but a part of the house of Ereshguna," his father reminded him.

"I know that, Father, but I intended to pay the bride-price from the profit I would bring home to Gibil from the caravan to the mountains of Alashkurru."

"You are but a part of the house of Ereshguna," Ereshguna repeated. "For the sake of this match, the rest of the house will gladly aid you."

"Father . . ." Sharur wished he did not have to go on, but saw no way around it. "Father, I do not know if Engibil will permit this. I do not know if the city god will let this be."

Ereshguna stopped in the middle of the Street of Smiths, so suddenly that a man walking behind him and Sharur almost bumped into him. After the fellow had gone his way, muttering under his breath, the master merchant asked, "Why should Engibil care how you gain the bride-price for Ningal? Why should it matter to the city god how you are wed to Dimgalabzu's daughter?"

"Because, Father," Sharur answered miserably, "I swore a great oath to Engibil before I set out for the mountains of Alashkurru, that I would pay Ningal's bride-price out of the profit I made from this caravan."

His father's breath hissed out in a long sigh. "What ever possessed you to do such a thing, son? Did a demon take hold of your tongue?"

"Yes," Sharur answered, "the demon of pride. I know

that now. I did not know it then. All the caravans on which I had ever traveled had gone well. I never dreamt the gods of other lands would turn their backs on us. I never dreamt the men of other lands would refuse to treat with us.''

"The demon of pride," Ereshguna repeated, his voice soft. "The men of the cities where gods still rule say this is the special demon of Gibil. The men of other lands where gods rule say the same."

"I have heard this." Sharur touched first one ear, then the other. "The Alashkurrut say we are so proud, we would sooner rule ourselves and put our god in the back part of our minds. I denied this all the time I was among them, but it holds some truth. When I swore the oath to Engibil, I did it not to affirm his power over me, as an Imhursaggi would have done, but to boast of my own power in the world. And now my oath brings me low." He hung his head.

"In my time, we never would have thought such a thought." The voice of his grandfather's ghost was shrill and accusing in his ears. "In my day, we never would have done such a deed."

"When I was a young man," Ereshguna said, "I might have had a thought like yours, Sharur, but I do not think I would have sworn an oath like yours. You and your brother are more your own men than I was at your age. Anything outside yourselves has less power over you than was so for me."

"And, when I go astray, I go further astray than you would have done," Sharur said.

Ereshguna set a hand on his shoulder. "Perhaps it is not so bad as you think. Perhaps we may yet set it right."

"But how, Father?" Sharur cried.

"Perhaps we can fulfill your oath to Engibil in another way," Ereshguna said. "As I said before, you are but a part of the house of Ereshguna. Perhaps we shall lend you the bride-price for your intended. There will be other days; there will be other caravans; there will be other times to profit. You can restore what is lent to you to the house of

Ereshguna. Thus you will have gained Ningal through the profit from a caravan.''

"But not through the profit from this caravan," Sharur said.

"No, not through the profit from this caravan," his father agreed. "But you will have the copper to give to Dimgalabzu for your intended. You will have the silver to give to the smith for his daughter. You will have the gold to give to him for Ningal. This will be good for the house of Ereshguna. This will be good for the house of Dimgalabzu." Ereshguna smiled. "And, son, this will be good for you. I have seen—who living on the Street of Smiths has not seen?—how you look at her when she goes by, and she at you as well."

Sharur bowed low before his father. "If you do this for me, I shall indeed repay you. You rescue me from my own pride; from my own foolishness you save me."

"You are my son." Ereshguna smiled again. "And you are a young man. The gods have never yet shaped a young man who did not need to be saved from his own foolishness now and again. Have we a bargain, then? I shall lend you the bride-price, and you shall repay it from profits yet to come."

"Yes," Sharur said joyfully.

*No.*

Had someone somehow cast a bronze bell twice as tall as a man, that one word might have tolled from it. The word echoed and reechoed inside Sharur's head, till he staggered and almost fell under its impact. Beside him, he saw his father stagger, too. He wondered briefly if Puzur the earthquake demon had chosen that moment to loose destruction on Gibil. But the tremor was inside him; the tremor was inside his father. Other men did not cry out, nor did the buildings on the Street of Smiths sway and topple.

*No.*

Again, the word rang through Sharur and Ereshguna. Sharur's grandfather's ghost heard it, too, though the ghost's terrified screeching seemed tiny and lost among those great reverberations.

"It is the voice of the god," Ereshguna gasped.

"Yes." Sharur shivered, as with an ague. Men schemed, men maneuvered, men labored for generations to gain a tiny space of freedom from the gods. Gods did not need to scheme or maneuver against men. Gods had strength. When they noticed what men were doing . . . Oh, when they noticed . . .

Engibil spoke once more, implanting his words in the minds of Sharur and Ereshguna: *I hold in my hands the oath of Sharur son of Ereshguna. I hold in my heart the oath of Sharur son of Ereshguna. The oath shall not be avoided. The oath shall not be evaded. Sharur son of Ereshguna swore in my name to pay bride-price for Ningal daughter of Dimgalabzu with profit from the journey he has just completed. There was no profit. There can be no bride-price. I shall not be mocked among my fellow gods. No god shall say of me, "See, it is Engibil, whose name men take in vain." Hear me and obey, men of Gibil.*

As abruptly as the god had seized Sharur and Ereshguna, so now he released them. They stared at each other, white-faced and shaking. "In all my years," Ereshguna said slowly, "in all my years, I say, I have never known Engibil to speak so."

"*I* remember things like this," Sharur's grandfather's ghost said shrilly, "and I remember *my* grandfather telling me they happened all the time in his day. I knew you clever people would get in trouble one fine day, I knew it, I knew it." The ghost sounded horrified and glad at the same time.

Sharur said nothing. He found nothing he could say. He looked to his father. Ereshguna said nothing, either, not for some time. That alarmed Sharur more than anything. No: that alarmed Sharur more than anything save the resistless voice of the god pounding inside his head. Nothing could have been more alarming than that. But seeing his father at a loss for words frightened him, too, underscoring the magnitude of what had just happened. Though a man grown,

Sharur had never lost the notion that Ereshguna could solve larger, more complicated troubles than he could himself. That, after all, was what a father was for.

When Ereshguna did not speak and then still did not speak, Sharur forced words out through numb lips: "What do we do now?"

His father gathered himself. "We had better do what we were going to do anyhow—we had better speak with Dimgalabzu the smith." He sighed and shuddered, still no more recovered than was Sharur from their encounter with Engibil. "Now, though, we shall have to give him a word we would sooner not speak, and also one he would sooner not hear."

"Is there no help for it?" Sharur cried, setting a hand on his father's thigh in appeal.

"I see none," Ereshguna said. "Come." Sharur saw none either, and so, all unwilling, he followed his father to the house of Dimgalabzu.


"Wait," Dimgalabzu said. Sweating as he stood close by the fire, he lifted a clay crucible from it with long wooden tongs, then, moving quickly, poured molten bronze into three molds, one after another. He had calculated his work well; the last of the metal filled the last mold. Dimgalabzu wiped his dripping forehead. "There. It is accomplished. Now we shall drink beer."

"Now we shall drink beer," Ereshguna agreed. Here inside the smithy, he sounded stronger and more sure of himself than he had out in the street.

Sharur also felt his own spirit revive here. As at the smithy of Abzuwas son of Ahhiyawas in the Alashkurru Mountains, he no longer noted the brooding immanence of hostile gods. Metalworking had a power of its own; without such power, how could something hard as stone be made to run like water and then turn hard once more, this time in a shape the smith determined?

Dimgalabzu clapped his hands. "Beer!" he called. "Beer

for Ereshguna the master merchant and Sharur his son. And let us have salt fish to eat with the beer.''

No slave brought the pot of beer, as Sharur had expected. No slave brought the bowl of salt fish, as he had looked for. Instead, Ningal fetched in beer; Ningal fetched in fish. Dimgalabzu did Sharur and Ereshguna honor, to let her serve them. She smiled at Sharur, saucily, over her shoulder as she went out once more. The smile was a knife in his heart.

He smiled back at her. That was twisting the knife.

After libations and invocations, he and his father and Dimgalabzu drank of the beer. They ate of the salt fish. Presently, Dimgalabzu said, ''What news have you for me, master merchant, master merchant's son?''

The smith smiled. His voice held no worry. He thought he knew what the word would be. He thought he knew the word would be good. Inside Sharur, the knife twisted again.

Ereshguna said, ''My old friend, we come to you with troubled hearts. My old comrade, we come to you with troubled spirits. Hear what has befallen us.'' He set forth the tale of Sharur's failed caravan to the mountains of Alashkurru, of the oath Sharur had given to Engibil, and of Engibil's awe-inspiring (''terrifying'' was the word Sharur would have used, but maybe they amounted to the same thing in the end) refusal to let the oath be altered or circumvented.

Dimgalabzu's lips skinned back from his teeth, farther and farther, as he listened, until at last he looked as if he were snarling. ''This is a hard word you give me, master merchant, a hard word in many ways. That the god should bar the arrangement you had in mind . . . that is hard. That the god should care enough to bar the arrangement you had in mind . . . that is very hard.'' Like any smith of Gibil, he was used to quiet from Engibil, quiet in which he could conduct his own affairs.

''It is very hard indeed,'' Ereshguna agreed. ''This happened, as I say, while we were coming here from the palace of Kimash the lugal. Kimash will find it hard news as well.''

''Yes,'' Dimgalabzu said. Even more than the smiths, the

merchants, or the scribes, the lugal depended on quiet from Engibil. Dimgalabzu shook his head. "That you cannot pay the bride-price for my daughter . . . that is hardest of all. Without the bride-price, there can be no wedding."

Sharur had known Dimgalabzu would say as much. Standing where Dimgalabzu stood, Sharur would have said as much. That did nothing to diminish his anguish at hearing Dimgalabzu say as much. He cried, "Could we not—?"

The smith held up a scarred, dirty hand. "Son of Eresh-guna, do not let this question pass your lips. Not even the peasants in the villages far from Gibil, not even the herders in the fields so distant they cannot see the city's walls, give up their daughters without bride-price. And Ningal is no peasant's daughter. My daughter is no herder's daughter. Without the bride-price, there can be no wedding."

To make Sharur's mortification complete, Ningal had come back into the room with a bowl of spicy relish for the fish. "Father—" she began.

"No." Dimgalabzu's voice was hard as stone. "Without the bride-price, there can be no wedding. My daughter shall not be the laughingstock of the Street of Smiths; my daughter shall not be a joke for the city. I have spoken."

"Yes, Father," Ningal whispered, and withdrew once more.

Desperately, Sharur said, "May I bargain with you, father of my intended?"

"I will hear your words," Dimgalabzu said, "though I make no pledges past that. Say on."

"If you cannot wed your daughter to me without bride-price, will you keep from pledging her to another, to give me time to see if I may not reverse Engibil's ban?"

"Were you not Ereshguna's son, I would say no." Dim-galabzu plucked at his curly beard. "Were you not in my daughter's heart to the point where that might trouble any future match, I would also say no." He licked his lips as he thought. "Let it be as you say. For the space of one year, let it be as you say. No more. Past that, I shall do as I reckon best."

Sharur bowed almost as low as he would have before Kimash the lugal. "Engibil's blessings upon you, father of my intended." Only after the words were out of his mouth and past recall did he wonder at the propriety of asking Engibil to bless Dimgalabzu when it was thanks to the god's interference that he and Ningal could not join in marriage as they had long planned and as they had long hoped.

Ereshguna also bowed to Dimgalabzu. "You have my thanks also, old friend. Things do not always go as we would have them go."

"There you speak the truth," the smith said. "We are not gods. And, even if we were gods, we would not be free of strife."

"How right you are." Ereshguna bowed again. So did Sharur. They took their leave of Dimgalabzu. As he turned to go, Sharur looked down the hallway from which Ningal had brought beer and fish and relish, in the hope of catching one last glimpse of her. He saw only the hallway.

Day followed day. Sharur worked with his father and younger brother, trading to the smiths the copper and ore and tin they had on hand, and trading with others the goods they got from the smiths in exchange. They even made a profit on most of their dealings, but that did not reassure them. "What shall we do when our supplies of metal are gone?" Tupsharru asked. "What shall we do when we have no more ore to trade?"

"We shall go hungry, by and by," Sharur said. His brother smiled, reckoning it a joke. Sharur did not smile in return. He smiled less often these days than he had before his caravan came home from Gibil without having been able to trade.

Then other caravans started coming home to Gibil without having been able to trade. Merchants from other cities did not bring their wares to the market square in Gibil, even merchants who had come each year for longer than Sharur had been alive. Nor did merchants from beyond Kudurru enter the city, as they had done more and more often in recent years.

Coming back one day from the market square—a square where, increasingly, Giblut bought from and sold to and traded with other Giblut alone—Ereshguna said, "Commerce has long been the lifeblood of this city. Now all the blood seems to drain out of Gibil, and none comes in. How can we lead the land between the rivers if commerce goes elsewhere?"

"Zuabu prospers, I hear," Sharur said. "Even Imhursag prospers, I hear. How can the Imhursagut prosper while we falter? Having their god bellowing in their ears all the time makes them stupid."

"Our god may be bellowing more and more in our ears," his father answered. "If Kimash the lugal cannot keep Engibil happy, the god will find a way to make himself happy. Then we and the Imhursagut shall be just alike."

"May it not come to pass," Sharur exclaimed. Engibil might make a better master than Enimhursag; as far as Sharur was concerned, Engibil could not possibly make a worse master than Enimhursag. But Sharur was used to being a free man, or a man as free as any in the land between the rivers. He did not want a god to rule his life.

Engibil did not care what he wanted. He had already seen that.

"May it not come to pass, indeed," Ereshguna said. "You and I say this. We are men who know freedom. We are men who do not want Engibil twisting our lives with his hand. But another in Gibil says this louder than you or I. Another in Gibil says this louder than you and I together."

"Kimash the lugal," Sharur said.

"Kimash the lugal," Ereshguna agreed. "We are men who do not want to be ruled. Kimash is a man who already rules. How would it be for him to have to give back to Engibil full mastery of this city?"

"It would be hard," Sharur said.

"It would be hard, yes," Ereshguna said. "And it might well be more than hard. It might well be dangerous. What will Engibil do, after three generations of lugals have kept him from full rule over Gibil? What will he do, after Kimash and Kimash's father and Kimash's grandfather have ruled in his place?''

''I do not know the answer,'' Sharur said. ''I am only a man, so I can not know the answer, not ahead of time. Even Kimash the lugal can not know the answer, not ahead of time. But I think, Father, that if I sat in Kimash the lugal's high seat, I would be a worried man.''

''I think you are right, son, and I think Kimash the lugal *is* a worried man today,'' Ereshguna replied. ''What will he do? What can he do?'' The master merchant plucked at his beard. ''I do not know what he can do. I wonder if he knows himself what he can do.''

Inadapa stood in the doorway to Ereshguna's establishment and waited to be noticed. As a man, he was not very noticeable. As a power in the city of Gibil, he was noticeable indeed. ''It is the steward to Kimash the mighty lugal!'' Ereshguna said, bowing himself almost double.

Sharur bowed, too. ''The steward to Kimash the mighty lugal honors us by his presence,'' he said. ''In his name and through him we greet his mighty master.'' He bowed again.

''Enter our dwelling, steward to the mighty lugal,'' Ereshguna said. ''Drink beer with us. Eat onions with us.'' He clapped his hands. A slave came running. Ereshguna pointed to Inadapa. ''Fetch a pot of beer for the steward's refreshment. Fetch a basket of onions for the steward's enjoyment.''

''You are generous to me,'' Inadapa said, drinking sour beer. ''You are gracious to me,'' he added, eating a pungent onion. ''By the honor you show to me, you also show honor to my master.''

''So we intended,'' Sharur said, ''for where you are, there also Kimash the mighty lugal is.''

Now Inadapa bowed. ''You are well spoken, son of Ereshguna. You are polite, master merchant's son. It is no

wonder, then, that my master, the mighty lugal Kimash, ordered me to bring you with me back to the palace of the
lugals, that he might have speech with you.''

"Did he?'' Sharur stole a quick glance at his father. "I
obey the mighty lugal in this, as I obey him in all things.
When you have drunk, when you have eaten, you will take
me to him.''

"When I have drunk, when I have eaten, I will take you
to him,'' Inadapa agreed.

"Does the mighty lugal also desire speech with me?''
Ereshguna asked.

Inadapa shook his bald head. "He spoke only of your
son, master merchant.''

"He is the lugal,'' Ereshguna said. "It shall be as he
desires, as in all things here in Gibil.''

Inadapa said nothing to that. Neither did Sharur. Had
everything in Gibil been as Kimash desired, the lugal would
have had no need to summon him to the palace.

After finishing his beer and onions, Inadapa declined
more of either. "Let us be off,'' he said to Sharur. "I am
glad to eat and drink with you, but I do not wish to make
the mighty lugal anxious for my return.''

"By no means.'' Sharur gulped down the last of his own
beer and rose from the stool on which he sat. "Lead me to
the palace. I am your slave, and the mighty lugal's slave as
well.'' *Better either of those than being Engibil's slave,* he
thought. He would never, ever say that aloud.

Inadapa rose, too. "We go, then.'' He bowed to Ereshguna. "Master merchant, your house is never to be faulted
for hospitality.''

With the steward, Sharur walked up the Street of Smiths
toward the lugal's palace. As he walked, he sometimes got
glimpses of Engibil's temple. The temple was larger than
the palace. Most of it was older, dating from the days when
Engibil had ruled his city: before there were lugals, some
of it from before there were even ensis. But Kimash, and
his father and grandfather before him, had not altogether
neglected the god's house, either, though they gave more

presents than they did building. Their hope had always been that greater luxury would compensate the god for losing power. For three generations, that hope had been realized. Now . . .

Now Sharur groveled in the dust before Kimash on his high seat sheathed in beaten gold. When he rose, the lugal asked, "Do I hear rightly that Engibil holds your oath tight to himself, and will not release you from it even to pay bride-price for your intended?"

"Mighty lugal, you do," Sharur answered. Neither he nor his father nor, so far as he knew, his grandfather's ghost had noised about the god's command. If Dimgalabzu had spoken of it to the lugal, however, the smith would certainly have been within his rights.

Kimash frowned. "The god uses you harshly," he observed. The frown got deeper. "All the gods use Gibil harshly these days. Our merchants return empty-handed from their journeys; no merchants from other cities, no merchants from other lands, come into our market square to trade their wares for ours. Our city suffers." He drew in a deep breath. "Did Engibil take it into his mind to cast me down from this high seat, many in Gibil would celebrate. Did the god take it into his mind to cast me out of this palace, many in the city would rejoice. Under Engibil's rule, they would reckon, trade would return. Under the god's rule, they would reckon, profit would grow."

"And they would become as the Imhursagut are," Sharur said. "Who among us would care to live as the Imhursagut live, with Engibil speaking from our mouths as Enimhursag speaks through theirs?"

"Who cares to live in a city without trade?" Kimash returned. "Who cares to live in a city without profit? Fewer men than you would suppose, son of Ereshguna."

"I would not care to live in a city without trade," Sharur said. "I would not care to live in a city without profit. But still less would I care to live as the Imhursagut live."

"It is because this is so that I have summoned you," the lugal told him. "Along with me, son of Ereshguna, you and your house stand to lose the most if Engibil should come to rule this city once more as well as reigning over it.''

Sharur bowed his head. ''What you say is true, mighty lugal. I have already lost, or nearly lost, a marriage my family, my intended's family, and I myself want very much, as you know.''

''Yes, I do know this,'' Kimash said, nodding. ''It is why I summoned you. It is why I give to you and to no other the task I hold in my mind.''

''What task is that, mighty lugal?'' Sharur asked.

Kimash answered indirectly: ''Son of Ereshguna, you were the first to bring back to Gibil word that men of other cities, men of other lands, would not treat with us. You were the first to bring back to Gibil word that gods of other cities, gods of other lands, were angry at us. I charge you with learning why this is so. I charge you with learning what we can do to make this so no longer.''

''Mighty lugal—'' Sharur hesitated.

''Speak,'' Kimash urged. ''Give forth. Say what is in your heart.''

''Very well. As you will have heard from me, mighty lugal, the gods of the Alashkurrut say they will not let the Alashkurrut trade with us because we are too much our own men and not enough men of our god. The only way to make this not so that I can see would be to become as the Imhursagut are.''

''Yes, son of Ereshguna, I have heard this from your lips,'' Kimash agreed. ''But I have for you a question of my own: how are we more our own men this year than we were last year? How are we less men of our god this year than we were last year? Why could the Alashkurrut trade with us last year and not this year? What has changed in so short a time, to set the gods of the Alashkurrut—and some of the gods of Kudurru as well, it is not to be denied— against us?''

Sharur stared at Kimash. Then, all unbidden, he prostrated himself before the lugal once more. His head against the ground, he said, ''Truly, mighty lugal, these are questions that want answering. When the gods spoke to me, I took their words for truth, and did not look behind them. By the way they spoke," he added, "I saw nothing but truth in their words."

"Rise, Sharur," Kimash said. "I would not deny the gods of the Alashkurrut told you the truth. I do not deny the mountain gods spoke truly. But was the truth they told all of the truth? Do gods not speak the truth and speak in riddles at the same time?"

"Mighty lugal, it is so," Sharur said.

"Of course it is so," Kimash answered. "The gods created man in the misty depths of time, and no man yet has learned why, not from that day to this. There are truths within truths within truths, as in an onion there are layers within layers within layers. This is the task I set you, son of Ereshguna: bite into the onion of truth. Go past that first layer with the teeth of your wit. Learn what lies beneath it. Learn, and tell me what you have learned."

"It shall be as you say." Sharur bowed to the lugal. "I will learn what I may as quickly as I may, and I will tell you what I have learned." He hesitated. "I do not think I will be able to learn all I need within the walls of Gibil. I shall have to travel beyond the lands our city rules."

"Travel where you will," Kimash told him. "I hope, though, that you will not need to return to the mountains of Alashkurru. I do not know if Gibil would be as it was when you returned from such a long voyage; I do not know if I would still sit on this high seat when you came back from such a great journey."

More than anything else the lugal had said, that showed Sharur how deep his worry ran. If Kimash feared Engibil might take back the city before Sharur could return from the land of the Alashkurrut, the power of the lugal truly hung by a thread. "Mighty lugal," Sharur said, the polite title reminding him as it was not intended to do of the limits to Kimash's might, "I hear you. Mighty lugal, I obey you. I shall not go to the mountains of Alashkurru. I shall remain in the land between the rivers. I shall go to the city closest to ours, that I may spend as little time on the road as can be.''

"It is well,'' Kimash said. "It is very well.'' By his expression, though, it was not well, nor would it be until and unless Sharur returned with the answers he needed. After coughing a couple of times, he went on, "May you have good fortune on your journey to Zuabu. May you learn what you seek in the city of thieves.''

"Mighty lugal, you misunderstand me,'' Sharur said. "I do not intend to go to Zuabu. I do not intend to travel to the city of thieves.''

"What then?'' the lugal asked. His eyes widened. "You do not intend to go to Imhursag? You do not intend to travel to the city drunk on its god?''

Sharur nodded. "I do. The Imhursagut I met on the road knew I would have trouble in the mountains of Alashkurru. Enimhursag knew I would have no easy time among the Alashkurrut. If answers lie within the land between the rivers, they will lie in Imhursag. If answers are to be found within Kudurru, they will be found among the Imhursagut.''

"You are bold. You are brave.'' Kimash's voice was troubled. "Even now, Engibil rests more than he acts. It is not so with Enimhursag. The god of Imhursag watches his city. If you cross from the land Gibil rules to the land where Enimhursag is lord, the god will know you for what you are. His eye will never leave you. His ear will always be bent your way. You shall not succeed.''

"Mighty lugal . . .'' Sharur paused. "Let me think. This thing needs doing; of that I am sure. How best to do it . . .'' He paused again. After a bit, he brightened. "Have I your leave, mighty lugal, to spend a little more time on the road to Imhursag than I might otherwise?''

"Imhursag is not so distant,'' Kimash answered. "What is in your mind?''

"Suppose, mighty lugal, that I do as you thought I would do: suppose I go to Zuabu, or to the land Zuabu rules. Zuabu and Imhursag are at peace; Enimhursag and Enzuabu have no quarrel. If I enter Imhursaggi land from Zuabu, to the eye and ear of Enimhursag I shall seem only another Zuabi myself. If he does not know me for what I am, he will take no special notice of me.''

''This is a good notion—or as good as a notion can be in bad times,'' Kimash said. ''No, son of Ereshguna, I shall not begrudge you the time you take traveling to Imhursag by way of Zuabu. Instead, I shall hope that you are able to turn the time into profit for yourself, for me, and for Gibil.''

He said not a word about profit for Engibil, which was one reason Sharur was so willing to do as he wished. The less the god interfered in Sharur's life, the happier he would be. He was certain of that; when the god had interfered in his life, it had made him very unhappy indeed.

''Do you require anything more of me, mighty lugal?'' he asked.

''I require that you succeed,'' Kimash answered. ''Gibil requires that you succeed. If we are not to return to what we were in the days before we learned to put tin in with copper, if we are not to return to what we were in the days before we learned to set our records down on clay, if we are not to return to the days before we learned to think our own thoughts and act on our own purposes, we all require that you succeed.''

Sharur took a deep breath. ''Mighty lugal, you tie a heavy load onto my back. I hope I am a donkey strong enough to bear the burden.''

''If you are not, where shall I find a stronger one?'' Kimash asked.

He did not put the question intending that it be answered, but Sharur answered it nonetheless, and without hesitation: ''Ereshguna, my father.''

The lugal pursed his lips as he considered that. ''No,'' he said at last. ''In this, I would sooner have you. I speak not of donkeys but of rams: the young ram will go forward where the old ram would falter.'' He chuckled under his breath. ''The young ram will go forward where the old ram would think twice. Be my young ram, Sharur. Go forward for me. Go forward, and lead the city toward safety.''

"Mighty lugal, you may trust in me!" Sharur exclaimed.

"I do," Kimash said simply. "Go now. Go for me. Go for Gibil."

"I shall go now," Sharur said. "I shall go for you, mighty lugal. I shall go for the Giblut." *And I shall go for myself, and for the sake of Ningal.* He did not say that aloud. Only later did he realize it was likely the chiefest reason for which Kimash sent him forth.

# 5

Sharur tugged at the donkey's lead rope. "Demons eat you!" he shouted in the best Zuabi accent he could assume. "Devils flay the hide off your bones! There lies the city, just ahead. If you want to rest, you can rest inside it."

The donkey brayed and looked stubborn and set its feet and would not go forward. A man with a couple of pots full of grain strapped to his back strode around Sharur as he went back to the animal and got it moving with a direct brutality of which Harharu would have disapproved. The others on the road to Imhursag—the road the donkey was doing its best to block—did not complain; on the contrary.

"You stupid thing," Sharur said, as the donkey resentfully started going once more. "You stupid, ugly thing. Under the shadow of the walls, you want to stop. I tell you, it shall not be." The donkey brayed, but kept walking.

In Sharur's view, the walls of Imhursag were not nearly so fine as those of his own city. They were not so high as Gibil's walls, nor did they compass round so broad an area. Much of the brickwork was old, and in imperfect repair. But that only made the temple of Enimhursag, thrusting step by narrowing step into the sky above the top of the wall, seem more massive and imposing by comparison. This was the god's city first, with men and their needs an afterthought.

Guards at the gate looked Sharur and the donkey over without much interest. "Where from?" one of them asked.

"Zuabu," he answered, and pointed southwest.

"What's the beast carrying?" the guard inquired.

Was Enimhursag looking out through the bored man's eyes? Was the god of Imhursag speaking through the bored man's lips? Sharur did not think so, but knowing was hard. Still, having succeeded with the lie—no, the half-truth, for the guard had not asked his home city—about his origin, he had not intended to speak anything but the truth here: "Bronze and bracelets and beads and pickled palm hearts."

"Where'd you come by all that stuff?" the Imhursaggi asked. He and his companions chuckled at that. The Imhursagut were men like any others . . . when Enimhursag let them be so.

As if his dignity had been affronted, Sharur drew himself up straight. "I traded for it—of course."

The guards laughed out loud. "Of course, Zuabi," their leader said. They didn't believe him. None of Zuabu's neighbors believed Zuabut when they proclaimed their honesty. The guard went on, "Just remember, friend, your light-fingered god won't protect you if you step out of line here. Enimhursag, the great lord, the mighty lord, loves thieves not."

His voice grew deeper, more rolling, more imposing when he mentioned his god—or was it the god delivering a warning through him? "I don't know *what* you're talking about," Sharur said in tones too arch to be taken seriously. Laughing once more, the guards waved him into Imhursag.

As he passed through the gateway into the city rival to his own, Sharur felt, or thought he felt, a tingle run through him. The hair on his arms and chest stood out from his body for a moment, as if lightning had struck not too far away. Then the feeling faded, and he might have been in any city of Kudurru.

Most of the Imhursagut, to look at them, were not much different from other folk of the land between the rivers. Peasants gaped at the number and size of the buildings Imhursag held. Potters shouted their wares. Customers shouted derision at them. A drunken woman slept in the shade of a mud-brick wall. Her tunic had hiked up to show her secret place. A small boy pointed and giggled. A dog lapped up what was left of the beer in the pot beside her, then lifted its leg against the wall. The small boy giggled louder.

Here and there, though, Enimhursag's priests—the god's eyes, the god's spies—strode through the streets. They shaved their heads. They shaved their beards. Sharur wondered if they ever blinked. He didn't think so. Whenever he saw one of them, he kept his own eyes cast down to the dirt of the street so as to draw no notice. He did his best not to imagine what would happen if Enimhursag realized a Gibli had sneaked into his city.

A gang of slaves was knocking down a mud-brick building. Only a single overseer watched them, and was paying more attention to a harlot sauntering along the street than to the workmen. Nonetheless, they labored steadily and diligently. In Gibil, a gang supervised with such laxness would have accomplished nothing.

One of the slaves, seeing the overseer's eyes following the rolling buttocks of the harlot, did lean on his coppershod digging stick for a breather. After a moment, though, the slave stiffened and began breaking up mud brick once more. "I pray your pardon, mighty lord," he muttered as he worked. "I am but a lazy dung fly, unworthy of your notice. I am but a lowly worm, not deserving of your attention." How the chunks flew from the brick!

Sharur shivered. No wonder the overseer could turn his gaze toward a whore's backside rather than keeping it firmly fixed on the work gang. Enimhursag watched the slaves, and held them to their tasks more thoroughly than the man might have done with lash and shouted curses. Sharur wondered if Enimhursag was keeping special watch on this gang because the building that would replace the one they were demolishing was to serve his cult, or whether the god simply surveyed all the slaves in his city.

The less Sharur spoke, the less chance he had of betraying himself to the people or to their vigilant god. He had hoped to be able to find the market square without talking to any of the Imhursagut. But the streets of Imhursag were like those of Gibil. They were like those of any other city in the land between the rivers. They bent and twisted back on themselves in ways no one who had not lived in Imhursag since birth—or no one whom Enimhursag did not guide—could hope to understand.

After passing the gang of sweating slaves and their inattentive human overseer for the second time, Sharur realized he might wander till nightfall without stumbling upon what he sought. No help for it, then, but to ask an Imhursaggi. He put the question to a graybeard carrying a large bundle of palm fronds.

"Not from here, eh?" the old man said. "No, I can tell you ain't, I can. You talk funny, you do. Well, from here you go . . ." His voice trailed away. Was he reviewing the plan of the city he carried in his mind? Or was he asking Enimhursag for the answer—and receiving it? Sharur did not inquire. Sharur would sooner not have known. The old man resumed: "Second left, third right, first left, and you're there."

"Second left, third right, first left," Sharur repeated. "I thank you. May your god bless you for your kindness."

"Oh, he does, lad, he does." The old Imhursaggi's smile was broad and happy. He liked living in a city where the god ruled directly. Sharur did not understand, but he did not argue, either. Thanking the man again, he led the donkey down the street.

The directions, whatever their source, were good. Imhursag's market square proved neither so large nor so noisy as that of Gibil. No, after a moment Sharur revised that first impression: Imhursag's market square might be small, but at the moment it was a great deal noisier than that of Gibil. Merchants from all over Kudurru and the surrounding lands thronged here, where the Giblut traded among themselves and large stretches of the square of Gibil were nothing but bare dirt and blowing dust. Seeing Imhursagut profit while his own people had to do without infuriated Sharur.

He found a tiny open area in the square of Imhursag, tethered the donkey to a stake driven into the ground not far away, and set out his own trade goods on cloths. That done, he began loudly crying their virtues.

Imhursagut and merchants from other cities and other lands wandered through the market square. Sharur quickly sold several pots of pickled palm hearts to an Imhursaggi tavern keeper. The man said, "Come to my place—I am Elulu—on the Street of Enimhursag's Elbow, just past the bend. My wife cooks palm hearts in many tasty ways."

"If I can come, I will come," Sharur said, bowing. The lie was as smooth as he could make it; he had no intention of going into a street named for any part of Imhursag's city god.

A couple of women traded him broken bits of bronze and copper for his beads. So did a couple of men, buying for their womenfolk. In such small dealings, the Imhursagut seemed little different from the people of Gibil. Without the eyes of the god on them, they were indeed simply people. They were also rather simple people; Sharur got more for the ornaments from them, and with less haggling, than he would have from Giblut.

Then one of the shaven-headed priests stopped in front of him. The man picked up a knife. He handled it like one knowledgeable of weapons. "This is fine metalwork," he observed.

"I thank you, sir, that I do." Sharur laid on the Zuabi accent like a peasant spreading manure thickly over his field.

"I would not have thought Zuabu could claim such skilled smiths." The priest's eyes moved back and forth, back and forth, from the blade he held in his hand to Sharur. Enimhursag was staring out of those eyes, too. "Tell me, if you will, whence came this blade. Tell me, if you know, where it was made."

"He who traded it to me said it came from Aggasher," Sharur answered. Not only was Aggasher farther from Imhursag than Zuabu, and so less likely to be intimately familiar to Enimhursag and his minion, it was also ruled by its goddess, and so more likely to be pleasing to the god and his priest.

"Aggasher, eh?" The priest felt of the knife. "Well, it could be. Metalworking makes the touch of a god hard to detect. Were it less useful, it would be banned. Perhaps, one day, it shall be banned anyway." Was that Enimhursag, thinking aloud through the priest's lips? Not all the sweat running down Sharur's back sprang from the heat of the day. But then the priest went on, "I have need of a good blade, Zuabi. How much will you try to steal from me for it?"

Against him, Sharur did not bargain so hard as he might have. He did not care to risk drawing Enimhursag's attention to himself. Even so, he would have been pleased in Gibil with the weight of silver he got for the dagger.

A man with a pot of beer strode through the market square, selling cups of his brew for bits of metal. Sharur gladly drank one. He did not think the beer was as good as they brewed in Gibil. He did not think anything in Imhursag was as good as its Gibli counterpart.

Not long after he gave the clay cup back to the beerseller so the man could refill it for his next customer, a couple of foreigners walked past his little display: Alashkurrut sweltering in their tunics. One of them was colored like a man of Kudurru; the other had lighter, ruddier skin and hair of a woody brown rather than the usual black.

"Good-looking blades there," the fair one said to the other in their own language. Sharur stood still as a stone and looked stupid, not wanting them to know he understood. The man from the western mountains went on, "They might almost be Gibli work."

His companion snorted. "Not in this city, Piluliumas," he said. "This city is Gibil's foe. No Giblut come here."

"Piluliumas, I know Gibli blades when I see them," Luwiyas said stubbornly. He turned to Sharur and spoke in the language of the land between the rivers: "You, trader. Where do these knives come from? What city do these swords call home?"

Bowing, Sharur answered, "I got these blades, knives and swords, in Zuabu. The man who traded them to me said they were made in Aggasher." Having told that story to the priest, he had to stick by it. Enimhursag might be listening.

"There, you see?" Piluliumas said. "Aggasher, not Gibil."

But Luwiyas said, "In Zuabu, they will sell you your own head and make a profit on it. In Zuabu, they will sell you someone else's head and say it is your own and make you believe it. If the god of Zuabu were not a god of thieves himself, his people would steal the jewels from his earrings."

Sharur had to work hard to keep his face straight and pretend he did not follow the Alashkurri. Luwiyas's opinion of Zuabut was identical to his own; the man must have had dealings with them. His friend said, "It could be so, I suppose. They do look like good blades. Shall we see what he wants for them?"

"Not now," Luwiyas answered. "We have asked about them, so he will seek too much for them. Let us come back tomorrow, as if by chance, and trade as if we do not care. He is no master merchant, or he would have more goods. He will be glad enough to trade with us then."

His companion bowed. "You are wise. It is good."

Sharur thought Luwiyas was good, too, his one mistake being the assumption that a chance-met merchant in the market square would not speak his language. The two Alashkurrut went off to disparage someone else's goods. Sharur had already intended to stay overnight in Imhursag; indeed, to stay in the city whose god hated him until he found answers to the questions Kimash had set him. Now he dared hope he might gain some of those answers sooner than he had expected.

As far as Sharur was concerned, the inn he chose for the night would have been reckoned poor in Alashkurru, a disgrace in Gibil. It was dark and dirty. The food ranged from bad to worse. The room to which the innkeeper showed him was so tiny and smelly and full of bugs, he carried his sacks of trade goods out to the stables and bedded down in the straw beside his donkey.

When the innkeeper refused to give back any part of what he'd paid, he shouted at the man. "You gave me copper for a night's food," the Imhursaggi said. "You gave me copper for a night's lodging. You have had food here. You have lodging here. Shall we go to the god? Shall we let Enimhursag decide?"

"No," Sharur said quickly. The innkeeper smirked, thinking that meant Sharur admitted justice lay with him. In fact, Sharur admitted nothing of the sort, but let himself be cheated to keep the god's eye from falling on him.

And, as he drifted toward sleep, he decided that perhaps he was not being cheated after all. He was, in fact, more comfortable than he would have been in that nasty little cubicle. He looked over toward the donkey. Though still without any great love for the stubborn beast, he said, "You are better company than that jackass of an innkeeper."

The donkey snorted. Sharur rolled over and fell asleep.

Some time later, his eyes came open, or, at least, he saw once more. Was he awake? Did he dream? He did not know. He could not tell. Normally, that alone would have told him he was dreaming. Everything he saw, though, everything he heard and felt and smelled, seemed too vivid, too real, for a dream. Everything seemed too coherent for a dream, too.

But neither was he in the world to which he usually awoke. He watched and marveled. Presently, he grew afraid.

He was moving through a green, growing field of barley. The stalks of grain, though, towered over his head as if they were the oaks and ashes and elms and other trees with peculiar names that grew in the mountain valleys of Alashkurru. Had he grown tiny, or had the barley become huge? He could not tell. He knew only that he had to keep walking through it, for he was going toward . . . going toward . . . He could not remember what he was going toward, only that getting there was important.

Then he did remember something else. Something—he could not remember what—would try to stop him. Something, if it got the chance, would do worse than try to stop him.

No sooner had that thought crossed his mind than something—*the* something he did not know—stirred the tops of the barley stalks, shoving them aside so that the sun stabbed down into the green-tinged twilight through which he moved. He scurried away from that light, for he did not want it to pin him to the ground. Whatever was up there would find him then.

Glistening with sweat in the sunlight, a hand and arm groped toward him. Each finger on that hand was longer than he was; he could have stood and danced on that immense palm. But if those fingers and that palm closed on him, he did not think he would dance. He did not think he would dance ever again.

He realized then, as he had not realized before, that he was not the only manikin moving through the field of barley. Others also scurried along beneath the growing grain. That enormous hand closed around one of them and lifted him up toward the light. A thin wail of terror rose, and then cut off abruptly. Sharur dove into a hollow in the ground. A cockroach already sheltered there. It was not much smaller than he; for a moment, he thought it would fight him to hold its hiding place. But then it fled, hairy legs flailing.

That immense hand descended once more. Blood now stained palm and fingers. A drop fell on Sharur as the hand passed over him. It went after the cockroach, whose motion must have drawn attention away from his hiding place. Looking up through the shifting barley stalks, he saw an intent, serious face as big as the world. He shut his eyes as tight as he could, not so much to keep the eyes in that face from seeing him as to keep himself from seeing them.

The hand groped after the cockroach. When it rose, though, it was empty; the scuttling bug had escaped. A great bellow of rage filled the sky, as if a thunderstorm cried out with the voice of a man.

\* \* \*

Sharur woke in the stable to the sound of his donkey—indeed, all the donkeys in their narrow stalls—braying frantically. His chest was wet. Some of the straw around him was wet. His first thought was that the donkey, in its fright, had kicked over or broken the pot of water the stablehands had left for it.

But that was not so; the light from a guttering torch outside the stall showed him the bowl where it belonged. It also showed him the liquid that splashed him was dark, not clear. A hot, metallic smell rose from it.

"Blood!" he exclaimed, recognition and horror mingling in his voice. He snatched up unstained straw from the floor, dipped it into the donkey's water pot, and washed himself as clean as he could.

While scrubbing at himself, he remembered the barley field. What had been hunting him through it, and what had that great hand caught instead of him? That it had wanted him he had no doubt.

Slowly, the donkeys calmed. As their racket subsided, Sharur heard more racket—the racket of men, outside the stable. He ran out into the night to find out what was going on.

"Lord Enimhursag!" people were shouting, and "The god!" and "The power of the god!" and "Who was the evildoer the god chose to punish?"

People were running from the inn as Sharur came out of the stables. Some of them had the same sorts of questions as did he. Others knew more, or said they did. "Squashed him flat!" one of them shouted. "Squashed him flat as a cockroach!" (Sharur shuddered.)

"He must have had it coming," someone else said—the innkeeper. He was carrying a torch. In its light, his eyes were wide and glittering. Catching sight of Sharur, he said, "You're a lucky bugger, Zuabi, and you had better believe it."

"Why?" Sharur asked. "What happened?"

"When that room didn't suit you—and curse me if I know why it didn't—I put another traveler from your city into it," the man answered. "The god only knows what crimes he'd committed—and the god made him pay for them."

"Reached right through the roof and squashed him flat!" that first fellow repeated, in a voice suggesting he'd had enough beer and then some the night before.

"Enimhursag knows a man's heart. Enimhursag sees a man's soul," the innkeeper said. "The god of our city is a just god. The god of our city is a righteous god. The god of our city is a mighty god."

*The god of your city is a stupid god*, Sharur thought. *The god of your city is a clumsy god.* Enimhursag had discovered that one man in Imhursag claiming to be a Zuabi was not what he seemed. (That was anything but stupid, a point on which Sharur chose not to dwell.) The god had tracked the false Zuabi to a particular inn. (That was anything but clumsy, another point Sharur would sooner have forgotten.) At the inn, though, Enimhursag had slain the wrong Zuabi, choosing the true instead of the false. (He might well have slain the right one, a point about which Sharur refused to think in any way whatever.)

"Was he kin of yours, this other fellow from your city?" the innkeeper asked.

Sharur thought for a moment before he answered. If he said yes, the innkeeper might let him look at or even take the effects of the other Zuabi, the true Zuabi, and who could guess what he might learn from them? But, on the other hand, if he said yes, he might draw Enimhursag's notice back to himself where the god now believed his troubles with Zuabut were over. That last consideration decided Sharur. "No," he said.

"An honest Zuabi," the innkeeper said. "Isn't that funny? Next thing you know, we'll be seeing a pious Gibli." He laughed loudly at his own wit. Sharur thought he heard other laughter, deeper laughter, echoing through and around that of the innkeeper. He told himself he was imagining that other laughter, and wished he could have made himself believe it.

"If the excitement's over, I'm going back to bed," he said, and forced out a yawn. He was not sleepy anymore; the yawn was as artificial as any of the expressions he wore while haggling over the price of a spearhead. Like those artificial expressions, this one served its purpose.

Before he lay down again, he shifted the straw in the donkey's stall to make sure he did not lie on any that was bloodstained. After he lay down, he sent a prayer in the direction of Enzuabu, apologizing that the god's subject had been taken in his place. And after that, to his surprise, he slept.

When he woke the next morning, he saw he had not done such a good job of cleaning himself as he had thought. But what had escaped his eye in the night had also escaped the eyes of the innkeeper and the guests who had spilled out of the inn after Enimhursag visited it in his wrath. He did better before letting anyone see him by light of day.

The barley porridge the innkeeper gave him for breakfast was bland and watery. He gulped it down anyhow, and then loaded trade goods onto his donkey and hurried out to the market square.

Arriving not long after sunrise, he found a better place than that from which he had done business the day before. He set out knives and swords and pickled palm hearts and started crying for customers. Before long, as if by chance, the Alashkurrut with whom he'd talked the day before came by. It wasn't chance, either on their part or on his: one of the reasons he reckoned the spot where he'd set up better than that which he'd had the day before was that it lay close to the display the men from the mountains had made for their own goods.

Bowing to them, Sharur said, "The gods give you a good day, my masters. How may I serve you?"

"Perhaps, since we are here, we will look further at these blades of yours," Piluliumas said, picking up one and hefting it. "I suppose I can say they are not the worst blades I have seen in the land between the rivers."

"You are generous to a small merchant." Sharur bowed again.

Piluliumas's companion plucked at the sleeve of his tunic. He spoke in the language of the Alashkurru Mountains: "I still say these blades look like Gibli work. What will our gods do to us if we bring back blades from Gibil?"

"You worry too much, Luwiyas. Metal's home is hard to tell," Piluliumas answered in the same tongue. "Besides, he said they were from Aggasher." The trader from the mountains shifted to the language of Kudurru: "You there, Zuabi—you said these swords were from Aggasher, not from Gibil?"

"Yes, I said that," Sharur agreed. "I said it because it is so."

Piluliumas looked happy. Luwiyas did not. "Will you swear in Enzuabu's name that this is so?"

"In Enzuabu's name I swear it," Sharur said at once. Enzuabu was not his god. His only hesitation over the false oath was some small concern that Enzuabu might catch and punish him when he went back onto Zuabi territory. But, for one thing, Enzuabu would not hear an oath made in Imhursag, and, for another, Sharur, having escaped Enimhursag's wrathful search in the night, thought he could escape Enzuabu, too.

Now Luwiyas bowed to him. "It is good. You have done us a favor. We will bargain with you for these blades." Piluliumas nodded.

Sharur held up a hand. "A favor for a favor. Is this not right? Is this not just?" When the Alashkurrut looked alarmed, he smiled reassuringly. "Nothing great, my masters. You asked a question of me. I would ask a question of you. Is this not right? Is this not just?"

"Ah. A question for a question." Piluliumas relaxed. "Yes, this is right. Yes, this is just. Ask your question, Zuabi."

"I shall ask." Sharur looked sly, as a Zuabi would in

seeking information about a rival city. "Tell me, men of Alashkurru, why have your gods so harshly turned against the Giblut? Why do you need to be so sure that nothing you buy, nothing you trade for, comes from Gibil? I have seen this with other men from the mountains as well as with yourselves, my masters, but have never found the chance to ask about it till now."

Luwiyas dropped back into his own tongue: "How much may we tell him?"

"We must tell him," Piluliumas answered in the same language. "A favor for a favor, a question for a question."

"Let the small gods speak, if they will." Luwiyas still sounded worried. "They will know what may be said. They will know what must not be said."

"They will know you are a man who runs from a lizard sitting on a rock," Piluliumas said tartly. "But still, let it be as you say." He returned to the language of Kudurru: "Trader from Zuabu, come see what we have brought to the land between the rivers. Trader from Zuabu, come hear the small gods we have brought from the mountains of Alashkurru. A favor for a favor, a question for a question: the small gods will answer you."

"I will come," Sharur said, hiding his worry. If the small gods the Alashkurrut had brought from the mountains recognized him as a man of Gibil, they would not tell him anything, or else they would tell him lies. If they recognized him as a Gibli, they might do him far more harm than that.

Playing his role as a Zuabi to the hilt, he fussily packed up his own goods, muttering about thieves all the while. Luwiyas said, "Few steal in the market square of Imhursag. Few risk the anger of Enimhursag."

"I am of Zuabu," Sharur said. "I take nothing for granted." The more he said he was from Zuabu, the more he made himself act like a Zuabi.

He convinced the two Alashkurrut. Laughing, Piluliumas spoke in the language of the mountains: "Zuabut will steal anywhere. They think their god protects all thefts. They may even be right."

"He will not steal from us," Luwiyas said, and set his hand on the hilt of his knife.

Sharur looked from one of them to the other, his face set in lines of blank incomprehension. Only when Luwiyas gestured for him to follow did he lead his complaining donkey after the two Alashkurrut. The men from the mountains had come down to Kudurru with guards and donkey handlers, as caravans from the land between the rivers went up to Alashkurru.

The guards looked bored, as Sharur's guards had looked bored up in the mountains. They were rolling dice in the dust of the market square, and tossing trinkets back and forth as they won or lost. They looked up at Sharur, decided he was harmless, and went back to their game.

"Here," Piluliumas said. "We have brought Kessis and Mitas with us from their home; we have brought them with us from our home. They are small gods of Alashkurru; they are small gods of our land. They will pay a favor for a favor; they will answer a question for a question."

One of the idols was carved from bone, in the shape of a dog. The other was carved out of a black, shiny stone, and looked something like a wild cat, something like a woman. Piluliumas and Luwiyas spoke together in their own tongue: "Small gods of the mountains, gods who watch your folk far from home, here is a man of Zuabu, a wise man, a worthy man, who would receive a favor for a favor, who would ask a question for a question asked of him."

"I am Kessis. He may speak." The bone lips of the dog-shaped idol moved. The voice was rough and growly. As was the way with gods, Sharur understood even though the words were strange.

"I am Mitas. He may speak." The half-cat, half-woman of stone had a voice of such allure, a fancy courtesan would surely have craved it.

"I thank you, small gods. I thank you, foreign gods. I am a man of the land of Kudurru. I am a man of the city of Zuabu," Sharur said. Kessis and Mitas were only small gods. They were only foreign gods. They would not know

the difference between one city and another in the land between the rivers. Sharur very much hoped they would not
know the difference between one city and another in the
land between the rivers. He went on, "Here is my question,
small gods, foreign gods. I have heard that the gods of
Alashkurru have grown angry at the men of Gibil, the men
of the city east of mine, and—"

"It is true," Kessis interrupted.

"Oh, yes, it is true," Mitas agreed. Her stone lips skinned
back from teeth like needles.

Sharur bowed. "Thank you, small gods. Thank you, foreign gods. Can you tell me *why* it is true? Knowing this,
we of Zuabu will gain great advantage over the Giblut."
Had he truly been a Zuabi, that would have been so. What
theft could be greater than a theft of knowledge?

Kessis's bone eyes rolled in their sockets. "He does not
know," the small god growled in astonishment.

"No, he does not know." Mitas sounded far more desirable, but no less surprised.

"Shall we tell him?" Kessis asked. "Should we tell him?
Will we anger the great gods if we tell him?" The dog-
shaped idol shivered. "I fear the anger of the great gods."

"He is not a man of Gibil," Mitas said soothingly. "He
is a man of Zuabu." Sharur stood very still, not wanting the
small gods to think of questioning that.

"Maybe he will tell what he learns to the Giblut," Kessis
said worriedly.

Both small gods turned their eyes toward Sharur. He had
to speak. He knew he had to speak. When he spoke, he
spoke without hesitation: "By all the gods of Kudurru, I
swear I shall not tell what you tell me to any man not of
my city." An oath to all the gods of the land between the
rivers, unlike one to Enzuabu, would bind him. But he had
managed to frame it in such a way as to make it serve his
needs and deceive the small gods of Alashkurru.

"It is good," Mitas purred. Sharur's blood heated when
he listened to her.

"Yes, it is very good," Kessis agreed.

He still hesitated, despite that agreement. Mitas spoke to Sharur: "Man of Zuabu, you know the Giblut do not give any gods, not their god, not your gods, nor yet the gods of Alashkurru, the honor they deserve."

"I have heard this, yes," Sharur said.

"This is one reason the gods are unloving in return," Mitas said, "but it is only one. You know the Giblut, when they trade in Alashkurru, trade not only for copper ore but also for other things—strange things, rare things, beautiful things, to take back to their city."

"I have also heard this is so, yes." Sharur nodded.

Kessis growled again: "One thing they took, they never should have taken. One thing a wanax or a merchant traded, he never should have traded. One thing that went to Gibil, it never should have gone to Gibil."

"What thing is this?" Sharur asked.

"It is a thing of the gods of Alashkurru," Kessis answered.

"It is a thing of the great gods of Alashkurru," Mitas added. Resentment flavored that wonderful voice. Mitas went on, "I am a small god because the great gods do not let me grow great. I am good enough for travelers to take with me on a journey. I am not good enough, I am not strong enough, to do more."

"You speak truth." Kessis still sounded and looked worried. "It is the same with me. But because we are not strong, because we are not great, we need to remember the great gods."

"Why? They barely remember us." Mitas showed those needle-sharp teeth again.

"What sort of thing went from Alashkurru to Gibil?" Sharur asked once more. "Why are the great gods of Alashkurru angry that it went from the mountains to the land between the rivers?"

"It is a thing of the great gods of Alashkurru," Mitas repeated, while Kessis let out growls that were close to frightened whimpers. "It is a thing into which the great gods of Alashkurru poured much of their power, to keep it safe."

Mitas's laugh was throaty and scornful, the laugh of a rich, beautiful woman rejecting the advances of a clod. "They poured in their power, to keep it safe, and now the thing is lost. And the thing can be unmade, the thing can be broken. The power can be spilled, the power can be lost, like beer soaking into the floor when a pot is dropped."

"Is it so?" Sharur said softly. "In the name of . . . Enzuabu, is it so?"

"It is so," Kessis answered. "Is it any wonder the great gods of Alashkurru hate and fear the Giblut? Is it any wonder they want no more Giblut coming to the land of Alashkurru?"

"What manner of thing is it that the great gods used to store their power?" Sharur asked. "Whence came it?"

"We know not," Kessis growled.

"It is a secret thing," Mitas added. She loosed that scornful laugh once more. "It is such a secret thing, even the man who kept it knew not what he kept; he was ignorant of the treasure he held. And so it went to Gibil, traded for a knife of bronze or a pot of wine or some other trifle, when it was worth as much as any three cities in the land between the rivers. And so the great gods are in a swivet; and so the mighty gods tremble. And so"—she laughed yet again— "it serves them right."

Sharur bowed low. "You have given me much to think on, Mitas and Kessis. You have given the folk of my city much to think on, small gods of Alashkurru."

"Small gods chafe under the rule of great gods hardly less than men do," Mitas said. Kessis's low snarl might have been agreement. It might as easily have been a warning to Mitas to watch her tongue.

Piluliumas said, "Zuabi, I will go back with you to the space you left in the market square. You have been here some little while. You have lost custom. I will go back with you and help you set out your goods once more."

"Man of Alashkurru, you are generous." Sharur bowed again. "I gladly accept your help." He took hold of the donkey's lead rope. "Let us go."

As they walked back toward the patch of dirt Sharur had vacated, Piluliumas said, "Zuabi, I will tell you a story. Hear me out before you speak. Think three times before you answer. Is it agreed?"

"Let it be as you say." Sharur nodded to Piluliumas. "I listen."

"Good," the Alashkurri said. "Let us suppose that a man from the mountains came down to this hot, flat land to trade. Let us suppose that, in a town square, he met a man who said he was from Zuabu, but who might have been from a different city, a city whose name I shall not speak. Do you understand so far?"

"I will hear you out before I speak," Sharur replied. "I will think three times before I answer." Piluliumas knew him for what he was, or thought he did. Sharur had no intention of confirming his suspicions.

Piluliumas seemed unoffended. "Good," he repeated. "Let us suppose that he had knowledge the man who said he was from Zuabu might find useful, but knowledge he could not pass to a man who was from a different city, a city whose name I shall not speak. He would ask no questions himself. He would seek to gain no knowledge himself. He would not make of himself a proved liar before the small gods of Alashkurru. He would not make of himself a proved liar before the great gods of Alashkurru. He would say, and say truthfully, 'The man said he was from Zuabu. I knew no differently. In the names of the small gods I swear it. In the names of the great gods I swear it.' Do you understand, man of Zuabu?"

"I think I do," Sharur answered. He kicked at the dirt. A puff of dust flew up. "May I ask a question of my own?"

"You may ask," Piluliumas said. "Because I am an ignorant man, I may not answer."

"Here is my question," Sharur said: "Why would a man from the mountains of Alashkurru care to help a man who said he was from Zuabu, but who might have come from a different city, a city whose name I shall not speak? There are some cities in the land between the rivers whose people the great gods of Alashkurru hate."

"There are some cities in the land between the rivers whose people the great gods of Alashkurru hate, true," Piluliumas agreed. "There is *a* city whose people they hate, at any rate. But the men of that city have traded in the mountains and valleys of Alashkurru for years. They have traded in the mountains and valleys of Alashkurru for generations. They have traded bronze, they have traded wine, and, sometimes not even knowing it, they have traded their words. Some of us have listened to those words and found them harder and sharper than bronze, sweeter and more splendid than wine. Do you understand, man of Zuabu?"

"Piluliumas, I understand," Sharur answered. And understand he did. Huzziyas the wanax had wanted to escape the power of the great gods of Alashkurru, but had been unable. Because he was a wanax, they watched him closely, watched him and controlled him. Others, perhaps, they did not watch so closely. Piluliumas—and how many more like him?—had to some degree broken free of their gods, as the men of Gibil had done. Yes, the gods of Alashkurru had reason to fear the Giblut. They had, in fact, more reason to fear the Giblut than Sharur had imagined.

Piluliumas said, "I have told you a story, a story to make the time pass by. It could be nothing more. See what a lucky man you are, that no one has taken your trading space while you visited ours?"

"I am a lucky man, Piluliumas," Sharur said. "I am a very lucky man."


"We are lucky men, Sharur," Ereshguna said. "We are very lucky men."

"That we are," Tupsharru agreed, beaming at his older brother. "Not only did you thrust your head into the lion's mouth by going up to Imhursag, not only did you find out what Kimash the lugal and the rest of us in Gibil desperately needed to know, but you also came home with a profit."

"If I can't make a profit trading against Imhursagut and foreigners, I am not a master merchant's son," Sharur said, and Ereshguna smiled at him. "The tale about being from Zuabu served me well. Zuabut are likely to have any sort of goods to trade, and no one asks many questions about how the goods came into their hands."

Ereshguna ran a hand through his beard. "These small gods of Alashkurru did not say what sort of thing had been carried down from the mountains here to Gibil?"

"No, Father, they did not. If they spoke truly, they knew not." Sharur paused to dip up a fresh cup of beer from the pot the Imhursaggi slave woman had brought at Ereshguna's order. After sipping, he went on, "I believe they did speak truly. They reckoned me a Zuabi who would use what they said against Gibil, not a Gibli who would use it for his own city."

"And yet that one Alashkurri knew you for what you were." Ereshguna stroked his beard once more. "Once men see other men free, they want to become free themselves. This is so in Alashkurru. This is so in cities of Kudurru ruled by ensis; I know as much for a fact. It could be so even in cities of Kudurru ruled by gods."

"It must be so," Sharur said. "Gods once ruled all cities. Even the rule of ensis gives men more freedom—or lets men take more freedom—than the rule of gods." He hunched his shoulders, remembering the voice of Engibil forbidding him to borrow from his father to pay Ningal's bride-price.

"Whatever this thing is, it must be a thing that came to Gibil in one of last year's caravans from Alashkurru," Ereshguna said, returning to the business at hand. "Last year, the gods of Alashkurru were friendly to us; not so this year. Likely, I would say, this thing came to Gibil in a caravan of the house of Ereshguna. We deal more with the Alashkurrut than any other merchant house of Gibil."

"Likely I brought this thing to Gibil myself," Sharur said. "But how do we go about finding out what it is? I will guess it is not an ingot of copper. I will guess it is not a sack of copper ore. These things would be changed and broken in the use of them. By what the small gods said, the power of the great gods is not lost from the thing in which they hid it, and the thing is not broken; they fear lest the thing be broken, and the power lost.''

Tupsharru said, ''If it is not copper, if it is not copper ore, it is likely to be a strange thing, a curious thing, a beautiful thing. If it is a strange thing, a curious thing, a beautiful thing, it may be anywhere in the city, for many Giblut prize these things and pay us well for them. But likeliest of all—''

''—Likeliest of all,'' Sharur finished for him, ''likeliest of all is that it lies on the altar of Engibil, or stored away in the god's temple, for Kimash the mighty lugal delights in giving Engibil such gifts.''

''This is good,'' Ereshguna said. ''This is very good indeed. If such a thing lies on the altar of Engibil, surely the god will know it for what it is. If such a thing is stored away in the god's temple, surely he will point it out to us.''

''If we return it to the gods of Alashkurru, they will no longer have reason to hate us,'' Tupsharru said. ''Our caravans will be able to go into the mountains. They will come home with copper and copper ore. The city will profit. The house of Ereshguna will profit.''

''*I* will profit,'' Sharur said dreamily. ''With my profit, I will pay Ningal's bride-price to Dimgalabzu the smith and fulfill my oath to Engibil.''

''Let us go to the temple and seek this thing,'' Ereshguna said. ''If we find it, Kimash the lugal will reward us for saving the city from its sorrow.''

They drained their cups of beer. They set them down. They got to their feet. It was then that Sharur had a new thought, a different thought. ''If we find this thing in the temple of Engibil, if we find it there and we break it . . .'' His father and his brother stared at him as he finished the thought: ''If we find it and we break it, we punish the gods of Alashkurru for slighting us.''

''What good would that do?'' Tupsharru exclaimed in horror. ''It would only make them hate us more.''

Ereshguna said nothing. "You see, don't you, Father?" Sharur asked. Slowly, unwillingly, Ereshguna nodded. By Tupsharru's wide eyes, he still did not follow. Sharur explained: "Into this thing, for safekeeping, the great gods of the Alashkurrut have poured much of their power. If we break the thing, we break the power and set the Alashkurrut free of their great gods."

"Only in Gibil, and only in your generation, my son, would such a thought come into the mind of a man." Ereshguna sounded awed and terrified at the same time. "I think Tupsharru has the better course. The Alashkurrut are only Alashkurrut. Who cares whether their gods rule them or not? If we find the thing, those gods are welcome to it. They will reward us for it, as your brother says, and Kimash the lugal will reward us for it as well."

"It may be so," Sharur said. "But if an Alashkurri like Piluliumas can free himself, if an Alashkurri like Huzziyas can tremble on the edge of freeing himself, how many in the mountains would be free if the great gods there were weakened?"

"Where is the profit in it?" his father asked.

"I care only so much for profit," Sharur answered. Now his father gaped at him, as if he had said Engibil did not exist or uttered some other manifest absurdity. He went on, "I care also about revenge. The gods of the Alashkurrut have wronged me. Let them pay."

"Aye, let them pay," Ereshguna said. "Let them pay compensation for the wrong."

"Let them pay pain for the wrong, as I have done," Sharur said. But now he wavered. Even a killer's family could avoid blood feud by payments to the victim's kin. He scowled. He kicked at the dirt floor. "Perhaps." His tone was grudging.

Tupsharru said, "We are pricing the lamb not born. We are pricing the sword not sharpened. We have not found this thing, whatever it may be. We do not know if we shall find this thing, whatever it may be."

"True!" Ereshguna seized on that with transparent

eagerness. "We do not know enough to have any certain plans yet. Let us go to the temple and see what we may learn. Let us go to the temple and see what Engibil may teach us."

"Yes, let us go," Sharur said, and left his home with his father and his brother. The way the god had refused to release him from his oath and let him borrow from his father to pay bride-price to Dimgalabzu left him less eager than he might have been to approach Engibil's house upon earth, but it needed doing, and he did not shrink from that which needed doing. Perhaps, as Tupsharru had said, finding the thing into which the Alashkurri gods had poured their power would let him make a profitable journey after all. And perhaps, as he had said himself, finding the thing would let him take revenge on the gods.

*Either way*, he thought. *Either way*.

Engibil's temple was larger than the palace of Kimash the lugal. The chamber at the top of the temple where the god dwelt, toward which the massive structure tapered in a series of steps, was the highest point in Gibil. From it, Engibil could look out across the whole city and across all the farmlands it ruled.

Bigger than the palace the temple might have been. It was not more splendid. For one thing, much of it was old. Because it was built of baked bricks rather than sun-dried mud brick—nothing but the best for Engibil—that was not so obvious as it might have been otherwise. The temple was not crumbling to pieces. But the brickwork had a faded, sun-blasted look that said it had been standing for a long time. No additions were going up, as they constantly were at the lugal's palace.

Hangings of rich wool dyed crimson and the savor of burnt offerings went some way toward concealing the aging bones beneath, as paint would on a woman. And, as a woman heavy with paint might be a long time realizing she was no longer beautiful, so Engibil, lulled by Kimash's splendid presents and those of the previous lugals, had not yet noticed he was less supreme in his city than had once been so.

Some of his priests understood that far more completely than he. The younger men in the priesthood were Kimash's creatures, more dedicated to lulling the god than to exalting him. The older servitors still revered him as they and their predecessors had done back in the days when he ruled Gibil through an ensi, but year by year death cut through their ranks, as the scythe cut through rows of barley at harvest time.

A younger priest, his head shaved like those of the priests of Enimhursag but his eyes clever and altogether his own, came up to the merchants in an outer courtyard. Bowing, he said, "I greet you in the name of Engibil, Ereshguna. In the name of Engibil I greet you, sons of Ereshguna. May the god's blessings be upon you all."

"I greet you in the name of Engibil, Burshagga," Ereshguna said, and bowed in turn.

"In the name of Engibil we greet you, Burshagga," Sharur and Tupsharru said together. They also bowed.

"How good when men are gracious," Burshagga said. "How pleasant when men are polite. How may this servant of Engibil also serve you?"

Ereshguna pointed to that topmost chamber. "If he be not otherwise engaged, we would speak with the god. If he be not otherwise busy, we would have words with him."

The priest frowned. Plainly, he had not expected that. "On what matter would you speak with the lord of the city?"

"On the matter that concerns Kimash the lugal," Ereshguna answered, his voice as soft as lambswool.

Burshagga's eyes widened. Now his bow was not the polite bow of greeting but the deeper bending that acknowledged authority. "Master merchant, if you are concerned with that matter . . . Wait one moment, please." He hurried away.

An old priest cocked his head to one side and examined Sharur and Tupsharru and Ereshguna. His beard was not gray but snowy white. Surely he remembered the days before Igigi had taken the rule of Gibil out of Engibil's hands and into his own. And, by the way he scowled at the three merchants, the men of the new, he remembered those days fondly, too.

Burshagga came back at a brisk walk. "The god is pleasuring himself," he reported. "That being completed, you may attend him." His eye fell on the white-bearded priest. "Have you nothing better to do than stand and stare, Ilakabkabu? Why don't you take yourself off to the boneyard and save us the trouble?"

"Because I am truly a man of Engibil," Ilakabkabu said. "I remember the god first, not a mere man who will be dead and stinking soon enough, soon enough." He drew himself up with a pride at the same time stubborn and impotent.

"I am a priest of the great god Engibil, as you are," Burshagga retorted. "I worship the great god Engibil, as you do. But I am not wedded to the past, as you are. I do not pant for the past as for a virgin bride, as you do. Go off to the boneyard, old fool; may your forgotten ghost go straight to the underworld."

"Engibil will remember my ghost," Ilakabkabu said. "Engibil will cherish it." He walked off at a stiff-jointed shuffle.

"Old fool," Burshagga repeated, this time to Ereshguna and his sons. "He would take us back to the days before lugals, to the days before metal, to the days before writing, if he had his way."

"Many things pull in that direction these days," Sharur said. Burshagga nodded indignantly. He had his own kind of righteousness, different from Ilakabkabu's.

"His years, if not his thoughts, may deserve respect," Ereshguna said mildly.

"Bah!" Burshagga said. But, before the priest could begin an argument, one of his colleagues came trotting up and pointed toward the uppermost chamber in the temple. Seeing the gesture, Burshagga grew businesslike once more. "Engibil will grant you audience now. This is, I remind you, on the matter that concerns Kimash the lugal, Kimash the mighty lugal."

He had his own way of getting the last word. As he turned to lead the merchants up to the god's audience chamber, Sharur studied him. Burshagga, too, was a man of the new. The old had been disagreeable and tyrannical. Burshagga looked to be proof that the new could also be disagreeable and tyrannical. Sharur shrugged. Even the gods had their weaknesses, their failings.

"Ascend Engibil's stairway!" the priest said. The stairway was one of four, one for each of the cardinal directions, that went up to the chamber of the god. It had one step for every day of the year. Despite being a man of the new, Sharur felt no small awe as he set his foot upon it. He had never gone up to an audience with Engibil before. Engibil had come to him—he remembered with a shiver the god's voice beating through him on the Street of Smiths—but he had never gone to the god, not like this.

Someone was coming down the long stairway as Sharur and Tupsharru and Ereshguna climbed it. A woman, Sharur saw; she was wearing tunic rather than kilt. As she drew closer, he recognized her: the beautiful courtesan who had stripped herself naked in the street for him and his caravan crew to admire when he came back to Gibil from the mountains.

He laughed under his breath. His brother looked a question at him, but he did not explain. He would not say what was in his thoughts, not here, not in the house of the god. Kimash the lugal had said he had ways of pleasing Engibil even without strange things, rare things, beautiful things from the land of the Alashkurrut. Remembering the lush ripeness of the courtesan's body, Sharur was certain she would have pleased him. No doubt she pleased the god, too.

And, as he drew closer still, he saw the god had also pleased her. She walked with slightly unsteady step, as if she were on the edge of being drunk. Her smiling lips were swollen, bruised; but for the smile, all the muscles of her face had gone slack with pleasure. She stared through Sharur and Tupsharru and Ereshguna, the pupils of her eyes enormous as a wild cat's at midnight.

After she swayed past Tupsharru, he laughed softly, too. "She was not a duckling, but she quacked like one," he murmured—a proverb about the sounds a truly kindled woman made in her ecstasy. Sharur nodded.

By the time he reached the top of the stairway, sweat bathed him. A fat old priest who had to make that climb was liable to fall over dead. Sharur glanced toward his father. Ereshguna was neither fat nor very old, but he lived his life in the city these days instead of leading caravans to distant lands. He was panting, but otherwise seemed all right. Sharur was panting a little himself. He nodded to his father. Ereshguna nodded back.

The god's chamber was a cube of baked brick with a narrow walkway around it. A door led into it from each of the cardinal directions. It should have been dimmer in there than outside; the chamber had no windows. But light streamed out from the doors: the light of the god. Sharur shivered again.

*Enter.* The word resounded inside Sharur's head, and, no doubt, inside Tupsharru's and Ereshguna's as well. It was as loud as the god's voice had been in the Street of Smiths, but not so terrifying. For one thing, here it was expected, as it had not been there. For another, here Engibil was inviting, not forbidding.

Sharur stood aside so his father and brother could precede him into the god's chamber. His heart beating fast, he followed them.

Engibil sat on a gold-sheathed chair like that of Kimash the lugal (after a moment, Sharur realized he had that backwards; surely the lugal's throne was copied from this one). The god was naked, perhaps because he had just had the courtesan, perhaps for no other reason than that it pleased him to be so. He had the form of a well-made man of about Ereshguna's age, but with all human imperfections removed. Sharur got only a quick glimpse before he, like Ereshguna and Tupsharru, threw himself flat on the floor in front of the god.

*Rise.* Again, the word filled the minds of the mortals who

had come before Engibil. *Rise, Ereshguna. Rise, Sharur and Tupsharru, the sons of Ereshguna.* As the three men got to their feet, the god went on, now moving his lips as if he were a man, "Seek not to beseech me to give back your oath, Sharur son of Ereshguna. Seek not to buy your bride with profit that never was."

"Great god, mighty god, god who founded this city, god who made this town," Sharur said through lips numb with fear, "that is not my purpose. That is not why I have come before you. Examine my spirit, great god. Look into my soul, mighty god. You will see I speak the truth. You will see I dare not lie before you."

Engibil looked at him. Engibil looked into him, as if looking into his mind was as easy as looking into his body. For the god, it was. Sharur felt penetrated, as he had penetrated the Imhursaggi slave woman. Engibil could have learned much Sharur would not have had him know. But he was searching only for the one thing and, when he found it, he withdrew.

"I see you speak the truth," he said. "I see you dare not lie to me. Speak, then, of the reason you have come before me. Speak, then, of your purpose. Or shall I examine your spirit once more? Shall I look into your soul again?"

"God who founded this city, I will speak," Sharur said hastily. "God who made this town, I will answer." Anything to keep the god from going through his mind as he went through clay tablets with writing on them.

"Say on, then." Engibil folded chiseled arms across massive chest.

Sharur took a deep breath. "Great god, you will know that my caravan brought no copper home from the Alashkurru Mountains. Mighty god, you will know I brought no copper ore to Gibil from the land of the Alashkurrut. Great god, mighty god, you will know the Alashkurrut would trade me no strange things, no rare things, no beautiful things to lay before you for your pleasure, to set on your altar for your delight."

"Yes, I know this," Engibil replied. "It does not please

me. The copper is of but small concern. The copper ore is of no great moment. That I fail to get my due angers me." His brows came down like thunder.

Sharur's eyes flicked to one side, toward his father. Ereshguna's face was blank, as it would have been in a dicker with another merchant. Sharur did his best to keep his own features similarly impassive. Behind that mask, anger sparked. The god cared nothing for what made Gibil the city thrive. The god cared only for what pleased him. No wonder Kimash had sent him the courtesan.

"Lord Engibil, I believe I know why the Alashkurrut would not treat with us," Sharur said. "I believe I know why the gods of the Alashkurrut would not let them treat with us."

"You will tell me how this came to pass. You will tell me why this is so."

"Great god, I will." And Sharur related what he had learned from Kessis and Mitas. He finished, "Mighty god, if this thing lies before you, we can give it back. Lord Engibil, if this thing is set on your altar, we can return it." He did not—he made sure he did not—think about destroying it.

Engibil's perfect features took on a look of puzzlement. "I recall no such object coming before me."

"Great god, are you sure?" Sharur blurted. "Mighty god, are you certain?" Only when he saw his father and brother staring at him in alarm did he realize that his words, if Engibil chose to construe them so, might be blasphemous. Who save a blasphemer could doubt anything a god said?

Engibil, fortunately, proved more interested in the riddle than in the possible affront. "I noted no great power trapped in any of the objects I received over this past year. I noted no great power trapped in any of the objects given to men of this city, and thus only indirectly to me, over the past year."

"Would you have noticed it, had you not been specially seeking it?" Sharur asked, affecting not to hear the god's casual assumption of ownership over everything and everyone in Gibil. "The man who traded it had no notion of what he was sending out of the mountains."

"A man!" Engibil's words dripped scorn. "What does a man know? What can a man know? A man beside a god is a mosquito, trying to suck the blood of time."

"But this is not a thing of men," Sharur reminded the god. What Engibil said was true, but, with writing, men gained memory as secure and long-lasting as that of the gods. Again, Sharur did not speak of that. Instead, he continued, "This is a thing of gods. Could the gods of the mountains not have concealed their power within it, hiding that power from both men and gods?"

Engibil frowned, not a frown of anger, but one showing Sharur had thought of something that had not crossed his mind. Engibil was immensely strong. Engibil knew a great deal. All the same, a truly blasphemous thought flicked into Sharur's mind—and then out again, as fast as he could send it away: the god was not very bright.

"I suppose it could be so," Engibil said. "I did not closely examine my gifts to see if they might have this power embedded in them. Why would I do such a thing, when I saw no need? Now I see a need. Now I will closely examine my gifts. You will come with me, even if you are only men. Come."

He rose from his throne and set one hand on Sharur's shoulder, one hand on Tupsharru's, and one hand on Ereshguna's. He was a god: if he needed an extra hand, he had one. Against Sharur's bare skin, the flesh of his hand did not feel like flesh, but like warm metal. Engibil's eyes blazed. As if Sharur had looked into the sun, for a moment he could see nothing but the light that poured out from them.

When his vision cleared, he found that his father and his brother and Engibil and he were no longer in the audience chamber at the top of the temple, but in a storeroom like the storerooms that made up so much of Kimash's palace. They proved not to be alone in the storeroom. A priest and a courtesan—not nearly so fine a courtesan as had ministered to Engibil's pleasure—had been about to lie down together. They both squeaked in astonished dismay.

Laughter rolled from Engibil in great waves. "Elsewhere!" he boomed. "Elsewhere, elsewhere." The priest and the courtesan fled. Sharur would have fled, too. The storeroom had a higher ceiling than that of the audience chamber. Here, instead of being man-sized, Engibil was half again as tall and all the more awe-inspiring.

Despite that, Sharur's first thought, one the god luckily did not read, was *What a lot of junk.* That was not completely fair, and he knew it. Many of Engibil's treasures were of gold and silver and precious stones. Those glowed in the light that poured out of the god. The lugals of Gibil, and the ensis before them, had given of the best they had.

But they had also literally followed the dictum *strange things, rare things, beautiful things.* The beautiful things were beautiful. The rare things were rare: Sharur gaped to see a necklace of huge, shimmering pearls. Caravans to distant Laravanglal would sometimes bring back from the east, along with the tin that hardened copper into bronze, a pearl or two, having paid enormous amounts of metal to gain them. Pearls as large as these, so many all together, each perfectly matched to its neighbors—Sharur had never known nor imagined the like.

And the strange things were . . . strange. Why any lugal would have chosen to give Engibil a piece of pottery shaped like a spider and painted with alarming realism was beyond Sharur. And the basketwork dog standing on its hind legs to display a large erection might have been funny the first time someone saw it, but after that?

Engibil said, "Where is this thing into which the gods of the Alashkurrut are said to have poured their power? Do you see it? Do you know which of my many treasures it is?"

"Great god, I do not know where it is," Sharur answered, looking to his father in consternation. "Mighty god, I do not know which of your many treasures it is." His eyes went now here, now there. So many pieces in the treasury were, or could have been, of Alashkurri work. He felt no special power in any of them. How could he? He was only a man.

Tupsharru spoke: "Lord Engibil, now that you are among your treasures, can you not feel the power poured into one of them?"

Engibil frowned again. He turned in all directions inside the treasure room, to the north, to the east, to the south, and last of all to the west. He reached out his hands—and in the reaching he had as many hands as he wanted—to the shelves and tables set against each wall, as if feeling of the objects set on each one. The frown deepened. At last, Engibil turned back toward Sharur and Tupsharru and Ereshguna. "I do not know what this thing is," the god said. "I do not know where it may be. I can feel nothing of it. Son of Ereshguna, are you sure the Alashkurri small gods were not playing a trick on you?"

"I am sure," Sharur said. Seeing his father give him a doubtful look hurt worse than having the god disbelieve him. "I *am* sure," he repeated.

"Maybe this thing is elsewhere in the city," Engibil said, "although, as I told you, I sensed it nowhere. Maybe the great gods of the Alashkurrut were playing tricks on their small gods."

"Tricks are all very well, great god," Sharur said. "But, mighty god, if not for the reason Kessis and Mitas gave me, why have the great gods of Alashkurru come to hate the people of Gibil? Why have even the gods of Kudurru come to despise the people of Gibil?"

"I have told you what I know," Engibil replied. "I have told you what I do not know. It is enough." He reached out and once more took hold of Sharur and Ereshguna and Tupsharru by the shoulder. In an instant, the three men and the god were back in the audience chamber atop the temple. "I dismiss you," Engibil said. "Go on about your lawful occasions, and seek no longer to circumvent my will."

His words beat against Sharur's mind like a windstorm. The young merchant had all he could do to nerve himself to ask the god whether he might speak. When he did, Engibil's eyes burned into his own until he had to struggle to hold his own gaze steady. At last, Engibil dipped his head in brusque assent. "I thank you, great god," Sharur gasped as the pressure of the god's will eased. "You are generous, mighty god. Here is what I would ask you: have I your leave to go on searching for this thing of which Kessis and Mitas told me?"

"If I, a god, cannot find this thing, why do you imagine that you, a mortal man, will have any better fortune?" Engibil demanded. "I do not believe this thing even exists, no matter what the small gods of Alashkurru may have told you."

"If it does not exist, my searching will do no harm," Sharur answered. "If it should exist, my searching may do some good." Was he contradicting the god? He did not worry about that until he had already spoken, by which time it was too late.

If contradiction there was, Engibil, fortunately, once more failed to notice it. "When mortals have so little time," he said, "I marvel at the ways in which they choose to fritter it away. Do what you will in this, son of Ereshguna. You will discover nothing, the reason being there is nothing to discover."

Sharur did a very human thing: he accepted the permission and ignored the scorn behind it. "I thank you, great god," he said, bowing low.

Now the fires of Engibil's eyes were banked, hooded. "I do not say you are welcome," the god replied. "Be gone from my sight."

# 6

"**My son,**" **Ereshguna** said as he and Sharur made their way back toward their home from the temple, "my son, in some things in life you will win, in others you will lose. I do not think you will win in this. If you keep at it, you will only bring grief down upon yourself. If you persist, you will only break your heart."

"Grief has already tumbled down upon me, like an avalanche in the mountains," Sharur answered. "The falling stones of grief have already broken my heart, as a pot breaks when it falls on hard ground. Unless I go on, my heart can never be whole again."

"The god asked of you a fair question," Ereshguna said. "If with his power he cannot find this thing that may or may not exist, how can you hope to do so?"

"If I cannot hope, what sort of man am I?" Sharur lowered his voice to a wary whisper. He covered the eyes of Engibil's amulet that he wore on his belt. "Was it a god who learned to free copper from its ore? No: it was a man. Was it a god who learned to mix tin with copper to make bronze? No: it was a man. Was it a god who learned marks on clay might last longer than a man's memory? No: for gods' memories fail not. It was a man."

"Power lies behind all those things," Ereshguna answered. "They may yet grow gods who feed from that power."

"May it not come to pass!" Tupsharru exclaimed.

"They may indeed grow such gods," Sharur admitted. "But they also may not. The power may remain in the hands of the men who work the metal. The power may remain in the hands of the men who inscribe the clay. Has this not been the hope of Giblut since the days of the first lugal?"

"It has," his father said. "I would not deny it. It is my hope now, no less than it is yours. But I do not see how the power in metalworking will help you find the thing of which the Alashkurri small gods told you. I do not see how the power in writing will help you find the thing into which Alashkurri great gods poured their power—if such a thing there be."

Sharur walked along for several paces before he spoke again. His strides were angry; his sandals scuffed up dust. At last, he said, "If I find this thing, I can take it back to the gods of the Alashkurrut." *Or I can indeed break it*, he thought savagely, but he did not speak that thought aloud. Ereshguna no doubt knew it was in his mind. "If I do not find it, how shall I find the bride-price for Ningal? Engibil holds my oath in his hand. He holds my oath in his heart. He will not let it go. If he does not let it go, I cannot buy the bride I desire. Dimgalabzu has given me a year, no more. Time is passing. Time is fleeting. I must find the thing."

"Many a man comes to grief, forgetting the difference between *must* and *shall*," Ereshguna answered. "That you want to find this thing—if thing there be, as I say—that you need to find it, no one can doubt. That you shall find it—if it be there for the finding—you cannot know."

"Your words hold truth, Father, as they always do," Sharur said. "But this I know, and know in fullness: if I search not for this thing, whatever it may be, I shall not find it. Therefore I *will* search, come what may."

Ereshguna's breath hissed out of him in a long sigh. "If you will not heed the god, perhaps you will heed your father. Son of my flesh, I tell you this is not a wise course. Son of my heart, I tell you this way heartbreak lies. I do not believe you will find the thing you seek. A man who turns aside from the road to chase a mirage is never seen again.''

"A man who walks past an oasis, thinking it a mirage, dies of thirst in the desert," Sharur replied. "If I do not wed Ningal, I know my heart shall break within me. If I search for the thing and fail to find it, perhaps my heart shall break and perhaps it shall not. If I search for the thing and do find it, of a certainty my heart shall not break. You are a merchant, Father. Which of those strikes you as the best bargain?''

"Bargains are for copper. Bargains are for tin. Bargains are for barley. Bargains are for wine of dates," Ereshguna said. "For my son's happiness, for my son's safety, I do not speak of bargains. I care nothing about bargains. With some things, a man should not bargain.''

"For your son's happiness," Sharur repeated. "Unless I do this, I shall not be happy. This I know. If I do it, I may be unhappy. I know this, too. I am a man. I may fail. Even gods fail. But I will try. I must try. What have I to lose?''

"Your life, my brother!" Tupsharru blurted.

Ereshguna walked on for several more steps. At last, he said, "Tupsharru is right. If you hold to this course, it could even be that you will lose your life.''

Before Sharur could reply, his grandfather's ghost spoke up: "Sooner or later, this is the fate of all men.''

Ereshguna looked exasperated. "Ghost of my father, how long have you been listening to us?''

"Oh, not long," the ghost replied in airy tones. "I was just coming up the street and saw the three of you coming down, looking glum as if your favorite puppy just died. If you want to talk about death, you should talk with someone who knows what he's talking about.''

"When a man rich in years dies, he will be a ghost rich in years, too," Ereshguna said, "for his grandchildren will recall him well, and he will be able to speak with them even when they grow old themselves, and will not sink down to the underworld to be forgotten by mortals until they die. But when a young man passes away, his stay as a ghost is also cut short, for only those of his age or older could know him while he lived on earth.''

Sharur's grandfather's ghost sniffed. ''The real trouble is, some people don't care to listen.'' Sharur could not see the ghost, but got the distinct impression that it indignantly flounced off.

His father said, ''I meant my words. You play no game here. If you seek a track where the god says there is no track, if you go on where the god bids you halt, you put yourself in danger. It may be that you put yourself in such danger, no mortal man may escape it.''

''I will go on,'' Sharur said. Maybe the shadows from the harsh sun above carved the lines in Ereshguna's face deeper than Sharur had ever seen them before, or maybe, for the first time, his father looked old.

Inadapa, the steward to Kimash the lugal, drank a polite cup of beer before getting to the business that had brought him to the Street of Smiths: ''The mighty lugal would speak with the son of Ereshguna over what passed in the temple of Engibil yesterday.''

Sharur drained his own cup of beer and rose from the stool on which he sat. ''I will gladly speak with Kimash. I will gladly tell him what passed in the temple of Engibil yesterday.''

''The mighty lugal will be glad to learn once more how readily you obey him,'' Inadapa said. ''Let us go.''

''I obey him as I would obey the god,'' Sharur said. He bowed to Ereshguna. ''My father, I shall soon see you again.''

''And I shall soon see you again,'' Ereshguna replied, returning the bow. His face was calm now, but Sharur could hear the worry in his voice, though he did not think Inadapa could. Sharur understood why his father sounded worried. He obeyed Engibil only grudgingly, under the compulsion of the god's superior strength. Such grudging, partial obedience, if given to Kimash, would be less than the lugal wanted.

"Let us go," Inadapa repeated; like any good servant, he was impatient in the service of his master.

Pausing only to put on his hat, Sharur walked with the lugal's steward along the Street of Smiths to the palace. As had happened when he went to the palace with his father, he had to wait while a stream of donkeys and slaves carrying bricks and mortar blocked his path. "The mighty lugal adds to his own glory," he remarked, to see how Inadapa would respond.

As usual, the steward's face was bland. "The lugal's glory is the glory of Gibil," he replied, and now he seemed to wait for Sharur's answer.

In most cities of Kudurru, a man would have said, *The god's glory is the glory of my city*. Men still did say that in Gibil, but how many of them meant it? If Kimash could go on building for himself even while Engibil sought to reassert his own power, the lugal must have thought his hold on the rule fairly secure.

Sharur said, "May the lugal's glory prevail." Inadapa weighed the words, as Sharur would have weighed gold brought in by a debtor. They must have brought down the pan of his mental balance, for he nodded once, in sharp satisfaction, and set no more word-lined traps for the master merchant's son.

As soon as the donkeys and slaves had passed, Inadapa led Sharur through the maze of hallways, past the endless storerooms and workrooms of the palace, to the audience chamber of Kimash the lugal. As Kimash had before, he sat on his high seat. As Sharur had before, he groveled in front of that high seat, lying with his face in the dust until the lugal bade him rise.

"I come in obedience to your summons, mighty lugal," he said, brushing dirt from his kilt.

"Yes, you do," Kimash agreed. He had the arrogance of a god, if not the inherent powers. "Speak to me of your journey to Imhursag, to the land of our enemies." Sharur told that tale, and also the tale of his visit to Engibil's temple. Leaning forward on his high seat, Kimash asked, "And did Engibil find this secret thing of which you spoke, this thing into which the great gods of the Alashkurrut poured their power?"

Regretfully, Sharur spoke the truth: "Mighty lugal, he did not. He found himself unable to tell it from any other offering he has received. He is of the opinion that the thing does not exist."

Kimash might not have had the inherent powers of a god, but he did own sharp ears and sharp wits. "He is of that opinion, you say. What of you, son of Ereshguna? Do you hold a different opinion?"

"I do, mighty lugal," Sharur answered. "I believed then, and I still believe now, that the Alashkurri gods intended no one to know this thing for what it was. The wanax or merchant who traded it to us knew it not, the trader who took it knew it not, and I think the god of the city also knows it not. But when will a god admit to ignorance? When will a god say he does not know?"

Kimash's chuckle was harsh as windblown sand. "When will a man admit to ignorance?" he returned. "When will a man say he does not know? Truly we are shaped in the image of those who made us; is it not so? Why do you believe your own thoughts, not those of the god, who knows so much more than you?"

As he would have done in a hard bargain, Sharur worked to hold his face still. What he concealed now was not the lowest price he would accept but dismay. Of all the men in Gibil, he had judged Kimash likeliest to believe him, likeliest to support him. Instead, the lugal made it plain he sided with Engibil.

Carefully, Sharur said, "Mighty lugal, as I answered before, this is a secret thing. Gods may keep secrets from gods. Even men may keep secrets from gods, provided always the gods do not know secrets are being kept."

"Speak not of this, son of Ereshguna, lest a certain god hear," Kimash said.

Sharur bowed his head. "I obey." Of all the men in Gibil, likely of all the men in Kudurru, perhaps of all the men in the world, the lugal kept the most secrets of that sort from the gods.

"Has your judgment not another reason?" Kimash asked. "Has your opinion not another source? The Diyala rises from many springs. The Yarmuk flows out of many streams. Do you not believe that, if this thing of which you speak exists, you will gain profit and favor not only from Engibil but also from the gods of the Alashkurrut? Do you not believe that, if this thing into which the gods of the mountains have poured their powers is real, you will be able to wed the woman you have long desired?"

"Yes, I believe those things." Sharur bowed his head again. "You are able to see deep into the heart of a man, mighty lugal; you would have made a formidable merchant." On his high seat, Kimash preened like a songbird displaying himself before a possible mate. But Sharur went on, "I do not believe this has clouded my judgment. I do not believe this has shaped my opinion. My views spring from what I have seen and heard, not from what I have hoped."

Kimash's frown was nearly as formidable as Engibil's. "There you make a claim not even the gods could make in truth. What man's views do not spring from what he hopes and believes?"

"The views of a man who follows truth," Sharur replied.

"Ah. Truth. But there is truth, and then there is truth. Remember the onion, son of Ereshguna." Now the lugal, who had seen as much of human frailty and as much of human desire as any man ever born, seemed almost amused. "From which layer of truth do your views spring? Is it not also truth that you wish to lie down in love with Ningal the daughter of Dimgalabzu the smith?"

"Yes, that is a truth." Sharur admitted what he could hardly deny.

"Does not this truth color your view of other truths, as a

man with an eye full of blood will see things red?'' Kimash asked.

''It . . . may,'' Sharur said reluctantly. He had always know the lugal was a formidable man, but never till now had all Kimash's strength of purpose been aimed at him and him alone. He felt very alone indeed.

''Ah,'' Kimash repeated. ''It is good to hear you say so much. Many would be too blind to their own failings to reckon that they had any. Well, here is what I say to you in return, son of Ereshguna. I say, give over your talk of secret things. I say, give over your dream of magic-filled things. I say, accept the world as you find it is here. I will reward you for your service to the city. I will repay you for your braving the city of the Imhursagut. Engibil has shown you that you may not have for your wife the daughter of Dimgalabzu. Choose any other woman in Gibil, son of Ereshguna, even if it be one of my own daughters, and not only shall you wed her, but the bride-price for her shall come from the treasury of the lugal. I have spoken, and it shall be as I say.''

''Mighty lugal, you are kind,'' Sharur said. ''Mighty lugal, you are generous.''

''All these things are true,'' Kimash said complacently. If the gods were not immune to flattery, how could a mere man escape its charms? The lugal went on, ''Then you will obey me, and give over your foolish search for a thing that is not and cannot be.''

''Mighty lugal, I—'' Sharur hesitated. Kimash, he realized, was also anything but immune to the problem of there being more than one possible layer to the truth. The lugal was astute enough to see that in others, but not in himself. One of his principal aims was to keep Engibil quiet and satisfied. Disagreeing with Engibil once the god had said he could sense no object into which the great gods of the Alashkurrut had poured their power would only stir him up and anger him. Therefore, Engibil had to be right and Sharur wrong. What Kimash wanted to be true influenced what Kimash believed to be true. But did it influence what *was* true?

"Then you will obey me," the lugal repeated, his voice now going deep and harsh. His eyes glittered. He was not, and made it very plain he was not, a man whom Sharur would have been wise to challenge.

"Mighty lugal, I—" The words stuck in Sharur's throat. Had he said them all, he would have put Ningal aside forever. He could not bear to do that. Instead of speaking, he bowed his head. Even if it was not, that looked like acquiescence. Did Kimash so choose, he could take it for acquiescence.

He did so choose. "Son of Ereshguna, it is good," he said, contented once more now that he thought he was being obeyed—even as Engibil was contented when he thought he was being obeyed, regardless of where the truth really lay. Smiling, he went on, "Is it not so, after all, that in the dark one woman is the same as the next?"

Sharur did not answer. He thought back to the Imhursaggi slave woman with whom he had lain after coming back from the mountains of Alashkurru. She had not been the same from one round to the next: fire when she reckoned she was serving the gods, ice when ministering to Sharur's lusts alone. That being so, how could Kimash presume to say another woman might—no, another woman *would*—satisfy Sharur as well as Ningal?

Kimash was the lugal. He could say what he pleased. Who in Gibil would presume to tell him he was wrong?

Again, he took Sharur's silence for agreement. "I thank you for your labor on my behalf and on behalf of the city of Gibil, son of Ereshguna. As I said, I shall reward you. You have but to choose, and the woman you desire shall be yours, even unto one of my own daughters. Go now, and speak to me again when you have made your choice. I await your return."

"The mighty lugal is generous. The mighty lugal is kind." Sharur bowed once more. *Generous indeed, to give me anything except what I truly want.*

"The house of Ereshguna is mighty in my aid," Kimash said—generously. He clapped his hands. "Inadapa!" The steward, who had gone, reappeared as if by magic. "Ina-dapa, conduct the son of Ereshguna to his home once more."

"Mighty lugal, I obey," Inadapa said. *Of course Inadapa obeys*, Sharur thought. *What else is he good for?* The steward turned to him. "Son of Ereshguna, I will conduct you to your home once more."

Sharur's eyes filled with sudden tears when he stepped from the gloom of the palace out into bright sunshine once more. He said, "You need not come home with me, steward to the lugal. Believe me, I know the way."

"Very well," Inadapa said, rather to Sharur's surprise: he had thought the steward would obey Kimash's instructions in all particulars, simply because it was the lugal who had given them. Seeing Sharur startled, Inadapa explained, "The mighty lugal gives his servitors many duties. The gods, however, give them only so much time in which to do those duties."

"Ah," Sharur said; that did indeed make sense. "Go back to your duties, then, Inadapa." But the steward had already gone.

Up the Street of Smiths Sharur trudged. Every step seemed harder than the one before, as if he were walking uphill, though the Street of Smiths lay on ground as level as any in Gibil. His father had told him to accept the word of the god. Kimash the lugal not only had told him to accept the word of the god but had sought to sweeten that with the promise of whatever woman in Gibil he wanted (save one woman only) and her bride-price as well.

*Believe the god. Listen to the god.* Sharur kicked at the dirt as he walked along. Gods could err, just as men could. Enimhursag had slain a Zuabi—the wrong Zuabi—at the inn where Sharur stayed, thinking he was slaying a spy. Engibil could miss magic that was meant to be missed.

Or Engibil might simply lie, although Sharur could see no reason why he would.

But Sharur seemed to be the only one who considered those possibilities. He thought he understood Kimash's reasons for neglecting them, just as Kimash thought he understood Sharur's reasons for believing them. Ereshguna? Well, Sharur's father had heard Engibil; he had not heard Mitas and Kessis. Sharur was the only one who had heard them, and what was his own word worth, against that of Engibil?

"No one believes me," he muttered, and scuffed along with his head down.

He did not see the fever demon perched on a wall, not till too late. Batwings flapping furiously, the demon flew into his face. Its foul breath filled his mouth. He staggered back in horror and dismay. Only too late did he reach for the amulet with Engibil's eyes he wore on his belt. Only too late did he drive the demon from him with the amulet. The demon fled, screeching, but triumphant laughter filled the screeches. The demon knew it had sickened him.

He knew it, too. His steps, already laggard, slowed still further. By the time he reached his father's house, he was staggering. Ereshguna was dickering with a smith. On seeing Sharur, he broke off in alarm. "My son!" he exclaimed. "What has happened to you?"

"Fever demon." Sharur got the words out through chattering teeth. Even in the heat of Gibil's summer, he shivered.

"Have to be careful of those demons," the smith said, clicking his tongue between his teeth. It was good advice. Like so much good advice, it came too late to do any good.

Ereshguna shouted for his slaves. Two men and the Imhursaggi woman with whom Sharur had lain came running at his summons. "Put Sharur on blankets," he told them. "Put wet cloths on his head. A fever demon has breathed into his mouth." The men helped support Sharur, who was wobbling on his feet, as he went into the courtyard and lay down in the shade of the southern wall.

"Fetch blankets, as the master said," one of the men told the other. "He should not lie on the naked ground." The second slave nodded and hurried off. So did the slave woman.

He came back, blankets in his arm, along with the woman, who carried rags and a pot of water. The two men raised Sharur, first at the shoulders, then at the hips, so they could get the blankets under him. "Is that not better, master's son?" one of them asked with a slave's solicitude, sticky as honey.

"Better," he said vaguely. His wits were already wandering. He told himself over and over he was a fool for not having seen the fever demon sooner. A man could die of the sickness a demon breathed into him. Regardless of how often he repeated them, no thoughts wanted to stay in his mind. He drifted from thinking he was a fool for not having seen the fever demon to thinking he was a fool for believing Kessis and Mitas to thinking he was a fool for not having gladly accepted Kimash's offer of one of his daughters and bride-price to boot to thinking he was a fool for worrying about women, considering how he felt.

Through it all, the one thing that did not change was that he thought himself a fool.

The Imhursaggi slave woman dropped a rag into the pot of water, then wrung it out and set it on his forehead. "It is cool," she said in her quiet voice. "It will help make you cool."

"I thank you," Sharur said. For a little while, when the damp linen first touched him, the demon's fever fled, and he was himself again, or someone close to himself. But the fever was stronger than a cold compress. It quickly came back, and his wits went their own way once more.

"Will you watch him?" one of the men asked the woman. "Will you tend to him?"

"I will watch him," she answered. "I will tend to him. It is easier work than most they might give me." The men went away. The woman soaked another compress, wrung it out, and set it on Sharur's forehead to replace the one that the heat of the day and the heat of his fever had dried. Her hands were cool and damp and deft. He noticed—as much as he noticed anything then. She sat beside him, humming a hymn to Enimhursag.

Somehow, he recognized it for what it was. Had his mind been fully under the control of his will, he would have known Enimhursag had no power here, not in the heart of the city of the god who was his rival. But he did not think of that. He had forgotten where he was. He thought of Enimhursag, and of Enimhursag's hunt for him. He thought Enimhursag was hunting him again, or perhaps that Enimhursag had never stopped hunting him.

He moaned and writhed on the blankets. The wet rag fell off onto the ground beside him. The Imhursaggi slave stopped humming. "Lie easy," she said, and put the compress back on his head. And, because he no longer heard the hymn, he did lie easy for a bit. But, seeing him relax, the Imhursaggi woman also relaxed, and began to hum once more. That brought fear flooding back, as melting mountain snow brought the Yarmuk's flood every spring.

Before long, though, his mother and his sister came out into the courtyard, both of them exclaiming over him. They dismissed the slave woman and took over caring for him themselves. "There—do you see?" Betsilim said triumphantly to Nanadirat. "He is better already."

His sister set a hand on his forehead. "He is still hot as a smelting fire," she said, worry in her voice.

"The demon only just now breathed its foul breath into him," his mother answered, sounding as if she was trying to reassure herself and Nanadirat both. "He will mend."

"He had better." Nanadirat stared fiercely down at Sharur. "I am so angry at him. How could he not spy a fever demon waiting to pounce?"

Betsilim wrung out a new compress and started to put it on Sharur, but he tried to roll away from her. "No, no," she said, as she had when he was very small. "You have to hold still. You have to rest."

He heard her and Nanadirat as if from very far away. Everything seemed very far away, his own body very much included. He had quieted for a moment when his mother and sister replaced the slave woman, but not because he preferred their touch to hers, only because he no longer heard her humming the hymn to Enimhursag. He tried to explain that to them, but forgot what he was going to say before the words could pass his lips.

His spirit drifted away from his body, almost as if he had become a ghost while still living. He wondered if ghosts were as confused as he was, then wondered what he had been wondering about, and then wondered if he had been wondering.

Huzziyas the wanax raised a cup to toast his health. An army of spearmen and donkey-drawn chariots drove another, identically equipped, army back against a canal, trapping it. Some men shouted Engibil's name. Some shouted Enimhursag's. Which were which? He could not tell. The army trapped against the canal broke like a shattered cup.

Ningal's face drifted over him like a full moon. He reached up to touch it and it broke like a shattered cup. He started to cry. Suddenly, without warning, everything went white. *I am dead*, he thought. *The fever has slain me. Now I am a ghost, as my grandfather is. I will hunt down that fever demon and pull off its wings. How it will wail!*

He heard it wailing already, though he had not yet begun the hunt. Then he heard a woman's voice—Ningal's? No, it was another's. "Fix that compress, Mother," Nanadirat said. "I don't think he wants it to cover his eyes. Did you hear him moan?"

"I heard him," Betsilim said. "The fever has sent him out of his head. But maybe you are right." Color and shapes—swirling, floating shapes with no plain meaning—filled Sharur's vision once more. Maybe he wasn't dead after all. The demon would escape, to sicken other people.

"How is he?" a man's voice asked. Huzziyas the wanax? Kimash the lugal? Engibil the god? Whoever it was, his voice sounded very much like that of Sharur's brother Tupsharru. But Tupsharru was not in the mountains of Alashkurru, was he? Sharur knew he was in the mountains, in the snowy mountains. How else could he have been so cold?

After a while, it started raining on him. So he thought at first, at any rate. Then he wondered whether the gods were angry at him or pleased with him, for it was raining beer. The gods talked among themselves. "Sit him up a little more, can't you? It's spilling all over him," a goddess said.

"I'm sorry," a god answered. "Here, try again." More rain or beer or whatever it was spilled on Sharur's face and chest.

"You have to drink, Sharur," another goddess said.

Dimly, he wondered why the gods had voices so much like those of his mother and sister and brother. They were gods, though. They could do as they pleased. And if they ordered him to drink, he could only obey. Drink he did, even if he choked a little doing it.

"There, that's better," the goddess who sounded like his sister said.

He had pleased the gods. He took that thought with him as he spiraled down into the dark.

When Sharur woke, he wondered for a moment whether the mud bricks of the house in which he had lived his whole life had finally fallen down. More to the point, he wondered if they had fallen down on him. He certainly felt as if something large and heavy had collapsed on him.

Raising his head took all the strength he had. Sitting not far away from him was his father. "Sharur?" Ereshguna said softly. "My son?"

"Yes," Sharur said—or rather, that was what he tried to say. Only a harsh, wordless croak passed his lips. Trying to speak made him feel how weak he was. Even holding his eyelids open took an effort.

But the croak seemed to satisfy his father. "You understand me!" Ereshguna exclaimed.

"Yes," Sharur said. This time, it was a recognizable word. Sharur noticed his mouth tasted as if someone had spilled a chamberpot into it. He lay back down flat; holding his head up seemed more trouble than it was worth. Those few moments of it were making him pant as if he had run all the way from Imhursag to Gibil.

Ereshguna ran: out of the courtyard and into the house, crying, "Sharur has his wits about him again!"

Then he came running back to Sharur, followed closely by Tupsharru and Betsilim and Nanadirat, with the house slaves a little farther behind. His family hugged him and kissed him and made much of him. He lay there and accepted it; he had not the strength to do anything but lie there and accept it. His mother and sister both let tears stream down their cheeks. A little at a time, he realized he must have come very close to dying.

"I'm all right," he whispered.

"You're no such thing," his mother said indignantly. "Don't talk nonsense. Look at you." He couldn't look at himself; that would have meant lifting his head again, which was beyond him. But Betsilim was doing the looking for him: "You're nothing but skin stretched over bones. I've seen starving beggars with more flesh on them."

He tried to shrug. Even that wasn't easy. Nanadirat asked, "If we give you bread and beer, can you chew and swallow?"

"I think so," he answered. "It was raining beer on me not so long ago. The gods made it rain beer on me not so long ago. I remember." He felt proud of remembering anything.

His mother and brother and sister seemed less impressed. With a distinct sniff in her voice, Nanadirat said, "That wasn't the gods. That was us. And it wouldn't have been raining beer on you if you'd drunk it the way you were supposed to."

"Oh," he said, feeling foolish. "I suppose a lot of the things I think happened didn't really, then. Huzziyas the wanax didn't come here to drink my health, did he? He raised the cup, and . . ."

Betsilim and Nanadirat were looking at each other. He recognized their expressions: they were trying not to laugh, and not succeeding very well. Betsilim said, "My son, I am surprised you remember anything at all of the past five days, even if you remember things that are not so."

"Five . . . days?" Sharur said slowly. "Was I out of my head for five days? It's a wonder my spirit found its way back to my body."

"We think so, too," Betsilim said, and started to cry again. Nanadirat put an arm around her mother's shoulder.

The Imhursaggi slave woman, who had gone into the house, came out once more carrying a tray. "Here is bread," she said. "Here is beer." She set the tray on the ground in front of Betsilim.

Tupsharru came up and supported Sharur in a half-sitting position. A god with his voice had done that while Sharur lay sick. No. Sharur laughed at himself. That had been—that must have been—his wits wandering again.

He looked down at himself, now that he could. He had indeed lost flesh, although he was not so thin as his mother made him out to be. Nanadirat held a cup up to his mouth. He took a sip of sour beer, then swallowed. That felt wonderful, like rain for a flower after a long dry spell.

But Nanadirat did not merely want to rain on him, to make him bloom. By the way she tried to pour beer into him, she wanted to flood him. Like a canal that had fallen into disrepair, he could not take in as much as she wanted to give him. To keep himself from drowning, he raised his arm. That did more than he had intended: not only did it stop her from giving him the beer, it knocked the cup from her hand. The cup flew against the wall that shaded him and shattered.

"Maybe he has not got his wits about him after all," Tupsharru said. But he sounded more amused than annoyed.

"I'm sorry," Sharur said, feeling very foolish as he stared at the shards of the broken cup. He remembered . . . But no, that had surely been nonsense, too.

"You need not be sorry," Betsilim said. "Your sister tried to give you too much too fast." She turned to the slave woman. "Fetch another cup."

"I obey," the slave said, as she had when Sharur ordered her to lie with him. She hurried back into the house.

"Bread, please?" Sharur said.

Betsilim tore off a piece of bread from the loaf that sat on the tray. Sharur reached out to take it. Instead of handing it to him, his mother put it straight into his mouth, as if he were a baby. Had he felt a little stronger, that might have made him angry. As things were, he chewed and swallowed without complaint. "Is it good?" his mother asked, again as she might have done when he was very small.

He nodded. "More?" he said hopefully, and Betsilim fed him again.

The Imhursaggi slave woman came out with a new cup to replace the one Sharur had broken. Nanadirat filled it with the dipper and offered it to him. This time, he drank without spilling any. It made him feel very strong. "Another cup?" he said.

"Yes, but this will be your last for now," his sister said. "Too much all at once after too long without much will make you sick again."

"I know how we'll be able to tell when he's truly better," Tupsharru said, mischief in his voice.

Betsilim was so glad for the words, she did not hear the mischief. "How?" she asked.

Tupsharru grinned. "When he wants the slave woman, not bread and beer."

Betsilim and Nanadirat both made faces at him. The slave woman looked down at the ground, no expression at all on her face. Sharur watched the byplay without caring much about it. He recalled desire, but it was the last thing on his mind.

He yawned. Maybe the beer was making him sleepy. Maybe it was nothing but his own weakness. "Let me down," he said to Tupsharru. He yawned again as his brother eased him to the blanket. He thought he stayed awake long enough for his head to touch it, but was never quite sure afterwards.

His sleep, this time, was deep and restful, with none of the fever dreams and visions that had troubled his illness. He woke in darkness, only pale moonlight illuminating the courtyard. He felt stronger. Without even thinking about it, he sat up by himself. That proved he was stronger.

He got to his feet. He wobbled a little, but had no trouble staying upright. A chamberpot sat on the ground not far from where he'd lain. He walked over and made water into it, then lay back down on the blanket. He hoped sleep would come again for him, but it did not. Mosquitoes buzzed. One landed on his chest; he felt it walking through the hair there. He slapped at it, and hoped he'd killed it.

His grandfather's ghost spoke in his ear: "You are like an owl, awake while others sleep. You are like a cat, prowling through the night."

"Hardly prowling," Sharur said with a low-voiced laugh. More often than not, his grandfather's ghost was a nuisance, bothering him when he would sooner have paid it no attention. Now, for once, he was glad of its company. Still speaking quietly, he went on, "I greet you. Is it well with you?"

"As well as it can be," the ghost answered. "I have only the memory of bread. I have only the memory of beer. I have only the memory of desire."

Sharur remembered what Tupsharru had said. "As things are right now, I also have only the memory of desire."

The laughter that came from his grandfather's ghost held a bitter edge. "You know not what you say. Soon enough, you will burn like a furnace again, and you will tip up the legs of that slave or give a courtesan copper to suck your prong. I have only the memory, not the thing itself. I shall never have it, never again."

"And even if I slake my lust, what will it mean?" Sharur asked, in his weakness after being ill matching the ghost's self-pity. "I shall not have the one woman I truly want."

"Having any woman is better than having no woman at all." His grandfather's ghost was not about to be outdone. "Having thin beer is better than having no beer at all. Having moldy bread is better than having no bread at all."

"You have the essence of beer. You have the essence of the bread," Sharur reminded him.

"It is not the same." The ghost's sigh was like the breeze blowing through the branches of a dead bush. "And you say nothing about the essence of a woman. Tell me, where shall I find the essence of a woman?''

''That I do not know.'' Sharur smiled in the darkness. ''Were there such a thing, many living men would seek it: I do know that.''

''And the house of Ereshguna would sell it. The house of Ereshguna would profit from it. I know my son.'' The ghost of Sharur's grandfather spoke with a sort of melancholy pride. Then it said, ''I am glad you remain among those with flesh on their bones. When your spirit ran free of your body, I feared you would join me here among the ghosts for some little while, and then drift down into the underworld, into the realm of the forgotten.''

On the blanket, Sharur shivered, though the night was not cold and though he was not feverish. ''Truly I had a narrow escape from death because of the foul breath of the fever demon,'' he said.

''Truly you had a narrow escape from death,'' his grandfather's ghost agreed. ''But while your spirit wandered, you saw more widely than you have while still wearing flesh.''

''I saw more confusedly than I could while still wearing flesh,'' Sharur said. ''Some of it, I suppose, might have been real. Some would have been the real, transmuted by fever. And some, surely, was nothing but fever.''

''Ah, but which was which?'' His grandfather's ghost used a sly tone Sharur had sometimes heard from his father when he had overlooked something. ''Which was real, and which the fever dream?''

''You sound as if you know the answer,'' Sharur said. ''Tell me.''

''The question is the essence, not the answer. I am a ghost. I am a thing of essences.'' Sharur's grandfather's ghost sighed again. ''But not the essence of a woman. Find a way to boil off the essence of a woman and the ghosts of men would give you whatever you wanted for it.''

''They would give the essence of gold, no doubt,'' Sharur said. ''Mortals are not things of essences. Tell me: I ask it of you again—which was real, and which the fever dream?''

"The question is the essence, not the answer," his grand-father's ghost repeated. "And now I shall go."

Sharur had not known the ghost was there until it spoke. He could not have proved it was gone now. Was it mocking him, or had it tried to tell him something important? Before he could decide, he fell asleep again.

Slowly, Sharur recovered from the sickness the fever demon had breathed into him. His strength came back, little by little; he ate bread and salt fish and drank beer to restore the flesh of which the fever demon had robbed him. One day, he noticed that, when the Imhursaggi slave woman brought him food and drink, he was eyeing her body. She noticed, too, and departed as quickly as she could. He thought about ordering her back, but in the end did not bother. Though desire had returned, it was not so urgent as to make him want to lie with her.

A few days after that, he left his home and went out into Gibil once more. His steps were slow and halting, so slow and halting as to make him realize that, while he had regained much strength, he was still a long way from having regained it all.

He bought beans fried in fat from a man who cooked them over a brazier set up on a small table he would carry from place to place. The fellow handed them to him in a twist of date-palm leaf. Eating gave Sharur an excuse to stand still and rest. His weakness angered him, but he could do nothing about it.

People and beasts of burden surged past him. He smiled to watch a couple of little naked farm boys with long switches chivvying ducks along toward the market square. The ducks fussed and complained, but kept on moving. Some of them, the lucky ones, might be kept for egg layers. The rest would soon be seethed or roasted. Though few foreigners came to Gibil these days, the Giblut still traded busily among themselves.

Sharur had almost finished his beans when a small, thin

fellow came up to the man who prepared them and said, "Let me have some of those, if you please." He opened his right hand to display several broken bits of copper. The cook held out his own hand. He took the copper bits, hefted them, nodded in satisfaction, and gave the newcomer a ladleful of beans in a leaf. The fellow beamed at him. "Thank you, friend. These'll fill the hole in my belly."

He spoke with a Zuabi accent. At first, that was all Sharur noticed about him, for it stood out these days. Then he took a longer look at the fellow. "I know you!" he exclaimed.

"No, my master, I fear you are mis—" The Zuabi stopped. His eyes went wide and round in his narrow, clever face. He bowed very low. "No, my master, I am the one who is mistaken. It is an honor to see you again."

"Come. Walk with me." Sharur ate the last of his beans, threw the date-palm leaf on the ground, licked his fingers clean, and wiped them on his kilt. "Tell me how you come to be in Gibil, when we last met outside Zuabu."

"As you might guess, my calling brings me here," replied the man who had tried to rob Sharur's caravan as it returned from the Alashkurru Mountains. He popped a handful of fried beans into his mouth.

"Yes, I might have guessed that," Sharur agreed. "And what, if you would be so kind as to tell me one thing more, have you come to Gibil to steal?"

"I should not tell you what I have come to Gibil to steal," the Zuabi thief said, "for Enzuabu commanded me to come to Gibil to steal it."

Sharur walked along without saying anything. He knew, as the thief knew, the Zuabi would not have been able to steal anything in Gibil without the mercy Sharur had shown, and without Sharur's letting him steal a token bit of jewelry to placate his god.

"I will tell you my name," the thief said. "I am called Habbazu."

"I will tell you my name," Sharur returned. "I am called Sharur."

They bowed to each other. Habbazu said, "And you are

the son of a master merchant? So your men said, back by Zuabu.'' Sharur nodded. Habbazu went on, ''And I am the son of a thief, and each of us follows his father's trade. Tell me, master merchant's son, if a thief could have robbed you and slain you while you lay sleeping but did no more than pass by in the night, what would you owe that man?''

''In Gibil, we do not reckon thievery an honorable trade,'' Sharur answered. ''A man owes it to himself not to do anything dishonorable. He does not need any other man to owe him anything for refraining.''

''We think differently in Zuabu,'' Habbazu said. ''With us, thievery is work like any other. If it were not honorable work, would the god of the city command us to undertake it?''

''I know little of the ways of gods,'' Sharur told him.

''Of course you know little of that—you are a Gibli.'' Habbazu raised a bushy eyebrow. ''The god of Gibil drowses. The god of Gibil sleeps.'' Sharur wished Engibil had been drowsier; he wished the god had been sleepier. The thief continued, ''If the god of Gibil were not a drowsy god, if he were not a sleepy god, I would not have come to—'' He broke off.

''—To steal something that belongs to the god?'' Sharur finished for him.

Habbazu walked rapidly along the narrow, twisting street. Sharur had to push himself to keep up with the thief, though he was larger and his legs longer. He got the feeling Habbazu could easily have escaped him, had he so chosen. Sweat rolled down his back. He got the feeling a playful three-year-old could easily have escaped him, had he so chosen.

Slowly, reluctantly, Habbazu said, ''Yes, I am charged to steal something that belongs to the god of Gibil.'' He held up a hand to keep Sharur from speaking. ''By Enzuabu I swear, master merchant's son, I have not come to Gibil to take anything of great value from the temple of Engibil. I have not come to Gibil to impoverish the god of the city.''

''Then why *have* you come?'' Sharur burst out. ''Has

Enzuabu ordered you to steal something that has no value?''

Before, Habbazu had looked uncertain about how much he should say. Now he looked uncertain in a different way. "It may be so," he answered. "For all I know, Enzuabu aims to embarrass Engibil before the other gods, to show that something once in the house of the god of Gibil is now in the house of the god of Zuabu. The gods score points off their neighbors no less than men."

"What you say is true," Sharur admitted. "If someone besides me had caught you, though, thief and son of a thief, what would your fate have been? Did your god care what your fate would have been? Or did Enzuabu think, *He is only a man. What does it matter if the Giblut torture him to death?*"

"I am Enzuabu's servant," Habbazu said with dignity.

"Are you Enzuabu's slave? Are you Enzuabu's dog? Are you an Imhursaggi, with the god looking out from behind your eyes more often than you do yourself?" Sharur asked. "Is your ensi no more a shield from Enzuabu than that?"

"I am not a slave. I am not a dog. Enzuabu be praised, I am not an Imhursaggi," the thief replied. "Even Engibil, I have heard, can give orders from time to time. When Engibil tells a Gibli he shall do this or he shall not do that, is the god obeyed, or is he ignored and forgotten?"

"He is obeyed." Sharur spoke in grudging tones made no less grudging because, had he dared ignore Engibil's command to him, he could have given Dimgalabzu the bride-price for Ningal.

"Then why complain when a man of another city also obeys his god?" Habbazu said. "How is he different from you?"

"He is different in that he might harm my god. He is different in that he might harm my city." Sharur moved slowly into the shade of a wall. "Shall we sit? I am recovering from the foul breath of a fever demon, and have not yet regained all my strength."

Habbazu sank down beside him. "It shall be as you say. I am obliged to you. I do not see, though, how I might harm your city. I do not see how I might harm your god, except perhaps, as I say, to make him a laughingstock before the other gods. No god dies of laughter aimed at him over a small thing. No man dies of laughter aimed at him over a small thing, either, though some men wish they could.''

"What is this small thing you would steal?'' Sharur asked. "What is this small thing Enzuabu would have you steal? You still have not told me what it might be.'' As a merchant will, he put other words behind the words he spoke, using his voice to suggest to Habbazu that, if the thing was small enough, he might stand aside while the thief stole it. He had no such intention, but had no qualms about creating the impression that he did, either.

And create that impression he did. Habbazu waggled his fingers in a gesture of appreciation. "It is the smallest of things, master merchant's son. It is the least of things, merchant of Gibil. Engibil would not miss it, were it to vanish from his temple. Your god would not note its passing, were it to disappear from his shrine. It is, after all, only a cup.''

"Mighty Engibil has among his treasures many cups he would miss greatly,'' Sharur said. "He has cups of gold and cups of silver, cups for drinking beer and cups for drinking date wine.''

"This is no cup of gold. This is no cup of silver,'' the thief from Zuabu assured him. "This is only a cup of clay, such as a tavern might employ. If it falls to the ground, it will shatter. Sharur, I speak nothing but the truth when I say that the god's treasury would be better off without such a worthless, ugly piece.''

"If it be worthless, why does Enzuabu want it?'' Sharur said, as he had before.

Habbazu shrugged. "I am not one to know the mind of the gods. I have given you my best guess: that the god of my city wants nothing more than to embarrass the god of yours before their fellows.''

It was, in fact, far from a bad guess, and better than any Sharur had come up with for himself—until this moment.

Keeping his tone light and casual, he asked, "Is it by any chance an Alashkurri cup?"

"Why, yes, as a matter of fact, it is." The thief gave Sharur a look both puzzled and respectful. "How could you know that?"

"I know all manner of strange things." Sharur got to his feet. It was a struggle, and he was panting by the time he made it; his body still craved rest. When Habbazu stayed on his haunches, enjoying the coolness of the shadowed dirt on which he sat, Sharur said, "Rise. Come with me. I think my father should hear the tale you tell. I think Kimash the lugal should perhaps hear the tale you tell."

"Kimash the lugal?" Habbazu spoke in some alarm. "What will he do to me?" Without waiting for Sharur's reply, he answered his own question: "He is a man claiming the power of a god. He will do whatever he likes to me. I am a thief, come to steal from his city. He will not welcome me with beer and barley porridge and salt fish and onions."

"Do you think not?" Sharur raised an eyebrow. "You may be surprised."

"I am surprised whenever I deal with Giblut," Habbazu answered. "Sometimes the surprises are for the good. Sometimes—more often—they run in the opposite direction."

"True, Kimash the lugal may not welcome you with beer and onions," Sharur said. "Instead, he may welcome you with gold and silver."

"You are pleased to joke with me, knowing you could have me slaughtered like a lamb because this is your city." Habbazu paused and studied Sharur's face. "No. You are not joking. You mean what you say. Why do you mean what you say?" His own face, sly and thin, radiated suspicion. He opened his mouth, then closed it again.

Sharur recognized those signs, having seen them many times before in dickers. Habbazu had drawn his own conclusion about why the lugal might welcome him with gold and silver. Whatever that conclusion was, he did not intend to share it with Sharur. No matter what else the thief was, he was no fool. His conclusion was likely to lie somewhere on the right road—that the cup was something which would work to Kimash's advantage and to Engibil's disadvantage. Sharur realized he had told Habbazu too much, but no man, nor even a god, could recall words once spoken.

He wondered if he should raise the alarm and have Habbazu hunted through the streets of Gibil. That would take no more than a shout. But Engibil had in his temple several Alashkurri cups. Which was the one into which the gods of the mountains had poured their power? Sharur did not know, and did not know how to learn . . . unless Habbazu could tell him.

"Come with me to the house of my father," he told the thief.

"I will come with you to the house of your father." Habbazu did rise then, and bowed to Sharur. "Perhaps what you desire and what Enzuabu desires may both be accomplished."

"Perhaps this is so," Sharur agreed, nodding. Enzuabu wanted the Alashkurri cup stolen from Engibil's temple. Sharur also wanted it removed from that temple. Sharur was willing to return it to the mountains of Alashkurru, though other notions had also crossed his mind. He was not sure what Enzuabu would do with it if it came into the thief-god's hands.

He did not ask Habbazu whether Enzuabu had spoken of his plans for the cup. Having already put more thoughts than he wanted into Habbazu's mind, he did not wish to give the thief any further ideas he had not already had.

Habbazu looked around with interest as he and Sharur made their way toward the Street of Smiths. "Poverty does not pinch Gibil," he remarked. "Hunger does not stalk this city. In Zuabu, they say women here are poor. In Zuabu, they say women and children here starve."

"Many people say many things that are not true about Gibil and the Giblut," Sharur answered. He looked at Habbazu out of the corner of his eye. "Many gods say many things that are not true about Gibil and the Giblut. If this were not so, Zuabi, would you be here now?"

"After all this time, I doubt my skeleton would have much meat left on its bones," the thief said coolly. "My ghost would be wandering my city, telling anyone who could hear what vicious, wanton murderers the men of Gibil were."

That struck Sharur as an honest answer. He shook his head in bemusement. Getting an honest answer from a thief was like plucking sweet, fat dates from the branches of a thornbush.

When they came out onto the Street of Smiths, Habbazu pointed down its length. "What is that great building there, the one that looks to be almost the size of the temple to your city god?"

"That is the lugal's palace," Sharur replied. "That is the building wherein the mighty Kimash makes his residence, as his father and grandfather did before him."

"All that, for a mere man?" Habbazu shook his head in slow wonder. Then his eyes lit, as if torches had been kindled behind them. "He must have many treasures. And how can a mere man guard what is his as well as a god?" Instead of being angry at the lugal for usurping the god's place, he saw that usurpation as an opportunity for himself.

"Do you know, Zuabi," Sharur said, "you are farther along the path toward thinking like a man of Gibil than you may suspect."

The thief drew himself up, the very image of affronted rectitude. "You have caught me," he said. "You have spared me. Do you think this gives you the right to insult me?"

"I meant it for a compliment," Sharur said mildly. That Habbazu made a joke of it meant he did not take it seriously, either, no matter what he said. Sharur thought Enzuabu would take it seriously. Wherever men looked first to their own advantage and only then toward service to their gods, there the unquestioned, unchallenged rule of the gods tottered.

And, as Habbazu walked along the Street of Smiths, he watched with keen interest. His eyes flicked to left and right, studying donkey trains, peering into smithies and shops. "We have smiths in Zuabu," he said after a while. "I do not think we have so many smiths as do you Giblut. We have merchants. I do not think we have merchants so busy as do you Giblut."

Sharur's chest puffed out with pride. "Trade here is slow these days, too," he said. Habbazu did not look as if he believed him, though that was simple truth.

Ereshguna was pressing a stylus into a tablet of damp clay when Sharur led Habbazu into his home. His father looked unhappy as he wrote, which likely meant he was reckoning up accounts. As trade with other cities and other lands declined, the accounts gave less and less reason for a man to look anything but unhappy.

Thus, when Sharur and the thief came in, Ereshguna set down the tablet with every sign of relief. "I greet you, my son," he said, bowing. He turned to Habbazu and bowed again. "And I greet your companion as well, though I have not yet had the pleasure and honor of making his acquaintance."

"Father, I present to you Habbazu, who visits Gibil from the city of Zuabu," Sharur said. "He practices the Zuabi trade. Habbazu, here is Ereshguna my father, the head of the house of Ereshguna."

Habbazu bowed. He had polished manners when he chose to use them. "I greet you, Ereshguna of the house of Ereshguna. Your fame is wide, as is the fame of your house. But you should be most famous for the mercy your splendid son showed a thief who intended to steal from his caravan outside Zuabu."

"Ah." Ereshguna's eyebrows rose. "You are not any Zuabi thief. You are that particular Zuabi thief. I did not know your name."

"Yes, I am that particular thief." Habbazu bowed once more.

"When I met him outside Zuabu, I did not know his name," Sharur said.

His grandfather's ghost shouted in his ear, and, no doubt,

in Ereshguna's: "Are you mad, boy? Has the sun baked the wits from your head? Have the demons of idiocy crept in through your ears and built a home between them? Why do you bring a Zuabi thief into this house? Do you want to wake up in the morning and find half the walls missing?"

"It will be all right, my father," Ereshguna murmured in the tone people often used when ghosts interrupted their conversations with fellow mortals. Habbazu looked up at the ceiling and said nothing. That tone would have been familiar to him, too. Ereshguna clapped his hands together and, raising his voice, called for bread and onions and beer.

He set out an extra, partly filled cup for the ghost of Sharur's grandfather, surely in the hope that, having consumed the essence of the beer, the ghost would grow gay or grow sleepy and would in any case shut up. To Sharur's relief, that hope, or at least the last part of it, was realized.

Having drunk, having eaten, Ereshguna asked Sharur, "Why has Habbazu come to Gibil to practice the trade of the Zuabut?" *Why did you bring him here?* underlay the words.

In a voice as light and casual as he could make it, Sharur said, "Enzuabu charged Habbazu to steal something from the temple of Engibil: a cup of baked clay that came to the god's house from the mountains of Alashkurru."

"Really?" Ereshguna said. Sharur nodded. So did Habbazu. Ereshguna plucked at his beard. "Isn't that interesting?"

"I thought so, Father," Sharur said, having been too well brought up to say something as impolite as, *What did I tell you?*

"Why such a fuss over one worthless cup?" Habbazu asked.

Sharur did not directly answer that question. Sharur could not directly answer that question, having sworn in the market square of Imhursag by all the gods of Kudurru that he would not. Instead, he said, "Think, thief. Would Enzuabu have sent you to Gibil to steal one worthless cup?"

"Who know what a god would do?" Habbazu returned.

"Who can guess what is in a god's mind?" But he leaned forward, his sharp-featured face alert. "Speaking as a mere man, though, I say you are likely right. And so I ask a different question: What is the true value of this cup that seems worthless?"

Again, Sharur did not answer. Again, Sharur could not answer. His father had taken no oath to speak of the power contained in the thing from the Alashkurru Mountains only to the folk of his own city. But Ereshguna said only, "We are not certain ourselves." Sharur thought that wise; the less Habbazu heard, the less Enzuabu would learn.

Being no fool, Habbazu noticed he was getting something less than straightforward answers. "You know more than you are saying," he remarked, although without any great rancor.

"Yes, we know more than we are saying," Sharur agreed. "You have come into our city to steal from our god. Should we be delighted at that? Should we drink ourselves foolish and dance in the street because of it? You have not come here to help Gibil. You have not come here to help the Giblut."

"This is so," Habbazu said frankly. His eyes flicked from Sharur to Ereshguna and back again, as they had flicked from donkey train to smithy as he walked along the Street of Smiths. In easy, relaxed tones, he went on, "If, though, you hated me as you might hate me, you would bind my hands and feet and deliver me to the temple of Engibil trussed like a hog for the slaughter, that the god of this city might punish me for my crime."

"Nothing prevents our doing that now," Ereshguna said.

"That is so, my master," Habbazu said with a polite bow. "But it is not the first thought in your minds, as it would be had I fallen into the hands of, say, the Aggasherut. They would have given me over to Eniaggasher at once, to let the goddess do her worst to me."

"We are not Aggasherut, for which I am glad," Sharur replied. He scratched his cheek, at the line where his beard stopped. "Shall we bargain, thief from Zuabu?"

Habbazu smiled at him. "What else have we been do-ing?"

Sharur inclined his head. "You speak the truth; there can be no doubt of it. The question is, how much loyalty do you owe to a god who has twice sent you to steal from Giblut and twice left you at the mercy of Giblut?"

"That is half the question," Habbazu said. "The other half is, how much loyalty do I owe to the Giblut who twice showed me mercy?"

"Even so," Ereshguna agreed. "Also to be remembered is the question of how much mercy the said Giblut will continue to show you."

"Believe me, my master, this question is never far from my mind," the thief said. "You still have not said what you would have me do. Until I learn this, how can I judge whether I am more loyal to Enzuabu or more grateful to you for your mercy?"

"That is a fair question," Ereshguna said slowly. Sharur nodded. It was, in fact, *the* question of the moment. Sharur felt fairly certain that he wanted Habbazu to steal the Alash-kurri cup from Engibil's temple if he could. Of what should happen after that, of what would happen after that, he was less sure.

He did not want Habbazu to take the cup back to En-zuabu. The god of Zuabu might keep it for himself or might return it to the great gods of the Alashkurrut. In neither case would Gibil or the Giblut gain any credit with those great gods.

If Habbazu stole the cup and promised to deliver it into the hands of Sharur and Ereshguna, could he be trusted? Or would he say he would help the Giblut who had been mer-ciful to him and then try to escape from Gibil with the cup and take it to the god who had ordered him to steal it?

If he did deliver it into the hands of Sharur and Eresh-guna, what should they do with it? Sharur knew returning it to the great gods of the Alashkurrut would be the sure course, the safe course. He did not know whether he cared about the sure course, the safe course. The notion of smashing the cup, letting the power of the gods spill out of it, held an appalling sweetness. Sharur had suffered. Why should not the gods of the Alashkurrut suffer in turn?

He glanced over to his father and saw the same questions in Ereshguna's eyes. Habbazu saw the intently thoughtful expressions on both their faces, too. "Perhaps, my masters," he said with surprising delicacy, "this is a matter you wish to discuss further between yourselves before telling me what you decide."

"Perhaps," Sharur said. "But perhaps, while we discuss this matter between ourselves, you will slide out the door and never again be seen by a Gibli who knows you for what you are."

Habbazu bowed. "Perhaps," he said with a broad smile.

Sharur's grandfather's ghost broke into the conversation: "Best thing you can do is knock the cursed Zuabi thief over the head and fling his body into a canal. No one will miss him, not in the least."

"No, ghost of my grandfather. It would not do," Sharur said. He said no more than that, not with Habbazu in earshot. But not only did the thief know too much, Enzuabu also knew too much. If Habbazu vanished, the god of Zuabu was only too likely to send forth another thief, one Sharur would not be able to recognize.

"My son is right, ghost of my father," Ereshguna said. His thoughts and Sharur's might have been twin streams of molten bronze poured into the same mold. After a moment, he spoke directly to Sharur in a low voice: "I think we have no choice but to let the thief pay a call on the temple. He and only he knows which cup among the many in Engibil's treasure contains the power of the Alashkurri gods. Once he has it, once we learn which it is, we go on from there."

"Father, I think you are wise. I too think we have no other choice," Sharur said, nodding. He turned to Habbazu. "You will pay a call on the temple. You will bring forth this Alashkurri cup. If we aid you, will you deliver it into our hands, not into the hands of Enzuabu?"

Habbazu hesitated. Had he agreed at once, with fulsome

promises, Sharur would have been sure he was lying. As things were, he could not say with certainty whether the thief lied or told the truth—which, no doubt, was exactly what Habbazu wanted. He scowled, angry at himself and Habbazu both.

At last, the thief said, "I will deliver the cup into your hands, not into the hands of Enzuabu. Were it not for your forbearance, Enzuabu could not have sent me here. Were it not for your mercy, Enzuabu could not have ordered me to Gibil. I remember my debts. I repay them."

"It is good," Sharur said, hoping the thief remembered debts to men more than whatever he owed to the god of his city.

"Speak to me of the priests of Engibil," Habbazu said. "Speak to me of their comings and goings. Speak to me of their prayers and offerings. Speak to me of their duties and rituals, that I may avoid them while they perform those duties and rituals."

Now Sharur and Ereshguna hesitated in turn. In revealing, would they also be betraying? And then, before either of them could reply, Engibil spoke, his voice resounding inside Sharur's mind as he said, *You shall come at once to my temple. You shall come alone to my temple. You shall obey me.*

# 7

"I will come at once to your temple. I will come alone to your temple. I will obey you," Sharur said, and he left his father's house, the house in which he had dwelt all his days, and he walked up the Street of Smiths toward Engibil's temple. When the god spoke in that way, a man could not disobey.

Engibil must have spoken to Ereshguna at the same time as he ordered Sharur to come before him, for Ereshguna neither exclaimed in alarm nor shouted out questions. Habbazu did both, but Sharur took no notice of Habbazu, not then. All he noticed was the god's resistless command.

As he walked up the Street of Smiths, his own thoughts slowly began to return. His will, however, remained enslaved to the god's greater, stronger will. He could not stop his feet from moving closer to the temple, one step after another. But he could be bitterly amused at his folly—and also at Habbazu's. So the thief had believed, as Sharur had believed, Engibil to be a drowsy god, a sleepy god? Would they had been right! Now Engibil, not so drowsy, not so sleepy, had caught them plotting against him. What would he do? *Whatever he wants*, Sharur thought. Fear made him tremble—all but his legs, which kept walking, walking, walking.

The temple loomed before him. The priest Burshagga stood waiting in front of the entrance as he approached. Sharur's mouth shaped words: "I am come at the command of the great god. I am come at the order of the mighty god."

"This I know," Burshagga answered. "I was commanded to wait here. I was ordered to bring you before the god the moment you arrived." His voice was steady, but fear had a home in his eyes. He was used to obeying the orders of Kimash the lugal, not those of Engibil.

Without another word, he turned and walked into the temple. Without another word, Sharur followed him into the temple, as he might have followed—as he often had followed—Kimash's steward Inadapa into the palace of the lugal. But he had never been so afraid, following Inadapa.

Through the forecourts of the temple they went, Sharur behind Burshagga. Other priests looked up from their tasks as the two men went by, as Kimash the lugal's servants and slaves might have looked up when Inadapa led someone past them. Sharur tried to read their faces. He saw nothing out of the ordinary, but that failed to reassure him. He reckoned the priests simply took his condemnation for granted. No man could successfully oppose a god's direct will. Kimash ruled by distracting Engibil's will, not by opposing it.

Up the many steps to Engibil's audience chamber strode Burshagga. Up the many steps to Engibil's audience chamber strode Sharur after him. Down the steps from Engibil's audience chamber strode no beautiful courtesan, not today. Sharur regretted that. He would have liked his last memories before the god condemned him to be of something beautiful.

His heart pounded as he reached the top of the stairway. He told himself that was because he had climbed one step for each day in a year. But he knew his heart would have pounded no less had Engibil chosen to meet him in the forecourt of the temple, down at the level of the ground.

Burshagga did not precede him into the audience chamber. He gestured to the doorway and said, "The god awaits you within."

Sharur already knew as much; Engibil's radiance, brighter than the sunshine, streamed out through the entranceway. Having no choice but to go forward, he went forward with the best show of spirit he could muster.

Inside Engibil's house on earth, the god sat on his gold-wrapped throne. Sharur cast himself down before Engibil. He felt no shame in doing so; he should have done likewise before the lugal on his throne.

*Rise.* The word resounded soundlessly inside Sharur's head. He could not have disobeyed even had he wanted to. Willing his limbs not to tremble, willing his face to show none of the fear he felt, he got to his feet.

"Great god, mighty god, god who founded this city, god who made this town, I greet you," Sharur said. "Tell me how I may serve you, and all shall be as you desire. You are my master. I am your slave."

"This I know," Engibil said complacently. It pleased him now to speak like a man, to move his lips and let sound come forth. "I have been reflecting on your case, Sharur. I have been contemplating your circumstances, son of Eresh-guna." He folded his arms across his massive chest, awaiting Sharur's reply.

That would have been easier to give, had Sharur had any idea how to answer. "Is it so, great god?" he said, temporizing as he might have done when a rival merchant said something unexpected and confusing during a dicker.

"Son of Ereshguna, it is so," Engibil replied. "Hear now the judgment I have reached concerning you."

Sharur bowed his head. "Great god, I will hear your words. Mighty god, I will obey your words." *What choice have I?* he wondered bitterly.

"My judgment, then, is this," Engibil said. "I have decided I held your oath in my hand too tightly. I have decided I held your oath in my heart too straitly. Thus I ease it; thus I loosen it. You have my leave to borrow from your father bride-price wherewith to pay Dimgalabzu the smith."

"Great god, may I—?" Sharur had intended to try to talk Engibil into reducing whatever punishments he ordained. That was probably hopeless, but, being a merchant and a scion of merchants, he had intended to try. Now what would have been his protest gurgled into silence after a bare handful of words.

He stared into the god's face. Engibil was, as always, divinely perfect, divinely awe-inspiring. Engibil also looked divinely pleased with himself, as if he had settled a problem to his own satisfaction. So, evidently, he had.

But it was not the problem because of which Sharur thought he had been summoned to the temple. He had to conclude, then, that Engibil had not been listening when he and Habbazu and Ereshguna discussed robbing the god's temple.

As Sharur stared at Engibil, so Engibil stared at Sharur. "Are you not pleased, son of Ereshguna?" the god demanded. "Is not your heart gladdened? In my generosity, I give you leave to wed the woman you desire."

He was indeed a lazy god. He could have searched through Sharur's mind to learn why the man before him did not respond as he had expected. Sharur imagined coming before Enimhursag if the god of Gibil's rival city needed to discover something. Enimhursag, if he saw anything out of the ordinary or suspicious, would have torn it from a man by force. But Engibil was content to ask.

And Sharur answered, "Oh, yes, great god, I am pleased. My heart is gladdened, mighty god. Truly you are generous, to give me leave to wed the woman I desire." He spoke the truth there, nothing but the truth. He spoke it as quickly as he could, too, to give Engibil no chance to change his mind yet again.

The god smiled on him; beneficence flowed out from Engibil in waves. "It is good," the god of Gibil said. "It is very good. Go now, son of Ereshguna. Go now, and give this news to your family. Go now, and give this news to the family of the woman you desire. May the two of you prove joyful together. May the two of you prove fruitful together. Go now. You have my blessing."

Sharur prostrated himself once more before the god of Gibil. Then he rose and, with profuse thanks, left the god's house at the top of the temple. Burshagga waited for him outside. "I gather you are a fortunate man, son of Ereshguna,'' the priest said as they began to descend the great stairway.

"I gather I am," Sharur agreed vaguely, being still too astonished for any more coherent reply.

Burshagga did not press him. No doubt the priest had seen many astonished men come out of the god's house. Had he seen one more astonished than Sharur, Sharur would have been astonished.

"The god has blessed the son of Ereshguna," Burshagga told the priests and temple servitors working in the courtyard while he and Sharur were walking out through it.

Ilakabkabu shuffled up to Sharur. "Are you worthy of the god's blessing, boy?" the pious old priest demanded.

"I gather I am," Sharur repeated. "Engibil thought I was."

"Be worthy in your heart," Ilakabkabu declared. "Be worthy in your spirit. Deserve well of the god, and he will do well by you."

"You give good advice," Sharur said politely. As in a dicker, he feigned feelings he did not have. He feigned them well enough to satisfy Ilakabkabu, who nodded gruffly, let out a sort of coughing grunt, and tottered back to the wall hanging he had been straightening.

"For once, I cannot disagree with my colleague," Burshagga said. "His words are true; his doctrine is sound."

"Any man can see as much," Sharur said. "Truly, I am blessed that Engibil chose to look kindly upon me. Truly, I am fortunate that the great god chose to grant my heart's desire."

Truly, Sharur had no idea why Engibil had chosen to look kindly upon him. Truly, he did not know why the great god had chosen to grant his heart's desire. So far as he knew, he had done nothing to deserve anything but anger from Engibil. Anger was what he had been braced—so far as any mortal could be braced—to receive from the god. After all, when Engibil so summarily ordered him to the temple, he and his father and Habbazu had not been singing the god's praises.

But Engibil had not known. Engibil had not even suspected. Gods were very powerful. Gods knew a great deal. But they were not omnipotent. They were not omniscient. Engibil had proved that.

Walking out of the temple, Sharur realized the gods of the Alashkurru Mountains had proved it, too. Had they been all-powerful, they would have recovered the cup in which they had hidden so much of their strength. Had they been all-knowing, they would have known some wanax or merchant might set the cup in a Gibli's hands.

For that matter, when Enzuabu sent Habbazu to rob Engibil's temple, the god of Zuabu had not known all he might have. He had not known the debt of gratitude his thief owed to a Gibli, or how that debt might affect Habbazu's actions.

Sharur still did not know how that debt of gratitude might affect Habbazu's actions, either. But Sharur did know he was not a god. Mere mortals were used to dealing with uncertainty.

When Sharur returned to the house of his family, he found Ereshguna and Tupsharru, Betsilim and Nanadirat all gathered downstairs, all of them looking as if they were about to begin the rituals for the dead. They all cried out together when he walked through the door. His mother and sister embraced him; his father and brother clasped his hand and clapped him on the back.

Habbazu was nowhere to be seen. "What became of the thief?" Sharur asked, when he was no longer kissing his parents and siblings.

"He saw you go out the door with the will of the god pressing hard upon you," Ereshguna answered. "He walked with me for a few more moments, and then, without warning, he fled. He was around a corner before I had any hope of pursuing him."

"Perhaps the power the god showed put him in fright," Sharur said with a grimace. "He thought of Engibil as a drowsy god; he reckoned him a sleepy god. He discovered

Engibil was not so drowsy, not so sleepy, as he thought.''

"It could be so," Ereshguna said. "In truth, Engibil has shown himself to be more interested in the city, more interested in the world, than we might have wished him to be.''

"Engibil has shown himself to be more interested in this family than we might have wished him to be," Betsilim exclaimed. "If not on account of this mysterious cup, why did the god summon you to his temple?''

"Why?" Sharur knew he still sounded bemused. He could not help it, for he still felt bemused. "The god summoned me to his temple because he is more interested in this family than we had thought him to be.''

"I am your mother. I gave you birth," Betsilim said sharply. "Do not think to twist my words into jokes.''

"Mother, I was not trying to twist your words into jokes," Sharur answered. "I told the truth. Engibil summoned me to his temple to give me leave to accept a loan from the house with which to pay bride-price for Ningal the daughter of Dimgalabzu.''

That startled his family into silence. He understood, being startled himself. Nanadirat broke the silence first, with a squeal of delight. She hugged Sharur again. Tupsharru spoke to the slaves: "Bring beer! No, bring wine! This news deserves better than our everyday drink.''

Ereshguna said, "This is splendid news indeed, news good beyond the wildest hopes I had when you left our home." He frowned a little. "It is news so good, I wonder what caused the god to change his mind.''

"Father, I wondered the same thing," Sharur said. "But, considering what I feared when Engibil summoned me before him—considering what we all feared when Engibil summoned me before him—I did not question him, nor did I question his judgment.''

The wine came then. The sweetness of fermented dates washed from Sharur's mouth the taste of fright that still lingered there. He drank several cups. His head began to spin. His head had been spinning, one way and another, the

whole day. He was still weak from his encounter with the
fever demon. Meeting Habbazu the thief on the streets of
Gibil had astonished him. When Engibil summoned him to
the temple, he had thought he would visit his family again
only as a ghost. When the god, instead of condemning him,
granted him favor, he found himself amazed all over again.

Ereshguna kept frowning—not in anger, Sharur judged,
but in continued perplexity. "Why did the god summon
you?" he said again, dipping a chunk of barley bread in the
honey pot. "Why?"

"Maybe Engibil decided he was wrong," Nanadirat said.
"Maybe the god decided he treated Sharur unjustly, and that
he should make amends."

Sharur laughed. He laughed and laughed. Some of it was
the wine laughing through him. Some of it was relief laughing through him. And some of it was nothing but amusement. "My sister, justice for a god is what the god says it
is: no more, no less," he said. "Gods do as pleases them.
They are gods. They can."

Nanadirat pouted. Ereshguna said, "Sharur is right. Engibil will have had some other reason. He laid down a firm
decree, and then he changed that firm decree. It is very
strange."

"But what reason could he have had?" Sharur asked.
"You are right, Father. That he should change his decree is
very strange. When I stood before him, I did not think on
how strange it was."

"You were thinking of what the god might do to you,
not of what he might do for you," Tupsharru said.

"So I was, my brother—so I was," Sharur agreed. "Now
that I am away from Engibil, though, I would try to understand why the god did as he did."

"Why he did it does not matter," Betsilim said. "Rejoice
that he did it, as your family rejoices. Rejoice that he did
it, as the family of Dimgalabzu the smith will rejoice when
the news reaches them." She looked sly. "Rejoice that he
did it, as Ningal your intended will rejoice when the news
reaches her."

Thinking of Ningal rejoicing did make Sharur want to rejoice. Thinking of wedding Ningal made him want to forget everything else. Thinking of wedding Ningal made him want to forget Habbazu the thief; it made him want to forget the Alashkurri cup in the temple of Engibil.

"Who will take the news to Dimgalabzu and his family?" Nanadirat asked. "May we all go together? I want to see Ningal's face when she hears."

"That is very forward of you, my daughter," Betsilim said, sounding disapproving and indulgent at the same time.

Tupsharru leered. "Sharur wants to see Ningal's face when she hears."

The kitchen slave dared to speak: "It will be a happy time." She would reckon it a happy time because, with Ningal come to the house, Sharur would not choose *her* to minister to his lusts even occasionally.

"Let's go now," Nanadirat said. "Bad news can wait. Good news should not."

"Important news, good or bad, should never wait," Ereshguna said.

At that, Sharur turned his head to look at his father. He found Ereshguna looking back at him. Both of them had intent, thoughtful expressions on their faces, very different from the joyful ones Betsilim, Nanadirat, Tupsharru, and the slaves were wearing (though the slaves' joyful countenances might well have been masks to please their masters, at least in part).

"Could it be?" Sharur asked.

"Have you got any better notion?" his father returned. "Have you got any other notion at all?"

"What are the two of you talking about?" Nanadirat asked impatiently. "When are we going over to the house of Dimgalabzu the smith?"

"Later," Sharur said, also impatiently. "Father and I need to talk about this."

But Ereshguna held up a hand. "No. Let us go now. We can talk about this later. If we go now, if we speak with Dimgalabzu now, and if the god is watching and listening, he will see he has accomplished that which he wished to accomplish. Later will be time enough to discuss the other. We have had the notion. It shall not escape our minds.''

Sharur inclined his head. ''Father, you are wise. As you say, let us go now. As you say, later will be time enough to discuss the other. The notion shall not escape our minds.''

''What *are* the two of you talking about?'' Nanadirat repeated. Neither Sharur nor Ereshguna answered her.

Dimgalabzu was grinding a sharp edge onto a spearhead when Sharur and his family walked into the smithy. Seeing them all there together, the smith set the spearhead down on his workbench. ''Well, well, what have we here?'' he said in surprise. He took a longer look at his guests. A slow smile spread across his face. ''What we have here is good news, unless I miss my guess.''

Ereshguna bowed. ''What we have here is good news indeed, my friend,'' he said. ''Engibil has smiled upon my son. Engibil has smiled upon the union of our families.''

''Is it so?'' Dimgalabzu's smile got wider, but then contracted. ''When last we spoke of this matter, there was a difficulty concerning the bride-price. Unless this difficulty has been eased, the union can not go forward.''

''This difficulty has been eased, father of my intended,'' Sharur said. ''The union can go forward. Today Engibil summoned me to his temple. Today the god released me from my oath. Today he gave me leave to accept from my family a loan for the bride-price to be paid for Ningal your daughter.''

''Is it so?'' Now the smith sounded astonished. ''How fortunate for you, son of Ereshguna. The god rarely changes his mind. The god rarely needs to change his mind. Why did he change his mind this time?''

''He said he had held my oath too tight. He said he had been too strait. Thus he chose to ease and loosen his hold on the oath.'' Sharur answered with nothing but the truth, straight from the god's lips. He did not look at his father.

The thought they seemed to share would have to wait.

"How fortunate for you, son of Ereshguna," Dimgalabzu repeated. The broad smile returned to his broad face. "How fortunate for all of us." He clapped his hands together and shouted for his slaves to bring beer and salt fish and onions for his guests. Then he went to the stairway. "Gulal!" he called. "Ningal! Come down! We have guests you should see."

Ningal and her mother came downstairs. They both carried spindles; they had been making wool or flax into thread. They exclaimed in surprise when they saw Sharur and his family in the smithy. They exclaimed in delight when Dimgalabzu explained why Sharur and his family had come.

"Is it true, Sharur?" Ningal asked softly.

"It is true," Sharur answered. Most of the time, his intended bride kept her eyes on the ground, as a modestly reared young woman was supposed to do in the presence of a man not of her immediate family. Every so often, though, she would look up at Sharur from under lowered eyelids. As he kept his eyes on her to the exclusion of all else, he caught the glances. They enchanted him.

Gulal, who stood beside her daughter, also caught those glances. She poked Ningal in the ribs with her elbow and muttered something pungent under her breath. Thereafter, Ningal glanced at Sharur less often and more circumspectly. But, to Sharur's delight, she did not stop glancing at him.

In came the beer and salt fish and onions. "Let us drink," Dimgalabzu boomed. "Let us eat. Let us rejoice that our two families are to be made one. Let us rejoice that the god has favored our two families' being made one."

They drank. They ate. They rejoiced. Gulal and Betsilim put their heads together and talked in low voices for some time. Every so often, they would look over at Sharur and Ningal and then go back to their intent conversation. He eyed them with considerable apprehension. Because they were only women, he felt foolish about that . . . until he noticed Ereshguna and Dimgalabzu eyeing them with considerable apprehension. If his father and the father of his intended worried about their wives, his own concern had reason behind it.

Dimgalabzu asked, "How did the god of the city come to release you from the oath he formerly held close?"

"If you mean to ask why the god chose to do it, father of my intended, you would have to enquire of him," Sharur replied. Whatever ideas he and his father had on that score, he was not yet ready to share them with Dimgalabzu. "If you mean to ask how he did it, he summoned me to his temple, as I told you, and told me of his change of heart there."

"How very curious," Dimgalabzu murmured. "Do not mistake me, son of Ereshguna; I am delighted that Engibil changed his mind. I am joyous that the god thought twice. But I am also surprised."

"I was surprised, too, when Engibil summoned me to his house on earth," Sharur said. He had also been horrified, but the smith did not need to know that. He wondered whether he ought to tell Dimgalabzu about Habbazu. For the time being, he decided, the father of his intended did not need to know about the Zuabi thief, either.

Ningal and Nanadirat put their heads together, as their mothers had done. Watching them whisper and giggle and point at him made Sharur want to sink into the floor. He glared. They giggled harder than ever. Having nothing better to do, he dipped up another cup of beer.

Gulal spoke up in a loud voice: "It is decided."

"Aye, it is," Betsilim agreed. Between the two of them, they sounded as certain—and as irresistible—as any god Sharur had ever met.

Gulal went on, "The wedding shall take place on the day of the full moon of the last month of fall: not only a day of good omen, but also one on which the son of Ereshguna is unlikely to find himself away from the city with a caravan."

Sharur did not think he was likely to find himself away from the city with a caravan any time soon. No other cities of Kudurru, no other lands around Kudurru, seemed willing to trade with Gibil. Still, his guess was that his mother had won the concession from Gulal, hoping trade would improve in what remained of the better weather. He supposed he should have thanked her. Instead, he grumbled to himself at having to wait so long for the wedding.

Whatever else Dimgalabzu was, he was not a foolish man, and, if he was not a young man, he once had been. He said, "Let Sharur and Ningal embrace now, before us all, in token that this arrangement is agreeable to them."

Gulal gave her husband a look suggesting she would have a good deal to say when she could speak to him in private. When Ningal stepped toward Sharur with a smile, Gulal gave her daughter the same look. Under Gulal's glare, the embrace was perforce brief and decorous. But an embrace it unquestionably was.

Tupsharru clapped his hands together. Nanadirat whooped. That embarrassed Sharur enough to make him let go of Ningal even sooner than he would have otherwise. Dimgalabzu looked pleased with himself. Gulal's expression said she was less furious than she had been before Sharur took Ningal in his arms.

Sharur bowed to the mother of his intended. His politeness made Gulal smile for a moment, till she caught herself doing it. Ningal saw that and smiled, too, at Sharur. He kept his own face carefully blank. A merchant often found it useful not to let the other side in a bargain see at a glance everything in his mind.

Ningal said, "The end of fall is not so far away. Every day that goes by brings it one day closer."

"You are right," Sharur said loyally. Altogether too many days would go by to suit him, but he would not disagree with his intended before she became his wife—nor, he hoped, too many times after she became his wife, either.

Ereshguna stared down into his cup of beer, as if it held the answers to all the questions in the world. A torch behind him flickered, making his shadow jump. Outside in the darkness, a cricket chirped. Farther away, a dog howled. Those were the only noises Sharur heard. His mother and sister and brother had gone up onto the roof to sleep. The slaves slept, too, in their stuffy little cubicles.

Sharur looked down at his own cup of beer. He saw no answers there. He drank. If he drank enough, that was an answer of sorts, but not the one he needed now. He sighed.

So did Ereshguna. The master merchant sipped, then said, "Son, tell me what is in your mind: why, in your reckoning, did Engibil choose the moment he chose to release you from your oath concerning the bride-price for Ningal?"

"Did we not have the same notion at the same time?" Sharur asked.

Ereshguna smiled. "Each of us had a notion at the same time. Whether we had the same notion, I cannot know until I learn what your notion was."

"That is so," Sharur admitted. "Very well, then. I will tell you what my notion was." Before continuing, he covered the eyes of the amulet to Engibil he wore on his belt. His father did the same with the amulet he wore. Whatever their notions were, neither of them wanted the god to know. As neither of them was sure about precisely how much good their precautions did, Sharur went on warily: "My notion, Father, is that the god chose to release me from my oath concerning the bride-price for Ningal to make me so joyous, I would forget about every other concern I had."

"Thus far we walk the same trail, like two donkeys yoked together," Ereshguna said. "But tell me one thing more. Do you think the god wanted you to forget every other concern you hold, or some concern in particular?"

"Father, your thoughts are as orderly as the accounts set down on our clay tablets," Sharur said, and Ereshguna smiled again. "I think Engibil wanted me to forget some concern in particular. I think the god wanted to distract me from helping Habbazu the Zuabi steal from his temple the cup, the plain cup, the ordinary cup, from the mountains of Alashkurru."

"Indeed, you are truly my son," Ereshguna said. "The same canal waters your thoughts and mine. That is the reason I also believe Engibil had for loosening his hold on the oath you gave him. I do not believe the god wanted Habbazu to go forward. I do not believe the god wanted us to help Habbazu go forward.''

Sharur scratched his head. ''Do you think, then, that Engibil discovered the cup from the mountains was an object of power because he learned the Zuabi thief sought to steal it?''

''I do not.'' Ereshguna sounded thoroughly grim. ''I think the god knew from the beginning the cup from the mountains was an object of power.''

Now his thoughts had got ahead of those of his son. Sharur raced to catch up. When he did, he stared at his father. ''You are saying the god knew this thing and told us he did not.'' From there, it was but a short step to the full and appalling meaning of Ereshguna's words: ''You are saying the god told us a lie.''

''Yes,'' Ereshguna answered in a voice soft and dark and heavy as lead. ''That is what I am saying.''

His fingers were pressed over the eyes of his amulet, so hard that his fingernails turned pale. Looking down at his own hands, Sharur saw their nails were yellowish white, too. ''But why?'' he whispered. ''Why would the god tell us a lie? Why would he not speak the truth to men of his own city?''

''I do not know that,'' Ereshguna said. ''Ever since you returned from the temple with your news, I have pondered it. I have found no answer that satisfies me.''

Though Sharur sat inside with his father, he glanced toward the temple. He could see it in his mind's eye as clearly as if all the walls between had fallen down, as clearly as if it were bright noon rather than black of night. He hoped Kimash had found some distraction for Engibil at this moment. Slowly, cautiously, he said, ''Perhaps the god intends to let lack of trade stifle the city. Perhaps he intends all of Gibil to grow poor, so that all of Gibil will be glad to have him back as its ruler.''

''Perhaps so,'' Ereshguna said. ''This thought, or one not

far different from it, also crossed my mind. It comes nearer to accounting for why the god is doing as he is doing than any other I have found. But I do not think it accounts in fullness for the god's acts.''

"How not?'' Sharur said.

"I will explain how not. I will set it forth for you,'' his father answered. "What troubles me is that, if Gibil grows poor, Gibil also grows weak. If Gibil grows weak, what will our enemies do? What will Imhursag do? What will Enimhursag do? Will the god of Imhursag not believe Gibil's weakness and Engibil's weakness to be one and the same?''

"Ah,'' Sharur said. "I see what you are saying. Yes, I think that is likely. Imhursag smarts from defeats at the hands of Gibil. Enimhursag smarts from defeats at the hands of Engibil. If Gibil grows weak, Engibil will also seem to have grown weak. The god of Imhursag and the Imhursagut will want their revenge.''

"Even so.'' Ereshguna nodded. "This is why I do not understand why Engibil would seek to weaken his city, even to regain his rule here.''

"Ah,'' Sharur said again. "Now I follow. Now your thought is clear to me. What could be so important to the god that he would sooner have his city humiliated than yield it?''

"That is half the riddle, but only half, and, I think, the smaller half,'' Ereshguna said. "What could be so important to Engibil that he would sooner have himself humiliated than yield it?''

Sharur inclined his head. His father had drawn a distinction that needed drawing. Sharur had seen how Engibil could be indifferent to whether or not the folk of Gibil prospered. The god even wondered whether such marvels as metalworking and writing, which helped the folk of Gibil prosper, were worthwhile, because they infringed on his prerogatives.

But one of the god's prerogatives was his standing among his fellow gods. If Gibil grew weak, Imhursag would defeat it. If Imhursag defeated Gibil, Enimhursag's power would grow and Engibil's would recede. The two neighboring gods truly did hate each other, like two families living in the same street whose children threw rocks at one another.

As Ereshguna had, Sharur asked, "What could make Engibil willing to take a step back—perhaps to take several steps back—before Enimhursag, with whom he has quarreled since time out of mind?"

"Whatever it is, it has to do with the cup into which the great gods of the Alashkurrut poured their power," Ereshguna said. "Of that we may be certain."

"Yes," Sharur said. Dimly, he remembered the cup that had figured in his fever dreams. Part of him wished he could recall more of those dreams. The rest of him wished he could forget them altogether, as madness he was better off without.

Ereshguna went on, "But we may be as certain of another thing: that we do not know why Engibil has such concern for this cup, which holds none of his own power, and that it may be—no, that it is—very important for us to learn the reason for his concern."

"Every word you say is true," Sharur replied. In a whisper, he added, "This is more than can be said of Engibil in this matter."

"So it is." His father also whispered. "Well, I shall try to say one more true thing, and then I shall drink the last of my beer here and go up on the roof to sleep. Here is the last true thing I shall try to say: I think we need to let Kimash the lugal know a Zuabi thief is prowling his city."

"My father, in this, too, you are right." Sharur drank the last of the beer from his own cup. He doused all the torches but one, which he and Ereshguna used to light their way upstairs.


When Sharur walked with Ereshguna to the lugal's palace the next day, he felt more nearly himself than he had since the fever demon breathed its foul breath into his mouth. He looked up and down the Street of Smiths as he walked along, hoping he might spot Habbazu. But the Zuabi thief did not show himself. Sharur wondered if he had already crept into Engibil's temple to steal the cup, and if he had escaped with it.

As they drew near the palace, Ereshguna raised an eyebrow. "Things are quiet here today," he remarked. "Things are quieter here today than I have seen them for a long time."

"Yes." Sharur nodded. "Where are the donkeys carrying bricks? Where are the slaves carrying mortar? Where are the workmen building the palace higher and broader?" Only a couple of guards stood in front of the entryway, leaning against their spears.

Sharur and Ereshguna came up to the guards. One of the men said, "How may we serve you, master merchant? How may we serve you, master merchant's son?"

"We would have speech with Kimash the mighty lugal," Ereshguna answered. "We have learned of a matter about which he must hear."

The guards looked at each other. One of them set his spear against the wall and went into the palace. When he returned, Inadapa followed him.

Bowing to the steward, Sharur said, "Good day. As my father told the guard, we would have speech with Kimash the mighty lugal."

Inadapa bowed in return. "Master merchant's son, I regret that this can not be." He shifted his feet and bowed to Ereshguna. "Master merchant, I regret that your request can not be granted."

"But the matter on which we would speak with the mighty lugal is both urgent and important," Ereshguna said, frowning.

"Master merchant, I regret that your request can not be granted," Inadapa repeated.

Ereshguna folded his arms across his chest. "Why can my request not be granted?" he rumbled. "If I may not see Kimash the lugal, I whose house has always supported the lugals of Gibil, who then may? If he is sporting among his wives or concubines, let him sport among them at another time: what I have to tell him will not wait. Should he judge me wrong, having heard me out, let his wrath fall on my head.''

"He is not sporting among his wives," Inadapa said. "He is not sporting among his concubines."

"Well, where is he, then?" Sharur asked. "Why can he not see us?"

Inadapa took a deep breath. "Master merchant's son, master merchant, he can not see you because he is closeted with Engibil. The god summoned him to the temple at first light this morning, and he has not yet returned."

"Oh," Sharur said, the word a sharp exhalation, as if he had been punched in the stomach.

"May he come back to the palace soon," Ereshguna said. "May he come back to the palace safe. May he come back to the palace as lugal."

"So may it be," Inadapa said fervently. If Engibil chose to arise from two generations and more of drowsiness, the first the folk of Gibil would know of it was when he began looking out of their eyes and thinking their thoughts for them, as Enimhursag did in the city to the north.

"When Kimash returns, faithful steward, please do tell him we would have speech with him at his convenience," Sharur said. That assumed Kimash would return to the palace as lugal, not as . . . *as Engibil's toy*, Sharur thought. He had to assume as much. Anything else would be disaster.

Inadapa bowed. "It shall be just as you say." He hesitated. "I hope it shall be just as you say." More than that he would not say, any more than Sharur would.

Sharur looked in the direction of Engibil's temple, though the great bulk of the palace hid it. Suddenly, in his mind's eye, the lugal's residence seemed transparent as clear water. If Engibil arose in his full might, how long would so great a building be given over to a mere man?

Ereshguna said, "When the mighty lugal returns from the temple, please send a messenger to let us know. We do have a matter of some importance to take up with him as soon as may be, provided . . ." He shrugged.

"It shall be just as you say," Inadapa repeated. He shook himself like a dog coming out of a canal. His big, soft belly wobbled. "May we soon come to live in more placid times."

"So may it be," Sharur and Ereshguna said together. Sharur did not think his father believed more placid times would come soon. He knew he did not think more placid times would come soon.

He and his father left the lugal's palace and started up the Street of Smiths toward their home. Now both of them kept stealing glances toward Engibil's temple. If the god took over the city once more, Sharur wondered whether he would leave those who had led Gibil's search for more freedom for mortal men enough of that freedom to flee to some other town.

Then he wondered how much difference it would make. Nowhere else in Kudurru had the new taken hold as it had in Gibil. Still, even under the thumbs of their city gods, men remained to some degree men. Here and there across the land between the rivers, no doubt, were ensis who longed to make themselves into lugals. If they had at their disposal merchants and smiths and scribes from Gibil, perhaps they might succeed.

Perhaps, too, they would fall short, as Huzziyas the wanax had fallen short in the mountains of Alashkurru. But some sparks might still smolder, to be kindled again one day a generation from now, or two, or ten.

Ereshguna's thoughts must have been much like Sharur's. When they came to a man dipping cups of beer out of a large jar, Sharur's father said, "Let us stop and drink. Who knows how long we have left to taste beer with our own tongues? Who knows how long we have left before Engibil tastes beer with our tongues, sees the city with our eyes, thinks with our minds?"

That not only made Sharur want to drink beer, it made him want to drink himself blind. He bought a second cup from the beer seller, and was drinking from it when a large, burly man strutted up to the fellow and loudly demanded some of his wares. Having got the cup, the burly man turned to Sharur and Ereshguna, saying, "Can't work all the time, eh, master merchant, master merchant's son?"

"No, Mushezib, we cannot work all the time," Ereshguna answered with a smile that seemed altogether natural and unforced. A merchant, after all, was trained not to show on his face everything he thought. Sharur admired his father's skill at concealment.

"Not much work for guards these days," Mushezib remarked. "Things are pretty quiet."

"If we have good fortune, caravans will resume before too long," Sharur answered. Caravans might also resume before too long if the men of Gibil did not have good fortune, but those would be caravans where Engibil looked out through the eyes of merchants, guards, and donkey handlers. The Imhursagut sent forth such caravans. Sharur chose not to dwell on them.

Mushezib's eyes brightened. "Is it so, master merchant's son?"

"It is so," Sharur said firmly, though he remained unsure whether it would be so. Then his eyes sparkled, too. He pointed to Mushezib. "And you are a man who can help make it so."

"I?" the guard captain asked. "How is this so? How can this be so. I take no part in the affairs of the great. I take no part in the quarrels of the gods."

"That is not so," Sharur said. "Do you recall the thief whom Enzuabu sent to rob our caravan when we returned from the Alashkurru Mountains?"

"Oh, aye, I recall him," Mushezib answered. "I would recall his ugly face even as I lay dying. With my last breath, I would curse him. You should have left his body in the bushes, a feast for dogs and ravens. You should have left his body in a canal, a meal for fish and snails."

Some of that, in among the bombast, was what Sharur

hoped to hear. "If you recall his face, you will know him if you see him again?"

"Master merchant's son, I will." Mushezib spoke with great certainty. "Nor am I the only one among the guards and donkey handlers who would."

Sharur smiled. So did Ereshguna, who must have seen where his son's thoughts were going. Smiling still, Sharur went on, "This is good news, Mushezib, for I must tell you that this thief, whose name is Habbazu, has come to Gibil to steal from Engibil's temple. I have seen him. I have had speech with him. But I could not bring him before the mighty lugal for justice, for he escaped me." That he had not intended to bring Habbazu before Kimash for justice was nothing the guard needed to know.

Mushezib's blunt, battered features grew dark with anger. "He is here? In this city? He has come to rob our god for Enzuabu? Master merchant's son, I will hunt him down. I will put word of him in the ears of our comrades who also saw him outside Zuabu. When we lay hands on him, the scavengers shall feed."

"No," Sharur said, and Mushezib's shaggy eyebrows rose in surprise. "No," Sharur repeated. "Bring him to the house of Ereshguna, that we may question him as he should be questioned."

"Gold awaits you if you bring him to my house," Ereshguna added.

"Question him as he should be questioned, eh?" Grim anticipation filled Mushezib's chuckle. "Question him with hot things and sharp things and hard things and heavy things, do you mean?"

"It could be so," Sharur answered, not altogether untruthfully. He still did not know how far Habbazu could be trusted.

Mushezib bowed to him. "Master merchant's son—" He also bowed to Ereshguna. "Master merchant, my comrades and I shall drop on this thief like a collapsing wall. We shall fall upon him like the roof beams of a house that crumbles."

"It is good," Sharur said, and Ereshguna nodded. Mushezib bowed to each of them once more and strutted off, a procession of one. By his manner, he expected to return momentarily to the house of Ereshguna with one large fist clamped around Habbazu's skinny neck. Sharur hoped he or another caravan guard or a donkey handler would soon return to the house of Ereshguna with Habbazu in his grasp.

"Do not raise your hopes too high," Ereshguna warned him. "Do not expect too much. These men saw Habbazu for a small part of one night some while ago. They may not recognize him even if he should walk past them on the street. And he is a clever thief, a master thief. He may not show himself at all, and he will surely be adept at escaping danger."

"Every word you say is true, Father," Sharur replied. "And yet—I will hope."

"How not?" Ereshguna clapped him on the back. "You are a man. I, too, will hope—but not too much."


Sharur was adding numbers on his fingers that afternoon when a man of about his father's age came through the doorway. "One moment, my master, if you please," Sharur said, as to any stranger. "Let me finish my calculation." He looked down to his hands once more.

"Take the time you need," the stranger answered, and Sharur forgot the calculation he had been making. The man's voice declared what a hasty glance had not—he was no stranger. There stood Kimash the lugal, not in a lugal's finery but in the rather dirty kilt and worn sandals a potter or a leatherworker might have worn.

"Your pardon, mighty lugal," Sharur gasped, and began to prostrate himself before the man who had ruled Gibil for most of his life.

"No. Wait," Kimash said. "Speak neither my name nor my title while I am here. Call me . . . Izmaili." He plucked the name from the air like a conjuror plucking a date from a woman's ear.

"I obey." Sharur wondered if he was not to call Kimash

lugal because Kimash was lugal no more. Had Engibil stripped the man of his title and his power? Would a dirty tunic and worn sandals be Kimash's fate forevermore?

Reading his thoughts as if they were syllables incised on clay, Kimash said, "You need not fear, son of Ereshguna. I still am what I was." He smiled at his circumlocution, then went on, "Barely, perhaps, but I am. No, a man who looks like me sits on my high seat in the palace. A man who looks like me wears my raiment. He drinks my fine date wine. He eats my delicate food. If he so chooses, he couples with my women—all but a few whose names I have not told him, and of whom I am particularly fond. If the god looks in the palace, he will see the lugal in the palace, doing the things the lugal does. I? I am Izmaili, a person of no particular account."

Sharur bowed, acknowledging Kimash's daring. "But," he could not help asking, "what if the god should summon the lugal to his temple while Izmaili, a person of no particular account, walks through the streets of Gibil?"

"Then we have a difficulty," Kimash said. "But I do not think that will happen, not today. The god and the lugal have already had a long talk today. Call your father, if you would." He smiled. "Izmaili, a person of no particular account, was told the two of you would have speech with him."

"It shall be as you say, my master," Sharur replied, as he might have to any customer who came into the shop. He raised his voice: "Father! The . . . a man is here to see you."

When Ereshguna came out, he recognized at once who the "man" was. As Sharur had done, he began to prostrate himself. As Kimash had done with Sharur, he bade Ereshguna stop and gave the name by which he would be known and the reason he was wearing both it and his shabby clothes.

Ereshguna nodded slow approval. "This is a bold plan, Izmaili." He hesitated not at all over Kimash's alias. "This is a clever plan, person of no particular account."

"For which praise I thank you—although why you

should value the thanks of a person of no particular account is beyond me.'' Kimash's eyes twinkled as he went on, ''Also beyond me is why the two of you would want to have speech with a person of no particular account.''

''Be that as it may, we do,'' Ereshguna said. Together, he and Sharur explained how Habbazu had come to Gibil to steal the Alashkurri cup from Engibil's temple, and how the Zuabi thief had fled when Engibil summoned Sharur to his temple.

Kimash listened intently. When Sharur and Ereshguna had finished, he said, ''For one who sits on the high seat in the palace, admitting he was wrong would come hard. For Izmaili, who is a man of no particular account, it is much easier. Son of Ereshguna, in the matter of this cup and its likely importance, you had the right of it.''

Sharur bowed, saying, ''You are gracious, Izmaili. We have men from my caravan, men who will know this Zuabi by his face, searching for him here in Gibil. Still, we do not know whether they will find him before he can enter the temple and seek to steal this cup.''

''You did well to put men on his trail,'' Kimash said. ''You did well to have men search for him. But, if he should enter the temple and steal the cup, is it not likely now that he would take it away to Enzuabu rather than setting it in your hands? He will be fearing that you have come under Engibil's power, even as you feared I had come under the god's sway.''

''That is likely, yes,'' Sharur said, and Ereshguna nodded.

''Then we shall have to warn Engibil's priests,'' Kimash said. ''Better that our god should have this thing than that a rival god in Kudurru should have it.''

Reluctantly, Ereshguna nodded again. Sharur said, ''What still perplexes me, Izmaili, is why the god should have denied any knowledge of the cup when we asked him about it.''

''This also perplexes me,'' the lugal admitted. ''I have no answer I can give you. The god lied for reasons of his own. What those reasons are, I cannot guess. I am, after all, only a man. I am, after all, only a person of no particular account." He seemed to enjoy having escaped for a little while the stifling ceremony with which the lugals of Gibil had come to imitate the homage given the city god. After a moment, though, he turned serious once more: "If your searchers catch this thief, have him brought before me."

A person of no particular importance would never have given an order in that crisp tone, a tone used by a man certain of obedience. "We shall do as you say, Izmaili . . . just as if you were the lugal," Sharur replied.

Kimash's eyes widened. Then he caught the joke, and threw back his head and laughed. "It is good," he said at last. "It is very good. Obey me as you would obey the lugal and all will be well. Now I will go back to the palace. I will see how much fine wine I have left. I will see how much dainty food I have left. I will see how many babies born next spring I will know to be a cuckoo's eggs, and not sprung from my seed at all." With a shrug of resignation, he left the house of Ereshguna and strode down the Street of Smiths.

"He is a bold man," Ereshguna said when the lugal was gone. "He is a clever man. He is a resourceful man. He is the right man to lead Gibil and to keep Engibil quiescent while we—" He broke off.

*While we mortals gather strength*, was no doubt what he had been on the point of saying. Saying such things while Engibil was less quiescent than he might have been was unwise. In any case, he knew Sharur could supply the words he did not speak aloud.

Sharur did supply those words without difficulty. "He is everything you have said he is," he agreed. "But, Father, is he a man before whom we want to bring Habbazu the thief if we lay hands on him once more?"

"You were the one who said we would do as Izmaili said, just as if he were the lugal," Ereshguna reminded him.

"Yes, I said that." Sharur shrugged. "What of it? If the god does not scruple to lie to me, should I scruple to lie to the lugal?"

Ereshguna whistled softly between his teeth. "Kimash may punish you for lying to him. Who will punish Engibil for lying to you?"

*I will*, Sharur thought, but those were words *he* would not say aloud. Instead, he answered, "If the lugal is warning the priests of Engibil's temple about Habbazu, would not giving the thief over to him be the same as condemning the thief to death?"

"That is likely to be so, yes." Ereshguna grew alert. "I see what you are saying, son. *We* want the Alashkurri cup stolen. Kimash, on the other hand, may well reckon that giving the thief over to Engibil for punishment, or punishing Habbazu himself, will gain him more credit with the god."

"It will gain him credit with the god of Gibil, yes," Sharur said, "but it will not help him or help us in our dealing with the other city gods of Kudurru, nor with the gods of the Alashkurrut."

"I wonder how much Kimash frets over that," Ereshguna said. "He is the lugal, the man who rules Gibil. Anything that helps him rule Gibil, he will likely do. Anything that gains him credit with Engibil helps him rule Gibil, so he will likely do it. He will think of the rest of us Giblut only after he thinks of ruling Gibil—so I believe."

"And I." Sharur's mouth thinned to a bitter line. "In that, the lugal is much like the god, is he not?"

Ereshguna looked startled. "I had not thought of it so. Now that I do, though, I see that there is some truth in what you say."

"We sometimes have the need to do this or that without the god's knowing it," Sharur said, and his father nodded. "If Kimash is much like Engibil, should we not sometimes have the need to do this or that without the lugal's knowing it?"

"Yes, that would follow from the first," Ereshguna answered. Before Sharur could say anything, his father held up a hand to show he had not finished. "You must also think on this, though, son: often, if we have the need to do this or that without the god's knowing it, the lugal will help us shield it from his eyes. If we seek to hide from the god and the lugal both and we are discovered, who will shield us then?''

"No one," Sharur answered, so bleakly that he startled Ereshguna again. "We Giblut have for long and long aimed to live as free as we could. If we are free, we are also free to fail." He grimaced. "Except we had better not."

Mushezib did not find Habbazu. The caravan guards who had served under Mushezib did not find Habbazu. The donkey handlers did not find Habbazu. Five days after Engibil had summoned Sharur to his temple and Habbazu had fled, the Zuabi thief returned to the house of Ereshguna.

One moment, Habbazu was not there. The next, he was. So, at any rate, it appeared to Sharur, who was searching for a particular clay tablet among the many in the baskets near the scales. When he looked up, Habbazu stood not three feet away, watching the search with sardonic amusement.

"You!" Sharur exclaimed.

"I," Habbazu agreed. He bowed to Sharur. "And you. Believe me, having seen you ordered to the house of your god, I am more surprised to see you safe among men than you could be to see me."

"How did you come here without being seen?" Sharur asked.

"I have my ways," Habbazu answered airily. "I am, after all, a thief sent forth by Enzuabu himself." He said no more than that. Maybe it meant the god of Zuabu had lent him powers or enchantments to help him escape notice. Maybe it meant he wanted Sharur to think the god of Zuabu had lent him such powers and enchantments.

At another time, Sharur might have spent considerable worry over the question of whether and to what extent Habbazu was bluffing. Now he had more important things on his mind. "The Alashkurri cup," he said. "Have you got it, or does it still sit in Engibil's temple?"

Habbazu lost some of his jaunty manner. "The Alashkurri

cup still sits in Engibil's temple." He sent Sharur an accusing look. "The god of this city is not so drowsy a god as I was led to believe in Zuabu. The god of Gibil is not so sleepy a god as I was led to believe in my city."

"As I told you, not everything about Gibil is as you may have been led to believe," Sharur said.

"The god is alert," Habbazu said. "The priests of the god are alert. This makes it harder for me to enter the temple, harder for me to reach the chamber within which the cup rests, harder for me to escape after I steal it."

"With the god and the priests alert, can you enter the temple?" Sharur asked. "Can you reach the chamber in which the cup rests? Can you steal the cup?"

"I can do all these things." Habbazu drew himself up with the sort of pride in his ability at his chosen trade that Sharur or Ereshguna might have shown over matters mercantile. "As I said, though, it will be harder for me. I will pick my time with care."

"Indeed," Sharur said, raising one eyebrow, "if you do not, you are liable to be captured, as the caravan guards captured you outside Zuabu."

Habbazu looked miffed. "That should not have happened. That should never have happened. The caravan guards were lucky to set eyes on me, luckier still to lay hold of me."

"As may be," Ereshguna said, coming downstairs. How long had he been listening? Long enough—he went on, "Who is to say Engibil will not be lucky enough to set eyes on you? Who is to say Engibil's priests will not be lucky enough to lay hold of you? They are alert, as the caravan guards were alert. Have you not noticed how often luck comes to those who are alert?"

"Oh, indeed, my master: I have noticed this many times," the thief said. "And I do not deny my task would be easier if the god's eye were turned elsewhere. I do not deny my task would be easier if the god's priests were to look in some different direction."

"Distracting the priests may not be too hard," Ereshguna

said. "They are, after all, but men. Distracting the god . . ." His voice trailed away.

"A question," Sharur said. "Habbazu, if you steal this Alashkurri cup, will you still deliver it into the hands of the house of Ereshguna and not into the hands of Enzuabu who sent you forth?"

"When Engibil summoned you to his temple, I repented of my promise," the thief admitted. "Now that I learn he did not summon you to punish you for consorting with me, I see that, though he may be alert, he does not rule every aspect of every life in Gibil, as Enimhursag does in Imhursag. And so, though shaken as by an earthquake, the promise stands."

"It is good," Sharur said. As he and his father and Habbazu spoke of the difficulty of distracting, so Engibil no doubt wondered how successful his effort to distract the annoying mortals would prove. He had succeeded in making Sharur happy by releasing the promise he held.

"As your father said, distracting the priests of the god may not be too hard," Habbazu said. "How, though, how do you propose to distract the god himself?"

"That will not be easy," Ereshguna said. "You may indeed have to prove how gifted a thief you are."

"To distract a god from watching over men and the concerns of men," Sharur said slowly, "it may be best to involve him with gods and the concerns of gods."

"This Alashkurri cup has involved Engibil with gods and the concerns of gods," Ereshguna said. "Without it, he would have been a drowsy god. Without it, he would have been a sleepy god. Without it, we could have gone on living our lives as we desired."

"There are other gods than the great gods of the Alashkurrut, other gods over whose doings Engibil has concerned himself for long and long," Sharur said. "If he were again to concern himself over their doings . . ."

"Enzuabu and Engibil do not squabble over the border between their lands," Habbazu said. "Zuabu and Gibil have gone on for many years without strife between them."

"That is so," Sharur agreed. "But if Engibil were to look to the north and not to the west, what would he see? Engibil and Enimhursag hate each other; Engibil and Enimhursag have long hated each other. In every generation, Gibil and Imhursag go to war against each other—often twice in a generation."

"In the past three generations, in the time while the lugals have ruled Gibil, we have beaten the Imhursagut in almost all these wars, too," Ereshguna said. "In the latest one, we beat the Imhursagut so badly, Enimhursag had to humble himself to beg for peace." He spoke with no small pride.

Habbazu said, "Strange how, though the power of your god in your city is less than it was, the power of your city among its neighbors has grown greater."

"Men matter, too," Sharur said: that, if anything, was the motto under which the Giblut had lived since Igigi became the first lugal. Sharur went on, "If Enimhursag were to believe Engibil's power badly weakened, though; if the god of the Imhursagut were to believe the Giblut divided by factional squabbles . . . would he not seek to regain what we have taken from Imhursag over the years? Would he not think he could but stretch forth his hand and what he had lost would be his once more?"

"But what would make him believe such a thing?" Ereshguna asked. "It is not so. If anything, as we have seen, Engibil is more active now than he has been for some time."

"Suppose a Gibli were to flee to the land of Imhursag," Sharur said. "Suppose a Gibli were to speak these words into Enimhursag's ear. Suppose a Gibli were to beg Enimhursag to arm the Imhursagut and come down into the land of Gibil and restore order, order that has been lost as water is lost when the bank of a canal breaks."

"What Gibli would be mad enough to do such a thing?" Ereshguna said.

"I would," Sharur answered.

Habbazu stared at him. "You would set your city at war with Imhursag. You would set your god at war with Enimhursag?"

"I would," Sharur said. "If Engibil's eyes travel north to the border with the land Imhursag rules, how closely will the god watch his temple? How much notice will he take of a certain skulking thief?"

"Ahhh." Habbazu let out a long breath of praise.

"But, my son, you would not go to speak to another merchant," Ereshguna said. "You would go to speak to a god. You would go to speak to a god who rules a city in his own right. You would go to speak to a god who can look deep into your heart and learn whether you speak truth. You would go to a god who can punish you terribly when he learns you are speaking lies."

"I would go to speak to a god who rules a city in his own right," Sharur said. "I would go to speak to a god whose own people fawn on him. I would go to speak to a god who will very much want to hear the words I speak into his ear. I would go to speak to a god who will very much want to believe the words I speak into his ear. Gods, like men, believe that which they want to believe. If he believes what comes from my mouth, he will not look deep into my heart and learn whether I speak truth."

Habbazu bowed. "Master merchant's son, no one will deny you are a man of courage. No one will claim you are a man without bravery."

"A man should be brave," Ereshguna said. "A man should not be foolhardy. A man should be wise enough to know the difference between the one and the other." By the way he looked at Sharur, he did not think his son passed that test. "If you are wrong in this, if Enimhursag goes through your mind like a man going through his belt pouch, all is lost. If you are wrong in this, you are lost."

"How better to distract Engibil than to embroil him with Enimhursag?" Sharur returned. "And Enimhursag is a foolish god. He is a stupid god. We have seen it in the way the Imhursagut fought the men of our city. We have seen it in the way our caravans constantly outdo those from Imhursag. We have seen it in the way I went into Imhursag and came out safe again. What I have done once, I can do twice."

"Enimhursag is a foolish god: true," Ereshguna said. "He is a stupid god: true. But he is a god, and he has the strength of a god. Remember this. You went into Imhursag and came out safe again: true. Enimhursag nearly slew you, though you disguised yourself as a Zuabi merchant. Remember this, too."

"What's this? A Gibli pretending to be a man of my city?" Habbazu exclaimed. "I am insulted. Zuabu is insulted." His eyes sparkled.

Ereshguna ignored him, continuing, "If you go to Enimhursag this time, you will go as a Gibli. If you go to the god of Imhursag this time, you will go as a man of the city he hates. Why should he not slay you out of hand?"

"He will hear me first, Father," Sharur said. "When has a Gibli ever fled to Imhursag? That alone will make the god of Imhursag curious enough to hear me. When has a Gibli ever begged Imhursag to strike against his own city? That will make the god of Imhursag glad enough to do it without looking too closely at why a Gibli might say such an outlandish thing."

Slowly, Habbazu said, "Master merchant's son, though the risk is real, as your father has said, I think your words may hold much wisdom."

Ereshguna was not yet ready to give up: "Son, would you start a war between Gibil and Imhursag without leave from Kimash the lugal?"

"I would," Sharur replied without hesitation. "Kimash the lugal has alerted Engibil and his priests against us."

"You would go to Imhursag, knowing you are now free to wed Ningal?" his father enquired. "You would throw away the chance to do what you have longed to do above all else?"

That was a stronger question than any Ereshguna had yet asked. Now Sharur did hesitate. At last, though, he said, "I would. Engibil tried to disrupt my wedding Ningal over this cup; what other reason could the god have had? Then, again on account of it, he reversed his course. We must have it. I shall return. I shall wed Ningal."

"I see I cannot dissuade you," Ereshguna said with a sigh. "You are a man. You have a man's will. Go on to Imhursag, then, if that is what you reckon you must do. I shall stay behind, and pray all follows as you hope."

*Pray to whom?* Sharur wondered. No one in Gibil but Imhursaggi slaves would pray to Enimhursag. Engibil would hope he failed. The great gods of the Alashkurrut would hope he failed. Very likely, the great gods of Kudurru, the gods of sun and moon, sky and storm and underworld, would also hope he failed. That left . . . no one. Sharur felt very much alone.

"Good fortune go with you," Habbazu said. Sharur wondered if he meant it. The thief would have done better for himself, would have obeyed the orders of his god, had he never encountered Sharur. Whether they were sincere or not, though, Sharur gladly accepted his wishes for good fortune. He would need as much as he could find.

# 8

A peasant grubbing at the ground with a stone-headed mattock looked up from his unending labor as Sharur strode north along the path. "Watch where you're going," the peasant warned. "Imhursaggi land starts just beyond that next big canal there." He pointed. "The Imhursagut aren't fond of men from Gibil, either, not even a little they're not."

"I know that," Sharur answered, and kept walking.

The peasant took an especially savage swipe at the dirt. "City man," he muttered, barely loud enough for Sharur to hear. "Has to be a city man. Men from the city never listen to anybody."

*He would probably be happier if Engibil told him what to do*, Sharur thought. *He doesn't seem to be very good at thinking for himself.* Everything that had happened in Gibil the past few generations—metalworking, writing, the rise of rulers who were merely mortal—was of no account to this man, and to thousands like him. Nothing that happened outside his own little village mattered to him, or to his neighbors.

Sharur came to the canal. The peasants working in the fields on the other side were Imhursagut. By looks, they were indistinguishable from the Giblut, save that rather more of them went altogether naked, being too poor to wear even a kilt of linen or wool.

Stripping off his own kilt, his sandals, and his hat, Sharur waded out into the canal. The muddy water was warm as blood. He did not know if he would have to swim in the middle of the canal; he had never come this way before. The water came up to his shoulders, but no higher. He had no trouble keeping his clothes dry.

He stepped up onto the northern, Imhursaggi, bank of the canal and stood there, naked and dripping. The breeze cooled him as it dried the water on his body. Only after he was dry did he don his hat and his sandals and his kilt again. By the time he had it round his middle, he was surrounded by Imhursagut.

Some had mattocks, some had digging sticks, some had nothing but their bare hands. All of them looked ready to beat Sharur to death. Their expressions were frighteningly alike, as if someone had used a cylinder seal to stamp out a long row of identical faces.

"You are a Gibli," one of them said. "You are an intruder. You are an invader. Why do you come to trouble the land of Imhursag? Why do you come to disturb the peace of Enimhursag? Answer at once, lest we tear you to pieces. Answer this instant, lest we smash you down."

"I do not come to trouble the land of Imhursag," Sharur answered: his first lie with his first words. "I do not come to disturb the peace of Enimhursag. I come to escape the city of Gibil, which has fallen into chaos. I come to escape the god of Gibil, who has gone mad."

That made the Imhursaggi peasants stare and mutter among themselves. Enimhursag did not look out of all their eyes all the time; at the moment, they were merely men, trying to make sense of the world as men will.

But the fellow who had threatened Sharur with tearing and smashing now took on the look he had seen in the trader from the Imhursaggi caravan, the look that said Enimhursag was present in his mind. He spoke slowly, as if listening to the god before uttering his words: "What nonsense do you speak? When I look into the land of Gibil, I see everything as it has always been. When I look into the land the Giblut stole from me, I see them doing as they have always done."

"In the farms around the city, everything is as it has always been," Sharur agreed, and he knew he was speaking the truth there. "In the land you can see, the Giblut do as they have always done. In Gibil, Engibil has gone mad, as I say."

"Giblut are liars. They suck in lies with their mothers' milk," Enimhursag answered through the peasant. "What lie do you give me now?"

"I give you no lie, god of Imhursag," Sharur replied, lying. "Hear me. Hear me speak truth. Judge for yourself: Engibil had in his hands, in his heart, an oath of mine. He would not let it go. He refused to let it go."

Out of the peasant's mouth, Enimhursag laughed a great laugh. "Why should he let it go? He is a god—not much of a god, being Engibil, but a god. You are a man—not much of a man, being a Gibli, but a man. He owes you nothing. You owe him everything."

Sharur bowed. "Let it be as you say, god of Imhursag. But hear me. Hear me speak truth. After the god of Gibil did as I said, hear what he did. After the god of Gibil did as I said, he summoned me to his temple and gave me back the oath he held in his hand, in his heart. He let it go. Is the god mad, or is he not?"

"Giblut are liars," Enimhursag repeated. "I do not believe what you say. I cannot believe what you say. No god would give back that which he had refused to give back."

Sharur took a deep breath. "Look into my mind, god of Imhursag," he said, knowing the risk he ran. He had not expected Enimhursag to be quite so dubious. "Look into my mind, god of the Imhursagut. See if Engibil held my oath and would not let it go. See if Engibil held my oath and then did let it go. Look for those two things. See if I speak truth."

Out through the eyes of the peasant poured Enimhursag's power. Sharur did not resist it. Sharur could not resist it. If Enimhursag chose to use that power to paw through everything in his mind, everything would be lost. But he had suggested to the god what he should look for. He put those things at the front of his mind, so Enimhursag might easily find them.

Find them Enimhursag did. "It is so!" the god cried through the peasant's lips. The other peasants exclaimed in astonishment at hearing their god agree with a man of Gibil. Sharur stood very still, trying not to think of Enimhursag pawing through the rest of his mind.

Trying *not* to think about something, Sharur discovered, was like trying not to breathe. He could, with great effort, do it for a short stretch of time, but after that the urge grew more and more demanding until . . .

Enimhursag withdrew. Sharur felt the god leaving his mind, as he had felt his body leaving the water of the canal. "It is so!" Enimhursag repeated. "You have told me the truth. Truly Engibil must be a god run mad upon the earth."

"So we of Gibil believe," Sharur said, not inviting Enimhursag to search his mind this time. "So we of Gibil fear."

"Men should fear the gods," Enimhursag said. "You of Gibil should fear Engibil. You of Gibil fear Engibil too little. But men should fear gods because gods are gods, not because gods are mad."

"Even so," Sharur said.

When the peasant through whom Enimhursag spoke nodded, Sharur did all he could do not to fall to his knees before the tough, unwashed Imhursaggi. The god spoke again: "And what would you have me do about the madness of Engibil?"

"Rescue us!" Sharur cried with all the passion he could muster, all the passion his training as a merchant enabled him to counterfeit so well. "Muster your valiant warriors. Come down and drive from his city the god who is now a terror to it. The Giblut will welcome you as lord. The Giblut will welcome you as liberator, freeing them from a master on whom they may no longer rely."

If Enimhursag was searching his mind at this moment, he was ruined, and he knew it. But he had read the god of Imhursag rightly. The eyes of the peasant through whom the god chose to speak glowed like the sun. "Vengeance shall be mine!" he cried in a great voice. "Vengeance on Gibil shall be mine. Vengeance on the Giblut shall be mine. Vengeance on Engibil shall be mine. The land Gibil, the Giblut, and Engibil have stolen from me shall be mine. And all the rest of the land of Gibil shall be mine as well."

The rest of the Imhursaggi peasants surrounding Sharur cast themselves down on the ground before the one who for the time being embodied their god. They shouted out their delight in the course Enimhursag had chosen for them and their city. How could they do otherwise, in a land where the god could look into their hearts and look out through their eyes whenever he chose, and where he frequently chose to do just that?

One of them asked, "Great god, source of our life, what are we to do with this Gibli who brought you this news you relish? Had the news not been to your liking, we should have slain him, but what are we to do with him now? What will you do with him now?"

Enimhursag might almost have been asking himself the question, as a man might ask himself a question while thinking aloud. Through the lips of the peasant he had chosen, he replied, "Take him to your village. Give him bread. Give him onions. Give him beer. Give him wine. Give him, for his pleasure, the loveliest of your maidens. I would reward him greatly. I *shall* reward him greatly, and more greatly yet after Gibil is in my hands."

Sharur glanced from the peasant in whom the god dwelt to his comrades. That Enimhursag had ordered them to give him food and drink—well and good. That their god had ordered them to give him not merely a woman but a maiden . . . How would they take to that?

"We shall obey in all things, as we always do," one of them murmured, and the rest nodded. They neither looked nor sounded angry or grudging. If the god ordered it, they accepted it. Sharur was glad Enimhursag was not looking into his mind at that moment.

"It is good," Enimhursag said, accepting the obedience

as no less than his due. "Yes, I shall reward this Gibli more greatly yet after his city is in my hands. I shall not rule there as I rule here, not at first. I shall not reach into all men's minds. I shall not reach into all men's hearts."

"What then, great god?" Sharur was curious to learn what Enimhursag planned to do if everything went as he hoped.

"I shall need time to tame the wild men of Gibil," the god replied. His plans filled his thoughts, and he was not shy about setting them forth. While he spoke of himself and what he wanted, he would not be troubling himself with Sharur and what Sharur wanted. He went on, "The wild men of Gibil have lived too long under the wild god, Engibil. The foolish god let them run every which way, as goats will if the goatherd sleeps. They cannot at once be made to obey and hearken as they should."

Sharur nodded. From the god's point of view, all that made good sense. Were Sharur a god planning to subdue a restless, restive city of men, he would have looked at the difficulties facing him the same way.

Engibil continued, "This being so, I shall set a man over them. I shall instruct the man, and the man will instruct the people. He will be my ensi. Perhaps his son will be my ensi. His grandson will be my slave, as all men in Gibil, tamed from their wildness, will then be my slaves."

Now Sharur had to make himself nod. If Enimhursag did conquer Gibil, such a scheme might well eventually subject the Giblut to him. Realizing that made Sharur remember anew what a dangerous game he was playing.

The peasant through whose lips the god spoke thrust out a forefinger. "And you, man of Gibil, you shall be my first ensi in Gibil. I shall instruct you. You will instruct the people. The riches of Gibil shall be yours for the taking. The women of Gibil shall be yours for the taking. Did I not say I should reward you greatly?"

"Great god, you did," Sharur replied, more than a little dizzily. Kimash the lugal had offered him a daughter, which would have tied him to the ruling house of Gibil. Now Enimhursag promised to make him the head of the ruling house of Gibil—the chief slave in a great house of slaves. Enimhursag did not bother to pretend otherwise. The god did not see the need to pretend otherwise.

"You have earned this reward," Enimhursag said. He—in the body of the peasant he inhabited—turned to the other peasants. "He has earned this reward. Take him to your village and make him glad."

In the lands Enimhursag ruled, men obeyed their god. So Sharur had always heard. So Sharur had seen when he went into Imhursag in the guise of a Zuabi merchant. So Sharur saw now, when the peasants, following the orders Enimhursag had given them, took him to their village and methodically made him glad.

These were men who, when he had waded across the canal from the land of Gibil into their land, had been ready to tear him to pieces. But, because their god accepted him, they now accepted him as well—completely, without hesitation, without reservation. As they walked back toward their village, they chattered and bantered with him as if he were one of their own. Because Enimhursag accepted him, he was one of their own.

The village might have been a peasant village outside of Gibil: a cluster of houses, a few of the finer ones built of mud brick, the rest of bundles of reeds and sticks. Ducks and pigs and chickens and naked children roamed the streets, all of them making a terrific racket.

Women came out of the houses to stare when some of their men returned from the fields at an unexpected time. Whispers ran through them, alarmed whispers: "A stranger. They have a stranger with them." Some of the women disappeared as quickly as they had come out. Others stared and stared. Sharur wondered how long it had been since the last stranger came into their village. He wondered if another stranger had ever come into their village.

Loudly, the peasant through whom Enimhursag had

spoken said, "This is a stranger whom Enimhursag delights to honor. This is a stranger whom the great god intends to reward greatly. This is a stranger whom the god commanded us to take to our village and make glad. We are to give him bread. We are to give him onions. We are to give him beer. We are to give him wine. We are to give him, for his pleasure, the loveliest of our maidens." He clapped his hands. "Now, let these things be done."

And those things were done, exactly as Enimhursag had said they should be. The women of the village brought Sharur bread. They brought him onions. The bread was freshly baked, and good. The onions filled his mouth with their strong flavor. When he asked for salt fish to go with the bread and onions, the women muttered among themselves. One of them said. "The god did not speak of salt fish. We shall make you glad as the god bade us make you glad."

"Salt fish would make me glad," Sharur said.

"We shall make you glad as the god bade us make you glad," the woman repeated. Sharur got no salt fish.

They brought him beer. They brought him wine. The beer was tasty. The wine, as he would have expected in a peasant village, left a good deal to be desired. He drank a polite cup of it, then went back to the beer. Out of the corner of his eye, he noticed the villagers worriedly muttering again.

"You have brought me beer, as the god bade you," he said, hiding his amusement. "I have drunk of your beer. You have brought me wine, as the god bade you. I have drunk of your wine. You have made me glad, as the god bade you. I am made glad. The god will be pleased with you." The villagers relaxed.

Sharur did not ask them to bring him the loveliest of their maidens. Had they forgotten that part of Enimhursag's instructions, he would not have minded. He still worried that the villagers would resent such an order, even from their god. He also worried that the maiden would resent it.

But, after he had eaten and drunk, the peasant through whom Enimhursag had spoken came up to him, leading a pretty young woman by the hand. "This is my daughter, Munnabtu," he said, "the loveliest of our maidens. As the god ordained, I bring her to you for your pleasure."

Her eyes were modestly cast down to the ground. Sharur could not see the expression on her face. He said, "If your daughter, Munnabtu, does not wish this, it need not be."

She looked up then, her eyes wide with astonishment. "The god has ordained it," she exclaimed. "What the god has ordained here shall be. What the god has ordained here must be."

When Sharur heard that, he knew he had not understood how completely Enimhursag ruled the people of Imhursag and its surrounding villages. He also knew he would cause more trouble by refusing Munnabtu than by taking her. And, if she was not quite so lovely as some of the loveliest women in Gibil, neither would taking her work a hardship on him. Far from it.

"What Enimhursag has ordained here shall be," he agreed. Munnabtu smiled at him. So did her father. He made himself smile back. Making himself smile back proved not too hard.

The villagers cleared out one of their huts for Munnabtu and him. Several women brought in blankets and rush mats. They giggled as they went out the door and closed it behind them. That helped ease Sharur's mind; women in Gibil would have done the same thing.

With the door closed, it was gloomy and stuffy inside the hut. "Let us begin," Munnabtu said forthrightly, and pulled her tunic off over her head. Her body, high-breasted, with a narrow waist and broad hips, had no flaw Sharur could find. She lay down and waited for him to join her.

He wasted no time in doing just that. Because he was a stranger to her, because she did not lie down beside him out of love, he expected her to be still and let him do what he would, as the Imhursaggi slave woman was in the habit of doing. But, as his hands roamed over her body, she sighed and pressed herself against him. Her mouth was eager against his.

"What Enimhursag has ordained here is sweet," she murmured, and then he saw that, because the god had ordained it, she gave herself to it with her whole heart, as the Imhursaggi slave had on that one occasion when Sharur went into her in fulfillment of his vow.

Munnabtu sighed again when Sharur's mouth, following his hands, moved down her belly toward the triangle of midnight hair between her legs. Presently, she gasped and arched her back and urged him on with more murmurs that were not quite words.

Her legs spread wide. He poised himself between them. When he entered her, he discovered she was truly a maiden. She stiffened and grimaced. "You hurt me," she said, sudden fear in her eyes.

He drew back a little, though he wanted nothing so much as to go forward. "I will be gentle," he promised, and returned to the barrier he would have to break.

Munnabtu grimaced again, and made as if to pull away from him. Then something in her face . . . changed. Sharur could not have described it more precisely than that. For a moment, Enimhursag looked out at him through her eyes. In a voice not quite her own, she said, "Go on. All will be well."

He almost pulled away then. Never had he imagined coupling with a woman in whom the god dwelt. But her thighs clasped his flanks; her legs caged him. Instead of pulling back, he did go on, and all was well. Herself again, so far as Sharur could tell, Munnabtu gasped when he fully fleshed himself in her, but she was no longer afraid. She gasped again, a little later, in a different way, and squeezed Sharur so tightly that he groaned in his pleasure and spurted forth his seed.

She was bleeding a little when he withdrew, but it did not trouble her. Pleasure suffused her features, pleasure and . . . something else? Now Sharur could not be sure. "The god helped me," she said. "Enimhursag helped me." Was it altogether her voice? Again, Sharur could not be sure.

He agreed nonetheless: "Yes, the god helped you." He could scarcely deny it.

She looked up at him from eyes shining under half-lowered eyelids. "And you helped me, man whom the great god ordered me to make glad. You made me glad in turn, though the god did not order you to do that. You could have taken your own pleasure without caring for mine."

"A man has more pleasure when a woman shares it," Sharur said.

"Ah." Munnabtu stretched. It was the sort of stretch that made him try to watch every part of her at once. It was intended to be that sort of stretch, for when it was done she sat up and asked, "Would you have more pleasure? Would you give more pleasure?"

Sharur's manhood stirred. Knowing he could take her again, he said, "Are you sure? You have just had your maidenhead broken. You may take more pain than pleasure if we go again so soon."

"I do not think that will be so, but if it is—" She shrugged. Her firm, dark-tipped breasts bounced only a little. "If it is, Enimhursag will make it right. The god watches over me."

They began again. This time, Sharur could not tell whether or not Enimhursag aided Munnabtu. Whether the god of Imhursag aided the woman or not, she enjoyed the passage as much as he did, and he enjoyed it a great deal.

"Have I made you glad, as the god ordered me to do?" she asked, smiling up at him as they lay together covered in sweat, their bodies still joined. It was not the smile of a god. It was the smile of a woman, a woman who knew the answer before she asked the question.

"You have made me glad," Sharur said. "You have also made me tired." He took his weight off his elbows and flopped down limply onto her. She squawked and laughed and pushed him away.

She pulled on her tunic before he redonned his kilt. Picking up the blanket on which they had lain together, she went out of the hut. Sharur followed a moment later, as Munnabtu faced shouts from the village: "The stranger whom Enim-hursag bade us make glad, is he made glad?"

"I *am* made glad," Sharur said.

"He *is* made glad," Munnabtu agreed, and displayed the blanket with the small bloodstain on it as proof. Everyone cheered.

Sharur would have been content—Sharur, in fact, would have been delighted—to stay for some time in the village near the border with Gibli land. That did not come to pass. After breakfast the next morning (bread, onions, beer, and wine: the peasants obeyed Enimhursag in every particular and went beyond his instructions in no particular), the god of the Imhursagut again spoke to him through Munnabtu's father: "Gibli who warned me that Engibil runs mad in his city, you will now journey to my city, to see how I make ready to repay him for the many affronts and humiliations he has afforded me. This man whose mouth I use shall be your guide."

"As you order, great god, so shall it be," Sharur replied, bowing to the peasant and to the god who inhabited him. He did not want to go to Imhursag. He would have a harder time escaping Imhursaggi soil from the central city than from regions near the border. But he dared not refuse Enimhursag.

He also wished Enimhursag had chosen a different guide; he would sooner have traveled with someone other than the father of the maiden he had deflowered the day before. But the peasant, whose name, he learned, was Aratta, still seemed content that he and Munnabtu had followed the god's wishes.

When Enimhursag had withdrawn from him, Aratta said, "I will bring bread and onions. I will bring beer and wine. Thus you will be glad on the road to Imhursag."

"Thus I will be glad on the road to Imhursag," Sharur agreed resignedly. He had come to the conclusion that arguing with Imhursagut was pointless, especially when they were convinced they were acting as their god required them to act.

He and Aratta were far from the only travelers on the road to Imhursag. As the day wore along, more and more men joined them, so that they walked as if in the middle of a dust storm that never subsided. Some of the men carried clubs with heads of stone or, rarely, bronze. Some carried spears. Some carried bows and wore quivers on their backs. About every other man with a spear or club also bore a shield of wicker or leather.

"Imhursag arms for war," Aratta said proudly. "Enimhursag arms for war. How the Giblut will cower! How Engibil will tremble!"

"Imhursag arms for war," Sharur echoed. By echoing one part of what his guide said, he let the man—and the god who might be, who probably was, listening through him—gain the impression he was echoing all parts of what Aratta said.

Gibil's peasant levies were not much different from Imhursag's peasant levies. Sharur did not think his people would cower. He did not think his god would tremble. He did hope Engibil would notice.

He came under the walls of Imhursag a little before noon the next day. What he saw outside the city convinced him that Engibil would indeed notice what Enimhursag purposed hurling against Gibil. Already a large encampment had sprung into being, an encampment that grew larger by the moment as men came in to it from the countryside and out to it from the city. With so many men moving busily through it, it put Sharur in mind of an anthill: a thought he carefully kept to himself.

Through Aratta, Enimhursag said, "See the might Imhursag brings to bear against the god run mad. See the might Imhursag brings to bear under the god who is the shepherd of his people."

"I see," Sharur said, and see he did. Not only was Enimhursag summoning the peasant levies who would, for the most part, spread over Gibil's fields to rob and burn, he was also gathering together the men who would fight battles in the van. Some were his priests, striding through the camp with bronze swords and bronze-headed axes, helmets of bronze or of bronze and leather on their shaved heads, corselets of bronze scales over leather protecting their vitals. Some were Imhursaggi nobles, also armored, who rode in four-wheeled chariots drawn by donkeys, from which they would ply the Giblut with spears and arrows.

"See the might a ruling god can bring to bear when he chooses," Enimhursag boasted. "See the force that will blow away the Giblut as the wind blows away chaff at harvest time. See the fierce, bold warriors before whom Engibil shall tremble. See the strong, brave warriors who will course Engibil as the hounds course an antelope."

"I see the might, great god," Sharur said. "I see the force. I see the warriors." He took a deep breath. "Truly it will be fine to have men who know and honor the strength and majesty of their god come into Gibil once more."

Had Enimhursag peered into his heart at that moment to learn whether he spoke truth, all his hopes would have crashed to the ground like a mud-brick house collapsing when its roof got too heavy. But Enimhursag, as Sharur had thought he would, had become convinced Sharur's story of Gibil in disarray and Engibil mad was so because he thought that was how things in the neighboring city should be, and no longer saw the need of examining the words of the Gibli who had come to Imhursag to bring him such wonderful news.

Through Aratta, Enimhursag said, "Come and be made known to my warriors. Let them see the man who will rule Gibil in my name after they drive the raving Engibil from the temple his presence now profanes. Let them see the ensi through whom I shall rule as the great god of Gibil."

"I obey," Sharur said, which was a reply always acceptable to Enimhursag. Sharur obeyed with something less than a heart full of gladness; the more who knew him here, the more he was kept at the center of Imhursag's army, the more difficult would his escape be.

But Aratta took his arm and led him through the milling hosts of Imhursag, crying out with Enimhursag's authority in his voice to clear a path for the man who had caused the god to assemble his army. He urged Sharur up onto a small swell of ground and went up there with him, calling to the growing army: "Warriors, see the man who will rule Gibil in Enimhursag's name after you drive the raving Engibil from the temple his presence now profanes. See the ensi through whom Enimhursag will rule as the great god of Gibil."

All the assembled warriors cheered. The peasant levies gaped at Sharur, as peasant levies throughout the land between the rivers habitually gaped on the rare occasions when they saw something new and unfamiliar. Enimhursag's priests examined him with eyes as sharp as those of hunting hawks. And the nobles of Imhursag sized him up as a potential rival. He could see that in the calculating expressions they carefully hid—but not fast enough—when his gaze lit on them. He did a much better job of hiding his own smile. Even in Imhursag, some folk looked to their own advantage, not merely that of the god.

He knew he would have to say something, with so many men staring so expectantly. Taking a deep breath, he called out in a loud voice: "Imhursagut, may you gain what is rightfully yours in the coming war against Gibil. May Enimhursag gain all the revenge rightfully his in the coming fight against Engibil." He suspected he and they had differing opinions on how much that was, but did not feel inclined to go into detail over the differences.

The Imhursagut took his words as he had hoped they would. The peasants cheered once more. The priests nodded in satisfaction; he took that satisfaction to mean Enimhursag was also satisfied with what he said. And the nobles looked as if they had bitten into plums not yet ripe enough to be sweet.

Through Aratta, Enimhursag cried, "We march against Gibil! We shall overthrow the Giblut! We shall cast down

Engibil! We shall liberate the city to the south from its mad god, who lets its men run wild.''

Now the cheers were loud and unending. When the god spoke, those he ruled agreed with and approved of what he said. It could hardly have been otherwise, as he helped guide them toward just such agreement and approval.

''In two days' time, we march against Gibil!'' Enimhursag shouted. The roar from his warriors left Sharur's ears stunned and ringing, as if he had been caught in the center of a thunderstorm. The priests led the peasants in a hymn of praise to the might and wisdom and splendor of their god.

Giblut going off to war praised Engibil, too, and asked for his aid against their foes. But no Gibli since the time of Igigi—and probably since long before the time of Igigi—would ever have sung, as the Imhursagut sang, ''With you, great god, we can do anything. Without you, great god, we can do nothing.'' Giblut took too much pride—aye, and too much pleasure, too—in doing things for themselves to think they were impotent when they did not lean on their god as a feeble old man leaned on his stick.

''When we cross into Gibil, the Giblut shall flee before us,'' Enimhursag said to Sharur. ''When we cross into Gibil, Engibil shall not stand against us.''

''So you have said, great god,'' Sharur replied.

''So I have said,'' Enimhursag replied complacently. ''So shall it be, for I, a god, have said it.'' He took Sharur's silence for agreement.


In two days' time, the army of Imhursag marched on Gibil. Sharur marched at its head, still accompanied by Aratta, through whom Enimhursag had chosen to speak for the time being. Behind him came the nobles in their slow, heavy chariots and the warrior-priests with their armor and axes and swords. Behind them, eating their dust, trudged the peasant levies who made up the bulk of the army.

More peasants joined Imhursag's army as it moved southwards. Some came in from the west, some from the east, and some, breathless with exertion, caught up with the host from behind, from out of the north. "Never have we gone to war with so great a host," Enimhursag declared through Aratta's lips. "Never have we gone to war with so valiant a host."

"They are as many as the ears of barley nodding in the fields," Sharur said, like any wise merchant quick to agree with the one in whose company he found himself. "Surely they will prove as valiant in battle as so many lions."

Aratta's lips shaped a smile. It was not quite a man's smile. It was the god's smile, written on the flesh of a man. Seeing it made Sharur's own flesh creep. Despite the effort it took, he smiled back.

He looked back over his shoulder at Imhursag's army. Enimhursag had believed him and acted on that belief even more strongly and quickly than he had hoped. Uppermost in his mind was the question of how he would escape the army when the time came. He felt like a hare in a pot, waiting in the market to be sold as someone's supper.

"Are they not splendid?" Enimhursag said. "Are they not magnificent? Are they not formidably armed and equipped?" The god paused, looking at Sharur through Aratta's eyes. Such moments always made Sharur fight to hold in his fear: would Enimhursag be content to look at him, or would the god look into him as well? This time, Enimhursag was looking at him, no more. The god went on, "You, Gibli, are not formidably armed."

"That is so." Sharur touched the bronze knife that hung on his belt. "I have no other weapon besides this."

"This should not be," Enimhursag said. A moment later, one of his warriors came trotting forward and pressed into Sharur's hands a bronze-headed mace. Enimhursag went on, "Now you have a proper weapon with which to chastise the wild folk and mad god of your city."

"Great god, you are generous. You are forethoughtful. You leave me in your debt." Sharur would have preferred a sword. If Enimhursag had chosen to give him a mace, though, he would take it without complaint. It was a better weapon than he had had before.

"I do indeed leave you in my debt," the god said. "When Gibil is mine, you shall repay me. When Gibil is mine, Gibil shall repay me. Gibil has owed me for long, for long."

Aratta's eyes blazed. Sharur looked down at the ground. What he felt now was awe, not fear. Seeing the power of the god in the man reminded him he was truly a wild Gibil madman to play this game.

Enimhursag's army moved no more swiftly than its slowest soldiers. The god halted the host well before sunset, too, so that his men might encamp far enough from the border to keep the Giblut from noticing anything out of the ordinary. That was sound generalship of the most elementary sort. Sharur was disappointed to find the most elementary sound generalship from Enimhursag.

Once in camp, Imhursag's peasant levies acted as the peasant levies of Gibil would have acted: they made themselves as comfortable as they could, got food and drink, and then either fell asleep or sat around the fires talking and singing.

The nobles slept in pavilions of wool and linen; slaves fanned them to keep them cool in the warm night. A few did not sleep, but gathered round Sharur, questioning him about the roads down toward Gibil and about the opposition they might face. "The Giblut have invented nothing new since we faced them last, have they?" one of the nobles asked anxiously. "I never did see such people for inventing new things."

"No, they have no new weapons," Sharur answered truthfully. The noble let out a sigh of relief.

One of Enimhursag's shaven-headed priests gave the fellow a reproving look. "The ingenuity of the Giblut is of no account. They are only men, toying with the things of men. We have the power of the god with us."

"Do not sneer at the things of men," the noble returned. "The grandfather of my grandfather died by the sword in a war against Gibil, back in the days when the Giblut had such things of men and we had them not.''

''We have them now,'' the priest said. ''Enimhursag has ordained that we should have them, and so we do.''

He missed the point entirely. The noble rolled his eyes, understanding that he missed the point entirely. But most of the other nobles, all the other priests, and Aratta in whom Enimhursag was dwelling nodded in approval at the priest's words. Sharur had noted before that Imhursagut thought more slowly than Giblut, not least because their god was doing part of their thinking for them. He saw it again here.

And the noble, who also saw it, bowed his head and said no more. Most of the Giblut whom Sharur knew would have gone on arguing. Justified or not, Giblut had confidence in their own wits. Confidence in their own wits was a large part of what made them Giblut.

Aratta lay down on the ground and fell asleep, as if he were still no more than a peasant. No. Sharur stared. Aratta floated a couple of digits above the ground, and slept on a cushion of air. When mosquitoes tried to land on him, they could not, but buzzed away unsatisfied. And when Sharur lay down, he discovered he did not touch the ground, either. Enimhursag granted him the same soft rest as he did to the man in whom he had chosen to dwell for the time being. Nor did insects bite him. He passed as luxurious a night as any in all his life.

The rising sun woke him. Beside him, Aratta was already awake and alert. Perhaps the peasant woke quickly every day. Perhaps, too, having the god looking out through his eyes roused him to early alertness.

Through Aratta, Enimhursag said, ''Today, we cross into the land the Giblut stole from Imhursag. Today, we cross into the land Engibil stole from me. Today, that land returns to its rightful owner.''

''Have you sent scouts into the land the Giblut rule?'' Sharur asked. ''Have you sent spies into the land that once belonged to Imhursag?''

Enimhursag shook Aratta's head. ''I have not done this.

In the land where I rule, I can at my will see through any man's eyes, hear through any man's ears. I can reach beyond my borders where the gods of the lands are not my enemies. But in the land of the raving Engibil, I am as one blind and deaf.''

"Ah.'' Sharur nodded, remembering how the family's Imhursaggi slave woman mourned the absence of Enimhursag from her spirit. He said, "If it please you, great god, I can go into Gibil, scout ahead, and then come back and tell you what I see. If an Imhursaggi tried this, he would give himself away, but I would not betray myself, having been born a Gibli.''

"Yes, you were born a Gibli,'' Enimhursag said, as if reminding himself. Sharur was acutely conscious it was the god studying him through Aratta's eyes. If Enimhursag did more than study him . . . But, after that measuring stare, the god went on, "Yes, go into the land Engibil took from me. Accompanying will be the noble Nasibugashi. He, too, will scout ahead. You were born a Gibli. You will protect him, so he will not betray himself.''

"It shall be as you say.'' Sharur bowed his head.

"Of course it shall.'' Enimhursag allowed himself no room for doubt.

Nasibugashi proved to be the noble who had wondered whether the Giblut would bring any new weapons to the war. Sharur judged him a shrewd choice on Enimhursag's part. He seemed more his own man, less drunk on the power of the god, than most Imhursagut. That would make him better able to act on his own in Gibil than others from his city might have been.

"Let us be off,'' he said to Sharur. "Let us be moving. The farther ahead of the army we get, the deeper into Gibil we can go, the more we can see, the more word we can bring back to the warriors and the god.''

"These things are true,'' Sharur said. Was Enimhursag looking out through Nasibugashi's eyes, too? Sharur had trouble telling, far more so than he had with Aratta. Perhaps Enimhursag's presence was lighter in the noble. Or perhaps

Nasibugashi had more personality of his own than did the peasant, making Enimhursag's presence harder to discern.

As Nasibugashi had urged, Sharur and he hurried out ahead of the host of Imhursag. When they walked through the village to which Aratta and the other peasants had brought Sharur after he crossed into Imhursaggi land, Munnabtu came out of her house and waved to him. "The god told me you were coming this way," she said, smiling. "Did I make you glad?"

"Truly, you made me glad," Sharur answered, and smiled back.

"You made her glad, too," Nasibugashi said. Was he only a man, judging by a woman's smile, or was the god speaking through him with certain knowledge? The latter, Sharur judged: he sounded very certain.

Sharur and Nasibugashi walked through the fields south of the village toward the canal that marked the border between Imhursaggi land and Gibli. The peasants working in those fields waved to Sharur almost as Munnabtu had done. When he entered Imhursaggi territory, their only thought had been to kill him. Now, because their god was well pleased with him, they, too, were well pleased with him.

On the southern side of the canal, Gibli peasants performed similar labor in similar fields with tools also similar save that rather more of them were bronze and rather fewer stone. Curious as magpies, they looked up from their work to see what the two men on the Imhursaggi bank of the waterway would do.

What Sharur did was slide off his kilt and shake his feet out of his sandals. After a moment, Nasibugashi imitated him. Together, the two men stepped naked into the warm, muddy waterway of the canal.

About halfway across, Nasibugashi let out a soft exclamation of surprise. "The god's voice fades in my ears," he murmured. "The god's presence fades from my mind. I am alone within myself, as I have never been before." He cocked his head to one side, as if listening internally. "I do not feel Engibil trying to fill the emptiness the loss of Enimhursag has left behind."

"No, you wouldn't," Sharur agreed. "Engibil isn't—there—all the time, the way Enimhursag is." Remembering the times when Engibil had spoken in his mind, he wished the god made his presence known even less often.

When the two men came up onto the Gibli side of the canal, peasants loped toward them. The peasants who had been working in the fields of Imhursag came down to the bank of the canal and stared across with round, wide eyes to see what sort of reception Sharur and Nasibugashi got.

"What are you two doing here?" one of the Gibli peasants asked. Unlike Imhursagut, he and his comrades seemed more interested in the new arrivals than angry about them. "Don't often see people coming this way, where their god can't yell in their ear all the time." He spoke with good-natured contempt.

"It's not so bad," Nasibugashi said. Sharur nodded; Enimhursag had indeed made a good choice in him. A more god-assotted Imhursaggi—a priest, say—would have been as bereft as a canal fish suddenly thrown up on land.

"What about you?" the peasant asked Sharur.

"I don't think it's so bad, either," Sharur said. "Shall we get out of the reach of all the big, staring eyes?" He nodded toward the Imhursaggi peasants, through whose eyes and ears Enimhursag was no doubt seeing and hearing.

One of those Imhursaggi peasants would have failed to understand what he meant, would have made him explain more than he wanted to explain, more than would have been wise to explain. As he had hoped they would be, as he had thought they would be, the Giblut were quicker on the uptake. "All right, we'll go for a walk," their leader said.

The Imhursagut kept staring after them. After a bowshot or so, they went up and over a tiny hillock, so that the border canal and the Imhursagut on the other side of it were no longer visible.

Sharur pointed to Nasibugashi and said, in bright, conversational tones, "This man is an Imhursaggi spy. You should seize him."

With commendable quickness, the Gibli peasants did just that. With equally commendable quickness, they also seized Sharur. Their leader asked, "And why should we listen to you, whoever you are?"

"Because, sometime before nightfall, Imhursag's army will swarm over the canal," Sharur answered. "Enimhursag sent us ahead to spy out the land."

Nasibugashi's eyes looked as if they would bug out of his head. "You betray the god!" he gasped. A moment later, he found something even more appalling to say: "You deceived the god!"

His horror convinced the Giblut to take Sharur seriously. That horror probably did a better job of convincing them to take Sharur seriously than anything he could have managed on his own. The peasant who had been doing the talking for his comrades asked, "Who are you, anyhow?"

"I am Sharur, the son of Ereshguna the master merchant," Sharur answered, which made Nasibugashi's eyes get even wider. Back in the lands of his own city, Sharur smiled an enormous smile. "I have indeed betrayed the god of Imhursag. I have indeed deceived the god of Imhursag."

"It is well done!" the peasant cried. He and his friends pounded Sharur on the back for fooling the god of the rival city. Sharur wondered what they would have done had they known he had fooled Enimhursag into launching an attack on Gibil.

"How did you deceive the god?" Nasibugashi asked. He sounded half astonished that Sharur should have imagined such a thing, let alone accomplished it, half curious to learn his exact method.

"Never mind." Sharur spoke to the Gibli peasants: "Spread the word that the Imhursagut are coming. Women and children should flee, men should get weapons, harry the invaders, and fall back on the main army, which will, I have no doubt, muster between the city and the invaders."

Some of the peasants—those who had been standing

around and those who had been holding Sharur—dashed off
to do as he had asked. Nasibugashi stared again. "Does not
the god of Gibil tell his people what needs doing?" he said,
astonished again.

Sharur and the peasants who still held the Imhursaggi
noble looked at one another and started to laugh. "Sometimes he does and sometimes he doesn't," Sharur answered.
"Sometimes the people figure out what needs doing before
the god does."

"How can this be?" Nasibugashi cried in honest bewilderment.

"Not hard at all," one of the peasants answered with
another chuckle. "Engibil is that kind of god—and we are
that kind of people."

"Be gentle with this one, as gentle as you can," Sharur
told them. "For an Imhursaggi, he is very much his own
man. Had he been born in Gibil, he would be his own man.
Had he been born in Gibil, he might well be a great man."

"As you say it, master merchant's son, it shall be," the
peasant said. "What shall we do with him now?"

"A good question." Sharur had not thought past laying
hold of Nasibugashi. He spoke in thoughtful tones: "He is
my captive. Perhaps I shall make him my slave and have
him serve me."

The Gibli peasants burst into laughter. The Imhursaggi
noble burst into curses as vile as any Sharur had ever heard
from caravan guards or donkey handlers. The curses made
the Gibli peasants laugh louder.

Sharur said, "Or, perhaps, I shall see whether his kin or
his god care to ransom him. He is a clever man; he would
make a clever slave, and might escape. He is a bold man;
he would make a bold slave, and might seek to slay me. For
now, let us take him back to Gibil. We can decide his fate
there."

"It shall be as you say," the peasants said as one. And
then, almost as one, they went on, "Master merchant's son,
you will reward us for helping you take him to the city?"

"I shall reward you for helping me take him to the city,"

Sharur promised. "The house of Ereshguna does not stint."

"No," Nasibugashi said bitterly. "The house of Ereshguna cheats."

"It is not so," Sharur said. "I am a Gibli. I serve my own needs. I serve the needs of Gibil. I serve the needs of Engibil."

"You are a Gibli," Nasibugashi agreed. "You put the needs of your god last. Were you a proper man, you would put those needs first."

"I am a proper man. I am a proper Gibli," Sharur said. "Now your god is out of your mind, Nasibugashi. Perhaps you, too, will learn to be a man first, a creature of the gods only afterwards."

Nasibugashi did not answer. Sharur studied him. Of all the Imhursagut he had met, this noble was the first who indeed might learn to be a man before he was a creature of the gods. Sharur wondered if his wisest course might not be to keep Nasibugashi in Gibil for a time, to let him learn what living in a city full of men who were their own men was like, and then to let him return to Imhursag, to see if he might sow the seeds of such a city under Enimhursag's nose.

"Let us go on to Gibil," Sharur said. One of the peasants gave Nasibugashi a push. Outrage still mingling with astonishment on his face, the Imhursaggi noble stumbled south toward Sharur's city.


Engibil might not have warned the folk of Gibil that the Imhursagut were invading, as Enimhursag had assembled the folk of Imhursag for the invasion. But news of trouble with Imhursag had far outsped Sharur's coming to the city. Already, peasants with spears and bows and clubs and shields were forming into companies to oppose the Imhursagut. Already, nobles in donkey-drawn chariots rode north toward the canal that marked Gibil's boundary with its hostile neighbor.

"Where are your warrior-priests?" Nasibugashi asked as

yet another chariot rumbled past, ungreased axles squealing.

"We have only a handful," Sharur answered. "Most of our priesthood serves the god in his temple. That is his home. That is where he needs servants. Men take care of the business of the city."

"Madness," the Imhursaggi noble said. "Madness."

"It could be so," Sharur said. "But I, a mad Gibli, deceived Enimhursag, and had no great trouble in doing so." He exaggerated there. He knew he exaggerated there. But Nasibugashi did not know and would not know he exaggerated there. He went on, "And, when we mad Giblut go to war with Imhursag, who these days comes off victorious?"

"It will be different this time," Nasibugashi said.

Sharur showed his teeth in what was not quite a smile. "I doubt it," he said. "Come—now we go into Gibil."

"Well, well," Ereshguna said when Sharur and the Gibli peasants led Nasibugashi into his presence. "Well, well. My son, you not only thrust your hand into the jaw of the lion again, you come home with a prize as well. He looks as if he will make a fine slave."

"Actually, I was thinking of ransoming him, if we can get a good enough price," Sharur said. "He is a noble in Imhursag; I am not sure how well he would take to slavery."

"A taste of the lash would probably convince him to obey—it does with most slaves," Ereshguna said, his voice dry. "Still, he is your captive, and so your property. You may do with him as you wish." He examined Nasibugashi more closely. "Mm—perhaps you are right. He does look to have a wild horse's spirit, doesn't he?"

Nasibugashi threw back his head and gave forth with the bugling cry of the donkey's untamed relative. Sharur and Ereshguna stared at him, then burst into laughter. Sharur said, "These men need to be rewarded for helping me bring this horse from the border with Imhursag to the city. I promised them we would repay them for their aid.''

"We shall do it," Ereshguna said at once. "We should
have done it even had you not promised." He gave all the
peasants small broken bits of gold.

They were loud in the praises of the house of Ereshguna.
One of them told Sharur, "Truly, master merchant's son,
you knew whereof you spoke when you told us your family
did not stint."

"How can you have so much gold, to give of it to peasants?" Nasibugashi asked as those peasants, rejoicing,
headed back toward their village. "The gods hate Gibil.
Folk from the surrounding cities, folk from the surrounding
lands, hate Gibil. They will not trade with Gibil. And yet
you have gold, to throw away to peasants. How can this
be?"

"I have honor," Ereshguna said. "I have pride. Were it
the last gold I possess—and it is far from the last gold I
possess, Imhursaggi—I would give it to these peasants for
the sake of my honor, for the sake of my pride. I am a man.
These are the things a man does. Do you understand that?"

"In Imhursag, these are the things the god would have a
man do," Nasibugashi said.

"I do not need the god to tell me what to do," Ereshguna
said. "By myself, I know what to do. This is what being a
man means."

"You Giblut are strange," the captive Imhursaggi noble
said. "Word by word, what you say makes sense. Idea by
idea, oftentimes what you say is madness."

Horns blared outside. A bronze-lunged herald shouted the
name of Kimash the lugal. Down the Street of Smiths came
Kimash, not in his usual litter but in a chariot with gilded
sides drawn by donkeys with gilded reins and harnesses. His
helmet, all of bronze, was also gilded, as was his armor, and
as was the bronze head of the spear he brandished.

People on the Street of Smiths cheered themselves hoarse
when Kimash and his retinue went past. The lugal's guards
were less splendid only than Kimash himself. Their gilded
shields and helmets sparkled in the sunlight. They looked

hard and tough and at least a match for any of the warriors
Sharur had seen in the Imhursaggi force.

"Great is the lugal!" cried the people. "Mighty is the
lugal! Strong in Gibil's defense is the lugal! The lugal and
his bold men will drive back the wicked invaders! The lugal
and his men will bring home slaves and booty! Engibil loves
the mighty lugal!"

"So this is what it means to have a lugal," Nasibugashi
said. "You have made him into a god, and mention the true
god of your city only as an afterthought." His lip curled to
show what he thought of that.

"No city can be without a ruler," Sharur said reasonably.
"We have a ruler who is one of us, not one who treats the
men and women of Gibil as if they were cattle and sheep
in the fields."

"We are the cattle of our god," the Imhursaggi noble
said. "We are proud to be the cattle of our god. Enimhursag
is our master. Enimhursag is our lord. We are his, to do
with as he would."

"We are *ours*, to do with as we would," Sharur answered.

Ereshguna pointed to Nasibugashi. "What shall we do
with this divine cow here?" he asked. "We, too, shall have
to go to war against the Imhursagut, you know, and we can
hardly take him with us."

"I know, Father," Sharur said with a sigh. He had succeeded better than he expected, and started a larger war between Imhursag and Gibil than he had thought he would.
As his father had said, Gibil would need every man who
could afford good bronze weapons and armor of leather and
bronze. He sighed again. "This is liable to interfere with
our other business."

"So it is," Ereshguna agreed. "That cannot be helped,
though, not when Gibil depends on its men to save it. And
I have a scheme for dealing with that other business."

"Have you?" Sharur said. "Good." Neither he nor his
father spoke of Habbazu or Engibil's temple or the cup
within Engibil's temple, not in front of Nasibugashi. Now

Sharur pointed to the noble he had captured. "Let us give him into the hands of Ushurikti the slave dealer for safe-keeping."

"Wait!" Nasibugashi cried. "You said I would not be a slave—well, you said I might not be a slave. Have you now changed your mind?"

"No," Sharur answered. "Ushurikti will house you and keep you from escaping until you may be ransomed. We will pay him for your keep, and add the cost to the ransom we receive for you. Only if your kin or your god refuse to ransom you will you be sold as a slave."

"It is good," Ereshguna said. "So it will be."

"It is *not* good," Nasibugashi said. "I believed you, Gibli. My god believed you. You deceived me. You deceived my god."

"I do not serve Imhursagut," Sharur said. "I do not serve Enimhursag. I serve the Giblut. I serve Gibil." Here, he did not bother adding that he served Engibil. He was used to deceiving his own god. Since he had done that for so long, deceiving another god came easier.

Ereshguna said, "Come. Let us take him to Ushurikti."

"Let us warn Ushurikti to watch him with care," Sharur said. "He may seek to run away, and he is clever."

"Were I so clever, would I be here?" Nasibugashi asked. Neither Sharur nor Ereshguna heeded him. They had no need to heed him. He was a captive, in a city not his own. oThey took him to Ushurikti the slave dealer.


Habbazu bowed to Sharur. "Master merchant's son, you have done what you set out to do. Engibil now surely heeds the northern border, not his own temple. This is surely the time to snatch from it the Alashkurri cup."

"No, my friend from Zuabu, it is not quite the time, not yet," Ereshguna said to the thief. "Here: see. We have fine gifts for you, better than any you could steal."

Sharur presented the gifts to Habbazu: a bronze sword, its hilt wrapped with gold wire, in a leather sheath; a helmet of stiff leather, reinforced with bronze plate; and a leather corselet with overlapping bronze scales. "All these are yours," Sharur said.

"They are very fine." Habbazu bowed. "You are indeed generous to me. Whether they are finer than any I could steal, I do not know. I have pride in my thieving, as you have pride in your trading. But they are very fine. Still, I must ask of you: why do you give me a warrior's tools, when I am not a warrior but a thief? Why do you give me these tools now, when thievery is needed? Why do you give me them now, when fighting is not needed?"

"Because fighting is needed: fighting against the Imhursagut," Ereshguna answered. "After we have beaten them, while Engibil's eyes remain on the northern border to make sure Enimhursag does not renew the fight, we shall hurry back to Gibil. Then indeed will thievery be needed."

Habbazu's skinny face twisted into a grimace of distaste. "You think that, if I steal this Alashkurri cup while you are away from Gibil, I will keep it for myself. You think that, if I steal this cup while you are away from the city, I will take it back to Enzuabu."

"Yes, we think that," Sharur agreed. "Did you stand where we stand, would you not think that as well?"

To his surprise, the question made Habbazu grin. "Well, perhaps I might, master merchant's son. Perhaps I might. Will you also pay me to fight for a city that is not mine?"

"We will," Ereshguna said, and then he grinned, too. "Who says you are not a merchant as well as a thief?"

"I say so," Habbazu replied with dignity. "Being a merchant is hard work. Being a merchant is also boring work. Being a thief is hard work, too, I cannot deny. But being a thief is never boring work."

"Not even when you have to wait and wait before you can commit your theft?" Sharur asked slyly.

"Not even then," Habbazu said. "While I wait, I commonly sit in taverns. I drink beer. I eat salt fish and onions. Sometimes I even eat mutton. If I see a pretty courtesan, I give her metal or trinkets to lie down on a mat with me and do as I desire. Perhaps some men would be bored with this life. If that be so, I am not among them.''

"That is not all there is to a thief's life," Ereshguna said. "If it were, all men would be thieves. No one would run a tavern. No one would brew beer. No one would catch fish or salt it. No one would raise onions. No one would herd sheep or butcher them. No courtesan would lie down on a mat for metal or trinkets if she could more easily steal them.''

"Master merchant, what you say is true, but it is true only in part," Habbazu answered. "Many men are merchants. How many of them lead the life of a master merchant like yourself? Only the handful who are also master merchants, as you are. Many men, too, are thieves. How many of them lead the life of a master thief like myself? Only the handful who are also master thieves, as I am.''

"Indeed, you are not to be despised in argument," Ereshguna said slowly.

"Indeed, he is not," Sharur agreed. "If he can fight as well as he can argue, the Imhursagut will have yet another reason to flee the might of Gibil.''

Habbazu said, "I am not part of the might of Gibil. I am part of the might of Zuabu." He held up a hand. Like his face, his fingers were long and clever. "If you would call me a Zuabi mercenary serving with Gibil, I should not quarrel over that.''

"How generous of you," Sharur said. He laughed to show he meant no offense. Habbazu laughed to show he took none. Sharur looked around. Shadows were thickening. Colors were fading. "Let us eat supper, then let us sleep. In the morning, we will march to the north with my brother Tupsharru. We will help beat the Imhursagut, and then we will return.''

No sooner had the words gone forth from his mouth than Tupsharru came into the house. "I see you have given Habbazu weapons," he said. "He will fight for us before he steals for us?''

"He will," Ereshguna said. "He is a Zuabi mercenary

serving with Gibil. He says as much, so how could it be otherwise?''

"You mock me," Habbazu said. "I am cut to the quick." He mimed staggering about after having taken a deadly wound.

When Sharur, Ereshguna, Tupsharru, and Habbazu set out the next morning, they were not alone. The Street of Smiths was emptying. The men who made the weapons for Gibil also carried them to defend their city. Even bald, heavy Dimgalabzu shouldered a long-handled ax with a great head.

"Going to chop down some of those Imhursaggi palms, are you?'' Ereshguna called on seeing the fearsome weapon.

"That I will," Dimgalabzu answered. "That we will, all we smiths. We shall fight in the first ranks. Being full of the power of metalworking, we dread less than others might the force Enimhursag can bring to bear against us."

"It is good," Sharur said. "Kimash the lugal is wise to arrange his line of battle so."

"It is good," Ereshguna agreed. "We have had great profit by fighting thus against the Imhursagut in our past few wars.''

Habbazu looked interested. Eventually, Sharur suspected, Enzuabu would hear of the way the Giblut fought against Imhursag, and why they fought thus. What the god of Zuabu would make of that remained to be seen.

Dimgalabzu also looked interested—in Habbazu. "Who is this man who marches with you and your sons?" he asked Ereshguna.

"His name is . . . Burrapi," Ereshguna answered. "He is a Zuabi mercenary. Sharur here became acquainted with him when leading caravans through the land of Zuabu. He was here in Gibil when word came that the Imhursagut have gone to war with us. We will pay him well to fight for the city.''

Habbazu took for granted being named by a false name. He dipped his head to Dimgalabzu. The smith gave a similar walking bow in return. Chuckling, Dimgalabzu said, ''Be careful that he has come here to fight, not to steal. You know what they say about Zuabut.''

''A few thieves have spoiled the reputation of all of Zuabu,'' Habbazu complained. Tupsharru coughed, as if at dust hanging in the roadway. Sharur and Ereshguna held their faces straight. They were both more experienced merchants than Sharur's younger brother. Sharur did not have an easy time of it, experience or no.

On they marched. The smiths, who were men with powerful upper bodies, did not use their legs so much in their work. They were also wealthy men. They clubbed together to buy a donkey in a village through which they passed, and loaded their weapons and accoutrements onto it. After that, they tramped along with lighter loads and gladder hearts.

Peasants marched north, too. Before long, the road became crowded, for other peasants, men and women and children, were fleeing south, often leading their livestock. ''The Imhursagut!'' they cried, as if men heading toward the foe with weapons in hand did not know whom they would be fighting.

In time, Ereshguna pointed toward the northern horizon. ''Smoke,'' he said. ''They are burning our fields. They are burning our villages. They will pay the price for burning our fields and villages.''

The Gibli camp not far from the border was a city in its own right, a city with guards and winding streets and with tents taking the place of houses. The mood inside the camp was confident. As someone past whom Sharur walked put it: ''We've beaten the Imhursagut plenty of times before. What can be so hard about doing it again?''

Kimash the lugal advanced with his force against the Imhursagut the next day. Sharur shouted to see the men from Imhursag drawn up on Gibli soil in a ragged line of battle. Then he shouted again, on a different note, for there near the head of the Imhursaggi force appeared Enimhursag, angry and armored and ten times the size of a man.

# 9

"**Enimhursag! Enimhursag!**" **the** Imhursagut chanted as their god strode with them toward the Giblut. But Sharur saw what they, perhaps, did not: Enimhursag did not stride out in front of them to take new land away from Gibil. Where his men had not gone before him, he had no power.

Some few of the Gibli peasants, not realizing this, fled before his awesome apparition. Beside Sharur, Habbazu asked in a shaken voice, "Where is Engibil, to withstand the god of Imhursag?"

"Engibil does not withstand in his own person the god of Imhursag," Sharur answered.

"Engibil has not withstood in his own person the god of Imhursag for many years," Ereshguna added.

"Not even in the days of my youth did Engibil withstand in his own person the god of Imhursag," Sharur's grandfather's ghost said, abruptly announcing his presence to his kin.

Habbazu could not hear the ghost, not having been acquainted with Sharur's grandfather in life, but what the living men said was enough—was more than enough—to dismay him. "Engibil will not withstand the enemy for his own city?" he cried. "Then truly you are lost! Truly all is lost!" He made as if to flee after the handful of Gibli peasants who had fled.

"No, all is not lost," Tupsharru said as Sharur set a hand

on the thief's arm to steady him. "Gibil and Imhursag have fought many wars since Engibil last withstood in his own person Enimhursag. We Giblut have won almost all those wars."

"This is so," Habbazu said slowly, as if reminding himself. Panic drained from his face, to be replaced by puzzlement. "I know this is so, but I do not understand how it can be so. How can men stand alone against men and a god and win?"

"We do not stand alone," Sharur said. "This is Engibil's land. He has dwelt on it longer than we. He aids in its defense. But we are not his slaves, as the Imhursagut are Enimhursag's slaves. We do not need him with us to go forward against the foe."

"And now," Ereshguna said, drawing his bronze sword with its gleaming edge, "it is time to talk no more. It is time to go forward against the foe."

Forward against the foe they went, Habbazu dubious and rolling his eyes but no longer ready to turn and run. Men without corselets, men without helmets, men without shields gave way before them, urging them up to the forwardmost ranks, the ranks where the men with the best gear were concentrated. As Dimgalabzu had said, many of those who fought at the fore were smiths; Sharur saw friends and neighbors from the Street of Smiths.

Others in the first ranks—the armor over the softer body of the army as a whole—were prosperous merchants (also friends and sometimes rivals whom Sharur knew) and scribes. The scribes were not so prosperous, but were fitted out with armor at Kimash's expense. Like the smiths, they were imbued with a certain resistance to Enimhursag's might by the power inherent in their trade.

On came the Imhursagut, still shouting their god's name. They, too, had wealthy men, armored men, in their front ranks. Enimhursag tramped among them, like a tower on parade. Off to either wing, archers in the donkey-drawn chariots exchanged arrows with one another and maneuvered to outflank the opposing army so they could disrupt it with their archery.

Enimhursag waved his sword and shouted abuse at the Giblut, as if he were a peasant woman in the market square spurning an offer for a bundle of radishes. "Have no fear, men of Gibil!" Kimash yelled in reply. His voice was small beside the gods, but large enough. "Do you see how his blade cannot go a digit's length farther than his frontmost line of men? He has no power over us, save that which his warriors can give him. Let us beat those warriors. Let us drive them back over the canal, and their foolish, loud-mouthed god with them. Forward the Giblut!"

"Forward the Giblut!" the men of Gibil cried, and stepped up the pace of their advance against the invaders.

Beside Sharur, Habbazu said, "You are all madmen, do you know that? When your line and the line of the Imhur-sagut collide, Enimhursag will be free to pick you like dates. The Imhursaggi god will be free to harvest you like barley." He did not give way as he spoke, though, but kept trotting along with the rest of the Gibli army.

"We have fought wars against the Imhursagut before," Sharur repeated. "We have won wars against the Imhursa-gut before. Remember that when our line and the line of the Imhursagut collide."

Moments later, the two lines did collide. Sharur picked the Imhursaggi he would meet from among several on his front: a rawboned fellow with streaks of gray in his beard who bawled "Enimhursag!" like a lost calf bawling for its mother. He wore a helmet and corselet and carried a mace with a flanged bronze head.

"Forward the Giblut!" Sharur shouted again, and swung his sword at the Imhursaggi. The foe turned it on his shield, then brought down the mace like a smith bringing down his hammer. Had it struck Sharur, it would have dashed out his brains regardless of whether or not he wore a helm. It did not strike him, for he skipped to one side.

The momentum of the blow made his foe stagger slightly forward. Sharur dropped his own shield for a moment. He reached out, grabbed a bushy handful of the Imhursaggi's grizzled beard, and yanked for all he was worth. The fellow cried out in pain and alarm. Sharur struck him in the side of the neck. Blood spurted. The Imhursaggi's cries became bubbling, soggy shrieks. He toppled, clutching at himself.

When the two lines met, all semblance of order in either one disappeared. The warriors who could reach their enemies flailed away with whatever weapons they had. The peasant levies who made up the bulk of both armies emptied their quivers as fast as they could in the general direction of the foe.

Beside Sharur, someone yelled, "I see what you mean!" Sharur almost swung at the man before realizing it was Habbazu. The Zuabi thief pointed up and up, toward the enormous figure of Enimhursag. "What good does his huge whacking sword do him?"

"Not much," Sharur answered. "He can mow down ten men at a stroke with it—but half of them, in this melee, will be his own men."

"Ah," Habbazu said. Then he added "God of my city, aid me!" because an arrow hissed past his face. And then, aplomb restored, he went on, "Yes, what good is he in this battle? Even if he stomps with his feet, he will trample his own men as well as the Giblut."

"Even so," Sharur answered, slashing at an Imhursaggi who stumbled back to escape the blade.

Despite Enimhursag's raging, despite his shouted exhortations that filled the field with thunder, the Imhursagut fell back all along the line. The fury of the Giblut matched theirs, while the men of Gibil had more corselets, more helmets, more bronze-faced shields, more bronze blades, more of the chariots that, though slow and awkward, were still faster and more maneuverable than men afoot, and allowed the Gibli archers in them to shoot at the Imhursagut from the flank.

"Forward the Giblut!" Kimash shouted, and the men of Gibil echoed the cry as they advanced: "Forward the Giblut!"

"We drive them!" Tupsharru yelled, his voice breaking in his excitement. "We drive them as a swineherd drives swine to the market." He had a cut on his left cheek, from which blood ran down into his beard. Sharur did not think he knew he had been hurt.

But Enimhursag was not altogether powerless: far from it. Having come far out from under the shadow of their own god, having often defeated the Imhursagut and driven north the border between Gibil and Imhursag, the Giblut could hardly be blamed for reckoning the god of their rivals reduced to impotence.

Then Enimhursag stooped over the battlefield, seized a Gibli in his left hand—the hand not holding that immense sword—lifted him on high, and cast him down. The god bent again, grabbed another Gibli, and smashed him to the ground as well.

Seeing the god's great hand descending to close on yet another man of his city, Sharur thought of his dream when he had gone up to Imhursag in the guise of a Zuabi merchant. There, too, something vast and terrible had reached down to pluck up tiny men and send them to their doom. Then Enimhursag had killed a true Zuabi merchant, not the false one he had, Sharur remained convinced, been seeking. Now—

Now, suddenly, Enimhursag let out a bellow of pain and rage; he rose without a Gibli clenched in his fist. Now his ichor dripped down onto the battlefield from a wounded forefinger. Another bellow rang out on the field, this one from Dimgalabzu the smith: "If your women haven't taught you to keep your hands to yourself, you great overgrown gowk, let a man do the job!"

Enimhursag reached down again, and succeeded in killing another Gibli. The success gave him confidence. It gave him, perhaps, too much confidence, for his next try resulted in another wound, this one worse than that which Dimgalabzu had given him. A Gibli scribe's voice rose in a triumphant cry.

The Imhursagut cried out, too, in dismay. "Our god is

wounded,'' moaned a man in front of Sharur. ''Our god bleeds!''

''You will be wounded,'' Sharur shouted at him. ''You will bleed.'' He flourished his sword and screwed his face up into a fierce and terrible grimace. When he took a step toward the Imhursaggi, the fellow spun on his heel and fled back through his own lines, throwing away his club to run the faster.

Sharur threw back his head and laughed. He was a young man at the forefront of a victorious army. When he had sneaked into Imhursag disguised as a Zuabi, he had been afraid. When he had gone openly into Imhursag to deceive the god, he had been afraid. He had been alone each time then. He was not alone now. He and his comrades, he and the men of his own city, were driving the enemy before them. No wonder, then, he laughed.

Also driving the enemy was one man not of his city. Grinning widely, Habbazu displayed a fine, heavy gold necklace. ''So long as you took that from an Imhursaggi and did not steal it from a man of Gibil, enjoy it and profit from it,'' Sharur said.

''A man who would steal from his friends is no gentleman,'' the thief replied. ''In this fight, the Giblut are my friends, for they help keep the Imhursagut from doing my body harm. I have this of an Imhursaggi, not from a Gibli.''

''It is good,'' Sharur said. Along with the nobles and smiths and scribes of Gibil, he pressed deeper into the wavering host of Imhursag, forcing the foe back in the direction of the canal that marked the border between Imhursaggi land and that of Gibil.

Then a shadow fell on his part of the battlefield. Involuntarily, Sharur looked up. The day, like most days in Kudurru from the beginning of spring to the end of autumn, had been bright and clear. For a cloud to pass in front of the sun was rare.

But no cloud had passed in front of the sun. Obscuring its light was the massive form of Enimhursag. Sharur stared up into the god's enormous face. That proved a mistake.

Enimhursag's eyes widened as he recognized the mortal who had led him and his city into this war.

"You liar!" Enimhursag shouted, his voice ringing in Sharur's ears. "You cheat! You trickster! You *Gibli*!" To his mind, that seemed the crowning insult.

He intended more than insult. With his left hand, the hand unencumbered by the sword, he reached down for Sharur. No green and growing stalks of barley hid Sharur from the god's search and anger now. If Enimhursag squeezed him in that man-sized fist, his blood would pour down onto the struggling Giblut and Imhursagut, as the luckless Zuabi merchant's blood had poured out of him after Enimhursag seized him by mistake.

Unlike the luckless Zuabi, Sharur was not taken asleep and helpless on his mat. He had a sword in his hand and he had the determination to use it. He swung it at the enormous thumb that curled down to grasp him.

The blade bit deep. Sharur yanked it free and slashed again. Enimhursag would have been wiser to try to smash him flat than to seek to lay hold of him. But the god had proved imperfectly wise in other ways as well. Wounded a second time, he bellowed like a bullock at the instant in which it is made into a steer: a cry of commingled pain and astonishment that without words said, *How could such a dreadful thing happen to* me?

More great drops of ichor splashed the ground by Sharur. Enimhursag's vital fluid did not have the harsh, metallic stink of human blood; it smelled more like the air just after lightning has struck close by—a smell that made the nose tingle on account of its power. If, after the battle was over, wizards could find the spots where the god had bled and dig up the ground into which his ichor had soaked, they might do great things with it.

That would be for later, though. For now, Sharur brandished his sword and shouted up to Enimhursag: "Go back to your own land. This land does not want you. Go back!"

All the Giblut took up the cry: "Go back! This land does not want you. Go back!"

Enimhursag howled in rage. He had expected the men of Gibil to welcome him as a liberator, to thank him for rescuing them from mad Engibil. But the Giblut not only did not welcome him, they not only did not thank him, they were handily defeating him and his people, and were defeating him by themselves, without even seeking the aid of their god.

Where that must have humiliated Enimhursag, it made Sharur proud. And yet, at the same time, it worried him. He had not wanted the Imhursagut to beat the men of his city. But he had wanted to draw Engibil's notice to the northern border of the land Gibil ruled. If the god of Gibil needed to pay no attention to the invasion, he would not be distracted from affairs in and around his temple, and Habbazu would have a harder time stealing the Alashkurri cup.

Sharur fought on. So did his fellow Giblut. Step by step, they forced back the Imhursagut. Enimhursag managed to slay a few more men of Gibil, but was also wounded again and again. Whenever the god tried to attack a smith or a scribe or some other man intimately connected with the new in Gibil, he found good reason to regret it.

Sharur briefly wondered if smiths and scribes would also be able to resist the power of Engibil. Before that thought had the chance to do anything more than cross his mind, he forgot it, for Engibil appeared on the battlefield.

He did not manifest himself as taller than a building, in the fashion of Enimhursag. He was, in fact, hardly more than twice as tall as a man. But his voice, like Enimhursag's, rang above and through the merely human din of the fighting. "Go home," he called to his fellow god, as the Giblut had done. "You have no business here."

"You are not a god, to give me orders," Enimhursag shouted back. "You are not even a god to give your own people orders. If men will not heed you, why do you think I will heed you?"

"The men of Gibil are doing as they should," Engibil said. "They are driving greedy invaders from their land.

They are doing as I desire. If they can do it without unduly troubling me, so much the better.''

"You are mad," Enimhursag said. "You let your men run wild. One day soon, they will run away with you."

"It is not so," Engibil said, though Sharur thought it might perhaps be so. "Kimash the lugal and I have an understanding."

"Aye, no doubt," Enimhursag said. "He does your job. While he does your job, you sleep. It is an understanding that requires no understanding: certainly it requires no understanding from you. This is as well, for you have no understanding to give."

"Mock me. Scorn me. Insult me. Revile me," Engibil said complacently. "Your city falters. My city thrives."

"Truly you are asleep—or perhaps I am speaking with the ghost of Engibil, who died some time ago," Enimhursag jeered. "Merchants from other cities of Kudurru shun Gibil. Merchants from lands beyond Kudurru shun Gibil. The gods from the land between the rivers shun Gibil and Engibil. The gods from lands beyond the land between the rivers shun Gibil and Engibil. And you say your city thrives!"

"My city thrives," Engibil repeated. "I know things of which you know nothing, and I say my city thrives. The proof lies before you: my men, the men of Gibil, move forward, while your men, the men of Imhursag, move back. You have puffed yourself up big as a pig's bladder blown up with air, but still my men wound you. See how you bleed."

Enimhursag looked at his left hand, which Sharur and other Giblut had cut again and again. "Yes, still your men wound me," the god said. "They wound me because they do not feel my power as they should. They have powers of their own, newfangled powers, godless powers, to set in the scales against my greatness, against my might, against my majesty."

Engibil laughed in the face of his rival god. "How great is your greatness, how mighty is your might, how majestic is your majesty if men wound you?"

"Laugh all you please," Enimhursag said. "Today, men of your city wound me. Tomorrow, beware lest they wound you."

Engibil did not reply. He folded his arms across his chest. So far as Sharur could tell, he exerted no special strength against the strength of Enimhursag. If anyone answered the god of Imhursag, it was Kimash the lugal, who cried, "Forward the Giblut!"

"Forward the Giblut!" the men of Gibil echoed, and the battle, which had hung suspended while the gods bickered, picked up once more.

Sharur traded sword strokes with an Imhursaggi who, though larger than he, was not skilled with his weapon. Taking the foe's measure, Sharur struck a clever blow. The sword flew from the Imhursaggi's hand. Sharur brought back his own blade for the killing stroke.

"Mercy!" the Imhursaggi cried. "Spare me!" He sank to his knees and set the palm of his hand on Sharur's thigh in a gesture of desperate supplication. "I am your slave!" Bending lower, he kissed Sharur's foot through the straps of his sandal. "Mercy!"

"Get up," said Sharur, who had no stomach for slaughter in such circumstances. "Go back through our line. Go back to our camp. Tell everyone as you go that you are the captive and slave of Sharur. If my people let you live long enough, I will give you over to Ushurikti the slave dealer, that I may profit from your price or ransom."

"You are my master." The Imhursaggi got to his feet. "I obey you as I would obey my god."

No one would get a stronger promise from an Imhursaggi. If Sharur's captive broke it . . . if he broke that promise, he would make a better Gibli than an Imhursaggi, anyhow. Sharur jerked his thumb to the rear. Still babbling praises and thanks, the man shambled away.

Habbazu said, "You might readily have slain him there. He is an enemy of your city. He is an enemy of your god. You would have gathered only praise."

"This way, I shall gather profit instead," Sharur said.

"Profit also has its uses. And, this way, I shall be able to ask Kimash the lugal for leave to go back to Gibil after the fight here is done, so that I may give my captive over to Ushurikti for safekeeping and for sale."

"You Giblut can be devious when you choose," Habbazu remarked. "It is as well that your god smiles not on thieves; were it otherwise, the men of your city would make formidable rivals for us of Zuabu."

"We judge man by man, not city by city," Sharur said.

"That is because your god does not roll his own cylinder seal across your souls so strongly as do the gods of other cities," Habbazu said. "This leaves you far more various from one man to another than are the men of Zuabu or Imhursag."

"It could be so," Sharur said.

"It *is* so." The Zuabi thief spoke with assurance. "You live among the men of your own city. I see them as an outsider, and see with my own astonished eyes how various you Giblut are." His eyes sparkled. "And now, another question: when you go back to Gibil to give your prisoner over to the slave dealer, may a certain retainer of such low estate he need not be mentioned to the godlike lugal accompany you?"

"What makes you think I know such a man?" Sharur inquired blandly. Habbazu glared at him, then started to laugh. Sharur went on, "Indeed, if I knew such a one, he might well accompany me when I go back to Gibil."

"Perhaps you will soon make the acquaintance of such a one," Habbazu said. At that moment, with Enimhursag bellowing to urge them on, the Imhursagut tried to rally. Habbazu said, "Perhaps we will both soon make the acquaintance of some large number of unfriendly men."

The Imhursagut fought fiercely, but the men of Gibil had more armor, better weapons, and, despite Enimhursag's exhortations, more confidence. The rally faltered. The Imhursagut began falling back once more.

Panting, Sharur was surprised to note how far the sun had sunk toward the western horizon. Panting hurt; he had taken a blow in the ribs from an Imhursaggi club. The blow had not been so strong as it might have, and had struck one of the bronze scales of his armor. Bruised he surely was, but he did not feel the grating or stabbing pains that would have warned of broken ribs.

Back and back the Imhursagut went, until they reached the tents of their encampment. They rallied once more in front of those tents, fighting now for the possessions they had brought into Gibil as well as for their god. With darkness looming, Kimash drew back from a final assault.

"He is wise," Habbazu said. "If you make Enimhursag desperate, who can guess what he might do?"

"I would rather not find out," Sharur said. "Kimash would rather not find out. It could even be that Engibil would rather not find out."

"It could even be, indeed, that Engibil would rather not find out," Habbazu said, nodding.

Leaving behind scouts to warn and companies of soldiers to resist for a time if the Imhursagut, contrary to expectation, tried to steal the war by night, Kimash led the bulk of his own host back to their camp. The wounded men among them groaned and cried; those who were unwounded sang songs of praise to their lugal, to their city, and, almost as an afterthought, to their god.

In the march back to the camp, Sharur found Tupsharru and Ereshguna. His brother bore no wound but the cut face Sharur had already seen; his father had bruised ribs almost identical to his own. "You should see what I did to the Imhursaggi, though," Ereshguna boasted.

At the camp waited the Imhursaggi whom Sharur had captured. He threw himself down before Sharur, crying, "I am your slave!"

"Of course you are," Sharur answered. "I am going to see if I can get leave from the lugal to take you back to the city and give you to the slave dealer there. I have no need for another slave of my own; the dealer will sell you or ransom you, and he and I will share the profit."

"You may do with me as you please," the Imhursaggi

said. "You spared my life when you might have slain me. I am yours."

Had capture ever been his fate, Sharur was certain he would have made a far more obstreperous prisoner than the abject Imhursaggi. But the Imhursaggi had been a slave before he was captured: a slave to his god. He was not getting a master for the first time, merely getting a new master. "Wait here," Sharur told him. "I will return soon."

He found Kimash the lugal surrounded by his guardsmen. The lugal raised in salute the cup he was holding. "Come, son of Ereshguna!" he called in expansive tones, waving for Sharur to approach. "Drink beer with me."

Someone pressed a cup of beer into Sharur's hand. He drank gladly; after a day of fighting in the hot sun, he was as dry as land to which no canal could bring water. "Mighty lugal," he said when the cup was empty, "have I your leave to go back to Gibil come morning, to take a prisoner, a captive of my sword, to the house of Ushurikti the slave dealer for safekeeping?"

"This will be the second Imhursaggi you have brought to Ushurikti, not so?" Kimash said. Sharur nodded, wondering if the lugal was angry at him for having captured Nasibugashi in the process of starting a war with Imhursag. But Kimash went on, "Aye, take this one back, too. Sooner or later, all the Imhursagut will be Gibli slaves, and deserve to be." As soon as his cup of beer was empty, he began another. He was not drunk yet, but soon would be.

Bowing his head, Sharur returned to his kinsfolk, his prisoner, and Habbazu. "Tomorrow we shall go down to Gibil," he told the captive, "you and I and my comrade here." He did not mention Habbazu's name; what the Imhursaggi did not know, he could not tell.

"It is good," the captive said. "Because you are generous, I still live. I still eat bread. I still drink beer. What can a man owe another man that is larger than his life? I know of no such thing. There is no such thing."

As a slave, he was liable to eat stale bread, and not much of it. As a slave, he was liable to drink sour beer, and muddy water dipped up from a canal as well. None of that seemed to bother him in the least. He had been a man of wealth in Imhursag, else he should not have held a bronze sword when he faced Sharur. Now, unless he was ransomed, he would be a man with nothing. Perhaps he failed to understand how far he had fallen. Sharur did not enlighten him; the more ignorant he was, the more tractable he would remain.

"If you and your comrade and your captive are not awake at earliest dawn, I shall rouse you," Ereshguna said as Sharur stretched out a mat on which to sleep. Like Sharur, his father did not mention Habbazu's name. A man could not be too careful. Word of the name might get back to Kimash. Or, for that matter, Engibil might be listening. Stretching, Sharur worried over that—but not for long.

When Sharur's father shook him awake, he did not want to rise. He rubbed his eyes and yawned as he made himself get to his feet. "Is the captive still with us?" he asked, looking around in the gray dimness of early twilight.

"Sleeping like a child," Ereshguna answered. "I have seen this in other Imhursagut, and in men from other cities where gods rule. They do not fret so much as we; their gods fret for them, as they do everything else for them. There are times when I almost envy them. Almost."

Sharur saw Habbazu sipping a cup of beer. The Zuabi thief looked very alert, and very much as if he did all his own fretting. He nodded to Sharur.

Ereshguna said, "Yesterday evening, after you lay down and as I was about to do the same, men came here from the pavilion of Kimash the lugal. They asked if we had ever laid hands on the thief we sought." He still named no names. Habbazu smirked. Ereshguna went on, "I told them no, and they went away. But it will be well when you and your comrade leave this camp, lest someone wonder if Habbazu the Zuabi thief and Burrapi the Zuabi mercenary are one and the same."

"Yes." Sharur stirred the sleeping Imhursaggi captive

with his foot. The man looked confused for a moment, then recognized Sharur and recalled his circumstances. He scrambled to his feet and clasped his captor's hand. Sharur gave him bread and beer for breakfast, then led him south, back toward Gibil.

Peasants by the side of the road, old men and striplings and women, called questions to the travelers as they tramped along. The peasants cheered to learn the Gibli army had beaten the Imhursagut in their first clash. The Imhursaggi captive was astonished. "Why has your god not told all the folk of Gibil of this victory?" he asked.

"Engibil doesn't do things like that," Sharur said. Whether Engibil *could* do things like that any more, he did not know. The god had not exerted himself so for generations. If he took back power in Gibil from the lugal, though, he would have to do such things. His laziness, which Sharur had seen, helped keep the people of Gibil free.

"How very strange," the Imhursaggi said. Habbazu caught Sharur's eye, but did not say anything.

"We like it this way," Sharur said, answering what his captive had said and what Habbazu had not.

"How very strange," the captive repeated. Habbazu started to laugh. Sharur gave him a dirty look. This time, though, he was the one who did not say anything.

When they got into Gibil, Ushurikti, who had not gone to war, bowed himself almost double before Sharur. "Ah, master merchant's son," the slave dealer said with a smirk, "are you going to bring me all of Imhursag to sell, one prisoner at a time?" He took a damp clay tablet out of a pot with a tight lid that kept its contents from drying out and incised it with a stylus. Sharur, reading upside down, saw the dealer write his name as the owner of the slave. Then Ushurikti asked, "And what is the name of this Imhursaggi?"

"I never bothered to ask him." Sharur turned to the captive. "What is your name, fellow?"

"I am called Duabzu, my master," the Imhursaggi replied.

"Du-ab-zu." Ushurikti wrote the syllables one by one. "Well, Duabzu, have you anyone in Imhursag who might ransom you? If your own people will pay a better price for you than I could get from a Gibli, you may go free."

"It could be so." Duabzu visibly brightened. "Perhaps, before long, I will again hear the voice of my god in my mind. Life would be sweet, were that to come to pass."

"He is not a poor man," Sharur said. "He swung a sword of bronze against me, till I struck it from his hand. No poor man would have swung a sword of bronze against me."

"This is so. No poor man could have afforded to own a sword of bronze to swing against you," Ushurikti said. "But whether this Duabzu has kin who would even want to pay ransom for him, that is a different question. When a man is captured, sometimes his kin prefer to reckon him as one dead, that they may make free with his inheritance." The slave dealer had surely seen more of the unsavory side of life than had most men.

Duabzu looked horrified. "My kin would never be so wicked as that. If they can afford your price, they will pay your price. Enimhursag would turn his back on them forever if they were so wicked as to refuse." He looked Sharur in the face. "In Imhursag, the god keeps men from being so wicked as that. I see the same is not true in Gibil."

"In Imhursag, the god keeps men from being men," Sharur answered. "Men are not all good, but neither are they all bad. Nor," he added pointedly, "are gods all good, no matter what they impose on men." Duabzu sniffed.

Ushurikti said, "You need not argue with this man, master merchant's son. You need not argue with this *slave*, master merchant's son."

"I know that," Sharur said. "I leave him in your hands. He invaded our land. He will pay the price. Someone, Gibil or Imhursaggi, will pay the price for him. You and I shall profit from that price."

"It is good," Ushurikti said. If Duabzu thought it was anything but good, he kept the thought to himself. Ushurikti led him away, back toward the little cubicle with the bar on the outside of the door where he would stay until sold or ransomed. Sharur wondered how close his cubicle would be to Nasibugashi's, and how many other Imhursagut would take up temporary residence with Ushurikti and other Gibli slave dealers.

To Habbazu, Sharur said, "Come, let us go back to my own house. You will be my guest there. You will eat of my bread. You will drink of my beer. You will use my home as if it were your own."

"You are generous, master merchant's son," Habbazu said, bowing. He answered ritual with ritual: "If ever you come to Zuabu, come to my own house. You will be my guest there. You will eat of my bread. You will drink of my beer. You will use my home as if it were your own."

"If ever I come to Zuabu, I will do these things," Sharur said. He wondered how welcome he would be in Zuabu, if ever Enzuabu learned Habbazu had given him the Alash-kurri cup instead of taking it back to the god. But ritual was ritual. Sharur continued with what was not quite ritual, but was polite: "If you feel the urge, lie down with our Imhur-saggi slave woman. If not eager, she is always obedient."

"Perhaps presents would make her more eager, or at least make her seem more eager," Habbazu said. "When a man lies down with a woman for his own amusement or for pay, having her seem eager is as much as he can expect."

"It could be so," Sharur said.

At the house of Ereshguna, the slaves brought Habbazu bread and beer. They also brought him onions and salt fish and lettuce and beans, and did so without being asked. Sharur smiled at that, remembering how the Imhursaggi peasants had done for him exactly what Enimhursag ordered them to do for him, and no more than Enimhursag ordered them to do for him.

Habbazu eyed the Imhursaggi slave woman with frank speculation. She recognized that for what it was, and some-how, without smearing dust on herself or using any other trick, contrived to look even more mousy and nondescript than she usually did. Habbazu turned away, as if he had smelled salt fish that had not been salted enough and was going bad. When he turned away, the Imhursaggi slave walked straighter. Sharur hid a smile.

Betsilim and Nanadirat stayed upstairs. For them to come down and greet a male guest who was not an intimate family friend, as Sharur and his father and brother were in the house of Dimgalabzu, would have been a startling breach of custom. Habbazu did not remark on their absence. He probably would have remarked had they made an appearance.

When the slaves had left Habbazu and him to their food and drink, Sharur asked, "Will you go to the temple of Engibil tonight, to see if you can make off with the cup while Engibil's eyes are turned to the north, to the fight with Enimhursag?"

"Master merchant's son, that was my plan," the Zuabi thief replied. "I think it best to do this as soon as may be."

"You thieves like the darkness," Sharur said. "It was in the darkness that you came to my caravan outside Zuabu."

"It is so," Habbazu agreed. "Darkness masks a thief. Darkness masks what a thief does." He sighed, a sound of chagrin. "Darkness, that night, did not mask well enough what a thief did."

Sharur's grandfather's ghost spoke in his ear: "Be wary of this man, lad. Be careful of him. He is a thief, and not to be trusted. He is a Zuabi, and doubly not to be trusted. Be wary, be careful, lest darkness hide what he does to you, not what he does for you."

"I understand all that," Sharur muttered impatiently, in the tones a living man used to address a ghost. Habbazu, realizing what he was doing, looked up to the ceiling and waited for him to be done. Sharur sighed, a sound of exasperation. His grandfather, querulous alive, was even more querulous as a ghost. Then Sharur brightened. He might yet make use of the suspicious ghost. "Ghost of my grandfather, will you go with the Zuabi thief into the temple of Engibil?" he asked, murmuring still, but not so softly as to keep Habbazu from hearing him. "Will you warn me if he tries to sneak off for his own purposes with what we seek?''

"No!" The ghost's voice in his mind was indignant. "I shall do no such thing. I wanted nothing to do with this man from the beginning. I want nothing to do with him now. I want you to have nothing to do with him now."

Sharur wanted to pitch the ghost through the nearest mudbrick wall. He knew that would not have hurt the immaterial spirit, but it would have made him feel better. Instead, he smiled broadly and said, "I thank you, ghost of my grandfather. That will help us. That will help us greatly."

"I told you, I am not helping you," his grandfather's ghost shouted at him. "You young people pay no attention to your elders." The ghost fell silent, and presumably departed in anger.

Habbazu, however, could not know that. Not having known Sharur's grandfather as a living man, Habbazu could not hear him as a ghost. The thief could hear only Sharur. He said, "I would not have cheated you even without the ghost watching over me."

"It could be so," Sharur answered, nodding. "I think it is so. But, because I am not sure it is so, I shall do what I can to protect myself. Were I trading wares for you here, would you not like to make as certain as you could that I was not cheating you?"

"Well, so I would," Habbazu said. "Very well; your grandfather's ghost will have no cause to complain of me."

"My grandfather's ghost always has cause to complain," Sharur answered, and Habbazu laughed, as if that were something other than simple truth.

"Most often," Sharur said in a low voice as he and Habbazu stepped out onto the Street of Smiths, "I go out at night with slaves bearing torches to light my way."

"Most often, when you go out at night, you want people to know you are going out at night," the thief replied. "This is a different business. You want to be silent as a bat,

stealthy as a wild cat, and quick as a cockroach that scuttles
into its hole before a sandal crushes it.''

"And what you need fear now is not the sandal of a
kitchen slave, but the sandal of Engibil," Sharur said.

"I fear the sandal of Engibil not so much, for you did
turn the god's eyes to the north," Habbazu said. "The way
you turned the god's eyes to the north . . . no Zuabi would
use such a way, but it worked. I fear the flapping sandals
of Engibil's priests. An old man who gets up to make water
at the wrong time could undo me."

"I thought you have ways to escape such mishaps,"
Sharur said.

"I do," Habbazu said. "And you, no doubt, have ways
to keep from being cheated in your trading. But sometimes
your ways fail. Sometimes my ways fail, as well. Did my
ways not sometimes fail, your guards would not have caught
me when I came to your caravan outside Zuabu."

Sharur nodded. "I understand. Each trade has its own
secrets. I hope, master thief, you will not need to use any
of yours."

"So do I," Habbazu said. "I like easy work as well as
the next man, as you must enjoy trading with fools for the
sake of the profit it brings you. I wish I were robbing Enimhursag's temple; with his eyes turned away from his city,
his priests, those who have not gone to war, will surely be
sluggish as drones. But you Giblut, you are alert all the
time."

"You speak in reproof," Sharur said. "It is not a matter
for reproof. It is a matter for pride. We do not need the god
dinning in our ears to make us do what we should do. We
are men, not children."

"You are nuisances," Habbazu said. "It is a matter of
risk. I am not fond of risk when that risk is mine."

"Ah," Sharur said, and said no more. Up the Street of
Smiths toward Engibil's temple they strode. Near the end
of the street, a large man stepped out of the deeper shadow
of the house. He looked in the direction of Sharur and Habbazu for a moment, then drew back into the shadows. As

Sharur walked on, he listened for the sound of rapid foot-steps behind him.

"I am lucky you are with me," Habbazu said. "Were I alone, that footpad might have set on me, for I am not large, and I look like easy meat." Suddenly, even in darkness, the edge of a dagger glittered in his hand. "A serpent is not large, either, and looks like easy meat. But a serpent has fangs, and so have I."

"I have seen your fangs," Sharur said. "So have the Imhursagut." He pointed ahead, and felt foolish a moment later: Engibil's temple could not have been anything but what it was. "We draw near."

"Yes." Habbazu had not been making much noise. Now, abruptly, he made none at all. He might have been a ghost, walking along beside Sharur. Truly, a master thief had talents of his own.

Sharur looked up and up, toward the god's chamber at the top of the temple. No light streamed out from its doors. Engibil was not in residence at the moment. Before Sharur could point that out to Habbazu, the thief waved him into a patch of deep shadow, nodded a farewell, and slid sound-lessly toward the temple.

Torches burned outside the main entranceway. Guards paced outside the main entranceway. Sharur wondered how Habbazu could hope to get in unseen. But Habbazu, appar-ently, did not wonder.

No cries rose from the temple guards. Whatever Habbazu was doing, it seemed to work. Sharur stood in the deep shadow and waited. He had no idea how long the thief would need to enter the temple, to find the cup, and to es-cape. He was not altogether sure whether Habbazu could do that, or whether he would face the wrath of Engibil's priest-hood and perhaps of the god himself. Again, though, Hab-bazu would not have attempted the theft without confidence he would succeed.

As Sharur waited, he stared up at the heavens. Slowly, slowly, the stars moved over that blue-black dome. The star everyone in the land between the rivers knew as Engibil's star was not in the sky. Sharur took that as a good omen: the god could not peer down from his heavenly observation platform and see Habbazu sneaking toward and into his temple.

Had the men who guarded that temple been caravan guards, they would from time to time have come out to check the shadowy places not far from the entrance to make sure no one skulked in them. They did not. They paced back and forth, back and forth. Perhaps they did not believe anyone would dare to try to sneak past them. Had Sharur been one of them, perhaps he would not have believed anyone would dare to try to sneak past, either.

He yawned. He was not used to being out by night, out in the darkness. The darkness was the time for men to sleep. The night was the time for men to lie quiet. It would not have taken much for Sharur to lie quiet against the wall. It would not have taken much for him to sleep.

He yawned again. The stars had wheeled some way through the sky. He glanced toward the east. No, no sign of morning twilight yet. He did not think he had been waiting long enough for the sky to begin to go gray, but he was starting to have trouble being sure.

Then, without warning, his grandfather's ghost shouted in his ear: "Be ready, boy! The thief comes!"

"Has he got the cup?" Sharur whispered, excitement flooding through him and washing away drowsiness as the spring floods of the Yarmuk and the Diyala washed away the banks of canals.

"What? The cup?" his grandfather's ghost repeated. "No, he hasn't got the cursed cup. He is pursued, boy— pursued. He'll be lucky to make it this far, is what he'll be."

"I did not think you wanted anything to do with him," Sharur said. "I did not think you wanted to go with him into the temple."

"I did not want anything to do with him," the ghost answered. "I did not want to go with him into the temple. But you are flesh of my flesh: flesh of the flesh I once had.

You were bound and determined to go through with this mad scheme. Since you were bound and determined to go through with his mad scheme, I had to help you as I could, even if I had said I would not.''

"For this I thank you, ghost of my grandfather,'' Sharur said.

"Do not thank me yet,'' the ghost said. "You are not safe yet. I have no flesh. I had no trouble leaving Engibil's temple. The thief is a living man. He will not find it so easy.''

"What will they do to him if they catch him?'' Sharur asked.

"Maybe they will simply kill him,'' his grandfather's ghost replied. "Maybe they will torture him and then kill him. Maybe they will torture him and then save him for Engibil's justice, for whatever time in which Engibil decides to mete out his justice. Whatever they choose to do, the house of Ereshguna will fare better if they have not got this choice to make.''

"Ghost of my grandfather, you speak truly,'' Sharur said with a shudder. What Engibil could wring out of Habbazu might well touch off a war between Gibil and Zuabu, and would surely bring ruin to the house of Ereshguna. The second possibility concerned Sharur far more than the first. He was a Gibli: his own came before his city, his city before his god.

He heard a thump, and then the sound of running feet—not headed in his direction. Cries came from the top of the temple wall: "There he goes! After him, you fools!'' Some of the guards at the entranceway ran off in pursuit of those fleeing footsteps. One man fell down, his armor clattering about him. Another tripped over him in the darkness, producing fresh clatters and horrible curses. The rest of the temple guards pounded on.

"A good evening to you, master merchant's son.'' The whisper came from right at Sharur's elbow. He whirled, and there beside him stood Habbazu.

"How did you come here?'' Sharur demanded, barely

remembering in his surprise to whisper also. "I heard you run off in that direction." He pointed.

Habbazu's laugh was all but silent. "You heard footsteps. Likewise, the priests and the guards heard footsteps. The footsteps you heard were not mine. Likewise, the footsteps the priests and the guards heard were not mine. Have you seen a mountebank, a ventriloquist, who can throw his voice so it seems to come from somewhere far from his mouth? The footsteps you heard—likewise, the footsteps the priests and the guards heard—seemed to come from somewhere far from my feet."

"How do you do that?" Sharur asked.

"Master merchant's son, this is not the time to linger and ponder such things," Habbazu replied. "Neither is this the place to linger and ponder such things."

"He is right. The thief is right," Sharur's grandfather's ghost said.

Sharur knew Habbazu was right without having his grandfather's ghost tell him. As quietly as he could, he withdrew from the place of shadow and stole back toward the Street of Smiths. Beside him, Habbazu was quieter still. Sharur was a quiet man; the Zuabi thief, again, might have been a ghost.

The ruffian who had thought of challenging Sharur and Habbazu as they went toward the temple did not come out when they retreated from it. Perhaps he had gone; perhaps he recognized them and concluded they were still a bad bargain. Either way, Sharur was as glad not to encounter him.

Once back safe in his father's house, Sharur allowed himself the luxury of a long sigh of relief. Instead of waking the slaves—waking them and making them aware he had come in during the middle of the night—he fetched beer and cups with his own hands.

Only after he and Habbazu had drunk did he ask, "What went wrong in the temple of Engibil, master thief?"

Habbazu looked disgusted. "Exactly the sort of thing I feared; exactly the sort of thing a thief can do nothing to prevent. There I was, moving toward the storeroom wherein the Alashkurri cup is secreted. There I was, eluding all the guards, eluding all the snares.'' He paused, then added, ''Were the god paying close attention to his house, it would have been harder. It was not easy, even as things were.'' He sighed.

''What went wrong, that a thief could do nothing to prevent?'' Sharur asked again.

''A doddering old fool, with a white beard down to here''—Habbazu poked his own navel with a forefinger—''came tottering out of his cubicle, as I had feared one might, most likely because his bladder could not hold the beer he had drunk with his supper and he needed to ease himself.''

Sharur thought of Ilakabkabu, whom the description fit as a swordhilt fit a man's hand. He said, ''Many of the older priests are very pious men. Having one of them see you would be the next thing to having the god see you.''

''So I found out.'' Lamplight exaggerated the lines and shadows of Habbazu's face, making it into a mask of woe. ''This old, white-bearded fool, then, saw me, and his eyes went so wide, I thought they would bug out of his head. Would that they had bugged out of his head! Would that he had been stricken blind years ago! However doddering he is, he still has a fine screech, like that of an owl in a thornbush. Other priests started tumbling out of their cubicles, and they all started chasing me.''

''How could you escape them?'' Sharur asked. ''It is not your house. It is the house of Engibil. Yet you eluded the priests of the god in his house. Truly you must be a master thief.''

''Truly I am a master thief,'' Habbazu agreed with just a hint of smugness. ''Truly I am a master thief of Zuabu, sent forth to steal by Enzuabu himself. I have ways and means most thieves have not.''

Again, he did not describe what those ways and means were. Sharur's trade had secrets of its own, too. He said, ''I am glad these ways and means let you get free.''

"Master merchant's son, believe me when I tell you that you are not half so glad as I am," Habbazu answered. "I did not know if these ways and means would suffice, not until I left the temple itself and found you faithfully awaiting me."

"Would another attempt soon be worthwhile?" Sharur asked. "Or will the priests and guards in and around Engibil's temple be too wary to do what you must do?"

"They will be wary," Habbazu said. "They will surely be wary. But, if we are to do this thing, we had better do it soon. Before long, by what I saw, the army of Gibil will have beaten the army of Imhursag. Before long, by what I saw, Engibil will no longer need to watch out for Enimhursag. Then he will watch out for his temple, and theft will grow more difficult."

"You said you could steal the cup even with the god at home in his temple," Sharur reminded him.

"Yes, I said that. I still think it is true. I still think I could steal the cup with the god at home in his temple," Habbazu said. "But, as I said just now, theft will grow more difficult with the god at home in his temple. And"—he hesitated, as if regretting the admission he was about to make—"I may have been wrong."

"Ah," Sharur said, and no more than *ah*. At least the thief could admit he might have been wrong. Many, perhaps even most, of the men Sharur knew would go ahead with a plan once made for no better reason than that they had made it. After a pause for thought, Sharur continued, "Then you are right. If we are to do this thing, we had better do it soon."

"It will not be easy, with the priests alerted," Habbazu said. "It will not be simple, with the guards on the lookout for a thief."

"That is so." Sharur sat in dejection, staring at the pot of beer. Then, little by little, he brightened. "It would not be easy, with the priests alerted," he said. "It would not be simple, with the guards on the lookout for a thief. If they are all looking in a different direction, matters may be otherwise.''

"Indeed, master merchant's son, you speak the truth there," Habbazu said, nodding. "Any thief or mountebank soon learns as much. Distract a man, and you will have no trouble stealing from him. Distract him, and he is easy to fool.''

"Merchants learn as much, too," Sharur said. "Who turned Engibil's eyes from the temple to the border with Imhursag?'' He waited for Habbazu to nod again, then went on, "We can turn the priests' eyes from the temple, too.''

"Tomorrow?'' Habbazu asked eagerly.

"That would be too soon, I think," Sharur answered. "But the day after . . .''

The square in front of Engibil's temple was not nearly so fine and broad as the market square of Gibil. It was, though, large enough to hold a surprising number of entertainers of all sorts. Musicians played flutes and pipes and drums and horns, each ensemble's tune clashing with those of its neighbors.

In front of one fluteplayer, a shapely woman wearing a linen shift so thin, she might as well have been naked, danced and swayed to the rhythm of his music. In front of another fluteplayer, a trained snake similarly danced and swayed. Sharur's eyes kept sliding back and forth from the woman to the snake as he tried to decide which of them moved more sinuously. For the life of him, he could not make up his mind.

"Come one!'' he called, a merchant out to make his sale. "Come all! Gibil wars against Imhursag, aye, but Gibil forgets not those who fight not. Here is an entertainment to lighten the hearts of those who wait within the city walls, to help them forget their worries.''

Boys paid with broken bits of copper shouted the same message—or as much of it as they could remember— through the streets of Gibil. Men who had not gone to fight the Imhursagut and women who could not go to fight the Imhursagut crowded into the open space in front of Engibil's temple to leave their cares behind for a time.

Jugglers kept cups and dishes and knives and little statues spinning through the air. An enterprising and nimble-fingered fellow used three cups and a chickpea to extract property from the spectators who tried to guess where it was hidden. He won so regularly, Sharur thought he had to be cheating. But Sharur could not see how he was doing it, and did not care to pay for instruction.

From the entranceway into Engibil's temple, the guards stared out eagerly at the performers before them. Priests also watched from the top of the wall around the temple, and from the high stairways within. From the corner of his eye, Sharur watched them watching. He made sure he watched them watching only from the corner of his eye.

He knew Habbazu was somewhere nearby. He did not know where. He did not try to watch for the Zuabi thief at all. Habbazu knew his own business best. Sharur was trying to give him the best chance he could to conduct that business without the risk of being disturbed.

Presently, priests began coming out of the temple and into the square. Some of them clapped their hands to the music. Some watched the snake sway. Some watched the pretty girl sway. Some proceeded to prove they were no better than any other man at guessing under which cup the chickpea lay.

After a while, the priest named Burshagga strode up to Sharur. The two men bowed to each other. Burshagga said, "Do I understand rightly that we have you to thank for this entertainment spread out before us?"

Sharur did his best to look self-effacing. "I thought those left in the city could use a bit of joy while our army repels the Imhursagut. I fought in the first battle, and came back to Gibil to put a captive into the hands of Ushurikti the slave dealer. Soon I shall return to the fighting. In the meanwhile, why should we not be as merry as we can?"

"I see no reason why we should not be as merry as we

can," Burshagga replied. "As I said, we have you to thank for this entertainment spread out before us. No less than men of other trades, priests enjoy merriment."

"This was my thought. This was why I decided to set the entertainment here," said Sharur, who did indeed want the priests merry—and distracted. But then he pointed in the direction of the entranceway. "Not all your colleagues, I would say, hold the same view."

There stood Ilakabkabu, his long beard fluttering in the breeze as he harangued several younger priests. "No good will come of this!" he thundered. "We do not serve the god for the sake of frivolity. We do not serve Engibil for the sake of merriment. We serve Engibil for the sake of holiness. We serve the god because he is our great and mighty master."

Burshagga looked disgusted. "I will go and settle that interfering old fool."

"I did not mean to cause such difficulties," Sharur said. That was also true—he wanted all the priests distracted, and none of them preaching against distraction. He strolled along toward Ilakabkabu in Burshagga's wake.

"Here, what are you doing?" Burshagga called to Ilakabkabu. "What foolish words fall from your lips now, old man?"

"I speak no foolishness," the old priest answered. "I say that we should prove our devotion to Engibil with prayers and sacrifices, not with jugglers and fluteplayers and squirming wenches." He gestured disparagingly toward the woman dancing in the thin shift.

"And I say Engibil does not begrudge his priests their pleasures," Burshagga said. "I am devoted to Engibil. No one can deny I am devoted to Engibil."

"I deny it," Ilakabkabu said. "You are devoted first to yourself, then to Kimash the lugal . . . lugal!" He laced the title with scorn. "And last of all, when you deign to recollect, to the god."

"Liar!" Burshagga shouted. "Son of a whore! You think that because you have been a priest since before men learned to till the soil, Engibil speaks to you alone. You think that, because you have been a priest so long your private parts have withered, priests are not men like other men. Our god is not a god who hates pleasure. Does Engibil himself not couple with courtesans when the urge strikes him?''

''What the god does is his affair,'' Ilakabkabu said stolidly. ''He is the god; he may do as he pleases. But for you to do as you please . . . you are only a man, and a priest besides. Do not add your shame to the disgrace the temple suffered of having a thief penetrate it as deeply as Engibil penetrates one of those courtesans you talked about.''

Priests and folk of the city gathered round Burshagga and Ilakabkabu. Wrangling priests were entertainment, too. Sharur listened with intent interest on his face. He listened with no trace of amusement or delight on his face. Ilakabkabu, no matter what he thought, was at the moment helping to do the work of distracting the temple for him.

Burshagga rolled his eyes. ''I do not think you ever saw that thief. I think you were imagining him, as I know you are imagining that you alone can see into the mind of Engibil.''

''And I think that, because you young men were too slow and too stupid to catch the thief, you pretend he was never there,'' Ilakabkabu retorted. ''You put me in mind of a wild cat when a mouse escapes it. The cat sits down and licks its anus, pretending it did not truly want the mouse.''

''You are the one who knows everything there is to know about the licking of an anus!'' Burshagga screeched. He grabbed a double handful of Ilakabkabu's long white beard and yanked, hard.

The old priest screeched, too. He brought up a bony knee between Burshagga's legs. Burshagga howled, but did not let go of Ilakabkabu's beard. In an instant, the two priests were rolling on the ground, gouging and kicking and hitting at each other.

Most of the Giblut laughed and clapped and cheered them on. Some of their fellow priests, however, eventually pulled them apart. They kept right on calling each other names.

Most of the priests seemed to side with Burshagga, as did Sharur—but he knew that Ilakabkabu had been telling more of the truth here.

Where was Habbazu? Sharur could look around now, as if to see who was coming to find out if the brawl would start anew. He did not see the master thief. He had not seen the master thief since the day's festivities began.

Where was Habbazu? Was he still waiting his chance? Was he skulking through the nearly deserted corridors of the temple toward the storeroom of which he knew? Was he sneaking out of the temple chamber with the nondescript Alashkurri cup in his hands?

Or had he already sneaked out of the temple with the Alashkurri cup in his hands? Was he even now leaving Gibil? Was he on his way back to Zuabu, on his way back to Enzuabu? How strongly did Enzuabu summon him? Where did he put his god? Where did he put his city? Where did he put himself?

Sharur knew what Habbazu had said. He also knew, better than most, that the truest test of what a man was lay in what he did, not in what he said. Sharur sighed. If Habbazu had deceived him . . . If Habbazu had deceived him, he would know before the sun set.

Burshagga and Ilakabkabu still shouted insults at each other. The insults Ilakabkabu shouted did nothing to keep more priests from coming out of the temple to enjoy the musicians and performers. As word of the unusual festivity spread through the city, those who sold food and beer also came into the open area in front of Engibil's temple. Sharur bought a dozen roasted grasshoppers impaled on a wooden skewer and crunched them between his teeth, one after another, as he watched a dog walk on its hind legs atop a ball carved from palm wood.

At its master's command, the dog climbed a stairway, jumped through a hoop, and did other clever tricks. Sharur applauded with the rest of the people gathered round it. It gave a canine bow, nose to the ground, forelegs outstretched in front of it. Then it ran over and stood, wagging its tail, beside the pot in which its owner was collecting his reward.

With a laugh, Sharur tossed a bit of copper into that pot. The dog bowed to him then. Its owner said, "Engibil's blessings upon you, my master, for your generosity." He bowed, too.

Sharur politely returned both the dog's bow and the man's, which made the people around him smile. Considering what Habbazu was doing or had done or would be doing, Sharur doubted that the dog trainer's prayer for Engibil to bless him would be answered. He did not speak his doubts aloud. He did his best not even to think of them.

A priest came running out of the temple, shouting in alarm. Sharur's heart leaped into his throat. Outwardly, he stayed calm. Nor did he show his relief when he heard what the priest was shouting: news that another priest of Burshagga's opinion and one of Ilakabkabu's were belaboring each other inside the sacred precinct.

"This is disgraceful!" Burshagga cried, rubbing at a scratch over one eye. "We embarrass ourselves before the people of the city."

"As you said to Ilakabkabu, you priests are men like other men," Sharur told him. "Other men will sometimes quarrel among themselves. The people of the city know that you priests will sometimes quarrel among yourselves."

Burshagga bowed low to him. "I thank you for your understanding, master merchant's son. I thank you for your patience. Would that all Giblut were as understanding and patient as you are. We should be a better people, were that so. As things are, most will use this as an excuse to laugh at the priesthood."

"Priests are men like other men," Sharur repeated. "Other men will be laughed at from time to time. So also will priests be laughed at from time to time."

Now Burshagga did not bow. He did not look pleased. He looked sour as milk three days old. "When people laugh at us, it diminishes the power of the god we serve. When people laugh at us, it diminishes the power of the lugal who appointed us."

He spoke of the god first now, and only afterwards of the lugal. But Sharur knew serving Kimash held a higher place in Burshagga's mind than did serving Engibil. Sharur would not have minded seeing Engibil's power diminished. On the contrary.

He also would not have minded seeing Habbazu. If he had embroiled Gibil and Imhursag in war, if he had managed this lavish distraction for the priesthood of Engibil—if he had done all that, only to have Habbazu flee with the cup to Zuabu and to Enzuabu, he would be embarrassed. He would deserve to be laughed at.

Burshagga sighed. "In the time of my sons, this will not matter. In the time of my grandsons, this will be a thing of the past. The old fools will be gone then, vanished from the priesthood. My sons and my grandsons will listen to my ghost haranguing them about the way things were when I walked the earth as a living man—they will listen, and they will laugh. And I, a ghost, shall laugh with them."

"You say that now," Sharur said. "You see that now. Will you say that when you are a ghost? Will you see that when you are a ghost? Or will you be angry when they laugh?"

"I am a man like other men," the living Burshagga said, and laughed. "It is likely, then, that I shall be a ghost like other ghosts. It is likely that, like other ghosts, I will be angry at the vagaries of the living, and angry when they fail to hearken to me in every particular."

Sharur laughed, too. "You are not altogether a man like other men, Burshagga. You are more honest than most. You see more clearly than most. You see farther than most."

"I see a master merchant's son who is flattering me," Burshagga said. "But I also try to see what is and what will be, not what I wish were so."

"Here," Sharur said, and waved to one of the beersellers. Buying a cup, Sharur handed it to Burshagga. "You see a master merchant's son who is buying for you a cup of beer."

"I see a master merchant's son who shows a proper and

pious respect for the priesthood.'' A twinkle in his eye, Burshagga drank the cup dry. "Ahh! It is good.''

"Which is good?'' Sharur asked. "The beer, or that a master merchant's son shows a proper and pious respect for the priesthood?''

"Both those things are good,'' Burshagga answered. He nodded to the beerseller. "Here, son of Ereshguna, I will buy you a cup of this beer, that you may learn for yourself whether it is good.'' And he did.

Sharur drank. As Burshagga had said, the beer was good. He and the priest exchanged bows and compliments. Burshagga went off to see if he could figure out under which cup the fellow with the nimble fingers had concealed the chickpea. Smiling, Sharur saw that the fellow with the cups and the chickpea had concealed one thing from Burshagga: that the game was unlikely to be as straightforward as it seemed.

With a shrug, Sharur bought another cup of beer for himself. If Burshagga did not know the fellow with the chickpea could make it appear wherever it would give him the greatest profit, Sharur did not intend to enlighten him. Every craft had its own secrets. The priest would learn these secrets from experience, and would pay for the privilege of learning.

Ilakabkabu came out of the temple once more, and began fervently preaching against the frivolous entertainment. He drew a considerable crowd. People clapped and cheered as he flayed them for their light-mindedness. Thus inspired, he preached more ferociously than ever. He did not notice he, too, had become part of the entertainment.

Burshagga gave up trying to find the furtive flying chickpea after several moderately expensive lessons. He came over and watched Ilakabkabu instead. He said not a word, but his mere presence inspired the pious old priest to new and rancorous heights of rhetoric.

"He talks like a man on fire,'' someone beside Sharur remarked. Sharur turned, and there stood Habbazu.

After staring, Sharur asked in a quiet voice, "Have you got it?"

The master thief looked offended that Sharur should doubt him. "Yes," he answered. "Of course I have it."

# 10

**Sharur and Habbazu** drifted out of the open area in front of Engibil's temple. They neither hurried nor dawdled; they might have been—indeed, they were—a couple of men who had had enough of entertainment and now needed to return to the workaday world in which they usually passed their time.

"Now that we have this thing, what shall we do with it?" Habbazu asked, taking care not to name the cup. "Shall we take it with us when we return to the fight? Shall we secret it away at the house of your father?"

"If we take it with us, it may perhaps be easier for the god to spot," Sharur answered. "The small gods of Kudurru told me there was little in it of power to be spotted, but I do not know precisely how much they knew, nor do I know how much power Engibil can put forth to seek the thing should he so will."

Habbazu nodded. "Wiser to hide it, then. Shall we go on to the house of your father?"

"I have a better notion yet," Sharur said. "Let us take it to the house of one of the smiths along the Street of Smiths. The power of metal, the power of smithery, make it harder for the god to peer into such places."

"That is so." Habbazu nodded again. "I have heard Enzuabu complain of it. What with you Giblut being as you are to begin with, it is probably even more true here than in Zuabu."

"Engibil complains of it, too," Sharur said. "If the gods had it to do over, I do not think they would let men learn to work metal. If they had it to do again, I do not think they would let men learn to write, either. But men have learned to do these things, and even the gods cannot have it to do over."

"This is also so," Habbazu said. "Have you the house of some particular smith in mind, a man whom you can trust with something as important as this? I would not—I do not—care to risk it with someone who would return it to the god or who would gossip so that its presence were noised abroad."

"Nor would I," Sharur replied. "I have in mind taking it to the house of Dimgalabzu, whom you have met."

"But Dimgalabzu is in the north, in the army of Gibil opposing the Imhursagut," Habbazu objected.

"So he is," Sharur said. "But he is also the father of Ningal, my intended bride. She of all people may be trusted not to return the cup to the god."

"I am glad to hear this is so," Habbazu said. "But she is a woman. Are you certain you can trust her not to gossip?"

"More certain than I am that I can trust you not to gossip," Sharur said, smiling to show he meant no offense. "You, master thief, I have known but a short time. Ningal I have known since we were both children getting filthy in the dust of the Street of Smiths."

"Very well. A point." Habbazu pursed his lips before continuing. "But can you likewise trust her kinsfolk? Can you likewise trust the slaves in her household?"

Sharur's grunt was not a happy sound. "That I do not know. I do know that anyone who trusts a slave too far is asking to be disappointed." Habbazu nodded once more. Sharur said nothing of Gulal, Ningal's mother. From what he knew of Gulal, she disapproved of everything. That meant she would likely disapprove of his leaving the cup in the house of Dimgalabzu.

His silence gave Habbazu the answer the master thief

needed. "If we do not leave the cup in the house of Dim-galabzu because people we can not trust are there, what shall we do with it?"

"Better then that we take it with us after all, I think," Sharur replied, forgetting what he had said not long before. "Being in among a great crowd of men may perhaps make it harder for the god to notice it, or so we can hope." If the god came after it and Sharur was close by, he could also try to break it. Again, he kept that thought to himself.

Habbazu laughed at him. "Since you say first the one thing and then the other, I judge that you are as unsure of the wisest course as I am."

Sharur laughed, too, ruefully. "Perhaps I was wrong ear-lier. Then again, perhaps I am wrong now." He wished he had thought of keeping the cup close by him earlier.

They walked past the house of Ereshguna. The house of Dimgalabzu lay a few doors farther up the Street of Smiths from Engibil's temple. When Sharur turned to go into the doorway, Habbazu walked on straight for half a step before spinning on his heel to follow. "I am sorry," Sharur said. "I forgot you did not know which house it was."

"No harm done," Habbazu answered. "Now I know which house it is. I shall not forget." Coming from a master thief as it did, that was a promise Sharur would have been almost as glad to do without.

With Dimgalabzu gone to war, the smithy was quiet: no hammering, no scraping, no hiss of melted bronze burning off beeswax as it poured into a mold, no great crackling roar from the fires. Because the fires did not blaze as they did when Dimgalabzu was at home and working, that lower chamber was also cooler than Sharur ever remembered find-ing it. It was not cool—it was far from cool—but he did not at once begin to roast in it as if he were a chunk of mutton on a spit.

"Where is everyone?" Habbazu asked in a low voice that suited the dim quiet of the chamber.

"I do not know," Sharur said. "A slave or two should be down here, if no one else. But slaves are lazy creatures.

Perhaps they are lying on their mats instead.''

"Perhaps they have sneaked away to the entertainment you arranged in front of Engibil's temple," Habbazu said.

"Perhaps they have." Sharur had not thought of that. He smiled; if the entertainment had distracted not only the priests but also Dimgalabzu's slaves, so much the better. He also kept a close eye on Habbazu, not wanting the master thief to practice his craft in this house.

A woman's voice came from upstairs: "Is someone down there?"

Now Habbazu eyed Sharur. Habbazu could not know whose voice that was. It could have been Ningal's. It could have been her mother's. It could have been a slave woman's. Sharur would know.

Sharur did know. Relief filled him. Now he had at least a chance to do what he had hoped to do. "It is Sharur the son of Ereshguna, and a friend," he called. Habbazu's eyes lit up. He mouthed Ningal's name. Sharur nodded.

But would his intended come downstairs by herself? Would Gulal, her mother, accompany her, as was customary? Would a slave woman accompany her if her mother did not?

She came down the stairs alone. Sharur's heart leaped. Habbazu spoke in an admiring whisper. "You are a fortunate man."

"I thank you," Sharur whispered back. He raised his voice: "Ningal, I present to you my comrade, Burrapi, a mercenary of Zuabu."

Habbazu bowed low. Politely, Ningal inclined her head. "Why do you and your comrade visit the house of Dimgalabzu?" she asked. By her tone, she meant, *I am glad to see you, but what is he doing here?*

"I brought in to Ushurikti the slave dealer an Imhursaggi prisoner I captured," Sharur replied. "Burrapi here accompanied me to help guard the man. Now we are going back to fight again. Before we go, we have something we need to leave with you."

"What thing is this?" Ningal asked.

Sharur nodded to Habbazu. Habbazu opened the pouch he wore on his belt—a larger pouch than most men might wear, but nowhere near large enough to draw any special notice—and drew from it the Alashkurri cup he had stolen from the temple of Engibil.

This being the first time Sharur had set eyes on it, he stared with no small interest. But, as Habbazu had said, as the small gods Mitas and Kessis had implied, it was nothing out of the ordinary. He had drunk beer from cups like it many times in the mountains of Alashkurru. It was of yellowish Alashkurri clay, ornamented with twisting black-glazed snakes. The potter who had shaped it and fired it had been a capable enough man, but he was no master.

Ningal's dark eyebrows rose as Habbazu handed her the cup. "What am I to do with this?" she asked.

"Keep it safe," Habbazu answered. "Let no harm befall it."

"Keep it secret," Sharur added. "Let not Gulal your mother know you have it. Let not Dimgalabzu your father, when he comes home from the war, know you have it. Let not the slaves of this household know you have it. If the servants of Kimash the lugal come through the Street of Smiths searching, let them not know you have it. If the priests of Engibil come through the Street of Smiths searching, let them not know you have it, either."

The eyebrows of his intended rose higher still, until for a moment they seemed almost to brush her hairline. "I had not thought anyone would speak thus of gold and lapis lazuli, let alone a common cup—except, I gather from your words, it is no common cup. What makes it other than a common cup, if one of outlandish style?"

Habbazu shot Sharur a warning glance. For his part, Sharur needed no warning. He said, "Better you had not asked this question. What you do not know, you cannot tell another."

"If you cannot keep it thus, give it to us once more, that we may take it elsewhere," Habbazu said. "For it must be safe. It must be secret."

Ningal did not return the cup. "It shall be safe here. You have no business doubting that." She looked indignant. "It shall be secret here. You may be certain of that."

Habbazu glanced once more at Sharur, saying without words, *You know her better than I. May we be certain of that?* "If Ningal says a thing is so, you may rely on it," Sharur said. He turned toward his intended and nodded. "It is good. Now we must go back to the fighting."

"May Engibil keep both of you safe," Ningal said. "May the god of this city hold harm away from both of you."

"May it be so," Sharur and Habbazu said together. Irony glinted in the master thief's eyes. Sharur nodded, ever so slightly, to show he understood. If Engibil detected what they had done, he would neither keep them safe nor hold harm away from them. He would be far more likely to put them in danger and bring harm down upon them.

Gulal's voice came from upstairs: "Who is it, Ningal?"

"A customer of Father's and his friend, Mother," Ningal answered. Strictly speaking, that was true, though what Sharur purposed buying from Dimgalabzu was Ningal herself. The words also gave Sharur and Habbazu the chance to slip out of Dimgalabzu's house unnoticed by anyone but Ningal. She nodded to them both as they left.

While they were making their way up the Street of Smiths toward the northern gate of Gibil, Habbazu said, "That is indeed a fine woman you have as your intended. Not only is she good to look on, she has sharp wits as well. Over the years, you will come to value the second more than the first."

Sharur made what he thought was a polite, noncommittal noise.

It must have been neither so polite nor so noncommittal as he had thought, for Habbazu burst into raucous laughter. "You think her wits will not matter so very much. You think on how she will look the night of her wedding, when you couple with her for the first time. You think of the pleasure your prong will know. Now, I have nothing against the pleasures of the prong—believe me when I tell you this is true. But believe me also when I tell you the pleasure you take in a woman's good looks fades far faster than the pleasure you take in her good sense. I have more years than you; I know whereof I speak.''

Sharur considered the marriage between his father and his mother. Betsilim had been a beautiful young woman, nor had the years robbed her too badly. But Ereshguna relied on her now in ways he surely had not when she was younger. That was not because he had lost capacity, but because he had come to respect hers. Thoughtfully, Sharur said, ''You may be right.''

''Ha!'' Habbazu said in surprise, and clapped him on the back. ''I did not look for you to admit even so much.'' Side by side, they walked on toward the gate.

Men came south from the fighting as Sharur and Habbazu walked north toward it. Some led dour prisoners who would become slaves, as Sharur had done a few days before. Some were hurt themselves, too badly to let them keep fighting but not so badly as to keep them off their legs.

''No, no big fights the last couple of days,'' one of the latter said. His right arm was bound tightly against his chest. When Sharur asked him how he had been injured, he looked sheepish. ''How, friend? I tripped over a spearshaft in camp and came down on this wrist, which broke. But when I get into Gibil''—he winked—''I shall tell them what a hero I was.''

''It is good,'' Sharur said, laughing. With a wave of his good arm, the man with the broken wrist trudged on toward the city.

Habbazu said, ''It is good indeed. If we return to the army before it fights another great fight, no one can possibly blame us for having been gone a few days.''

''You speak the truth,'' Sharur said. Lowering his voice, he continued, ''Nor has there been any great hue and cry coming up the road from behind us. I take this to mean either that your theft has gone undiscovered or that, it having been discovered, the priests know not in which direction to search.''

"Either of those would suit me well enough," Habbazu replied. "Better that the theft go undiscovered, of course, but not tracing it to me would do—will do."

They reached the Gibli encampment the next morning. "Good you have returned, my son," Ereshguna said. "Good you remain in the city no longer. The Imhursagut regain their insolence; Enimhursag regains his arrogance. They will, I think, soon come forth in battle once more."

"When they do, we shall defeat them," Sharur said confidently. He gestured; at his urging, Ereshguna and Tupsharru put their heads close to his. He went on in a whisper, and an oblique whisper at that, "Good also we went down to the city. We accomplished all that we hoped to accomplish. Duabzu the Imhursaggi captive is in Ushurikti's hands. He will bring a good price or a good ransom. And . . ." His voice trailed away. Some things he preferred not to say, even obliquely.

Tupsharru looked puzzled for a moment. Ereshguna did not. He asked, "And is it with you?" For obliquity, that was hard to match. Sharur shook his head. Tupsharru suddenly grunted, realizing what his father and brother had to be talking about. Ereshguna asked, "Where have you put it, then?"

Sharur hesitated. Every merchant's instinct in him screamed that that had to remain as secret as it could. He glanced over at Habbazu. The master thief's face bore no expression whatever. Sharur understood what that meant: Habbazu did not want the secret spread more widely, either.

Gently, Ereshguna said, "The Imhursagut, as I told you, will soon come forth in battle once more. May the gods decree otherwise, but, if you should fall, my son, and if Burrapi the Zuabi mercenary should also fall, who then would know where it is?"

"Ah," Sharur said. He glanced over at Habbazu again. Almost imperceptibly, Habbazu nodded. Despite that nod,

Sharur revealed as little as he could: "Ningal the daughter of Dimgalabzu would know."

"Would she indeed?" Ereshguna murmured. "Would she indeed? But not Gulal, her mother? Not the slaves of the household?"

"No, not Gulal, her mother," Sharur said. "Not the slaves of the household, either."

Tupsharru grunted again. "Burrapi the Zuabi mercenary!" he exclaimed. "Servants of Kimash the lugal were here the other day, asking about Burrapi the Zuabi mercenary. Since he was not with us, since we could not produce him, they were easily satisfied, and soon returned to the lugal's pavilion."

"Kimash and his men are no doubt curious to learn whether Burrapi the Zuabi mercenary and Habbazu the Zuabi master thief are by chance the same man," Ereshguna said.

"What an absurd idea," Habbazu said indignantly. Sharur, Ereshguna, and Tupsharru all laughed.

Tupsharru said, "If it please the Zuabi mercenary, he might now return to his native city, whither we would send him no small reward."

Habbazu shook his head. "So long as I may do so, I would sooner stay. What we have done does not affect you only. It affects my god, it affects my city, it affects me."

"What you say does not dishonor you, nor your city, nor your god," Ereshguna said. Habbazu bowed. Sharur noted what neither his father nor the thief seemed to see: that Habbazu had named Enzuabu first, then Zuabu, with himself last, while Ereshguna, a Gibli to the core, reversed the thief's order.

"Perhaps," Sharur said, "you would be wise, Hab... ah, Burrapi, not to make your return to this encampment widely known. You might do best to stick close to our fire here."

"Now this is good advice, prudent advice, and I shall take it," Habbazu said. "A thief oftentimes needs to move in secret. A thief frequently needs to hide himself in plain sight."

"What if the men of Kimash the lugal come searching for you again?" asked Tupsharru, who was inclined to worry and to borrow trouble.

"I am now forewarned against the men of Kimash the lugal," Habbazu said. "Let them come searching for me again. Again, they shall not find me."

"The master thief does not presume to tell us how to get the best price for an ingot of bronze or a pot of date wine of high-medium grade," Ereshguna said to Tupsharru. "I, for my part, shall not presume to instruct him how best to manage his own affairs."

"I understand, Father," Sharur's younger brother said, and hung his head.

"Has Engibil been active here along the border since Burrapi and I went down to the city of Gibil?" Sharur asked hopefully: the more active along the border the god was, the less interest he would have had in looking into his temple when Habbazu robbed it, and the less interest he would have had in looking into it after Habbazu robbed it as well.

Ereshguna and Tupsharru both nodded, which brought a smile not only to Sharur's face but also to Habbazu's. Ereshguna said, "Engibil has been active indeed. Yesterday morning, he and Enimhursag began screaming insults at each other. They were both so loud and fierce, we thought they would come to blows themselves rather than leaving it to the men of their cities to fight it out. In the end, though, they took it no further than screams, and I am just as well pleased at that."

"Why?" Sharur said. "If Engibil slew Enimhursag, we would not have to endure wars with the Imhursagut every generation."

"If that happened, you would be right," Ereshguna agreed. "But what if Enimhursag slew Engibil? We do not *know* what would happen if the two gods did battle each other, and I am satisfied to remain ignorant."

Sharur wondered if Gibil might not be better off were

Engibil to be slain. Could a city go on with only a lugal and no indwelling god at all? No city in the land between the rivers had ever done such a thing. No city or town or fortress anywhere in the world had ever done such a thing, so far as Sharur knew. Maybe no one anywhere in the world had ever imagined such a thing before.

Of itself, his right hand slid down to cover the eyes of the amulet to Engibil. The god probably would not pick this moment to examine his thoughts. But he wanted to make as sure of that as he could. Having Engibil learn what he was thinking now would be . . . *disastrous* wasn't nearly a strong enough word.

"On this matter, I am also just as well pleased not to know," Habbazu said. "Too much power, too much danger, were god to fight god straight up."

Tupsharru said, "Maybe that's why gods made men in the first place—to give them tools with which they could challenge each other without meeting face to face."

"No one knows why the gods made men in the first place," Ereshguna said. "Priests do not know. Sages do not know. Scribes do not know. Merchants do not know. I have heard it said that even the gods do not know, or do not remember. Whether this be so or not"—his craggy features crinkled into a smile—"I do not know."

"My brother's idea makes as much sense as any I have heard," Sharur said. "It makes more sense than most I have heard."

"This does not prove it is true." Ereshguna and Habbazu spoke together. Master merchant and master thief looked at each other in some surprise, then started to laugh.

Ereshguna said, "Here we are, two older men, trying to restrain the enthusiasm of younger men. When we were younger men, the older men would try to restrain us."

"Even so," Habbazu said. "And when your two fine sons are older men, they, too, will try to restrain the enthusiasms of the young."

He and Ereshguna laughed again. Sharur and Tupsharru exchanged indignant glances. Sharur did not think that, when he grew older, he would try to hold back those younger than himself. He wondered if his father, when a young man, had also doubted he would do any such thing. Looking over at Ereshguna, Sharur thought he probably had had those doubts. Despite them, Ereshguna had changed. Maybe that meant Sharur would change, too. He hoped not, but maybe it did.

Brazen trumpets roused the Giblut the next morning. Ram's-horn trumpets roused the Imhursagut—a different sort of braying. Along with those harsh blasts from the Imhursaggi camp came the cries of Enimhursag himself, easily audible across the space between the two encampments: ''Rouse, men of Imhursag! Today I lead you to victory over the liars and cheats of Gibil!''

Sharur smiled to hear the outrage in the god of Imhursag's voice. Much of that outrage, he knew, was aimed straight at him. He had lied to Enimhursag, saying Engibil had run mad and the Giblut wanted a new divine overlord. He had cheated Enimhursag, getting him to invade the land of Gibil on those false pretenses.

Engibil's voice was nowhere to be heard. Kimash's bronze-lunged heralds cried out the lugal's orders: ''Smiths and scribes and merchants to the front! As we fought before, so shall we fight again.''

On went the armor of bronze scales over leather. On went the helmet, of similar design. Wearing both, Sharur felt as if he had been thrown into one of Dimgalabzu's furnaces. Sweat poured off him, a river of sweat, a river that seemed to flow as powerfully as the Yarmuk.

''Forward the Giblut!'' Kimash shouted. The army he led echoed his war cry: ''Forward the Giblut!''

''Enimhursag!'' the warriors of Imhursag shouted back. ''Enimhursag!'' As he had done on the first day of the fighting, the god of the Imhursagut towered over his men, huge, menacing—and, Sharur thought, less dangerous than he ap-

peared. Along with the rest of the Giblut, he jeered at Enimhursag and reviled him.

Axles squealing, the donkey-drawn chariots of the Giblut
began to maneuver against those of Imhursag. Kimash had
more chariots with him than did the Imhursagut. Before
long, Sharur was sure, the elite archers of his home city
would overpower their foes and pour shafts into the opposing army from the flank. If it had happened so in the earlier
battle, it was likely to happen again in this one.

But, he soon discovered, even Enimhursag, the champion
of the old in all ways, did not always precisely repeat himself. The god of Imhursag could not advance beyond the
frontmost line of his warriors. But that did not mean, as it
had meant in the earlier battle, that he could exert no power
beyond the frontmost line of his warriors.

Enimhursag stooped alongside a tiny canal only a couple
of cubits wide. When he rose, his enormous hands were full
of mud. As a small boy might have done, he shaped the
mud into a ball—but this ball was more than half as big
around as a man was tall. The god flung it at a Gibli chariot.

It hit the donkeys and knocked them kicking. The chariot
itself flipped over, spilling the archers out into the dirt. Enimhursag stooped, rose, and shaped another ball of mud. He
aimed and let fly.

This time, the mudball squarely struck a chariot. The car
shattered. The donkeys ran wild, braying their terror. One
of the men who had been in the chariot somehow staggered
to his feet. The others did not move.

The Imhursagut cheered themselves hoarse. Enimhursag
methodically began to form still another ball of mud. Ad-
vancing beside Sharur, Ereshguna said, ''The god of the
Imhursagut has found something dangerous to do. But he
has not found out how to do it in the most dangerous way.''

As if thinking along with Ereshguna, Kimash cried,
''Close with them! Let us meet the Imhursagut sword to
sword, mace to mace, body to body! Close with them! Forward the Giblut!''

Forward the Giblut went, at a trot. Enimhursag threw at

another chariot and missed. His curses were enormous. He
threw again, and smashed a car to kindling. No Giblut staggered from that wreck.

Enimhursag needed longer to realize he was making a
mistake than had either Ereshguna or Kimash the lugal. The
Gibli army had almost closed with the Imhursaggi force before the god threw the first mudball into that crowded mass
of men. It bowled over a dozen, maybe more, not far from
Sharur. Some of them could still scream. Some would be
forever silent. The men who were not hurt ran on, toward
the Imhursagut.

Enimhursag let fly with yet another missile. It smashed
down another double handful of men. By then, though, the
front ranks of the Giblut, Sharur among them, crashed into
the armored nobles and priests and traders at the head of the
Imhursaggi force. All the Giblut hurled themselves forward
with desperate energy—the sooner they mingled with the
Imhursagut, the sooner the god of Imhursag would have to
leave off throwing balls of mud at them for fear of hitting
his own men.

An Imhursaggi priest, crying out his god's name, swung
his ax at Sharur as if he intended chopping down a date
palm. Sharur had to skip back; he had no hope of beating
that stroke aside. "Enimhursag is my protector!" the priest
shouted, drawing back the ax to strike again.

Before he could swing it a second time, Sharur slashed
at him. The priest's armor turned the first swordstroke. The
next, which was aimed at his neck, he had to block with the
handle of his ax.

Then a wounded Imhursaggi stumbled into him from the
side, throwing him off balance. Sharur's blade bit deep.
Blood filled the priest's beard. He toppled with a groan, the
ax falling from nerveless fingers. "Enimhursag does not
protect you well enough," Sharur said. "Enimhursag does
not protect Imhursag or the Imhursagut well enough."

If Engibil was on the battlefield, if Engibil was even
watching the battlefield, he gave no sign of it. If anyone was
going to protect the men of Gibil, they themselves had to

do it. And so they did, crying out Kimash's name—and also Engibil's—as they smashed into and through the Imhursagut.

Many men from Sharur's city—smiths and scribes and merchants—instead of fleeing from Enimhursag, made straight for him. They stabbed and slashed at his feet and hacked away at his ankles with axes. Ichor poured from the wounds they made.

The god of Imhursag bellowed in rage and pain. He stomped several Giblut into the dirt. In so doing, though, he also stomped into the dirt several of his own priests. His most devoted followers did their best to place their own bodies between the god they loved and the ferocious Giblut. Destroying the priests in that way seemed to wound Enimhursag as sorely as anything the men of Gibil could do to him.

Sharur, too, fought his way toward Enimhursag. He knew the stroke he wanted to deliver against the god who ruled the city rival to his own. "The back of the heel," he muttered. If he could cut through the tendon there, Enimhursag would fall, no matter how large he was. He would fall the harder, indeed, for being so large.

An Imhursaggi stood close by Enimhursag's ankle. He blocked the way against Sharur—or he did until Dimgalabzu's ax slammed through his armor and his ribs and crumpled him to the ground. "I thank you, father of my intended," Sharur shouted, and hewed at the tendon that went up the back of Enimhursag's enormous leg.

Enimhursag roared like a lion. He bellowed like a bull. His ichor, smelling of thunderstorms, splashed onto Sharur. It was hot, but it did not burn. Instead, it made him tingle and quiver all over. Under his helmet, his hair stood on end. It was indeed as if lightning had struck close by.

But the god of Imhursag did not topple. The god of Imhursag did not fall. Sharur was only a mortal man, and had not the strength to cut that mighty tendon through and through. The wound pained Enimhursag. It failed to cripple him.

"Let me have a try!" Dimgalabzu cried, and swung his ax as Sharur had swung his sword.

Enimhursag roared again. This time, Sharur thought he heard fear along with pain and fury. The Giblut were tiny next to the tremendous self he had chosen, but they had found a way of hurting him that might do real harm. He glared down at Sharur and Dimgalabzu, hate suffusing his face.

"Go back to your own city!" Sharur shouted. "Go back to your own city, and leave us Giblut alone!" He chopped at the god's heel tendon again.

Had Enimhursag kept his wits about him, he could have crushed Sharur and Dimgalabzu under his foot, as he had crushed other Giblut. But he might also have crushed men of his own city—men who, like the fallen priest, still strove to protect him. And the realization that the Giblut truly might endanger him rather than being only nuisances must have struck terror into his outsized heart.

Instead of trampling the men who tormented him, the god turned and, in a few great strides, withdrew from the battlefield. Sharur sent up a cry of exultant joy: "Enimhursag flees!"

"Enimhursag flees!" Dimgalabzu echoed with a great bass shout. In a moment, all the Giblut took up the cry: "Enimhursag flees! Enimhursag flees!"

"Enimhursag flees!" The Imhursagut shouted it, too. In their voices was no exultation. Horror choked their cries. Dismay filled them. Fear made them quaver. "Enimhursag flees!" Perhaps the Imhursagut had not imagined such a disaster could befall them. When it did, they had none of the self-reliance the Giblut might have possessed with which to withstand it.

"Enimhursag flees!" The Imhursaggi line wavered as courage drained from more and more of the Imhursagut. If their god would not defeat the men of Gibil, how were they to do so without his aid? Most of them saw no answer to the riddle. Most of them ran away, too, howling their terror.

Here and there, a man or a clump of men still stood

boldly. Here and there, a few brave warriors tried to stem the rout. The Giblut swarmed over them and cut them down. Even as Sharur slew a man of that forlorn rear guard, he knew a moment's sorrow. The men who stood, the men who fought on after their god abandoned them, were the men most like those of Gibil, the men most fully themselves and least tiny reflections of Enimhursag.

He and the men of his city rolled over those partly emancipated Imhursagut and after the warriors who fled. This time, the men of Imhursag did not pause to defend their encampment. A few did snatch what they could from their tents, but only a few. More of those were nobles than Imhursaggi peasants: the nobles, of course, had more possessions over which to concern themselves.

"Forward the Giblut!" Kimash shouted as his own men swarmed into the camp the Imhursagut were abandoning. "Forward! Later will come the time to loot. Presently will come the time to plunder. Now comes the time to finish the foe. Forward the Giblut!"

Most of the men of his city obeyed him and kept on pursuing the Imhursagut. Some, however, stopped and stole whatever struck their fancy. The Giblut, for better and for worse, were their own men first, men of their city second.

Habbazu, in this regard, also proved to be his own man first. When Sharur had gone to swing his sword against Enimhursag's heel, he had lost track of the Zuabi master thief. Now Habbazu, catching up to him, glittered with gold and sparkled with silver, having festooned himself with necklaces and armlets and rings. Grinning at Sharur, he said, "I have made a profit on this day that any master merchant would envy."

"See that you do not purchase this profit at the cost of your life," Sharur answered. "If you make your arm so heavy with silver and gold that you cannot lift it either to attack or to defend, then bronze may be your end. You would wish yourself better served by it and less well by precious metals."

Habbazu answered by swinging his own bronze sword in

Sharur's face. The blade had blood on it. "Fear not," the thief said. "The Imhursagut will bear witness that I am not too burdened to battle. Several of them will bear witness only to those who knew them well enough in life to hear them moan and complain as ghosts."

"Good enough, then," Sharur replied, and slogged on after the broken army of Imhursag.

No more than the men of his city had Enimhursag lingered at the army's encampment. The god of Imhursag fled ahead of his warriors toward the broad canal that marked the border between the territory of Gibil and the land he ruled. He crossed the canal in a couple of enormous strides; the water bore his weight as readily as land had done.

Once back on the soil his city ruled, the soil he ruled himself, he turned back toward his army and shouted in a great voice: "To me, my children! To me, my chicks! Back to our land—to the land of the pure, to the land of the good, to the land of the honest. Away from the land of Gibil— away from the land of serpents, away from the land of scorpions, away from the land of liars."

"Away from the land of Gibil!" the Giblut jeered. "Away from the land of warriors, away from the land of heroes, away from the land of men."

But the Imhursagut could not cross the wide canal without wetting their feet, as Enimhursag had done. They had to wade in and flounder across. Gibli archers gleefully plied them with arrows as they waded, as they floundered.

When those arrows were aimed at men who were more than halfway across the canal, and more particularly at men dragging themselves up onto land on the Imhursaggi side, many of them went wide or fell short—more than could be accounted for by bad shooting.

"Enimhursag protects them," Ereshguna said as he came up alongside Sharur. The older man looked and sounded very tired; he was breathing in great panting gasps. But he still thought clearly. Sharur could not remember an occasion on which his father had failed to think clearly. Ereshguna went on, "Now they are on Imhursaggi land. Now they are on land Enimhursag possesses as his own. The Imhursaggi god has greater powers on land he possesses as his own.''

"And yet land Enimhursag once possessed as his own is now Gibli land," Sharur answered. He stamped his foot on the muddy ground near the edge of the canal. "This land we stand on now is land Enimhursag once possessed as his own. He possesses it as his own no more; it is now Gibli land." He pointed north. "If Kimash the lugal wills it, we may make more land Enimhursag once possessed as his own into Gibli land. Once more, we have beaten the god and his folk in war."

"Once more, we have beaten them," Ereshguna agreed. "If Kimash the lugal wills it, I shall go on into Imhursag. I shall go on into the land Enimhursag possesses as his own. But the fighting there will be harder, for it is land the god has held for long and long, land he has made his. I hope Kimash will decide routing the Imhursaggi army and humiliating the god of Imhursag are punishments enough."

"And I." Sharur nodded emphatically. "We have other things with which to concern ourselves." He said no more than that. Engibil might be listening. Engibil might come to the northern border of the land of Gibil to jeer at Enimhursag over his failed invasion. Or Engibil might come to the northern border of the land of Gibil in search of the stolen Alashkurri cup. If he did come in search of the cup, he would come in wrath. Sharur wanted to do nothing that would draw his notice.

Kimash came up to the banks of the canal. Donkeys in gilded harness drew him in his chariot, which was likewise adorned with gold leaf. With his armor and helmet also gilded, he glittered almost—almost—like a god. Cupping his hands before his mouth, he shouted across the canal: "Go home, men of Imhursag! Go home, god of Imhursag! You are not welcome here. You have seen you are not welcome here."

Sharur cheered. So did the rest of the Giblut drawn up along the canal. Mixed with the cheers were jeers for the god of the rival city, and also jeers for the men who fought at his command.

"You Giblut are mad!" Enimhursag shouted back. "You should be slain like mad dogs, lest your madness infect all the land between the rivers."

"We have beaten you," Kimash replied. "If you dare set foot on Gibli soil once more, we shall beat you again." The Giblut raised another cheer. Enimhursag shook his great fist at them, but remained silent. The lugal went on, "Stay on the soil that is yours, and we shall have peace. You may ransom prisoners we have taken; those not ransomed will be sold as slaves in the usual way. The booty from your encampment is ours, of course."

Enimhursag's scowl was fearsome, but still the god said nothing more. Ereshguna murmured, "Kimash, it seems, does not wish to cross over into Imhursaggi land. It is good."

"I suppose so," Sharur said, "though, thinking on it, Engibil might be happy and busy and distracted if he had to begin to rule new lands we had won for him with spear and sword."

"He would not do the fighting, though," his father replied. "He would not battle alongside us as Enimhursag has battled for the Imhursagut. He would merely enjoy the benefit of our labors. As I say, I am contented with the way things have gone."

"Perhaps you are right, Father," Sharur said. "And whether I am contented or not, it is the way things have gone, and I must accept it."

No sooner had he said that than Enimhursag turned his back on the land of Gibil: the god also accepted the way things had gone, whether it contented him or not. Recognizing that, some of the Giblut cheered. Others jeered again, loudly and lewdly. Enimhursag's great shoulders slumped.

Suddenly, the god's gigantic form disappeared. Some of the men of Gibil exclaimed in surprise. "Has he perished?" someone near Sharur asked.

"No," Sharur said in a loud voice, so many could hear.

"Usually, the god sees and speaks through one of the Imhursagut, picking the man or woman best suiting his purpose at the time. The rest of the Imhursagut will obey such folk, knowing Enimhursag inhabits them. That he no longer wears the great body proves he intends to fight no more."

"It is over," Ereshguna agreed. "It is over, and we have won the day."

Sharur and Ereshguna took no part in the plundering of the Imhursaggi camp on the way back to their own. "I would sooner not quarrel with men of my own city over trinkets," Ereshguna said. "Let others squabble over them; chances of finding anything worth trading or keeping are not good now. I would sooner return to our own encampment and drink dry a pot of beer."

"It is good," Sharur said, and went on with his father.

Tupsharru and Habbazu went in among the abandoned tents to see what they could find. In addition to the precious prizes he had already gained, Habbazu came back with a gilded helm, a fine bronze sword, and a dagger with a hilt inlaid with silver. Tupsharru carried an ax with a handle similarly inlaid back to the Gibli camp.

"Perhaps we were wrong," Sharur said to Ereshguna, eyeing the plunder with admiration.

"Perhaps we were," Ereshguna said. "But I have beer in my belly. I have bread in my belly. It is not perfect, but it will do."

Habbazu, who was dipping up a cup of beer for himself, bowed to Ereshguna. " 'It is not perfect, but it will do,' " he repeated, cleverly mimicking the master merchant's intonations. "There speaks a man who has lived in the world and taken its measure."

"I have lived in the world," Ereshguna said. "Whether I have taken its measure is for others to say, not for me. What I will say is that, over the years, the world has taken my measure: taken my measure, aye, and cut and trimmed and pounded me to serve its purposes."

"That is the way of the world." Habbazu glanced over toward Sharur and Tupsharru. "Your sons, I think, are still too young to agree in fullness."

"Likely you are right." Ereshguna also glanced toward Sharur and Tupsharru. His gaze was affectionate, not calculating.

Sharur said, "What I think is that Burrapi the Zuabi mercenary should disappear from this camp, and disappear soon. I think someone who answers to a different name should go down to the city of Gibil and take up lodging above a tavern or with a family that will let him use a room for pay. I think it would be best if he did this before the servitors of Kimash the mighty lugal come asking questions concerning that mercenary."

Habbazu inclined his head. "You may be young, son of Ereshguna, but you give good advice. I have seen this before. I now see it again." He drank down the beer, got to his feet, and bowed again to Ereshguna and then to his sons. "I shall not wait a moment. It shall be as if Burrapi the Zuabi mercenary had never been. With the loot Burrapi the mercenary has won, someone who answers to a different name will take up lodging in the city of Gibil. In Gibil, a stranger will call on the house of Ereshguna. Perhaps, though, he will seem somehow familiar." He bowed once more, to all the men of the house of Ereshguna together, and then went off whistling the tune the fluteplayer in the square in front of the temple of Engibil had played as an accompaniment to the dancing girl's lithe swaying.

"That was indeed a good notion," Ereshguna said. Sharur beamed, pleased at the praise.

How good a notion it was, Kimash showed within the hour. Two of the lugal's largest and burliest retainers appeared before the tent Sharur, Ereshguna, and Tupsharru shared. The bigger of the two growled, "Kimash the mighty lugal requires the immediate presence of the Zuabi mercenary named Burrapi. No excuse will be tolerated." To emphasize that, he set his right hand on the hilt of his sword.

Ereshguna said, "I must offer an excuse nonetheless: he

is not here. I have not seen him since the battle ended.''

"He was seen in the battle," Kimash's guardian said. "He was seen after the battle, plundering the tents of the Imhursagut."

"If he found enough booty to satisfy him, he is likely to be on the way to Zuabu by now," Sharur said. "He fought for gain, not for love of the city."

"Did he ever speak of a man named—?" The first guard turned and whispered with the other, then nodded. "Named Habbazu, that was it."

Solemnly, Sharur, Ereshguna, and Tupsharru shook their heads. The second guard spoke for the first time: "His silence proves nothing. The two Zuabut could have been plotting together, plotting for the benefit of Zuabu, plotting to harm Gibil and the interests of Gibil."

"I had not thought of that," Ereshguna said, solemn still. Kimash's conclusion was close to the mark, but not on it.

"That is why Kimash the mighty lugal rules Gibil," the first guard said. "He is a man who thinks of everything."

"No doubt you are right," Sharur said. Kimash's retainers spoke of him as if he were a god. Even Inadapa, steward to the lugal, spoke of him that way—and Inadapa was clever enough in his own right to understand perfectly well that Kimash was a man like himself. Most rulers in Kudurru either were gods themselves or were men through whom their city gods spoke. To rule in his own right, Kimash had to ape divinity.

His guards, though, did not seem to think he was aping it. The first one said, "The mighty lugal will send pursuers on the Zuabi's trail. They will drag him down like the dog he is. The mighty lugal has said he desires the Zuabi brought before him, and so the Zuabi shall be brought before him." He might have been stating a law of nature.

"No doubt you are right," Sharur said again, in the tones of polite agreement he would have used had an Alashkurri wanax come out with some obvious absurdity that would not ruin a dicker.

Kimash's retainers swaggered away. Ereshguna said,

"Son, you were indeed wise to send Habbazu down to Gibil as quickly as you did."

"I thought Kimash would link Habbazu and Burrapi in his mind," Sharur answered. "He did not link them in quite the right way, but with Habbazu in his hands he would soon correct his mistake."

Tupsharru said, "I wonder when Engibil will realize something out of the ordinary has happened." He went into no more detail than that; no telling if the god was listening.

Perhaps Engibil did hear him, and went searching to discover what had happened that was out of the ordinary. Or perhaps the god, having seen that Gibil's northern frontier no longer faced danger from Enimhursag and the Imhursagut, returned his chief attention to Gibil and, in Gibil, to the temple wherein he dwelt.

His voice was a great deal more than twice the size of a man's. It might have been articulate thunder crying out: *"I have been robbed!"*

Sharur wanted to run. Sharur wanted to hide. Running from Engibil was futile. Hiding from Engibil was useless. By their expressions, Ereshguna and Tupsharru felt exactly as he did.

Since running from the god was futile, since hiding from the god was useless, all three of them stayed where they were. Through lips likely as numb with fear as Sharur's, Tupsharru whispered, "Engibil has ways of squeezing the truth from a man even the torturers of Kimash the lugal cannot match."

"There is truth, and then again there is truth," Ereshguna answered, also in a whisper. "Remember it. Give as little as you can. We are in danger. We are not yet lost."

Tupsharru and Sharur both nodded. Sharur's younger brother knew little directly concerning the stolen Alashkurri cup, and could truthfully deny questions assuming such direct knowledge. Sharur knew his own position was riskier. He knew too much, altogether too much.

And Engibil knew he and Ereshguna knew too much, altogether too much. Telling Kimash that Habbazu was in Gibil had been a mistake. The lugal, seeking to shore up his own shaky position, had warned the god. He had not said who had given him that news, or Engibil would already have descended in wrath upon the house of Ereshguna. But, should Engibil enquire of Kimash, Sharur was sure the lugal would appease the god with him and his father and brother sooner than facing Engibil's anger himself.

So it proved. The god of Gibil did not immediately visit the tent wherein Sharur, Ereshguna, and Tupsharru rested, but neither did he long delay. He appeared without warning: one moment, he was nowhere nearby; the next, air blown out by his arrival stirred Sharur's hair and whiskers. "Men of the house of Ereshguna!" he boomed. "Was it you who told Kimash of the coming to Gibil of a certain Zuabi thief? Answer with the truth." He pointed to Sharur, Ereshguna, and Tupsharru in turn.

Engibil was a drowsy god, but a god nonetheless. Sharur suddenly found himself incapable of lying: an awkward predicament for a master merchant's son. He answered with the truth: "Yes, we were the ones." He could have done nothing else.

"How did you know this master thief when you saw him?" Engibil demanded.

"He had tried to rob my caravan when it was passing through Zuabu," Sharur said. "He failed—my guards were alert—but I knew his face when I saw him again in Gibil."

"*My* guards were not so alert," Engibil said petulantly. "Why did he want to steal whatever it was he wanted to steal?" Having denied that the Alashkurri cup was anything out of the ordinary, the god did not care to mention it now. Sharur noted how unspecific he was.

He answered, "Great god, he wanted to steal it for Enzuabu." That was true. Habbazu had later changed his reasons, but Engibil had not asked about that.

"Do you know where the thing that was stolen is now?" Engibil asked.

"No," Sharur replied. As Ereshguna had remarked, there was truth, and then again there was truth. Only Ningal knew *exactly* where the cup lay. If Sharur interpreted Engibil's questions literally enough, he could evade most of the strictures the god had set on him.

Engibil rounded on Ereshguna and Tupsharru. "Does either of you know where the thing that was stolen is now?"

"No," Sharur's father said. Sharur's brother shook his head. They had both interpreted the question as Sharur had done.

"You can not lie to me," Engibil said. "I know you can not lie to me. Even if you are less firmly in my grip than I might like, you can not lie to me."

"That is so, great god," Sharur said—truthfully. His father and brother nodded. Like him, they had given Engibil the exact truth, or what they could construe as the exact truth.

The god frowned. "This is not what I had been led to believe by others," he said. "I had thought you would know more than you do."

"Perhaps, mighty god, it was those others who were mistaken," Sharur said. The truth was that Engibil was indeed a lazy god. He asked only a handful of questions and then, when the men of the house of Ereshguna succeeded in evading them, decided not to bother asking any more. He could easily have found questions Sharur and Ereshguna and Tupsharru would have been unable to evade—or, for that matter, he could have torn answers from their minds by force.

He did neither of those things. He said, "Perhaps they were. They also told the truth, or what they thought to be the truth. But a man may be honestly mistaken, as a god may be honestly mistaken." He tried again, in a way, asking Sharur, "Do you know where this Zuabi thief is now?"

"No, great god, I do not," Sharur answered. Habbazu was surely somewhere between the encampment here and Gibil, but where? Had he stopped to rest? Was he buying beer in a village? Sharur had no way of knowing, not when the thief was out of his sight.

Engibil asked the same question of Ereshguna and Tupsharru in turn, and received the same reply. Then, as much to himself as to the men of the house of Ereshguna, the god said, "I shall watch the western border. If the thief tries to take the thing that was stolen back to Zuabu, I shall learn of it. If he tries to take the thing that was stolen back to Enzuabu, I shall know."

And then he was gone, as suddenly as he had appeared. Sharur, Ereshguna, and Tupsharru looked at one another. As one, they sighed. As one, they turned toward the pot of beer. Ereshguna happened to be standing closest to it. He dipped up cups for himself and his sons. As one, they drank.

None of them said anything for some time. Engibil had gone, but they could not tell whether he had left behind some small part of his presence to listen to whatever they might say. Sharur quickly emptied his cup of beer, then filled it again.

At last, Ereshguna broke the silence, saying, "I am glad the god has realized we know so little about this theft and about the thief."

"As am I," Sharur agreed, and Tupsharru nodded.

Ereshguna went on, "I hope Engibil will have some sharp things to say to those who told him we knew more than we proved to know."

"So may it be," Sharur and Tupsharru said together, speaking to a listener who might or might not be there. Sharur added, "I hope the great god does keep a close watch on the western border, that he might capture and punish the thief if he tries to take the thing that was stolen back to Zuabu."

He could lie once more—he felt that—but he spoke the truth there. If Habbazu stole the cup from the house of Dimgalabzu, Sharur would sooner have seen it in Engibil's hands than in Enzuabu's.

Now Tupsharru and Ereshguna said, "So may it be." No matter how reliable Habbazu had shown himself to be, trusting a Zuabi came hard.

Sharur said, "I hope Kimash the mighty lugal will soon

permit us to return to Gibil. Now that we have forced Enimhursag to flee, now that we have plundered the Imhursaggi camp, we have no great reason to linger near the
border with Imhursag. We who dwell in the city can return
to our homes. We can return to our trades. The peasant
levies who fought alongside us can return to their villages.
They can return to their fields. We can be assured we shall
have a good harvest, and food for all.''

"That would be good," Ereshguna agreed. "That
would—''

Before he could say anything more, Engibil reappeared.
"You!" the god said, and pointed straight at Sharur.

"I serve you, great god." Sharur dropped to his knees
and then to his belly, though he doubted whether the forms
of respect would do him any good. Engibil had to have
learned something to return to the encampment of the Gibli
army. Sharur resolved to give the god as little as he could,
knowing how little such resolve was liable to mean.

Engibil said, "You were outside my temple when the
thing that was stolen disappeared. You were outside my
house when the thief dared rob it.''

"Great god, I had gone down into Gibil to put a prisoner
into the hands of Ushurikti the slave dealer," Sharur said.
"Mighty god, while I was there, I put on an entertainment
for the people left behind in the city, and especially for the
priests who serve your house on earth." Unless Engibil
forced it from him, he would not admit he knew exactly
when the cup disappeared from the god's temple.

"It was during this entertainment that the thing that was
stolen was raped away," Engibil said. "What do you know
of this? Tell me the truth.''

Sharur had to obey. "Here is the truth that I know, great
god," he said. "I know that, while the entertainment was
under way, I never once set foot inside your temple. I never
entered your house on earth. Your own priests, your own
servants, saw me in the open space outside your temple.
They will say as much. I never saw any thief enter your
temple. I never saw any thief leave your house on earth.

When I left the open space outside your temple, the entertainment was still going on.''

Every word of that was the truth. Every word was as misleading as he could make it. Engibil frowned, again not receiving the answer he had expected or hoped for. ''Do you wonder, son of Ereshguna,'' he said gruffly, ''that I ask these questions of you when you had seen a Zuabi thief and when you were close by my temple when the vile thief struck?''

''You are a god,'' Sharur said. ''How can a man wonder at anything a god may choose to do?''

''You can not,'' Engibil said. ''You must not.'' And then he was gone once more.

''I am glad you told the god the truth that you knew,'' Ereshguna said. ''I am glad you were able to tell the truth with such . . . precision.''

''So am I, Father,'' Sharur replied, still shaking a little. ''So am I. Has that beer pot yet gone dry?''


Kimash the lugal made the Gibli army's return to the city of Gibil into a triumphal procession. At every village along the road south from the Imhursaggi border, men dropped out to return to their usual labor in the fields. At every village, Kimash made a speech praising the warriors, praising the people of Gibil as a whole, and praising himself.

At every crossroads along the road south from the Imhursaggi border, men turned off to the right or left to go back to their villages. At every crossroads, Kimash halted the whole army so he could make another speech. Again, he extolled the warriors, the Giblut, and himself.

The speeches were not quite identical, one to another, but they were similar. After a while, Sharur stopped paying close attention to them. ''I wonder if he can find anything new to say when we finally get to Gibil,'' he remarked as the army started moving after yet another halt.

''More likely, he'll simply run all of these speeches

together, for the men and women of Gibil will not have heard them,'' Tupsharru said.

''And then, once he has done that, he will go into the south and make all these speeches yet again,'' Ereshguna said. ''He is not a god like Enimhursag, to speak into the ears of all his people at once. Naturally, he wants all the folk of Gibil to know he has driven back the Imhursagut. If he wants them to know, he must tell them himself.''

''And tell them, and tell them, and tell them,'' Sharur said with exaggerated weariness. Ereshguna tried to send a reproving look his way, but broke down and laughed before the expression was well formed.

Although the lugal's endless bombastic oratory made the march down from the Imhursaggi border seem to take forever, the baked-brick walls of Gibil, and Engibil's temple and Kimash's palace towering above them, at last came into sight. Kimash halted the army outside the north gate to the city and ordered the warriors who had armor to don it and those who had only weapons to carry them.

''He does indeed wish to make the bravest show he can,'' Sharur said.

''Only one sort of show is worse than no show at all,'' his father said, ''and that is a poor show.''

Kimash left himself in no danger of making a poor show. As his fighting men entered Gibil through the north gate, a great-voiced herald cried, ''Behold! Mighty Kimash returns in triumph, having made Enimhursag flee!'' Riding in the chariot all adorned with gold, Kimash waved to the men and women lining the narrow, winding streets of the city.

And the people cheered. Not all of them, no doubt, loved Kimash. Some surely longed for the days when Engibil did much of their thinking for them. But no one in the city of Gibil could possibly have longed for Enimhursag to do much of their thinking for them. The rivalry between their city and that of the vanquished god was too deep and went back too far for any of them to have hoped he won. Beating Enimhursag was the best way Kimash could have chosen to make the Giblut think well of him.

Into the market square marched the warriors of Gibil. The men and women who had not fought crowded in with and after them. Servants brought a platform from the lugal's palace. Kimash climbed up onto it and looked out over the crowd. He was wise in the ways of men, and proved wise enough not to do as Tupsharru had said he would. Instead of stringing together all his earlier speeches, he kept things short and to the point: "Warriors of Gibil residing in the city, I release you to your families and friends for the praise you so richly deserve. Warriors of Gibil dwelling south of the city, I bid you stay this day before resuming your homeward journey. Let this day be a day of feasting, a day of drinking, a day of revelry, a day of celebration. I, Kimash, lugal of Gibil, have spoken. I, Kimash, lugal of this city, have declared my will."

Again, the people of Gibil were glad to follow where the lugal led. Those who had gone to fight and those who had stayed behind all shouted and clapped their hands. Warriors embraced their fathers, their brothers, their wives, their mothers, their sisters, their children. Some headed for taverns. Some headed for brothels.

Sharur headed for home, along with Ereshguna and Tupsharru. They had not gone far when they met Betsilim and Nanadirat. Sharur hugged his mother and younger sister. He looked around hopefully, to see if Ningal was somewhere nearby. On a day of revelry, a day of celebration, he might with propriety hug his intended, too. But, to his disappointment, he did not spy her.

He also looked around for Habbazu. He did not see the Zuabi thief, either. He did not know what that meant, or whether he should worry. When Habbazu chose not to be seen, he was not seen. But he also might have fallen into the hands of Engibil, or those of Engibil's priests, or those of Kimash's servitors. He might even have escaped to Zuabu in spite of Engibil's watching the border.

Ereshguna and Tupsharru were also looking this way and that. Ereshguna smiled sheepishly when his eyes met Sharur's. He said, "I suppose it does not matter," and

Sharur had a very good notion of what *it* was.

"I suppose the same thing," Sharur answered. "I truly hope it does not matter."

"What are the two of you talking about?" Betsilim demanded.

"Nothing very important," Sharur answered. He could not remember the last time he had lied to his mother, but he lied now without hesitation. He did not think he had ever lied to his mother in his father's presence. Ereshguna heard him lie, and let it go without contradiction.

While Betsilim and Nanadirat went out, the Imhursaggi slave woman had labored in the kitchen. The returning men of the house of Ereshguna sat down to a feast: roast mutton, roast duck, a salad of onions and lettuce and radishes, fresh-baked bread with honey for dipping, and wine and beer to wash everything down. Sharur ate till just this side of bursting.

So did Tupsharru. Despite that, though, he eyed the slave woman in a marked manner. After a while, he and the slave disappeared. "He is intent on conquering Imhursag again," Ereshguna said dryly.

Sharur laughed. Nanadirat giggled. Betsilim gave her husband a look that said she didn't think the joke was funny, or maybe just that he had better not try to reconquer Imhursag in that particular way.

Presently, Nanadirat and Betsilim, both a little wobbly on their legs, went up to the roof to sleep. Tupsharru had not come back. He'd teased Sharur for taking the slave woman twice after coming home from his trading journey to the mountains of Alashkurru. Now, coming home from the war, Tupsharru seemed to be imitating his brother.

When Sharur got to his feet to go upstairs, too, Ereshguna held up a hand. "Wait," he said. "The thing you left behind . . . when do you plan to get it back from where you left it?"

He picked his words with obvious—and necessary—care, not wishing to draw Engibil's attention to them in any way. Sharur answered with similar caution: "My father, I do not know. As I have said, and said truly, I do not know just where that thing is now. I will have to go to the person to whom I entrusted it to get it back.''

''I understand,'' Ereshguna said. ''That may not be so easy, not when others have returned to the house. But I hope you will do it as soon as you may. If we do not take it back into our hands, others may take it into theirs.''

''I shall attend to it,'' Sharur promised. He yawned. ''But not tonight.''

''No, not tonight,'' Ereshguna agreed. He and Sharur both got to their feet and went up to the roof to sleep.

# 11

Sharur's dreams were strange. He realized that he had not known anything nearly so peculiar since the delirium through which he had drifted after the fever demon breathed its foul breath into his mouth. He wondered if he was delirious again. He did not think so, nor had he been so very drunk when he went up to the roof and lay down on his sleeping mat.

Voices called to him from a vast distance, their words echoing and indistinct. Some were male, some female; some might have been either, or both at once . . . or neither. He did not think they were speaking the language of Kudurru, but it was a language he understood, or should have understood. Maybe that was because he dreamt. Maybe . . .

He needed a while, but finally recognized the tongue that dinned inside his head: it was the speech of the Alashkurru Mountains. With that recognition, he heard the voices more distinctly, as if the men and women using that speech had suddenly come closer.

Men and women? Not all the voices had fit into either category. Up until he realized what language they were speaking, Sharur had seen only blurry flashes of light and color, like a distant landscape fitfully illuminated with lightning bolts.

Now those flashes and colors came closer and closer, too. They and the voices surrounded Sharur, who seemed to be looking up from the bottom of a great bowl at shapes that slowly congealed into faces and bodies. The faces peered down at him as he peered up at them.

"He knows us," one of them said: a woman—no, a goddess. As she spoke, her entire form became more plain to Sharur. She was nude, with enormously bulging breasts and, below them, an even more enormously bulging belly. Sharur did indeed know Fasillar; he had had dealings with the Alashkurri goddess of birth in the town of Zalpuwas. Now she went on, "He knows who we are."

"You are the gods and goddesses of the Alashkurrut," Sharur said, or thought he said—in a dream, how could he be sure?

"We are the gods and goddesses of the Alashkurrut." The speaker this time had a man's voice, a deep man's voice. He wore copper armor and carried a bronze sword. Tarsiyas, the war god with whom Sharur had had dealings in the town of Tuwanas, spoke with touchy pride: "We are the great gods and goddesses of the Alashkurrut."

Sharur bowed low to him and to Fasillar and to the other deities, whom he still perceived less clearly. "I greet you, great gods and goddesses of the Alashkurrut," he said; even in a dream, politeness to gods was a good idea. "What do you want with me?" Being in a dream, he could at least feign ignorance.

"You have something of ours," Fasillar said.

"You have something of ours," Tarsiyas agreed. "The thing of ours that you have, you have secreted away in a dreadful place."

"In a dreadful place you have secreted away the thing of ours that you have," Fasillar echoed. "We tried to send a dream your way before. We could not send a dream your way before. We had not the power to send a dream your way before, not from out of that dreadful place. You were too far from us. Even now, when you are so close, we can barely send a dream your way."

Tarsiyas nodded his fierce head. "You have met us face to face. Only because you have met us face to face can we send a dream your way at all. We have cried out to Engibil, but Engibil hears us not. He is a god. He sleeps not. He has no dreams in which to hear us.''

"He has not met us face to face, as you have," Fasillar said. "He is deaf to us. He hears us not."

Hiding the Alashkurri cup in the house of Dimgalabzu had truly proved a good idea. The power of the gods was at a low ebb along the Street of Smiths, and lowest in the smithies. Though he knew he was but dreaming, Sharur did not smile. Instead, he asked his own question once more: "What do you want with me, great gods and goddesses of the Alashkurrut?''

"Give back the thing of ours that you have." Fasillar and Tarsiyas spoke together, echoed by the rest of the great gods and goddesses of the Alashkurrut.

"Give back the thing of ours that you have, and we shall reward you," Fasillar said.

"Fail to give back the thing of ours that you have, and we shall punish you," Tarsiyas added, his grim features growing grimmer.

"What will you do to reward me?" Sharur asked. "What can you do to punish me? I am in Gibil. You are in the Alashkurru Mountains.''

"One day, you shall come again to the Alashkurru Mountains," Fasillar answered. "Would you sooner be rewarded or punished when you do?"

"I would sooner be rewarded, great goddess," Sharur answered. "I would sooner not be punished, mighty goddess."

"There, you see?" Tarsiyas rumbled. "I knew this was a wise mortal. I knew this mortal would be able to tell where he would have bread and meat to eat, where he would have had only crumbs and bones."

When last Sharur had seen and spoken with Tarsiyas, the Alashkurri war god had not praised him. Tarsiyas had reviled him for seeking to seduce Huzziyas the wanax away from the path of obedience to the gods. Belligerence had fit Tarsiyas's nature. Conciliation did not. A conciliatory Tarsiyas put Sharur in mind of a lion sitting down to a meal of bread and lettuce and dates.

Sharur realized he was thinking more clearly than he was used to doing in dreams. In his ordinary dreams, though, he did not talk with the great gods of the Alashkurrut. "Give back the thing of ours that you have," Fasillar repeated. "Give it back, and all the women you bed shall bear you many sons and shall come through the pangs of childbirth safe and unharmed."

"Give back the thing of ours that you have," the rest of the Alashkurri gods said in blurry chorus. "Give it back, and all..." The chorus broke down, presumably because each god or goddess was making a different promise, one set in a domain over which that deity held power.

"What are your promises worth to me?" Sharur asked. "You are great gods. You are mighty gods. But you are the gods of the Alashkurrut. You are the gods of the Alashkurru Mountains. You are not the gods of the men who live between the rivers. You are not the gods of Kudurru. Your power rests in the mountains. You have no power here between the rivers."

Tarsiyas glared at him. Now the Alashkurri war god looked and sounded fierce once more. "You are a mortal. You are only a mortal. Soon you will be a whining, carping ghost. Soon you will be gone, gone from this world, gone from memory in this world. Speak no words of who has power and who has not."

"What you say is true, great god," Sharur answered politely. "What you say is the way of the world, mighty god." He had to keep on being polite. Any man who openly opposed a god was liable to come to grief. That, too, was the way of the world. But, though Sharur was only a mortal, where power lay here was not so obvious. He had the thing the great gods of the Alashkurrut wanted, and they were not the gods of this land. They would have to satisfy him before he even thought of satisfying them.

Fasillar must have recognized that, for she said, "What other boons might we grant you, man of Kudurru? What other favors might we give you, man of Gibil?"

Had Sharur chosen to ask the Alashkurri gods to lift their

ban against his city's merchants, he was sure they would have promised to do it. He wondered, though, whether he might not have at his disposal another way to lift the ban. All he said was, "I do not know"—a merchant's canny answer.

"Send the thing of ours that you have back to the Alash-kurru Mountains, and we shall grant you all the good fortune lying in our power," Fasillar promised. "You shall be rich, you shall be beloved, you shall be healthy, your days in this world shall be long."

"Keep the thing of ours that you have, send it not back to the Alashkurru Mountains, and we shall inflict on you all the ill fortune in our power," Tarsiyas vowed. "You shall be poor, you shall be despised, you shall be sickly and pul-ing, your days in this world shall be short and filled with torment."

Had Tarsiyas not threatened him, Sharur's dream-self would have held its peace. As things were, though, he grew angry, as he would have grown angry while awake. He said, "Suppose, great gods of the Alashkurrut, that I do not send the thing of yours that I have back to the Alashkurru Moun-tains. Suppose, mighty gods of the Alashkurrut, that I do not keep the thing of yours that I have. Suppose, great gods, mighty gods, that I break the thing of yours that I have. What then?"

Tarsiyas gasped. Fasillar gasped. In the background, all the great gods of the Alashkurrut gasped. All the mighty gods of the Alashkurrut gasped.

Sharur gasped—and found himself awake on the roof of the house of Ereshguna, staring up at the stars. Unlike his fever dreams, this dream he would not forget, not to his dying day.

When morning came, Sharur intended to go straight to the house of Dimgalabzu to recover the cup he had left with Ningal. Before he finished his breakfast porridge of barley and salt fish, though, and before he finished the cup of beer he was drinking with it, Inadapa the steward of Kimash the lugal strode into the house of Ereshguna.

"I greet you, steward to the mighty Kimash," Sharur said, rising from his stool to bow to Inadapa. "Will you eat porridge of barley and salt fish with me? Will you drink a cup of beer with me? While you eat, while you drink, will you tell me what brings you to the house of Ereshguna so early in the day?"

"I greet you, Sharur son of Ereshguna," Inadapa said. "I have eaten, thank you. I breakfasted at first light of dawn, the better to serve the mighty Kimash through the whole of the day. But I will gladly drink a cup of beer with you, and I will tell you what brings me to the house of Ereshguna so early in the day, for it concerns you."

Sharur dipped up a cup of beer with his own hands and gave it to Inadapa. "I listen," he said, and spooned up more porridge.

Inadapa drank and nodded approval. "The house of Ereshguna brews good beer, as I have known for long and long. Kimash the mighty lugal has ordered me to bring you before him as soon as may be."

"I obey the lugal. I obey the lugal's steward." Sharur ate one more mouthful of porridge, then rose from his stool again. "Let us go."

"Kimash the mighty lugal will be glad for your obedience." Inadapa hastily finished the beer Sharur had dipped up for him, smacked his lips, and echoed the younger merchant: "Aye, let us go."

When they got to the lugal's palace, it was as it had been on some of Sharur's earlier visits: workmen swarmed everywhere, some with bricks, some with mortar, some building scaffolding of reeds to support brickwork already made or to support artisans running up new brickwork.

"Kimash the mighty lugal no longer stints himself, I see," Sharur remarked. "It is good." He meant what he said; the time when Kimash had gone easy because Engibil was reasserting himself had been difficult and alarming for all those in Gibil who favored the new and flourished because of it.

"Truly it is good." Inadapa's nod was emphatic. "The mighty lugal rejoices in his munificence and in his strength." What that meant was that Kimash rejoiced in Engibil's weakness and preoccupation, but his steward was far too canny to let himself say—probably far too canny even to let himself think—any such thing.

"For what purpose has the mighty lugal summoned me to his palace?" Sharur asked, as Inadapa led him through the maze of passages within the palace.

"Whatever the purpose may be, the mighty lugal did not see fit to enlighten his lowly servant as to its nature," Inadapa answered. "Soon you shall come before him. Soon he shall tell you his purpose. Soon you shall hear it from his very lips."

"Soon I shall hear it from his very lips," Sharur agreed. Perhaps Inadapa was merely doing as he usually did when bringing men before the lugal. Perhaps Kimash did not want Sharur to know ahead of time why he had been summoned, in the hope that he would not be able to prepare plausible answers for the questions the lugal intended to put to him.

In the throne room, Kimash sat on the raised seat covered in gold leaf. Sharur went down on his face in the dust before him. "I am here at the mighty lugal's command," he said, not raising his head. "I have come at the mighty lugal's order."

"Rise," Kimash said. "You are as obedient as you should be. You are as obedient as every Gibli should be."

"I am pleased to obey the commands of the mighty lugal," Sharur said as he got to his feet. *Better to obey your commands than those of the god*, he thought. He would not let himself say that, but it was there, and Kimash no doubt knew it was there.

Kimash clapped his hands. Inadapa hurried back into the throne room. "Fetch us beer and roasted grasshoppers," the lugal said. Inadapa bowed and hurried away, returning shortly with the food and drink. After crunching his way through a skewer of locusts, Kimash asked, "Have you seen either Habbazu the Zuabi thief or Burrapi the Zuabi mercenary since your return to Gibil?"

"Mighty lugal, I have not," Sharur answered truthfully.

A thoughtful look on his face, the lugal started on a second skewer. Presently, he said, "You convinced Engibil that you know nothing of the theft from his temple."

"He asked me questions," Sharur said. "Because of his power, I had to answer them with the truth."

"There is truth, and then again there is truth," Kimash replied, sounding very much like Sharur's father. "And, gods being as they are, Engibil no doubt relied too much on his power and too little on the common sense that men, having no such power, must develop and cultivate. The 'truth' a god will accept does not always stand up under a man's inspection."

"Here, though, all is well so long as the god accepts it," Sharur said.

"Perhaps, and then again perhaps not." The lugal chose to use his previous phrasing once more. "Engibil is satisfied, aye, but I still wonder whether you and the other men of the house of Ereshguna and the two Zuabut, the thief and the mercenary, obeyed me as completely as I have the right to expect." He stared down at Sharur from his high seat.

Sharur felt like a mouse on whom a hawk's gaze falls from the sky. But he bore up under the lugal's inspection. Kimash was but a man. Enimhursag had searched for Sharur from on high. After that, facing Kimash's doubts, if not easy, was by no means impossible.

"From what I have seen, thieves, generally speaking, obey only themselves," Sharur said. "And if Engibil is busy looking for a thief along the western border of Gibil's lands, he will not be busy within the city of Gibil. He will not be busy trying to take the rule in Gibil out of the hands of the mighty lugal and into his own hands once more."

"This is so," Kimash said. "Aye, this is so." Sharur pulled a locust off a skewer and popped it into his mouth. While he was eating, his expression could not give him away. He could not deceive Kimash by feeding him truths that were useless or misleading, as he had done with Engibil. But he could distract the lugal and get him to think of other things than those perhaps dangerous to the house of Eresh-guna.

After eating another grasshopper and sipping at his beer, Sharur said, "The mighty lugal's refreshments are of the finest."

"For those whom it pleases me to honor, nothing is too fine, no reward too great," Kimash said. "This brings me to another matter: indeed, to the other matter on account of which I had you summoned here. You will recall that, in exchange for your not pursuing the presence of the Alash-kurri cup in the temple of Engibil, I promised you a marriage tie to any woman in the city of Gibil, this to include even my own daughters."

"Yes, mighty lugal, I do recall that," Sharur said with a sinking feeling.

"I am glad you recall it," Kimash said. "The cup has stirred its own uproar, thanks to the Zuabi thief, but I do not think it is an uproar to threaten my position on the throne. And so, I am pleased to tell you that the promise of a marriage to any woman in the city of Gibil, this to include even my own daughters, still holds."

"Ah," Sharur said, and then "Ah" again. He wondered how, or if, he was to get out of this one without offering the lugal deadly insult. After some thought, he decided the truth offered his best hope. "You will recall, mighty lugal, that my oath to Engibil prevented me from making final marriage arrangements for Ningal the daughter of Dimgal-abzu the smith."

"Yes, of course," Kimash said. "That is why, out of the kindness and generosity of my heart, I offered you a marriage tie to any other woman in the city of Gibil, this to include even my own daughters." He bore down heavily on the last phrase; he plainly sought an alliance between his own house and the house of Ereshguna.

"The mighty lugal is kind." Sharur bowed. "The mighty

lugal is generous.'' He bowed once more. *The mighty lugal is conveniently forgetful*, he thought. Part of the reason for Kimash's offer, as the lugal had himself admitted, was to bribe Sharur out of pursuing his own course of action and into pursuing that which Kimash desired.

''Take advantage of my kindness, then,'' the lugal urged. ''Take advantage of my generosity.''

Sharur sighed. He could not deflect the moment any longer. With yet another bow, he said, ''Mighty lugal, were matters otherwise, otherwise even in the slightest degree, nothing would delight my heart more than doing exactly as you say. But with—''

''Wait.'' On the instant, Kimash went from affable to thunderous. ''Do you mean you refuse my offer? Do you mean you spurn my offer?''

''Mighty lugal, I mean nothing of the sort,'' Sharur replied, though that was indeed what he meant. ''As I told you before, the god prevented me from making final marriage arrangements for Ningal the daughter of Dimgalabzu the smith.''

''Even so,'' Kimash said. ''Those arrangements being prevented, what could possibly keep you from accepting the offer I made to you?''

''Were those arrangements still prevented, nothing could keep me from accepting the offer you made to me,'' Sharur replied, feeling sweat break out on his forehead. ''But mighty Engibil, in his own generosity, returned to me from his hands and from his heart the oath I had made in his name, and will suffer me to pay bride-price for Ningal to Dimgalabzu from the store of wealth of the house of Ereshguna, not from the profit I unfortunately failed to make on my last trading journey to the Alashkurru Mountains.''

Kimash's eyes went wide and round and staring. ''The god . . . returned to you from his hands and from his heart the oath you had made in his name?'' He sounded astonished, as Enimhursag had before him on hearing the same news. ''I can hardly believe it.''

''Believe or do not believe as best suits you, mighty

lugal," Sharur said. "But, whether you believe or do not
believe, I speak the truth. Because I speak the truth, I cannot
take advantage of your kindness. I cannot take advantage of
your generosity."

"Engibil returned your oath." Kimash shook his head.
He had the aspect of a man who had just come through an
earthquake: shaken but doing his best to preserve his equi-
librium, no matter what might happen next. "You realize I
can enquire of the god whether you lie."

"Of course, mighty lugal," Sharur said. "Enquire all you
like. Engibil will tell you I speak the truth."

"Engibil returned your oath from his hands?" Kimash
still did not sound as if he believed it. Perhaps he thought
that repeating it over and over would help persuade him it
was true. "Engibil returned your oath from his heart? Engibil keeps oaths. He holds oaths. He returns them not."

"This time, mighty lugal, he did return my oath." Sharur
knew why the god had returned his oath, too, or thought he
did. Just as Kimash had done, so Engibil had sought to
distract him from pursuing the matter of the Alashkurri cup
in his temple storeroom. As far as he was concerned, Ningal
made for a far more attractive distraction than any Kimash
had set before him. In terms carefully oblique, he said as
much: "As I have long desired to wed Ningal the daughter
of Dimgalabzu, I shall do so now that the great god, the
mighty god, has in his generosity given me leave to pay her
the bride-price as circumstances have compelled me to pay
it."

"A match with the house of Dimgalabzu will surely
prove advantageous to the house of Ereshguna," the lugal
said. "But will it prove as advantageous as a match with
the house of Kimash?"

A match with the lugal's daughter would swiftly raise the
house of Ereshguna high among the nobles of Gibil. But
Sharur was sure it would not put the treasures of Gibil into
his hands or those of his father. And what rose swiftly could
fall swiftly, too. Sharur knew that only too well.

Bowing to Kimash, he once more picked his words with

great care: "Mighty lugal, having long desired this match, as I said before, and having obtained for it the blessings of my father, of the father of my intended, and of Engibil himself, I very much hope to go forward with it."

Kimash sighed. "You are a stubborn man. You are hard to turn aside. If you prove as stubborn in matters of the heart, if you prove as hard to turn aside in matters of your affections, the woman you wed will have little to complain of you. Before you settle once and for all time who that woman shall be, though, would it not please you to make the acquaintance of the daughters of the house of Kimash?"

Sharur bowed again, very low this time. Kimash was offering him an extraordinary concession, and he knew how extraordinary it was. "You are kind beyond my deserts, mighty lugal," he murmured. "But I must tell you that, since Dimgalabzu and my father, since Gulal and my mother, have completed all arrangements for the wedding save only the nuptial feast, I do not see what point there might be to my meeting your no doubt lovely daughters. I think the meeting would be likelier to cause distress on all sides than to cause joy."

"It could be so, son of Ereshguna; it could be so," Kimash said with another sigh. "If that is the way you look on it, likely it *will* be so. Forcing a man to do what he truly does not wish to do is the surest way I know to make him into an enemy. Do as you wish, then, and may it be well for you, and for me, and for Gibil."

"I thank the mighty lugal for his forbearance," Sharur said. Only after the words had left his mouth did he realize that Kimash worried about making him an enemy. That the lugal should worry about him in any way was one more amazement out of many.

Instead of directly answering him, the lugal clapped his hands together. Inadapa appeared in the throne room in a way Habbazu might have envied: one moment he was not there, the next he was, or so it appeared to Sharur. Kimash said, "The two of us have finished our discussion. Escort Sharur back to the house of Ereshguna."

Inadapa bowed. "Mighty lugal, as you say, so shall it be." He turned to Sharur. "Come. I shall escort you back to the house of Ereshguna."

"I thank you, steward to the mighty lugal." Sharur bowed to Inadapa, and then again to Kimash. "And, once more, I thank the mighty lugal."

Inadapa led him out through the corridors of the palace and out past the guards at the entranceway, who respectfully dipped their heads to the steward and to Sharur. Just outside the palace, Sharur and Inadapa had to wait while another gang of laborers and artisans went past. Only when the two men were walking up the Street of Smiths toward the house of Ereshguna did Inadapa say, "Do I understand correctly, then, that you shall not unite your house with the house of Kimash?"

"Steward to the lugal, you do," Sharur replied. "Having made all arrangements to wed the daughter of Dimgalabzu the smith, I did not see how I could in good conscience break them." *Nor did I want to break them, though that is not your affair.*

"And the mighty lugal permitted this?" Inadapa asked. He had been hanging around the throne room; he must have heard almost all, if not all, of what had passed between Sharur and Kimash. Yet now he sought confirmation, as if unable to believe what his ears had told him.

"The mighty lugal permitted this," Sharur agreed. "In his forbearance, in his generosity, in his kindness, he permitted it."

"I heard it," the steward said. "I understood it. Having heard it, having understood it, I still have trouble believing it. For the mighty lugal to turn aside from a course on which he had settled is as untoward as for Engibil to give back an oath—which, from what you say, also came to pass. Truly, son of Ereshguna, your affairs of late have been extraordinary."

"There, steward to the mighty lugal, I can only say that you speak the truth," Sharur replied. If anything, the steward understated the truth: fortunately, he did not know all of it.

"Here we are, at the doorway to the house of Eresh-guna." Inadapa bowed to Sharur. "I now return to serve Kimash the mighty lugal once more, though I do not expect to be so amazed in his service again any time soon." He set both hands on his ample belly, shook his head, and went back down the Street of Smiths toward the palace.

Sharur walked through the doorway. As soon as he was inside the house of Ereshguna, he was very glad Inadapa had not accompanied him on those last few steps, for there, talking animatedly with his father, stood Habbazu the thief.

"I greet you, master merchant's son," Habbazu said with a bow.

"I greet you, master thief." Sharur politely returned the bow.

"Your father has told me you have not yet recovered the cup we gave to your intended to hold for us in the house of Dimgalabzu, unless you chanced to do so while returning from the palace of Kimash," Habbazu said.

"My father speaks the truth, as he usually speaks the truth," Sharur answered. "Nor did I recover the cup while returning from the palace of the mighty lugal." He opened his hands to show they were empty. "I might have tried to recover the cup, but Inadapa, Kimash's steward, accompanied me from the palace, and so I had no chance to go alone to the house of Dimgalabzu."

"Yes, I can see how having the steward along would make regaining the cup more difficult." Habbazu's voice was dry.

"A bit, yes," Sharur said, and the master thief smiled to hear his own tone so neatly matched.

Ereshguna said, "Before you came back from the palace, son, I had just asked whether Habbazu had recovered the cup you gave to your beloved to hold for you in the house of Dimgalabzu."

"And I had just said no," Habbazu added. "I did not feel so brief an introduction to your intended would have persuaded her to give me the cup in your absence, and I would have had a difficult time explaining my presence to Dimgalabzu her father."

"Yes, I can see how that might be so, even if you have made his acquaintance as Burrapi the mercenary," Ereshguna said. "Is that the same name you used when you met Ningal?"

"It is," Sharur and Habbazu said together.

"Well, that is good, at any rate." Ereshguna nodded approval.

To Habbazu, Sharur said, "Considering the trade you practice, you might have recovered the cup without meeting either Ningal my intended or Dimgalabzu her father."

"I am, as you say, a master thief." Habbazu bowed to Sharur. "I am a master thief who has the aid of Enzuabu, the master of thieves. But I would hesitate to steal from a smith's house in Zuabu. Still more would I hesitate to steal from a smith's house here in Gibil. Some of the protections I have from the god work less well around smithies than almost anywhere else."

"Working in metal as they do, smiths deal with raw power of their own," Ereshguna said. "Perhaps this power will become a divine power, but perhaps it will not. Because the powers of the gods are weaker around smiths and scribes—whose power over words is likewise not divine, or not yet divine—they were among the men whom Kimash set in the first ranks against Enimhursag, as you saw."

"Yes, I did see that," Habbazu said, nodding. "The weakening of the gods' powers worked to their advantage then. It would work to my disadvantage, did I try to, ah, visit the house of Dimgalabzu by stealth."

That Habbazu might hesitate before trying to rob a smith's house did not mean he would not try, not after he had robbed a god's temple. Sharur found another question to ask him: "When you lay down to sleep last night, did you have strange dreams?"

The master thief had been on the point of saying something else. He stopped with his mouth open, looking extremely foolish for a moment. Then, gathering himself, he replied, "Since you ask it, I shall answer with the truth, and the truth is that, yes, I did have strange dreams when I lay down to sleep last night."

"As did I," Sharur said, nodding. "Tell me something more, then: were these dreams you had when you lay down to sleep . . . crowded dreams?"

"Crowded dreams indeed," Habbazu said. "The very word I should have used. As best I can recall, I have never had such crowded dreams in all my days."

"And in these dreams," Sharur persisted, "did those who crowded them insist that you restore to them something they said was theirs?"

"So they did," Habbazu said. "Aye, master merchant's son, so they did. They grew quite insistent, as a matter of fact. They also promised great rewards if I restored to them something they said was theirs. And then"—he frowned— "it was very strange."

"How so?" Sharur asked. Here, for the first time, the words of the master thief took him by surprise.

Habbazu's frown deepened and grew quizzical. "It was very strange," he repeated. "In my dream, I was in converse with this crowd, as I say. At times, they threatened me; at times, they sought to cajole me. And then—all at once, it was as if the lot of them let out a great gasp of fright and fled. I do not know what might have frightened them. Certainly, I did not frighten them. I did not know any way to frighten them. But frightened they were. And frightened I was, too. I also let out a great gasp of fright. When I opened my eyes, I found myself alone on my sleeping mat."

"Ah." Now Sharur smiled. "I think we must have been dreaming our crowded dreams at the same time, master thief."

"Why do you say this, master merchant's son?" Habbazu asked. "Did the crowds in your dream also take fright?"

"They did—and I made them take fright," Sharur

answered. "We were speaking of my possibly restoring something they said was theirs, and we were speaking of my possibly keeping something they said was theirs. Then, in my dream, I asked what would happen if I broke something they said was theirs. They took fright. When I opened my eyes, I, like you, found myself alone on my sleeping mat."

"If you . . . broke something they said was theirs." Habbazu spoke the words slowly, as if he had trouble bringing them out. His face bore an uneasy mixture of admiration and dread. "Son of Ereshguna, this I will tell you, and tell you truly: only a Gibli could think of such a thing."

Ereshguna, who had been some time silent, spoke up: "Only a Gibli of my son's generation could think of such a thing. My heart stumbled within me when I first heard this notion, too."

"And, you having heard it more than once, what does your heart do now?" Habbazu asked.

"It still quivers," Ereshguna replied, "but it no longer stumbles. We of Gibil have a way of growing used to new notions."

"*That* I have seen." By Habbazu's tone, he did not intend the words as a compliment.

Ereshguna studied him. "Do you know, master thief, that you have shown yourself capable of growing used to new notions as quickly as most Giblut?"

"Have I indeed?" Habbazu considered that. "Well, perhaps I have. What of it?" He looked a challenge at Sharur and Ereshguna.

Sharur took it up. "What of it? you ask. Let me ask you a question in return: suppose that, after all this business is done—however it may finally end—you return to Zuabu. Will you feel easy, living once more under the rule of Enzuabu? Will you feel comfortable, living once more under the strong hand of your city god?"

"Enzuabu is not Enimhursag," Habbazu said. "He is the lord of Zuabu. He is the ruler of Zuabu. He is not the toymaker of Zuabu, compelling men to move here and there as if they were tiny clay figures."

"I never claimed he was," Sharur replied. "I do not claim he is. What I asked was, Enzuabu being as he is, will you feel easy, living under his rule? When he orders you to rob this one or to leave that one alone, will you be glad to obey him as you have always obeyed him?"

"He is my god," Habbazu said. "Of course I shall obey him." Then he realized that was not quite what Sharur had asked. "Of course I shall be glad to—" he began, and then stopped. He gave Sharur a sour look. Sharur saw the pans on either side of the scales in his mind swinging up and down, up and down, and finally reach a balance he had not expected. Habbazu's expression grew more sour still. "I have associated too long with Giblut. I have had too much to do with the ways of Giblut. Giblut and the ways of Giblut have corrupted me."

Ereshguna and Sharur both smiled. "You have associated too long with free men," Ereshguna said. "You have had too much to do with the ways of free men. Without quite knowing it, you have become a free man yourself."

"If that is what you call it, perhaps I have," Habbazu said. "I would not presume to argue with my host."

"Well, then," Sharur said, "in that case, does your heart still stumble within you at the notion of breaking something those in your dream said was theirs?"

"Of course it does," Habbazu answered at once. "If you were not a mad Gibli, your heart would stumble within you, too. To be free, or largely free, of your city god is one thing. To strike a blow against those in my dream"—he would not say, and Sharur could not blame him for not saying, *to strike a blow against the gods*—"is something else again. No wonder, then, that my heart stumbles within me."

"No wonder," Ereshguna agreed. "Let me, then, ask a different question: regardless of whether your heart stumbles within you, do you think we should go ahead and break something those in your dream said was theirs?"

"Truly, that is a different question." Habbazu plucked at his beard as he thought. At last, he said, "Perhaps it might not be so bad, if we could be sure of escaping the wrath of those closer to us.''

''We cannot be sure of that,'' Sharur said. ''We cannot be sure of any such thing. We can only hope—and act.''

''If we do break something those in my dream said was theirs, I can never go back to Zuabu,'' Habbazu said. ''I can never go back to Enzuabu. How can I tell the god of my city I have disobeyed him? How can I tell him I have chosen my own will, my own path, rather than his?''

''You were the one who said Enzuabu was not Enimhursag,'' Sharur replied. ''I believed your words. I accepted that you spoke rightly. Do you tell me now that you were mistaken?''

Habbazu shook his head. ''Enzuabu is not Enimhursag, to rule every tiny thing in the city. But neither is Enzuabu Engibil, to do as near nothing in the city as he can. When he lays down a command, he expects obedience.''

''Well, so does Engibil,'' Sharur said. ''The difference between them is, Engibil lays down a command but seldom.''

''And besides,'' Ereshguna said, ''have you not obeyed the command your god laid down, master thief? Have you not stolen from the temple of Engibil something those in your dream said was theirs?''

''I did steal it from the temple of Engibil, yes,'' Habbazu said, ''but I did not bring it to Enzuabu. He will fault me for failing to fulfill the greater part of the promise; he will not shower me with praises for fulfilling the lesser part. I shall live out my days in exile from my city.''

''You shall live out your days a free man, or a man as free as he can hope to become in a world wherein gods hold the upper hand whenever they care enough to use it,'' Ereshguna said.

''In other words,'' Sharur said, ''you shall live out your days as a Gibli.''

Habbazu's eyes twinkled. ''Master merchant's son, I hope you will forgive me, but I prefer your father's way of putting it.''

"Go ahead—mock this city after you have fought for it in war," Sharur said, laughing. He quickly grew more serious. "If, now, we break something those in your dream said was theirs, we also help to make into free men those who live a long way away from the land between the rivers."

"If they live a long way away, why should I care about them?" Habbazu asked. "I did not care much about you Giblut until Enzuabu sent me to this city to rob the temple of the god."

"And now, though you did not care much about us Giblut, you are practically a Gibli yourself," Ereshguna said. "Did this not teach you that you should not neglect folk for no better reason than that they live a long way away?"

"It did not," Habbazu admitted. "Perhaps it should have."

"Shall we go, then?" Sharur asked. "Shall we recover from the house of Dimgalabzu something those in your dream said was theirs?"

That was the question Habbazu could neither evade nor avoid. He sighed. "Aye. Let us recover this thing." He sighed again. "And, once it be recovered, I shall, as you say, begin to become a Gibli." He sighed once more after that. "Well, no help for it, I suppose."

Dimgalabzu bowed to Ereshguna. He bowed to Sharur. In some surprise, he bowed to Habbazu. After the men had exchanged polite greetings, the smith said, "I did not look to see you here in Gibil, Burrapi."

Habbazu gave an airy wave of his hand. "A man who is always where you look to see him is a boring sort of man. Would you not agree, master smith?"

"I had not thought of it so." Dimgalabzu's expression was bemused. "Perhaps you speak the truth, or some of the truth. Still, I did not look to see you *here*, not with . . ." His voice trailed away.

Sharur had no trouble completing the sentence Dimgalabzu

was too polite to finish. *Not with Kimash's men looking for you*, was one likely way it might end. Another, as likely, was, *Not with the god of Gibil pursuing you.*

"Father of my intended, the man from Zuabu is with us for good reason," Sharur said. "He has good cause to be here."

Dimgalabzu folded thick arms across his wide chest, which was shiny with sweat. "I would hear of the good reason the man from Zuabu has to be with you," he said. "I would learn of the good cause he has to be here." Behind his thick beard, his features revealed nothing.

"He came with me after our first fight with the Imhursagut, helping me to guard an Imhursaggi prisoner I was taking to Ushurikti the slave dealer," Sharur said. "While we were in the city, he and I, we left something here in your house for safekeeping. Now we have come to get it back."

The smith's bushy eyebrows rose. "You left . . . something . . . here . . . in my house for safekeeping?" he rumbled. "What was this thing, and why did you presume to leave it here in my house?"

Neither of those was a question Sharur much cared to answer. Of the two, he preferred the second. "Father of my intended," he said, "we presumed to leave it here in your house not least because your house is the house of a smith."

He watched Dimgalabzu bite down on that until he had chewed it up and extracted all the nourishment from it. The house of a smith, by its very nature, was a house into which a god had trouble seeing. Dimgalabzu did not need long to figure out why Sharur and Habbazu might have chosen such a house for that which they wanted to leave in safekeeping. His eyes widened. "This thing you left here in my house for safekeeping," he began, "is it . . . ?"

Ereshguna held up a hand before Dimgalabzu could finish the question or Sharur could reply to it. "Some things are better left unasked," Ereshguna said, "even in the house of a smith. Some things, too, are better left unanswered, even in such a house."

The words, taken alone, were remarkably uninformative.

Yet Dimgalabzu had no trouble drawing meaning from them. The smith was not a young man, but he was a man of the new. He did not rush out into the Street of Smiths shouting that the thing stolen from the temple of Engibil now lay hidden in his house. In a quiet, thoughtful voice, he asked, "Why had I not heard you left something here in my house? Why did Gulal my wife not tell me? Why did Ningal my daughter not tell me? Why did my slaves not tell me?"

"Gulal your wife did not tell you because she did not know, or so I believe," Sharur said. "Your slaves did not tell you because they did not know. Ningal your daughter did not tell you because I asked her to tell no one."

Dimgalabzu's eyebrows rose again. He plucked at his elaborately curled beard. "Ningal my daughter obeyed you very well," he said. "Ningal my daughter obeyed you better than she is in the habit of obeying me." His chuckle was a rumble deep down in his chest. "Ningal my daughter obeyed you better than she is likely to be in the habit of obeying you when she becomes Ningal your wife."

Ereshguna chuckled at hearing that, too. So did Habbazu. Sharur ignored them. He ignored them so ostentatiously, they laughed out loud. He also ignored that, saying to Dimgalabzu, "Father of my intended, you asked why you did not know I had left something at your house. I have told you."

"So you have," the smith said. "So you have." He plucked once more at his beard. Sharur waited to see what he would do next. Ereshguna and Habbazu also stood quiet, waiting. Dimgalabzu asked, "When you get this thing back, what will you do with it?"

The question made Ereshguna flinch, ever so slightly. It made Habbazu look away from both Dimgalabzu and Sharur. Sharur answered, "I do not yet know. We shall have to see what looks most advantageous."

Dimgalabzu grunted. "Since I do not even know what sort of thing this is, how can I judge whether your answer is good or bad?" He sighed. "Only one way to find out, I suppose. Ningal!'' As Sharur had found on the battlefield, the smith could raise his voice to a formidable roar when he so desired.

"What is it, Father?" Ningal's voice came from above. A moment later, she hurried down the stairs, a spindle still in her hand. When she saw Sharur and Ereshguna and Habbazu, she nodded to herself. After sending a quick smile toward Sharur, she said, "Ah. I think I know what it is."

"Do you, my daughter?" Dimgalabzu said. "Do you indeed?"

"I think I do, yes," Ningal said brightly, pretending not to notice her father's tone. She turned to Sharur and went on, "The servants of Kimash did come to this house while you were fighting the Imhursagut. I told them I knew nothing. The priests from the temple of Engibil also came to this house while you were fighting the Imhursagut. I likewise told them I knew nothing."

"It is good." Sharur bowed to her. "I am in your debt."

Habbazu bowed to Ningal. "We are all in your debt."

"I do not yet know whether this is so," Dimgalabzu said. He rounded on Ningal. "My daughter, why did you agree to hide this thing, whatever it may be, in our house? Why did you agree to tell no one of it?"

"I could not ask you what to do, Father, for you were in the field against the Imhursagut." Ningal looked and sounded the picture of innocence and obedience—unless one noticed, as Sharur did, the sparkle in her eyes. "After a woman leaves her father's home, she owes obedience to her husband. Being my intended, Sharur is almost my husband, and so I obeyed him in your absence—all the more so because he asked nothing dishonorable of me."

"Why did you not ask your mother?" the smith demanded.

"How could I, Father, when Sharur asked me to speak to no one?" Ningal said in tones of sweet reason. "I would not have been obeying him had I done so."

"You are not yet Sharur's wife," Dimgalabzu said. "You have not yet gone to live in the house of Ereshguna." He muttered something his mustache muffled, then shook his head like a man bedeviled by gnats. "Let it go, let it go. We could argue for long and long, you and I, and we would end up where we began." Glancing over to Sharur, he asked, "Do you see how this goes, intended of my daughter?"

"Yes, I see," Sharur answered. "Once we are wed, though, everything will be smooth as fine clay, smooth as rock oil between the fingers."

Dimgalabzu, Ereshguna, and Habbazu laughed uproariously. Sharur and Ningal looked miffed. "Let it go," Dimgalabzu said again, still laughing. He turned to his daughter. "Very well, you obeyed this fellow, with his words smooth as fine clay, his words smooth as rock oil between the fingers."

"Do not mock him, Father!" Ningal said. "Do not mock his words!"

"What is a young man for, if not to be mocked?" Dimgalabzu held up a hand before Ningal could say anything. "Never mind, never mind. Since you obeyed him, since you secreted away this . . . thing, whatever it may be, find it now and give it back to him, that he may take it away from here, that we may do our best to pretend it never was here."

"I shall obey you, my father," Ningal said. Her tone of voice remained in perfect accord with her words, but her expression warned that she was less serious than she sounded.

She picked up a stool and carried it over to the wall, into whose clay several shelves had been set. The highest of those, well above the height of a man, was too tall to be convenient, not least because one had to stand on a stool to see what was at the back of the shelf. One of the things at the back of the shelf proved to be the Alashkurri cup, which Ningal now brought down.

"Let me see this thing," Dimgalabzu said. Ningal's eyes swung to Sharur to make sure it was all right before she handed the cup to her father. The smith examined it, then gave it back to her. "I had expected something all of gold and silver, encrusted with precious stones. Why so much fuss, why so much mystery, over a foreign cup of cheap clay?"

"I will answer if you insist," Sharur said, "but I hope you do not insist, for naming certain things draws notice to them."

Dimgalabzu grunted. Sharur's answer was not an answer, and yet, in a way, it was. The smith thought for a while before finally saying, "Very well, then. What you tell me does not surprise me, not considering what I saw and heard at the encampment close by the border with Imhursag. You shall tell me in full one day, but not today."

"I thank you, father of my intended," Sharur said, bowing.

"Father, what did you see and hear at the encampment close by the border with Imhursag?" Ningal asked. "You have said nothing of this."

"Nor shall I say anything of this, not now," Dimgalabzu answered. "I shall tell you in full one day, but not today." He turned to Sharur. "Were you wise, son of Ereshguna, to embroil my family in this without my leave?" He had made his own guesses about the cup and its provenance, guesses liable to be good.

Sharur bowed again, apologetically. "Perhaps I was not wise, father of my intended, but I could not have embroiled your family with your leave, for, as Ningal your daughter has said, you were at the encampment close by the border with Imhursag. No harm has come of it, for which I am very glad." He spoke nothing but the truth there.

Dimgalabzu let out another grunt. Sharur's words were not quite an apology, but were soft enough to make it hard for the smith to take offense. "Let it go," Dimgalabzu said yet again. "Take that cup out of here, and let it be as if that cup had never been here."

"So may it be," Sharur said.

"So may it be," Ereshguna echoed.

"So may it be," Habbazu said, adding, "May the god of Gibil always reckon this cup has never been here. May the god of Gibil never learn where this cup has been.'' That prayer brought a fresh chorus of "So may it be!" from everyone else in the room.

Sharur, Ereshguna, and Habbazu bowed first to Dimgal-abzu and then to Ningal. They left the house of Dimgalabzu. Sharur wanted to run back to the house of Ereshguna, to minimize the time during which the Alashkurri cup was out on the Street of Smiths. But running might have drawn the notice of other men on the Street of Smiths, and might also have drawn the notice of Engibil. Sharur walked, and walked sedately, keeping up a front no less than he did in a dicker.

When he and his father and the master thief reached the house of Ereshguna, though, he did sigh once, loud and long, with relief. So did Ereshguna. So did Habbazu. Eresh-guna asked, ''Where will you now put this cup, son? What place have we that can match the house of a smith for hold-ing such things safe?''

''We still have a pot or two of Laravanglali tin, have we not?'' Sharur asked. He did not wait for his father to reply; he knew where the metal was stored. He carried the cup over to one of the big clay pots, opened it, set the cup inside on the dark gray nodules of tin, and replaced the lid.

''It is good.'' Ereshguna nodded. ''It is very good. The presence of metal makes a god as shortsighted as a mortal man. Tin is especially good since it has such power of its own, the power to strengthen copper into strong, hard bronze even though tin is neither strong nor hard itself.''

Habbazu also nodded approval. ''This hiding place will indeed conceal the cup from a searching god,'' he said. ''The question of what to do with the cup now that it is back in our hands still remains.''

Another question that still remained, as far as Sharur was concerned, was how to make sure the cup did not come into Habbazu's hands alone. The master thief might yet repair his position with Enzuabu if he brought the cup to his own city god—and if he could sneak it past Engibil, assuming Engibil was still watching the western border of Gibli territory and had not lazily gone back to fornicating with courtesans in his house on earth.

Ereshguna said, "If we break the cup, it stays forever broken. We must think hard before undertaking a step that may not be revoked."

"This is so," Habbazu said. "The very idea of breaking the cup, the very idea of choosing my will over the will of the gods, turns my liver green with fear."

"You would break something that belongs to the gods?" In Sharur's ears—and no doubt in Ereshguna's ears as well—the voice of Sharur's grandfather's ghost was a frightened screech. "Are you mad? What will your punishment be when the gods learn of what you have done?"

"They are only foreign gods, ghost of my grandfather," Sharur said in the mumble mortals used to talk with a ghost when other mortals who could not hear that ghost were present. "And, if we break this thing, the foreign gods will not have the power to punish us."

"Foreign gods!" Now Sharur's grandfather's ghost let out a disdainful sniff. "You have no business dealing with foreign gods in the first place. Leave them alone and pray they leave you alone, is all I can say."

Ereshguna sighed. "Ghost of my father," he said in a mumble like Sharur's, "when you lived among men, you traveled to the mountains of Alashkurru. You dealt with the Alashkurrut. You dealt with the gods of the Alashkurrut. We follow in the footsteps you laid down."

Habbazu could follow only one side of the conversation, but smiled in a way suggesting he had no trouble figuring out the other side. Sharur's grandfather's ghost said, "Aye, I traveled to the mountains of Alashkurru. Aye, I dealt with the Alashkurrut. Aye, I dealt with the gods of the Alashkurrut. And I hated the mountains of Alashkurru. They were too high and rugged. I hated the Alashkurrut. They were too haughty and foreign. I hated the gods of the Alashkurrut. They were even more haughty and even more foreign. I would sooner have had nothing to do with any of them."

Sharur schooled his features to stay straight. Laughing at

a ghost who complained about how things had been while he yet lived was rude. But Sharur recalled how many times his grandfather, while a living man, had told him stories of the Alashkurrut, stories that showed far more lively interest than hatred. Pointing that out now would be useless, so he stayed quiet.

Ereshguna said, "Nothing is yet decided, ghost of my father. Nothing will be decided today, I do not think. We shall take time for thought, and then do as we reckon best."

"It is the Zuabi who led you into this," the ghost said shrilly. "It is the Zuabi who sneaked into Engibil's temple. This thing you think of breaking must be the thing he thought of stealing. He is a foreigner, too, and has no business in Gibil." The ghost roared like a lion, as if seeking to frighten Habbazu away. But Habbazu could not hear him, and stayed where he was.

"All will be well, ghost of my grandfather," Sharur said. "Truly, all will be well."

Habbazu still looked as troubled as the ghost sounded. "I am afraid," he said. "All choices look bad to me now. To take the cup back to the mountains, to smash it—both fill me with dread. Even taking it to Enzuabu, as I had first thought to do, sets me to trembling like a leaf in the wind."

"We can act in our own interest and be free, or we can be tools of the gods," Sharur said. "Do you see a third choice, master thief?"

"If you leave only those choices, doing either the one thing or the other, no," Habbazu answered. "But could it not be that what is best for the gods will also prove best for mortal men?"

"A good question," Ereshguna said.

"A very good question," Sharur's grandfather's ghost agreed, so loudly that Sharur was almost surprised Habbazu could not hear him. "Maybe I was wrong. Maybe not all Zuabut are cheats and fools all the time."

*Maybe you approve of this Zuabi's words because he says things like the things you say*, Sharur thought. But he did not argue with the ghost of his grandfather. He saw no point to arguing with the ghost of his grandfather. Arguing with a mortal man rarely changed his mind. Arguing with a ghost was a waste of breath.

After some thought, Sharur spoke to Habbazu: "What you say could be, master thief. We ourselves would draw great benefit from doing as the gods desire. But would our sons and grandsons, would *their* sons and grandsons, thank us for it?"

"I do not know," Habbazu replied. "I can not know. Neither do you know. Neither can you know. But I see you are trying to think like a god, to think of what will be long after you are gone." The master thief sighed. "I honor you for the effort. Let us think on this once more until morning, and then, if we have not found some compelling reason to change our course . . . let us break the cup."

"Father?" Sharur asked.

Ereshguna also sighed. "Habbazu has spoken well. Let us think on this once more until morning, and then . . ." He did not say the words, as Habbazu had said them, but he nodded. His eyes went to the jar of tin nodules wherein the Alashkurri cup rested. So did Habbazu's. And so did Sharur's.

Sharur knew he lay sleeping on the mat on the roof of the house of Ereshguna. He did not seem to be there, though. He seemed to have returned to the company of the gods of the Alashkurru Mountains. He was not afraid. For one thing, he half expected—more than half expected—the Alashkurri gods would bring this dream to him once more. For another, he knew it was only a dream. Nothing bad—nothing too bad—could happen to him in a dream.

"Why do you hate us so?" Fasillar demanded. She folded her arms over her bulging belly, as if to say without words, *How can you hate someone who aids in bringing new life into the world?*

The question was one that had a great many possible answers, as far as Sharur was concerned. He chose the softest

one he could find. Yes, this was only a dream. Yes, the
Alashkurri gods had scant power here. But they were gods,
and power was what made them gods. "I do not hate you,
gods of the Alashkurrut," he said.

"Then why do you seek to tamper with that which is not
yours?" rumbled Tarsiyas, all shining in his armor of copper.

"Why do you not return that which is not yours to those
to whom it rightly belongs?" Fasillar added.

"Why did you gods make life so hard for Giblut in the
mountains of Alashkurru?" Sharur returned. "Why have all
the gods made life so hard for Giblut outside of Gibil?"

"Because you took that which was not yours to take,"
Tarsiyas said angrily. "Because some fool of a mortal gave
you that which was not his to give. Because—" He started
to go on, but checked himself.

Fasillar said, perhaps, that which he had begun to say but
which he had held back: "Because, in taking that which
was not yours to take, you have put us, the great gods of
the Alashkurrut, in fear. It is not right that mortals should
put the great gods in fear."

"No, indeed. It is not right," Tarsiyas echoed. He shook
his fist in the direction from which Sharur was perceiving
him. "What is right is that the great gods should put mortals
in fear. That is the natural order of things. That is how things
should be. That is how things must be." He shook his fist
again.

If he thought his bombast and ferocious bluster were putting Sharur in fear, he was right. If he thought bombast and
bluster would make Sharur more inclined to send the cup
back to the mountains of Alashkurru, he was wrong.

Fasillar must have sensed as much, for the Alashkurri
goddess of birth put on her face a look of such pleading,
such piteousness, that even Sharur, knowing full well the
expression was assumed, could hardly resist melting under
it. "Will you not do as you should?" she said. "Will you
not do as we ask? Would you deprive the Alashkurrut of

the overlords they need? Would you deprive them of the gods they cherish?''

Sharur thought of Huzziyas the wanax, who so wanted to trade with the Giblut that he was willing to do so by subterfuge. Only when Tarsiyas directly forbade him to engage in such trade had he desisted. Did he need the gods as overlords? Did he cherish them? Sharur had his doubts.

''Do you think we cannot take vengeance if you seek to harm us?'' Tarsiyas said now. ''Do you think we shall have no power left with which to punish anyone who tries to do us wrong?''

That was exactly what Sharur thought. That was exactly what Kessis and Mitas, the small gods of the Alashkurrut, had told him. Had they not told him, he would have thought so anyhow. The way the great gods of the Alashkurrut were behaving said more plainly than any overt words how much they feared being brought low were the cup to break.

''You have spoken much,'' Sharur said. ''Will you answer now a question of mine?''

''You may ask it,'' Fasillar said. ''Whether we answer and how we answer will depend on what it is.''

''I understand,'' Sharur said. That was, as far as he could see, the first sensible response the gods of the Alashkurrut had given him. ''Here is my question, then: why did you set so much of your power in this one cup?''

''To keep it hidden,'' Fasillar replied at once. ''To keep it secure. To keep it stored away where no one, god or man, would think to look for it.'' The goddess's mouth twisted. ''This worked less well than we hoped it would.''

''To keep any cowardly wretch from stealing it,'' Tarsiyas added. ''This also worked less well than we hoped it would.''

''From all that I have heard, from all that I have seen, from all that I have learned, this cup was not stolen from the mountains of Alashkurru,'' Sharur said. ''This cup was fairly given in trade by an Alashkurri to a Gibli, and so it came to Gibil.''

''This cup was given by an idiot,'' Tarsiyas roared. ''This

cup was given by a fool. This cup was given by a dolt whose mother was a sow and whose father was a lump of dung. Speak to me not of the man by whom this cup was given." The god's face turned the color of his burnished copper armor. Sharur wondered if a god could suffer a fit of apoplexy. Had Tarsiyas been a man, Sharur would have judged him ripe for one.

Fasillar took a gentler line: "Mortal, you can not deny that this cup was stolen from the temple in which it was placed. You can not deny it was raped away from the god's house in which it dwelt. This was not right. This was not just. The cup should be restored to us, its rightful owners."

In his dream, Sharur bowed. "Goddess, you cannot deny that we Giblut and the city of Gibil have suffered harm for what one of us did unwittingly. This was not right. This was not just. We are entitled to compensation or we are entitled to vengeance. When a surgeon cuts a man with an abscessed eye and causes him to lose the eye, the surgeon pays compensation or has his hand cut off. The victim and his family choose the penalty. That is right. That is just."

"We have offered compensation," Fasillar said. "We can offer more. Come to the mountains of Alashkurru, and we shall fill the packs of your donkeys with copper ore. We shall fill them with copper. We shall fill them with silver. We shall fill them with gold. The mountains of Alashkurru are rich in metals. We shall share the riches with the men of Gibil."

Tarsiyas turned his angry face toward Fasillar. "No!" the war god shouted at the goddess of birth. "The Giblut are liars. The Giblut are thieves. The Giblut will make our own people like unto them if they keep coming into the mountains of Alashkurru. What good will it do us to have our cup back when in two generations our own people will be made like unto the Giblut? They will learn to ignore us. They will learn to pay us no heed."

"If we have not the cup back, if the cup be shattered, they will pay us no heed in less time than two generations," Fasillar answered. "How can we do anything but deal with the Giblut, and with this Gibli in particular? What choice have we?''

"But the Gibli will not deal with us!" Tarsiyas howled.

"Not if you keep trying to put him in fear," Fasillar said.

"That has nothing to do with it," Tarsiyas said, which was in large measure true. "The Giblut have grown too used to taking gods lightly. They think themselves equal to gods. They think themselves superior to gods. Worse: they think themselves in no need of noticing gods. Have they tried to steal, have they tried to destroy, Engibil's store of power? No! They have not even bothered. They—''

"Be still," Fasillar snarled, growing angry in turn. "Be still, or we shall see a generation of nothing but women born in the mountains. Who will fight your precious wars then, when women have too much sense for them?''

Tarsiyas shut up with a snap. Sharur had no idea whether Fasillar could do such a thing. He did not know whether Tarsiyas had any such idea, either. The Alashkurri war god was not inclined to take the chance, though, which struck Sharur as uncommonly sensible of him.

Fasillar turned her attention back to Sharur. "What will you do, man of Gibil?" she asked. "Will you take the road that leads to riches and delight, or will you run wild into chaos and madness and danger?''

Tarsiyas also started to say something to Sharur. Fasillar sent a sharp glance toward her fellow deity. Tarsiyas said not a word. Had he been Tarsiyas, Sharur also would have said not a word. Fasillar looked in his direction once more, awaiting his reply.

He did not want to come straight out and defy a god. He did not dare to come straight out and defy a god. Neither was he altogether certain he *ought* to defy the gods of the Alashkurrut. "I will do that which seems best to me," he said slowly.

All at once, he was awake on the roof, under the stars. He wondered whether that meant the gods of the Alashkurrut had believed him or despaired of him. He wondered, too, which they should have done.

# 12

There on the counter, beside the scale that weighed out gold and silver, copper and tin, stood the snake-decorated clay cup from the Alashkurru Mountains. Sharur had gone downstairs to check on it and take it from the pot of tin after he woke from his dream, fearful lest Habbazu should have stolen it either for reasons of his own or because of urgings from the gods too strong for him to withstand.

But the Zuabi thief had not disturbed the cup in the night. Now, in the clear light of morning, he stared at it along with Sharur and Ereshguna and Tupsharru. Sharur's eyes went for a moment from the cup to the scales close by. The cup was more precious than anything he or his father or his brother set on the balance pans of the scale, but its value was not measured in keshlut.

"Now we come down to it," Ereshguna said in a heavy voice.

"I am afraid. I am not ashamed to admit I am afraid," Habbazu said. Beside him, Tupsharru sipped on a cup of beer and nodded.

"I am also afraid," Sharur said. "But I have grown tired of being afraid." *Afraid of the gods*, was what he meant, but he was also afraid to say that aloud. His father and brother and the Zuabi thief understood him: of that he was sure. He went on, "I would like to set men free. To how many is that chance given?"

Ereshguna said, "Strange to think that, if we set men free

by doing this, they are men far from Gibil, men far from the land between the rivers.''

"Yes, it is strange," Sharur agreed. Something Tarsiyas had said during the dream the night before still rolled back and forth in his mind. Did Engibil have an object wherein he stored his power, as the gods of the Alashkurrut had stored theirs in this cup? Did other gods have such objects? Did, for instance, Enimhursag have such an object hidden in his city?

"Are we truly resolved to do this thing?" Ereshguna asked.

Habbazu was silent. Tupsharru was silent. Sharur said, "Father, I think we are. Freeing men anywhere will in the end help free men everywhere." Habbazu did not contradict him. Tupsharru did not contradict him. And, in the end, Ereshguna, whose contradiction he would have taken most seriously of all, did not contradict him, either.

"Who will do it?" Habbazu asked. His voice was surprisingly small and surprisingly shaky. He had come further out from under the shadow of his city god, probably, than any other Zuabi. He was further out from under the shadow of his city god, probably, than many Giblut were out from under the shadow of Engibil. But he was not so far out from under the shadow of his city god as were Sharur, Ereshguna, and Tupsharru.

"I will do it," Sharur said, and his voice was surprisingly small and surprisingly shaky, too. He did his best to strengthen it: "Most of the troubles we have known of late have sprung from my travels. Let us hope that, once the deed is done, the troubles will also be done."

"We are men. We shall always have troubles," Ereshguna said. Habbazu nodded. After a moment, so did Sharur and Tupsharru. Ereshguna went on, "Let us hope that, once the deed is done, *these* troubles will also be done."

"Aye," Sharur said. "Let us indeed hope that."

He looked around. His eye fell on a bronze vase decorated with reliefs of lions and crocodiles, and with a proud line of writing around the rim: DIMGALABZU MADE ME. Though they could not have read the inscription, the men of the mountains of Alashkurru would have cherished such a vase—had their gods let them trade with the Giblut. Now they would cherish the vase for a different reason, one they would never know. Sharur picked up the vase by the neck and hefted it in his hands. It was of a good size. It was of a good weight.

"It is made from bronze," Tupsharru said, nodding at his choice. "That is right. That is fitting."

"It is made from bronze, and it has syllables cut into the bronze," Ereshguna said, also nodding. "That is very right. That is very fitting."

"Such was my thought," Sharur said, and he nodded in turn. "Metal and the written word: these are the powers of men. They did not come to us from the gods. We found them for ourselves."

Still holding the vase by the neck, he walked over to the counter and stood in front of the cup in which the great gods of the Alashkurrut had hidden so much of their power. Suddenly, he stared at the cup—was that a cry of appeal he had heard? He rubbed at his left ear with his left hand, but the cry had not sounded in his ears, and he knew as much.

But he was not the only one to have heard it. "They know what you are about to do," Habbazu whispered. "They know. Even here, they know."

"They know," Ereshguna agreed. "They know, and they fear."

That steadied Sharur. With a grunt of effort, he brought the upended vase down on the cup. The cup broke into a thousand sharp-edged shards of clay. They flew all around the room. One of them bit into Sharur's hand, as if the great gods of the Alashkurrut were taking what vengeance they could.

It was but a small vengeance, though—a tiny vengeance. When the vase smashed down on the cup, Sharur heard another cry, or the beginning of another cry, but after only an instant it guttered down to a low wailing and was gone, as a torch will gutter out after burning all its fuel.

"What a wailing and crying and gnashing of teeth!" Sharur's grandfather's ghost exclaimed. "What a howl of anguish! What a shriek of despair! My ears still ring with it, or they would if I still had ears."

"That cry was heard in your realm, too, ghost of my father?" Ereshguna asked.

"Heard?" the ghost said. "I should say it was heard. It echoes yet, and makes me tremble and shake. How could you have been bold enough, how could you have been mad enough, to do as you did?"

Now that Sharur had done it, he wondered the same thing himself. Nervously, he asked, "Will others in your realm know who did this? Will the gods be able to tell who did this?"

"I saw you do it," his grandfather's ghost replied. "I heard the gods of the Alashkurrut cry out when you did it. Everyone in my realm from the mountains of Alashkurru to the swamps of Laravanglal, I daresay, heard the gods of the Alashkurrut cry out when you did this, so great was that cry. So great was that cry, I think, that no one who did not see you do it will be able to know whence precisely it came."

"For this news I thank you, ghost of my grandfather," Sharur said sincerely.

"For this news you are welcome, my grandson," the ghost told him. "But I say this plainly: it is news you have by luck, not by design. Did you think on what this cry would be like in the world beyond the world of the living?" The ghost answered its own question before Sharur or his father or his brother could speak: "No, you did not. Manifestly, you did not."

Since he was correct, neither Sharur nor Ereshguna nor Tupsharru argued with him. In musing tones, Sharur said, "I wonder what is happening in the mountains of Alashkurru now. If Tarsiyas, say, was speaking in his temple, was he suddenly struck dumb? If Fasillar was aiding a woman in childbirth, will the woman have to finish giving birth alone?"

"Those are good questions," Ereshguna agreed. "I also wonder what will become of the people of the mountains of Alashkurru now that their great gods have lost this power. If such befell the Imhursagut, many of them would go mad, no longer having the god to take charge of their lives."

"Some there may do that," Sharur said. "I do not think many will. Huzziyas the wanax, for instance, is a man much like Habbazu here, a man who has come a long way out from under the shadow of his gods and who would have come further had he but had the chance. Now he has the chance. The land of the Alashkurrut may know some chaos for a time, but the Alashkurrut are not like the Imhursagut."

"I wonder what Enimhursag thinks of men and the things men say after you tricked him," Tupsharru said. "He will surely be less trusting of those from beyond his city. I wonder if he will also be less trusting of those from within his city."

"A point," Sharur said, nodding. "I wonder if he will be less trusting of those from within his city whom we captured in the late war. I wonder if he will think they have been corrupted, living among us Giblut. I wonder if, thinking them corrupted, he will let their kin pay ransom for them."

"If he will not let their kin pay ransom for them, then Ushurikti will sell them as slaves, as will other dealers in the city, and we Giblut shall have new backs and new hands to do our labor," Tupsharru said. He smiled and added, "And we shall have profit from the Imhursagut Sharur captured."

Habbazu smiled, too, in a different way. "Here you boast of setting the Alashkurrut free, but you also boast of profit from selling the Imhursagut as slaves."

"They are not slaves of the gods," Sharur said. "They are the slaves of men, in the same way that a lugal rules in Gibil rather than a god or even an ensi."

"That a lugal rules in Gibil rather than a god or even an ensi may be an improvement—or, then again, it may not," Habbazu said. "But will any man who is sold into slavery tell you it is an improvement over his earlier lot?''

"If he is starving and sells himself to a master who will feed him, yes," Sharur said. "If he is not a man but a child whose father sells him to a master who will feed him where the father can not, yes again."

"Hmm," Habbazu said, and then "Hmm" again. "You argue well—and why should you not? You are a Gibli, after all."

"You steal well—and why should you not? You are a Zuabi, after all," Sharur returned. He and Habbazu both laughed. He went on, "I will tell you another man who will say slavery is an improvement on the lot he might have had: Duabzu the Imhursaggi, whom I captured with the sword when I might have slain him with it."

"Well," Habbazu said this time, and then "Well" again. "Perhaps you are right. Perhaps I spoke too soon."

"Perhaps you did," Sharur said. "Perhaps you did."


Ushurikti bowed low when Sharur came into his establishment. The slave dealer's face was red, and he wheezed a little as he straightened. Like Dimgalabzu, he was prosperous enough to be plump: an upstanding pillar in the community that was Gibil. "How may I serve you, son of Ereshguna?" he asked. "Will you drink beer with me? Will you eat bread and onions with me?"

"I will gladly drink beer with you. I will gladly eat bread and onions with you," Sharur replied. Ushurikti clapped his hands. One of his own personal slaves—not one of the men and women in whom he traded—fetched food and drink. After Sharur had refreshed himself, he asked if he might see Nasibugashi and Duabzu.

Ushurikti's mobile features twisted into a sorrowful frown. "Truly my heart grieves, my master, that I cannot give you everything you desire on the instant. I have lent them, among others, out to Kimash the mighty lugal, and they are hard at work repairing canals that have begun to fall into decay. They eat of the lugal's bread. They drink of the lugal's beer. As they cannot eat of my bread or drink of my beer while they labor for the mighty lugal, I do not add their maintenance on these days to their ransom.''

"You are an honest man," Sharur said, and Ushurikti bowed again. Sharur went on, "With mention of ransom, though, you come to the question I would ask you concerning Nasibugashi and Duabzu and other Imhursaggi captives who did not fall to me: is Enimhursag permitting their kin and their friends to ransom them?"

"Ah." Ushurikti bowed yet again. "This is a most astute question indeed, master merchant's son, though of course I should have expected nothing less from one so clever as yourself." He smiled an ingratiating smile. He was also a merchant, and knew the value of flattery.

So did Sharur, who hid a smile at seeing the techniques he used himself now aimed at him. He noted that, despite the flattery, the slave dealer had not answered his question. He tried again: "What does Enimhursag say about ransoming prisoners? Will he permit it, or not?"

"All I can tell in that regard is this: the god of Imhursag will permit it—or not," Ushurikti replied, now looking somewhat less happy because he was compelled to admit his own lack of omniscience.

"How do you mean?" Sharur asked. "You have succeeded in confusing me, I will tell you so much."

"I am also to be numbered among the confused," Ushurikti said. "I would not deny it. I could not deny it. As is the custom between Gibil and Imhursag after our wars, I have written to the kin of those Imhursagut whom we captured, seeking ransom for their loved ones. As is also the custom between Gibil and Imhursag, I have written to the temple of Enimhursag in Imhursag, asking leave to seek ransom for those Imhursagut whom we captured. For long and long, this has been but a formality, with agreement always promptly forthcoming, else I should have written to the god at his temple before writing to the captives' kin.''

"But not this time?" Sharur said.

"But not this time," the slave dealer agreed.

"But Enimhursag has not refused to let the Imhursagut ransom their kin," Sharur persisted. "Had he done so, you would have told me plainly." *I hope you would have told me plainly.*

"Enimhursag has not refused, but neither has Enimhursag assented," Ushurikti said. "Enimhursag has not responded at all. In most such times, the god will say aye while my courier waits at his temple; sometimes he will even say aye through a chance-met man while my courier is still on the road toward the city of Imhursag. But my courier delivered the customary letter, and the god told him he would respond in his own time. That time has not yet come round."

"How strange," Sharur said, and the slave dealer nodded emphatic agreement. "I wonder why."

"So do I," Ushurikti replied. "It is a puzzlement. It is most unlike Enimhursag, of all the gods there be, to break custom. He has ever been one to stand for doing things as they were always done."

"That he has; it is one of the reasons he hates Gibil and the Giblut so," Sharur said. He scratched his head. "I wonder if he fears letting the Imhursagut whom we captured return to his city, lest they tell their kin we live better and more pleasantly than they. For, having been to Imhursag, I speak the truth when I say we do live better and more pleasantly than the Imhursagut. No one who has seen Gibil and Imhursag both could doubt it."

"Not even a slave?" Ushurikti asked.

"Not even a slave," Sharur declared.

Ushurikti also scratched his head. He plucked at his beard, a caricature of a man thinking hard. At last he said, "It could be so, master merchant's son. It could well be so, in fact. It makes more sense than any notion I have had for myself. And, while I have never seen Imhursag, I have had enough dealings with Imhursagut and with Enimhursag himself to know that I would never want to live in a city with those men and ruled by that god."

"Nor would I," Sharur said.

"But I will tell you something else," Ushurikti said, "and

that is that, even here in Gibil, living is not always so easy as we wish it would be. Why, not long after you and that Zuabi mercenary brought that Duabzu fellow in to me, the priests of Engibil came through here like locusts—locusts, I tell you—in search of something they said had been stolen from the god's temple. *I* think they only wanted the chance to snoop, and I shall not change my opinion. As if I, a reputable trader, would for a moment harbor stolen property, human or otherwise, here in my establishment.''

"I heard the priests of Engibil and also the servants of Kimash the mighty lugal were searching through the city for some such thing,'' Sharur said. "I do not know much about this, for I had already gone back to the camp in the north and to the fighting we did there.''

"Of course.'' The slave dealer's head bobbed up and down. "But I mind me, master merchant's son, that the priests were asking a good many questions about this Zuabi. All Zuabut being thieves, my guess is that they wanted to blame the crime—if crime there was—on him so they would not have to do anything more in the way of proper looking themselves.''

"It could well be so,'' Sharur replied. Ushurikti was indeed a man of no small weight in the city—if he believed something that cast scorn upon Engibil and his priests, he would help make others in Gibil do likewise, which would in turn help reduce the influence of the god and his priesthood.

"I should say it could,'' Ushurikti said now. "Why, at that entertainment you put on outside the god's house on earth—for which, honor to you and to your generosity—did you hear that white-bearded fool of a priest ranting and raving against everything that makes life worth living? If he had his way, life would not be worth living.''

"No doubt you are right,'' Sharur said. "Old Ilakabkabu is more sour than a pickled onion.'' And yet, the old priest had been far closer to correct about Habbazu's attempted thievery of two nights before the entertainment—and about much else besides—than had Burshagga, who was a man of

the new. But being right had done him no good, a twist of
fate Sharur savored.

"Ha!" Ushurikti said. "Well put, master merchant's son.
Well put. I shall send a messenger hotfoot to the house of
Ereshguna when the lugal restores to me Nasibugashi and
Duabzu, in whom you have an interest, or when I hear from
Imhursag—or rather from Enimhursag—on the matter of
ransoms."

"You are gracious." Sharur bowed. "I know I may rely
on you. You are a conscientious man."

Ushurikti beamed. "Praise from a man who is praise-
worthy is praise indeed. Insofar as I can make it so, everything shall be as you desire."

"For your kindness and your care, I am in your debt,"
Sharur said. After exchanging more polite formulas with the
slave dealer, he went on his way. He had not learned what
he had come to learn, but he had learned that what he had
come to learn was there to be learned. That, too, was knowledge worth having, and he took it back with him to the
house of Ereshguna.


A druggist came into the house of Ereshguna and asked
Sharur, "Have you any of that powdered black mineral from
the mountains? You know the one I mean: the one I mix
with perfumed mutton fat and sell to the women, that they
may darken their eyebrows and eyelashes with it, and perhaps paint beauty marks on their cheeks or on their chin."

"My master, I believe I do, but it has been some little
while since anyone asked me for it, so I shall have to rum-
mage about to find it." Sharur duly rummaged on shelves
and through storage jars, and at last came up with a small
pot ornamented with the face of a woman with entrancing
eyes. "Here you are: first grade, finely ground. How much
do you require?"

Before the druggist answered, he took a tiny pinch of the
powder, brought it up to his face to examine it closely, and
rubbed it between forefinger and thumb to see just how

finely it was ground. At last, grudgingly, he nodded. "It is as you say it is. Weigh me out four keshlut."

"It shall be as you say," Sharur replied. As he piled the cosmetic powder on one pan of the scales to balance the four little bronze weights on the other, he went on, "The price is two thirds of the weight in silver."

The druggist screamed at him. He had expected nothing else, and screamed back. They settled on a price of one half the powder's weight. Sharur would have settled for even a little less than that, which was nothing the druggist needed to know. The man took broken bits of silver from the pouch on his belt and set them on the scales until he had two keshlut there.

"It is good," he said. "I have had three women ask me for this paste in the last two days, and I have been embarrassed to go without." Contented, he took the powder, which he had stored in his own little jar, and departed.

Another man pushed past him into the house of Ereshguna, a stalwart fellow of about the age of Sharur's father. Sharur did not recognize him till he took off his straw hat and fanned himself with it. "Ah," Sharur said, bowing as he might have to any new customer. "You have not honored us with your presence for some little while, Izmaili."

"And yet you remember the name I give myself. No wonder you are a master merchant's son, soon, no doubt, to be a master merchant yourself." Izmaili—as Kimash the lugal preferred to call himself when he went out into Gibil without the trappings that made him as nearly divine as a man could be—smiled and nodded.

"You are kind and gracious," Sharur said. "How may I serve you? Would you like some cosmetic powder, as the druggist before you did?"

"I thank you for the thought, but no; I have come to the house of Ereshguna for a rather different reason." Kimash's voice was dry.

"I am your servant, as I am the servant of any man who comes to the house of Ereshguna to buy or to sell," Sharur replied.

"I fear I have come neither to buy nor to sell," Kimash said. "While another sits where I often do"—an allusion to the impostor who occupied the lugal's high seat while he in turn impersonated an ordinary man—"I have come to pass the time of day, to gossip."

"Shall I bring you beer, then, Izmaili?" Sharur asked. "Shall I bring you salt fish? Shall I bring you onions? Would you care to drink while you pass the time of day? Would you care to eat while you gossip?"

"I would be grateful for beer and for salt fish and for onions," Kimash said, though in the palace he was no doubt used to the daintier viands the man who took his place on the seat might now enjoy. Sharur fetched the beer and food with his own hands, not wanting to summon a slave who was liable to recognize the lugal and do some gossiping of his own, gossiping that could get back to Engibil's ears.

Kimash drank beer and ate salt fish and onions with every sign of enjoyment, as if he were a shopkeeper or an artisan or a peasant rather than likely the single most powerful man in the land between the rivers. Sharur ate and drank with him, and presently, when the beer in his cup had nearly reached the bottom, he spoke to Izmaili who was Kimash as if he were a shopkeeper or an artisan or a peasant who had come into the house of Ereshguna: "So. What have you heard? What do you want to know?"

Kimash smiled again. He bit into an onion and breathed odorous fumes into Sharur's face. "What have I heard? I have heard that something once missing is now gone for good. What do I want to know? I want to know whether what I have heard is true."

"Ah," Sharur said, and then said nothing more for some little while. At last, doing his best to remain casual, he went on, "And where might you have heard such a thing as that?"

"I heard it from someone who labors in the house from which the thing disappeared," Kimash answered elliptically. *Burshagga told him, having learned from the god*, Sharur thought: *Burshagga or some other man of the new among the priesthood.* If breaking the Alashkurri cup had alarmed Sharur's grandfather's ghost, what must it have done to Engibil? What must it have done to gods throughout the land of Kudurru? The ghost had said no one, ghost or demon or god, would be able to tell whence the cry of anguish from the Alashkurri gods had come, for which Sharur was heartily glad.

He answered, "The man who labors in that house did tell you the truth, as a matter of fact." How would Kimash respond to that? The lugal had sought Habbazu in the same way as had Engibil; he had sought the master thief as if he were a servant of the god.

But Kimash slowly clapped his hands together—once, twice, three times. "It is good," he said. "It is very good. The gods who suffered this are not our gods. The gods who suffered this dwell far away. But with men in one place freer, men everywhere breathe more easily. My great-grandfather was an ensi, through whom Engibil spoke. *His* great-grandfather was a priest, to whom Engibil gave orders as Enimhursag gives the Imhursagut orders today."

He did not directly name himself, or what he was, or how he did what he did. Sharur spoke with similar care: "Today the lugal speaks in his own voice, but must ever be wary, lest the god seek to seize once more the power he has let slip between his fingers. But how will things be in the days of the lugal's great-grandson? And how will things be in the days of *his* great-grandson?"

"Even so," Kimash said softly. His eyes glowed. "Even so. How *will* things be in the days of his great-grandson? Who then will be wary of whom?"

"That is surely an . . . interesting question," Sharur said. He imagined Engibil reduced to the status of a demon of the desert, or perhaps to that of a small god like Kessis or Mitas, able to change a man's luck for good or ill but not much more—certainly unable to aspire to the rule of a city. He imagined lugals ruling in other cities in the land between the rivers. He imagined even stubborn gods feeling men from their own cities chopping at their heels as Sharur had chopped at Enimhursag's heel during the second battle against the Imhursagut.

Kimash said, "The road will not be easy. The road will not run straight. The gods will see in which direction it runs. They will try to turn us back along it. They are strong. They are dangerous. They may yet win. If Engibil truly did choose to rise up in wrath now, who knows whether we Giblut could hope to withstand his anger and his might?"

"So the lugal feared earlier this year," Sharur said, continuing to speak of Kimash as if he were someone else. "But, from what I have heard, the god had not the will to rise up in wrath, even if he had the strength."

"What you have heard and what I have heard are one and the same," Kimash said. "Distracting the god has always been the lugal's greatest need. I do hope, though, that distracting the god shall not always be the lugal's greatest need."

"Might . . . ah, Izmaili, I think it may not be so," Sharur replied, and told the lugal what Tarsiyas had indiscreetly revealed about the thing in which Engibil had secreted away so much of his power.

"Well, well," Kimash said. "How interesting." For a moment, Sharur was disappointed at getting no stronger response. Then Kimash leaned toward him and demanded, "Do you know what sort of thing this is? Do you know where it may be found?"

"I know neither of these things," Sharur answered. "I do not think I was meant to know such a thing even existed. The Alashkurri god spoke of it in a temper to a goddess. But I heard. In my dream, I heard. And what I heard in my dream, I remember."

"Well, well," the lugal said again. "This is no small matter you have set before me. I am glad I am only an ordinary man, and do not have to concern myself with such." His smile declared how far apart lay the words that came from his mouth and the thoughts that formed behind his eyes.

Sharur had thoughts of his own, too. He turned one loose:

"I wonder how a man who is not an ordinary man, a man who does have to concern himself with such, would go about finding this thing, whatever it may be?"

"Right now, I do not know. Right now, I can not guess," Kimash said. "But such a man will surely concern himself with such a thing before any great stretch of time has passed."

"This I believe," Sharur said. "Even searching for such a thing without great hope of success, a man might make a better bargain with a god than otherwise."

"Truly you are a master merchant's son," Kimash said. "Truly you shall soon become a master merchant yourself."

"That is a generous thing for a person of no consequence such as yourself, Izmaili, to say," Sharur replied with a bow. Kimash, recognizing that he had in fact been addressed in his proper rank, graciously inclined his head.

Sharur started to say something more, but then paused, weighing whether he should. Kimash noticed, but misunderstood his reasons. In a cautious voice, the lugal asked, "Has the god seized your wits, son of Ereshguna? If it be so, can you find some way to let me know it is so?"

"It is *not* so," Sharur declared. "I am sorry if I alarmed you, but it is *not* so. On the contrary. I have another thought you may perhaps find worth hearing."

"I listen." Kimash inclined his head once more.

"Hear my words, then," Sharur said, exactly as if he were speaking to Izmaili the man of no particular consequence rather than to Kimash the lugal of Gibil. "The great gods of the Alashkurrut had this thing, into which they poured a great part of their power for what they thought to be safekeeping. The great gods of the Alashkurrut likewise let slip that Engibil has such a thing, into which he has poured a great part of his power. Could it be that all gods have such a thing, into which they have poured a great part of their power for what they think to be safekeeping?"

Kimash stood some time still and silent. Then he stepped forward and kissed Sharur on both cheeks. "It could be. It could be indeed." His smile might have appeared on the face of a lion spying a fat gazelle that did not spy it in turn. Slowly, he went on, "I wonder if Enimhursag has such a thing, into which he has poured a great part of his power for what he thinks to be safekeeping."

That same smile stole across Sharur's face. "If Enimhursag has such a thing, I wonder who would be more eager to find it and destroy it: we Giblut, or the Imhursagut the god has oppressed for so long?"

"If the Imhursagut were more like us Giblut, my wager would be on them," Kimash replied. "As things are . . ." He shrugged. "Perhaps they could do with suitable instruction."

"Provided, of course, that an Imhursaggi will listen," Sharur said. "Provided that an Imhursaggi will profit from instruction. Such a thing is possible, I suppose, but by no means sure."

"Indeed not," Kimash said. "In their resolute stupidity, the Imhursagut very much resemble their god, just as the Zuabut resemble Enzuabu in their inveterate thievery." He paused and looked thoughtful once more. "I wonder why we Giblut do not resemble Engibil, who is as lazy and lackadaisical as Enzuabu is thievish and Enimhursag stubborn and stupid."

"Folk whose god is lazy and lackadaisical needs must do for themselves what that lazy, lackadaisical god will not do for them," Sharur replied. "We are as we are because Engibil is as he is. And, because Engibil is as he is, we now draw near the point where we can live without him." He lowered his voice to a whisper for that last sentence—the Giblut might have been drawing near such a point, but they had not yet reached it.

"My great-grandson," Kimash murmured. "*His* great-grandson." He raised an eyebrow at Sharur. "Remember, son of Ereshguna, my great-grandson could be your grandson."

"That could be, yes, but for him to do as you do"—*to sit on the throne of Gibil*, Sharur meant, but would not say—"your male line would have to fail, which I pray it may never do. And, now that Engibil has assented to the match my family made for me, I am, as I have told you, content and more than content with it.''

"I had gathered that your match was among other things a love match. Now I see it must be so indeed,'' Kimash said. "Only a love match would make a man turn away from power when it is offered to him like a pot in the market square.'' He seemed to remember himself and the role he had assumed. "Fortunately, I, Izmaili, a person of no particular account, do not need to concern myself with such things.'' He bowed and departed.

Sharur stared after him. He had expected the lugal to be more annoyed at the destruction of the Alashkurri cup, but Kimash had accepted that without a qualm once it was accomplished. He had also accepted Sharur's avoidance of a marriage alliance more readily than Sharur had thought he would.

Maybe the thought of truly bringing Engibil to heel once and for all pleased the lugal more than any lesser disappointment bothered him. Had Sharur dwelt in the palace rather than in the house of Ereshguna, he knew how much that thought would have pleased him. As a matter of fact, it pleased him quite a lot even though he did dwell in the house of Ereshguna. And the thought of truly bringing Enimhursag to heel once and for all pleased him even more.

Ushurikti frowned. "Are you sure you wish to do this, master merchant's son? You consigned these slaves to me for sale. I shall have to charge the house of Ereshguna not only for their maintenance while in my hands but also for a part of the price I could have expected to realize from such sale.''

"Unless it be a very large part, I shall not object,'' Sharur replied. "Unless it be an extortionate part, I shall not complain.''

"We can settle that in due course,'' the slave dealer said. "First, though, tell me, if you would, why you have suddenly decided to set these two Imhursagut free instead of profiting from them.''

"I have a message I wish to send back to Imhursag, and they are the fitting ones to bear it," Sharur said.

"You must be the judge of that, of course," Ushurikti replied, "but you must also recall that they are at present laboring in the south for the mighty lugal, and are not here at my establishment.''

"I do indeed recall that," Sharur said, "but they are laboring in the south for the mighty lugal because they are slaves, or are presumed to be slaves. If you send a runner to the south with word they are in fact to be freed, will the runner not be likely to return to Gibil with them trailing after him as sheep trail after a wether?''

"Likely he will, master merchant's son." Ushurikti looked calculating. "As you are doing this of your own will, it is just that *you* send a runner to the south and *you* pay him to bring Duabzu and Nasibugashi back to Gibil.''

"Let it be done as you say," Sharur answered resignedly. Ushurikti instructed the runner where in the south the two Imhursaggi captives were laboring for the lugal. Sharur gave him a clay tablet to show to whatever foreman Kimash had set over them, authorizing their release. He rolled his stone cylinder seal over the bottom of the damp tablet, confirming it had come from him. The runner trotted off, his sandals kicking up puffs of dust as he went.

He returned three days later, with the two Imhursagut trailing after him just as Sharur had foretold. When Ushurikti sent word they had arrived, Sharur hurried over to the slave dealer's establishment. There he found the men he had captured, both of them anxious to learn what he would do with them.

"Can it be true?" Duabzu asked. "Can you really intend to set us free?" Now that he had tasted the life of a slave, he was no longer so eager to endure it as he had been when Sharur spared his life on the battlefield.

"Have we then been ransomed?" Nasibugashi added. For an Imhursaggi, he seemed, as he had always seemed, uncommonly alert and aware of the consequences of actions in the world around him.

"You are to be freed," Sharur replied, and both Imhursagut cried out. Sharur went on, "You are not to be ransomed. I set you free without being paid even so much as a barleycorn." They cried out again, this time in astonishment. Sharur held up a hand. "I have one condition, and one only, I set on your freedom: you must both deliver and spread widely through Imhursag a message I shall give you."

Duabzu got down upon his belly and touched his forehead to Sharur's foot. "In the great and mighty and terrible name of Enimhursag, I swear I shall obey you as a son obeys his father." Nasibugashi swore the same oath, though he did not humble himself before Sharur in the same way.

"It is good," Sharur said. "Here, then, is the message: somewhere in the land of Imhursag is some small, hidden thing into which Enimhursag has poured a great part of his power for safekeeping. I do not know what it is. I do not know where it is. I do know that, should it be broken, a great part of Enimhursag's power will be broken with it. Deliver and spread widely through Imhursag this message I have given you, as you have sworn to do."

Duabzu looked appalled. "But this is a message that might prove dangerous to the great god. This is a message that might bring harm to the mighty god." By way of reply, Sharur smiled at him. That only made him look more appalled. He had sworn an oath by the god he loved, the god who ruled him absolutely, but to fulfill it he would, as he said, have to endanger the god.

Nasibugashi said, "I see now what I have seen again and again since being deceived into entering Gibil in the first place: this city has a larger store of clever men, men who are ready for anything and to turn anything to their advantage, than does Imhursag. Imhursag would be a better place if we had more men of this sort."

"Imhursag would be a place more like Gibil if we had

more men of this sort.'' Duabzu's shudder plainly gave his opinion of that.

To Nasibugashi, Sharur said, ''I do not know whether you will take this for good or ill, but you strike me as being more nearly a man of this sort than most Imhursagut I have seen.''

''I do not know whether to take this for good or ill, either,'' Nasibugashi replied.

''Enimhursag will surely know whether to take this for good or ill.'' By Duabzu's tone, he had no doubt how the god of Imhursag would take it. Sharur suspected Duabzu was right, too. If Enimhursag saw what Duabzu and Nasibugashi carried in their minds, his wisest course might be to strike them both dead the instant they crossed into land he ruled.

But, while that might keep Enimhursag safe for the time being, it would also make Imhursag fall further behind Gibil not only in the art of war but also in the art, if art it was, of producing men such as those to whom Nasibugashi had alluded. If Imhursag fell further behind Gibil, sooner or later the Giblut would be in a position to overrun their rivals and find for themselves the thing into which Enimhursag had poured a great part of his power for safekeeping. And when they did . . .

Sharur would not have wanted to be the god of Imhursag, nor to be faced with the choices the god of Imhursag was facing. When he remembered the choices with which the god of Imhursag and the other gods had faced him, though, he was far from altogether sorry to confront them with worries for a change.

''You have sworn your oath. I expect you to obey it when you return to the land of the Imhursagut,'' he said to Nasibugashi and Duabzu. ''Return to the land of the Imhursagut you shall. I set you free. I release you. No one shall make any claim on you. No one shall molest you. Go now, and return not to Gibil unless you should come as peaceful traders.''

The two Imhursagut left the establishment of Ushurikti

the slave dealer, Nasibugashi walking straight and tall, Duabzu almost slinking after him. Duabzu was afraid. Duabzu, Sharur thought, had good reason to be afraid.

Ushurikti said, "Master merchant's son, now I see why you have done as you have done. You have given Enimhursag poison hidden inside a date candied in honey; in freeing two men for him, you may have freed his city from him. I bow before your cleverness." He suited action to word. "This, of course, does not mean I abandon my claim for compensation over what I might have expected to earn from the sale of these two men."

"Of course," Sharur said. "I expected nothing different."

"You had better not have expected anything different." Despite an unprepossessing, pudgy build, Ushurikti drew himself up to his full height. "Am I not also a Gibli, even as are you? Am I not also a merchant, even as are you?"

"You are a Gibli, even as I am. You are a merchant, even as I am." Sharur clapped the slave dealer on the shoulder. "And together, you and I have this day struck no small blow for all Giblut."

"May it be so," Ushurikti said, "as long as I get my profit, too."

A commotion in the street outside the house of Ereshguna made Sharur glance up from the tablet on which he was inscribing measures of barley received in exchange for some of the tin that had been stored in the pot where he'd hidden the Alashkurri cup. "Come on, you lug!" a man with a deep voice shouted. "Don't think you can give me and my pal the slip, because we cursed well won't let you! Now move, before something worse happens to you."

A moment later, Mushezib, the guard captain on Sharur's caravan to the Alashkurru Mountains, strode into the house of Ereshguna. With him came Harharu, the donkeymaster on that caravan. And jammed between them, like salt fish and lentils and sesame seeds between two rounds of flatbread, perforce came Habbazu the master thief.

Mushezib had hold of his right arm. Harharu had hold of his left arm. If he tried to escape, they would tear him in two, as a man at a feast might tear a leg of roasted duck in two.

"Here's that lousy Zuabi wretch, master merchant's son," Mushezib boomed. "Harharu and I were drinking a quiet cup of beer together when the fellow came swaggering by, bold as you please. Harharu gets the credit for spotting him, because I didn't. But I'm the one who jumped on the son of a thousand fathers, so I guess we ought to split the reward you promised."

"I had almost given up looking for the thief, master merchant's son," Harharu said, "and then he strolled past my nose when I thought he must surely have gone back to Zuabu. I am glad I was able to help put him in your hands."

Habbazu said not a word. He looked at Sharur with large, reproachful eyes. Sharur, for once in his life, had trouble finding words himself. He had offered the reward for Habbazu's capture. He had offered the reward, and then he had forgotten about it. The men to whom he had offered it, though, they had remembered.

He saw only one way to disarm their suspicions, and that was to play along with them. "Well done," he said. "Well done for being so faithful, well done for being so vigilant. I said I would reward you. Reward you I shall. I promised gold. Gold I shall give you, gold in equal measure."

He found two rings, thin bands of gold. Setting them on the scales, he discovered one was heavier than the other. He weighed the heavier one, then took it off the scales, set the lighter one on the pan in its place, and added tiny scraps of gold until they and the ring balanced the weights in the other pan. The heavier ring he gave to Harharu. The lighter ring and the gold scraps he gave to Mushezib.

"You are generous, master merchant's son," Harharu said, bowing.

"Truly you are generous," Mushezib agreed. "But can we leave this wretch of a Zuabi with you now that we have gained our reward? He is liable to rape away all your stock in trade.''

''What good would it do him, when he has seen he cannot escape the vigilance of the Giblut?'' Sharur said. ''You may leave him here with me. I will tend to him as is most fitting.''

''Ha!'' Mushezib said. ''In that case, he'll be sorry he was ever born.''

''The master merchant's son has not explained his purposes to us,'' Harharu pointed out.

''He doesn't need to explain them to me. I can figure them out for myself,'' Mushezib said. After giving Habbazu the sort of look he would have given to offal he needed to wipe from the soles of his sandals, he strode out of the house of Ereshguna. By his manner, he might have been a great captain who had just led the Gibli army to victory against Imhursag, not a guard captain who had just laid hands on a single thief.

Having dealt with donkeys for so many years, Harharu was less confident he could immediately understand everything that went on around him. He let go of Habbazu and said, ''I hope our capturing the thief after so long a time still suits your purposes, master merchant's son.''

''Did it not, would I have given you gold?'' Sharur returned. ''Did it not, would I have set a ring of precious metal on your finger?''

''I am not so quick to judge purposes as my comrade,'' Harharu said. ''Whatever yours may be, I pray they prosper.'' He bowed to Sharur and followed Mushezib out onto the Street of Smiths.

Habbazu turned his dark gaze on Sharur. Sharur coughed and looked away and drummed his fingers on his thigh and did everything else he could to convey without words how embarrassed he was. Habbazu, now, Habbazu had words: ''In a way, learning how greatly I am desired is heartening, but only in a way. Were you a beautiful woman seeking me so, I should have come closer to finding it worthwhile. Even then, though, having my arms all but pulled from their sockets would be no small sacrifice.''

"I set the men seeking you long before you stole the thing from the place wherein it was kept,'' Sharur said, speaking obliquely from long habit. "When they did not find you, the thought in my mind was that they would not and could not find you, and so I did not call them off. This was an error on my part. I see as much now, and I am sorry for it.''

"I have heard few apologies in my life,'' Habbazu said, "and I have heard fewer apologies still that sound as if those who make them speak from the heart, not from the tongue alone. Now I press new syllables into the clay tablet of my memory.''

"Master thief, you are gracious. Habbazu, you are generous,'' Sharur said. "I shall spread the word throughout the city that you are to be hunted no more. I shall spread the word to caravan guards and donkey handlers that you are to be left alone.''

"I might wish you had done this sooner. I *do* wish you had done this sooner,'' Habbazu said. "Still, that you do it at all speaks well of you.'' He paused. "I hope your noising my name abroad in the city does not bring me to the notice of the lugal. I hope your speaking of me to caravan guards and donkey handlers does not bring me to the notice of the temple and the god.''

"You need not fear the lugal,'' Sharur said. "Now that the deed is done, he is glad it is done. As for the temple and the god . . .'' He told of letting Kimash know that Engibil had stored a great part of his power as the gods of the Alashkurrut had stored a great part of theirs.

"Is this so?'' Habbazu murmured. "Is it so indeed? I did not hear the gods of the Alashkurrut speak thus in any dream I dreamt. And yet . . . and yet it makes sense that it should be so, eh? If some gods do thus, should not all gods do likewise?''

"So it would seem,'' Sharur replied. "So I believe. But of proof I have none.''

"If the gods of the Alashkurrut do thus and Engibil does likewise, would it not follow that Enimhursag also does likewise?" Habbazu said. Seeing Sharur's predatory smile, the master thief grinned back, a grin that made him look very much like a preternaturally clever monkey. Slowly, that grin faded, to be replaced by a thoughtful expression. "And would it not follow that Enzuabu also does likewise?"

Sharur stepped forward and set a hand on Habbazu's shoulder. "I congratulate you, my friend. Now you have become more surely a Gibli for the rest of your life than ever you were before. If you enter into Zuabu with this thought in your mind, if Enzuabu sees this thought in your mind as you enter into Zuabu, what will become of you?"

He had sent Nasibugashi and Duabzu toward Imhursag with this thought in their minds and without a qualm in his own. Them he had used as weapons against Enimhursag, as he had used a sword in the recent fighting against the god of the Imhursagut. Habbazu was not merely a weapon. Habbazu had become an ally and, in an odd way, a friend.

"What will become of me?" the Zuabi repeated. "Less than you think, master merchant's son. Do you not know, do you not remember, that the god of Zuabu is also the god of thieves? Do you not think that the god of thieves is able to protect his own from those who would steal it?"

"A point," Sharur admitted. "Surely a point. And yet, how great a point? Is he able to protect his own from those who would steal provided that they are many and diligent and seek their goal for generations if need be?"

Habbazu's mobile eyebrows sprang upwards. "I do not know. I wonder if Enzuabu would know. Being a god, he would also be sure he could defeat any one man, and he would be right in being sure. But can he defeat, can he deceive, all men over all time? Would such a thought even cross his mind? I do not know."

"Being a god, he is sure to be arrogant," Sharur said. "Having held so much power for so long, gods think they shall easily hold all power forever. Certain potsherds that have been swept away should teach them otherwise."

"Hmm," Habbazu said. "Perhaps I would do best to stay in Gibil after all—provided, of course, that you can keep these Gibli ruffians from assaulting me in the street while I pursue my lawful occasions."

"You are a Zuabi master thief," Sharur exclaimed. "How can you possibly pursue lawful occasions?"

Spoken in a different tone of voice, that would have been an insult. As it was, the two men grinned at each other. Habbazu said, "Whatever occasions I pursue, I shall now go and pursue them. Have I your gracious leave to do that— if, as I say, I am not to be manhandled the instant I show my face outside your door?"

"You have my gracious leave, certainly," Sharur said. "Whether you prove to have Mushezib's gracious leave, or Harharu's, is liable to be a different question."

"They took me by surprise, as you did earlier." Habbazu looked annoyed at himself. "Now I know their faces. Now I know their voices. Now I know their movements, even if I spy them moving in a crowd. They shall not lay hands on me again, I assure you."

"I have no doubt that you know your own affairs best," Sharur said.

Habbazu nodded, walked out the door, and might as well have disappeared. It was indeed almost as if a demon had wrapped a cloak of invisibility around him. Sharur went to the doorway. He looked up the Street of Smiths. He did not see Habbazu. He looked down the Street of Smiths. He did not see Habbazu. If he did not see Habbazu, he did not think Mushezib and Harharu were likely to see Habbazu, either. He went back into the house of Ereshguna and incised fresh syllables on clay with his stylus, meticulously recording the weight of the gold he had given to the caravan guard and the donkeymaster. Whatever else happened, accounts had to balance.

"Accounts have to balance," Dimgalabzu the smith said at the threshold to the house of Ereshguna. Behind him stood

Gulal, his wife, in a pleated shift of white linen, with a gold necklace round her neck, gold hoops in her ears, gold bracelets on her wrists, and gold rings on her fingers. Behind her stood Ningal, similarly dressed, similarly arrayed, with a scarf of filmy stuff draped over her head so that it hung down from either side and held in place by golden hairpins.

"Accounts have to balance," Ereshguna agreed. Behind him stood Betsilim, his wife, in finery not identical to that of Gulal but conveying a like impression of prosperity. Behind her stood Tupsharru and Nanadirat, also richly dressed, excited grins on their faces. Behind his own brother and sister stood Sharur, a nervous grin on his face. Had he not stood there, had Ningal not come to the house of Ereshguna, all the gathering, all the finery, would have been pointless.

"And accounts do balance," Dimgalabzu boomed. "The house of Ereshguna has duly paid to the house of Dimgalabzu the bride-price upon which the two houses agreed when we likewise agreed to the betrothal of the son of Ereshguna and the daughter of Dimgalabzu. In token of the due fulfillment of the said agreement, I offer to you, Ereshguna, your choice of these identical, fully executed contracts." He held out a pair of clay tablets to Sharur's father.

Ereshguna carefully examined the two tablets to make sure they were in fact identical. Dimgalabzu waited while the master merchant did so. He knew Ereshguna trusted him, but, in marriage as in any other business dealing, trust was no substitute for care and consideration.

"It is good," Ereshguna declared after he had read both tablets through. As custom required when all was in order, he reached out with his left hand to set one tablet in Dimgalabzu's right. That left each of the two men holding his copy of the marriage agreement in his right hand. Ereshguna held his up above his head. As Dimgalabzu did the same, Sharur's father said, "May the omen likewise be good."

"So may it be," Dimgalabzu said.

"So may it be," echoed Dimgalabzu's wife and daughter.

"So may it be," echoed Ereshguna's wife and sons and daughter.

Sharur said, "Father, I know I am in your debt. Rest assured, I shall repay this debt as soon as may be." Those were not words usually found in the marriage ritual, but they seemed to fit here. He had also learned from experience: he did not swear in Engibil's name that he would repay the debt within any particular time, nor with goods gained in any particular fashion. He did add, "I hope trading up in the Alashkurru Mountains next travel season will be better than it was in the travel season just past."

"It could hardly be worse," Tupsharru exclaimed.

"I likewise hope it will be better," Ereshguna said smoothly. "I hope the Alashkurrut will be as eager to trade with us as they have been in the past, and that they will now have every opportunity to do so."

That was as harmless and as careful a way of saying that the great gods of the Alashkurrut would henceforth lack the power to prevent such trade as any Sharur could have imagined. Dimgalabzu looked shrewd. "This would have somewhat to do with the cup that was briefly in my house, would it not?"

"What cup could you mean?" Ereshguna sounded as innocent and as ignorant as if he were hearing for the first time that the world held such things as cups.

"What cup do you mean?" Gulal's question, on the other hand, was as pointed as a serpent's fang. Sharur realized Ningal had never told her mother about the Alashkurri cup. He realized Dimgalabzu had never told his wife about the Alashkurri cup. He realized Dimgalabzu would probably have several more sharp questions to answer after the wedding feast was over.

But that would be after the wedding feast was over. Betsilim took charge now with effortless ease: "Let us feast. Let us be merry. Let us celebrate at last the joining of our two houses, the joining so long expected and now at last come to pass."

Gulal still looked unhappy. Gulal, in fact, looked sour as beer of the third quality, sour as date wine that had gone over into vinegar. But she would do nothing more than look sour now, not unless she wanted to make herself hateful before her husband and also hateful before the family into which her daughter was marrying. She knew better than that. She bided her time. Sharur was glad he was not Dimgalabzu. Dimgalabzu did not look so glad that he was Dimgalabzu.

Betsilim clapped her hands. Slaves began carrying in from the kitchen the feast they had prepared. One bore a large copper platter of roasted mutton, including such dainties as heart and liver and sweetbreads, eyes and tongue and brain. Dimgalabzu admired the platter as much as he did the meat piled high upon it. It was a product of his smithy, its use a subtle compliment to him from the house of Ereshguna.

The Imhursaggi slave woman came out next, with loaves of bread set one beside another on a wickerwork tray. And such loaves they were!—not the usual flat, chewy bread made from barley flour, but soft and fluffy and baked from costly wheat, bread that would not have disgraced the lugal's table. "That does look very fine," Dimgalabzu said, patting his big belly in anticipation. "Very fine indeed. Ah, I see honey and sesame oil for dipping. Truly the house of Ereshguna stints not."

Betsilim let out an indignant sniff at that. "The very idea!" she said. "If the house of Ereshguna stinted at the wedding of its eldest child, what would folk along the Street of Smiths say of us? They would say we were niggards. They would say we were misers. They would say we cared only for holding what was ours, and not for giving of what was ours when the time came to pass. They would say these things, and they would say them truly. We do not wish this, no indeed."

"My husband meant no offense," Gulal said, glaring at both Dimgalabzu and Betsilim. "My husband meant only praise." She glared at Dimgalabzu once more. Sharur got the idea she enjoyed glaring at Dimgalabzu whenever she found the chance. For his own sake, he was glad Ningal had a more easygoing disposition.

But Dimgalabzu would not take Ningal home with him

once the wedding feast and ceremony were done. Ningal would stay in the house of Ereshguna. Sharur glanced over toward his intended bride. She was glancing over toward him at the same time. When their eyes met, they both looked down to the rammed-earth floor in embarrassment.

Betsilim, for her part, went from clouds to sun in the space of a couple of heartbeats. "I understood you, father of my son's intended," she said, smiling brightly. "Let me assure you, I took no offense."

Now Sharur glanced toward Ereshguna. The two men, one younger, one older, exchanged small smiles. What Betsilim had meant was, *Let me assure you, I shall waste no chance to put you in your place.*

Gulal saw that, too. Her formidable black brows came down and together in a frown. But, with Betsilim outwardly so affable, Ningal's mother could do nothing but frown. Sharur's mother had won this round of the game.

The slaves of the house of Ereshguna kept bringing in more food: roasted locusts and ducks, boiled ducks' eggs, stewed beans and peas and lentils and cucumbers, fresh garlic and onions and lettuces of several varieties. They brought in jars of beer of the first quality, and jars of date wine as well. The feasters ate until they were very full. They drank until they approached drunkenness.

Dimgalabzu patted his capacious belly once more. He looked from Ningal to Sharur. "Having eaten so much, will you be able to do your bride justice on the first night?" he asked with a leer and a chuckle.

Tupsharru laughed at that, and poked Sharur in the ribs with his elbow. Sharur said, "Father of my intended, you may rely on it." Dimgalabzu was not a young man; perhaps he would have trouble doing a woman justice after such a feast. If so, Sharur felt sorry for him. He had no doubt of his own capacity—and his chance to prove it would not be long delayed.

Ningal modestly cast her eyes down to the ground once more. Having known her since childhood, Sharur also knew she had a mind of her own and, under the right circumstances or anything even close to the right circumstances, was not in the least bit shy about saying exactly what she thought and behaving exactly as she found best. These were not the right circumstances, nor anything even close to the right circumstances. Sharur's own manners here were far more formal than they would have been at any other time, too.

Dimgalabzu drank cup after cup of beer. He drank cup after cup of date wine. Smiling, he said to Sharur, "In the morning, I will wish my head would fall off, so I would not have to feel it thumping like a drum. But that will be in the morning. This is now. Now I feel very good indeed."

He felt good enough to pay very close attention to the way the Imhursaggi slave woman walked when she went back to the kitchen to bring the feasters more bread. He paid close enough attention to make Gulal speak sharply to him, though she did so in a low, polite tone of voice. Even after that, he kept watching the slave woman. After a bit, Tupsharru went over to him and murmured something into his ear.

"Ah? Is it so?" Dimgalabzu said, looking as if he had bitten into a plum and found an unexpected rotten spot. "What a pity, what a pity."

Nanadirat patted Sharur on the knee. "What did Tupsharru tell him? Why does he look so disappointed?"

Sharur looked at his younger sister. Looking at her, he realized she was not so young as that. One day before too long, someone's father would be dickering with Ereshguna over bride-price for her. To Sharur, who automatically thought of her as an annoying brat, that realization came as no small shock. Because of it, he answered her seriously rather than with an evasion or a joke: "You know what men and women do when they are alone together."

"Of course I do." Nanadirat tossed her head. "We wouldn't be having this wedding feast if men and women didn't do that when they were alone together."

"That's right, we wouldn't," Sharur agreed. "What I think Tupsharru was telling Dimgalabzu is that the

Imhursaggi slave woman takes no pleasure in lying with a man, and gives a man who lies with her as little pleasure as she can.''

"Oh." Nanadirat thought about that. Sharur waited for her to ask how Tupsharru would know, or, for that matter, how Sharur could make such a good guess about what Tupsharru had said to Dimgalabzu. She did neither. She simply nodded. She might be his younger sister, but she was a woman, and she knew what women knew.

After the fine wheat bread was all eaten, the Imhursaggi slave woman came out yet again, this time with a bowl of apple slices candied in honey. With great ceremony, Betsilim passed a slice to each of the feasters. "May the union between our two houses prove as sweet as this candied fruit," she said.

"So may it be," everyone echoed. Gulal added, "Engibil grant that it be so. The gods grant that it be so."

No one corrected her. No one disagreed with her, not out loud. Sharur hoped the gods would bless the marriage, too. If, however, the gods remained silent on the matter, he intended to go on with his life as best he could anyhow.

Everyone looked around, as if searching for something, anything, else that wanted doing before the marriage ceremony should be completed. No one said anything. Sharur presumed that meant no one found anything. Ereshguna glanced over to him and nodded, ever so slightly.

Sharur got to his feet. Ningal got to her feet. They stood side by side before their families. Sharur did his best to keep his voice steady and firm, as if he were describing the virtues of a bronze axhead to an Alashkurri wanax. Despite his doing his best, his words came out in a soft, nervous squeak: "I, Sharur the son of Ereshguna, stand here with Ningal the daughter of Dimgalabzu in the presence of witnesses who will see and remember that we so stand."

"You do. The two of you do." Ereshguna and Betsilim, Dimgalabzu and Gulal, Tupsharru and Nanadirat all spoke together.

Sharur took the lengths of veiling that hung at either side

of Ningal's head and brought them together in front of her face. "She is my wife," he said, and then made himself say it again, for no one, very likely including Ningal, could have heard him the first time.

"She is your wife," the members of the two families agreed, as formally as before.

From behind the veil, Ningal said, "He is my husband." That was not part of the marriage ritual, and no one echoed it. Nevertheless, Sharur was glad to have her affirmation.

Ereshguna rose then, a wide smile on his face. "And now, my son, my daughter-in-law, come with me, that you may consummate the wedding you have celebrated." Not only did Sharur and Ningal follow him, so did their families and even the slaves of the house of Ereshguna, all calling advice so ribald, Sharur's ears burned.

The slaves had cleared jars and pots and baskets from what was normally a storeroom. They had set stools in all the corners of the room, a lamp burning brightly on each one. In the center of the floor lay a sleeping mat. On the sleeping mat lay a square of fine linen, to serve as proof of the ending of Ningal's days as a maiden. Everyone pointed to the square of cloth and shouted more bawdy advice.

Sharur closed the door. That only meant everyone outside shouted louder than ever. He saw someone had thoughtfully put a bar and brackets for it on the inside of the door. Ignoring the racket in the hallway, he set the bar in the brackets. Behind the filmy veil, Ningal nodded.

He turned to her and parted the veil he had closed. "You are my wife," he said. "You are my woman."

Her answering smile was nervous and eager at the same time. "There is something we must do before that is truly so," she murmured.

"And so we shall," he said. He freed the veiling from her hair and let it fall to the ground. That done, he pulled her shift up over her head. The lamps shed plenty of light to let him admire her for a moment before he stepped out of his own kilt.

He stepped forward and took her in his arms. Her body

molded itself to his. His mouth came down on hers. His right hand closed on her left breast, his left on her right buttock. The kiss went on and on. Ningal sighed, deep in her throat.

Sharur's grandfather's ghost shouted in his ear: "By the gods, boy, do you call *that* a kiss? And *squeeze* her there, don't just pat her. Anyone would think you were a virgin yourself, the way you're going at it. What you have to do is—"

He couldn't even chase the ghost out beyond the barred door. He had to try to pretend it was not there and make the best of things. And he did.